Dragon
Ghosts

Also by Lisa McMann

» » « «

THE UNWANTEDS SERIES

The Unwanteds

Island of Silence

Island of Fire

Island of Legends

Island of Shipwrecks

Island of Graves

Island of Dragons

» » « «

THE UNWANTEDS QUESTS SERIES

Dragon Captives

Dragon Bones

Dragon Ghosts

Dragon Curse

» » « «

FOR OLDER READERS:

Don't Close Your Eyes

Visions

Cryer's Cross

Dead to You

LISA McMANN

THE UNWANTEDS QUESTS

Dragon Ghosts

Aladdin
NEW YORK   LONDON   TORONTO   SYDNEY   NEW DELHI

ALADDIN

An imprint of Simon & Schuster Children's Publishing Division
1230 Avenue of the Americas, New York, New York 10020
First Aladdin paperback edition February 2020
Text copyright © 2019 by Lisa McMann
Cover illustration copyright © 2019 by Owen Richardson
Also available in an Aladdin hardcover edition.

For information about special discounts for bulk purchases, please contact Simon & Schuster Special Sales at 1-866-506-1949 or business@simonandschuster.com.
The Simon & Schuster Speakers Bureau can bring authors to your live event. For more information or to book an event contact the Simon & Schuster Speakers Bureau at 1-866-248-3049 or visit our website at www.simonspeakers.com.
Book designed by Karin Paprocki
The text of this book was set in Truesdell.
Manufactured in the United States of America 0120 OFF
2 4 6 8 10 9 7 5 3 1
The Library of Congress has cataloged the hardcover edition as follows:
Names: McMann, Lisa, author.
Title: Dragon ghosts / by Lisa McMann.
Description: First Aladdin hardcover edition. | New York : Aladdin, 2019. | Series: [The Unwanteds quests ; 3] |
Summary: "Devastated by loss and hampered by war, Fifer struggles to regroup and continue the search for her twin. Meanwhile Thisbe, pounded by images of Grimere's dark history, contemplates her abandonment and considers leaving Rohan behind in a risky move that could take her home . . . or to her death."— Provided by publisher.
Identifiers: LCCN 2018027311 (print) | LCCN 2018035121 (eBook) |
ISBN 9781534416000 (eBook) | ISBN 9781534415980 (hardback)
Subjects: | CYAC: Adventure and adventurers—Fiction. | Magic—Fiction. |
Brothers and sisters—Fiction. | Twins—Fiction. | Dragons—Fiction. | Fantasy. |
BISAC: JUVENILE FICTION / Action & Adventure / General. |
JUVENILE FICTION / Fantasy & Magic. | JUVENILE FICTION / Social Issues / Friendship.
Classification: LCC PZ7.M478757 (eBook) | LCC PZ7.M478757 Dt 2019 (print) | DDC [Fic]—dc23
LC record available at https://lccn.loc.gov/2018027311
ISBN 9781534415997 (pbk)

To booksellers everywhere,
with love and thanks

Contents

Dragon
Ghosts

The Gray Shack

When the world of Artimé turned gray, Henry Haluki knew that Alex was dead.

The medicinal herbs he'd been picking turned to weeds in his hands, and the ground beneath his knees became hard and cracked. The enormous mansion swirled and disappeared, leaving a small shack in its place. Hundreds of Artiméans who'd been inside the mansion spilled out of the shack's doorway and burst through its windows, trying to keep from being crushed. The walls strained and bulged as if they were about to explode.

Henry stared for an instant, trying to comprehend what

LISA McMANN

was happening, and then he dropped the weeds and ran toward the chaos to help. As he went, he realized that his hospital ward and everything in it would have disappeared along with the mansion. He reached into his healer's coat pockets to see what medicines he carried with him, but those magical products had vanished too. His heart sank.

Cries and shouts rose from all over the property. It was impossible to know where to start helping. Henry looked around frantically as it dawned on him that his and Thatcher's adopted young Unwanteds were probably somewhere in the disaster. His breath caught as he thought about how scared everyone must be. With Alex gone, he had to step up.

With Alex gone. Not just away. Gone. For good.

A sharp pain speared through Henry. He slowed and stumbled forward, crumpling into the agony of the realization. A horrendous sob exploded from him, the sound of it lost in the chaotic din. *Alexander Stowe, head mage of Artimé, is dead.* Henry clutched his chest and tried to breathe, blinking the tears away. Then he got up and pushed through the growing crowd around the shack. He had to keep going.

"Henry! Over here!" Sean Ranger was inside, holding his

young son out the broken window and looking frantic. "Can you take Lukas? I can't find Ava!"

Henry rushed up and took the boy. Sean used his sleeve to clear out the rest of the glass, then helped a few others get through the window. He disappeared into the shack to look for his daughter.

"Go on," a man by the window said to Henry. "Move out of the way so we can get more people out."

Overwhelmed, Henry hurried away from the disaster with Lukas. The five-year-old was crying. He was missing a shoe, and he had a bruise turning purple on his arm and one on his cheek. A thin trickle of blood ran down his leg. Henry set the boy down and examined him. Finding his injuries to be minor, he tried soothing him. "There," said Henry, distracted and looking anxiously for his teens to surface from the stampede. "It's going to be okay." With relief, Henry spotted one of his and Thatcher's recently adopted girls, Clementi Okafor, at another window helping others out. Her natural spiral curls had a layer of gray dust on them, and her black skin shone with sweat. Henry caught sight of Clementi's brother Ibrahim, from the same purge group of Unwanteds, assisting her from the inside. "Thank goodness," Henry murmured. Hopefully the rest were close by.

Lukas sniffled, drawing Henry's attention back. "Where's Ava?" asked the boy. "I want my dad."

"She's . . . She'll be coming any minute. Your dad is going after her. It's just a little shack, so it shouldn't be too hard. They'll find us out here."

"Everybody fell on each other," said Lukas tearfully. "I got hit in the face."

Henry sucked in a breath, imagining what it must have been like to have the entire population of Artimé, on multiple floors and in a variety of additional magical rooms that took up no space, suddenly and entirely converge in the single gray shack when the mansion disappeared. He kept seeing more and more people struggling to get out. With other Artiméans rushing forward to help at the exits, there wasn't much Henry could do at the moment but stare and feel the horror he'd felt when he was ten years old—the first time Artimé had disappeared and Alex had taken him under his wing.

Alex is dead.

The reminder hit him like a sucker punch to the gut. It

repeated over and over in his thoughts. He tried to rationalize—tried to come up with reasons why it couldn't be so. Maybe Alex had just gotten too far away from home and had moved outside of his magely range, assuming there was one. Silently Henry counted the days since Alex and Thatcher and the rest of the rescue team had left, and he knew Alex would have been in the land of the dragons for a while. So it didn't seem likely that he'd somehow be out of range now if he hadn't been yesterday.

Alex. Is dead.

Sean came running over to them, bloodied and battered, with six-year-old Ava in his arms. She seemed to be okay, with just a few cuts and scratches on her arms and one of her legs. Henry checked her injuries and made sure she was all right. Then he looked up at Sean with dread, not sure what to say in front of the children.

Sean held Henry's gaze for a moment, then shook his head sorrowfully. "He's . . . gone. He's got to be."

Henry swallowed hard. Hearing Sean say it made it seem real. Permanent. Sorrow enveloped him. But fear did too. If Alex was dead . . . what about Thatcher? And Lani? And

Carina and the others on the rescue team? Were they dead too? He pushed the horror of that thought aside and nodded. "We need to get to Aaron—bring him over here right away. He knows the spell. He has an extra robe."

"Henry," said Sean, "we *can't* get to him. The tubes are gone. We'd have to take a ship. It'll take days."

"Can't we send a seek spell—" Henry cut himself off, annoyed and disheartened. "Sorry. Of course not." He thought for a moment as his anxiety built. "Who else knows what to do?"

Sean looked up. "Claire Morning does. She has a robe. She's familiar with the spell, too."

"Is she in Artimé?" Henry's eyes swept the area.

"I don't think she came today."

"Let's go to Quill and find her, then." Henry glanced back at the chaos surrounding the shack, confirming that, like Sean's and his kids', most people's wounds were superficial. His adopted Unwanteds would be all right—they'd been through worse. And there were people helping at all the exits. He spotted a few of the nurses assisting the injured, but without medicine or the hospital ward, they couldn't do much.

Neither could Henry. "Hang on a minute," he told Sean. He ran over to one of the nurses to explain where he was going and put her in charge while he was gone. "Keep an eye out for the rest of my kids, will you?" he asked. "Clementi and Ibrahim are there by the east window, but they're the only ones I've seen emerge so far."

"Of course," said the nurse, knowing it was more important for Henry to go after Claire so they could get the magic back as quickly as possible. Before chaos turned to disaster.

Sean and Henry each took a child on their backs and turned toward Quill, where Claire Morning now lived. At the sight of the larger part of the island, they both gasped, because they'd forgotten something else.

Quill was gone too. Everything there looked even worse than in Artimé. It was nothing but old burned land and sooty rubble. And angry, nonmagical Quillens were coming toward them in droves.

The Time Before

It had happened once before, when Henry was ten. Hours after Mr. Marcus Today, the first head mage and creator of the magical world, had been killed and Artimé had vanished, Henry's mother had died of injuries sustained in a skirmish with the Restorers of Quill. Henry's sister, Lani, had been taken captive on Warbler Island, leaving Henry with his grieving father, Gunnar, who was also trying to regain control of Quill.

The mess of problems that had surrounded Henry in those awful days had left a permanent, invisible bruise on his soul. He'd clung to Alex as a shadowy helper. Fetching him cups of water or a bit of broth if he could get some. Trying to come to grips with his losses when everyone else was feeling losses too. Comfort had been scarce. Artimé had seen its worst in the way people treated one another.

It had taken weeks for Alex to decipher the strange spell that Mr. Today had magically sent to the boy's pocket in the moment before he'd died. Sky had helped Alex—the world might still be gone if it hadn't been for her. People had turned desperate. Water and food had been nearly nonexistent. But they had survived . . . most of them anyway.

With Ava and Lukas on their backs, Henry and Sean forged a path through the increasing crowd of upset Quillens. The people of Quill were not magical, but the world they lived in was. When Quill had been destroyed by fire, Alex had come to the aid of the contentious neighbors, pushing the boundaries of Artimé's magical world to cover the soot and burned-out buildings and whatever else had been left. He'd created magical houses and workplaces and fields and even a lighthouse for them, and the people of Quill had accepted these things begrudgingly, having no other choice. They'd been tiresome

9 « Dragon Ghosts

LISA McMANN

and grumpy neighbors, but peaceful since then. Most of the Artiméans had at least a few family members there. But Quill's focus on what was important strayed far from Artimé's, and the two places, despite sharing an island, were still quite opposite.

As they traveled, Sean and Henry scanned the crowds for signs of Claire, hoping she was already on her way to Artimé. The shock they both felt was numbing. Henry could hardly fathom what had happened. All he wanted was for the magic to be restored as quickly as possible so he could send a seek spell to Thatcher. If he got one in return . . . well, it would mean at least they weren't *all* dead. Henry's throat caught. The desperate need to know if Thatcher and the others were alive was all consuming. He had to shove it down and get through this.

Sean felt the same way about Carina and Seth. "At least we were more prepared this time," he said. "I just can't believe . . ." He choked on the words, then kept going. "I can't believe Alex is . . . gone." He glanced up at Ava on Henry's back, not wanting to say anything to scare the young ones even more than they already were, especially since no one was 100 percent certain that Alex was dead. But Ava wasn't paying attention.

Rather, she was looking around in wonder and fear at the desolate burned-out mess of land that used to be Quill. She'd never seen it like this before.

It was slow going, pushing upstream the whole way. After an hour or more they came to a huge gathering of angry Quillens blocking the path, demanding to have their houses back. At the center of the gathering, hundreds of feet away, was Gunnar Haluki, Henry's father, looking frazzled. Beside him was Claire Morning, the musical instructor, raising her voice in a way she'd told many singers to avoid doing in order to protect their vocal folds. But now she was forced to do whatever it took to be heard.

"You must let me through!" Claire insisted. "I can't help you unless you let me get to Artimé! I need to talk to the people there. Please make way!"

The crowd around her grumbled louder.

Henry touched Sean's shoulder. "I'll go help them." He carefully lifted Ava off his shoulders and handed her to Sean so she wouldn't get stepped on. Then he shouted with authority, "Coming through! Move it! Look out!" which was uncharacteristic of him, but as it was a new distraction, it worked. He pushed people aside, row after row all the way to the center, and caught his father's eye. Gunnar looked relieved to see him.

Henry reached Claire first and took her hand, then beckoned for his father to come and grabbed his hand as well so they wouldn't get separated. They weaved through the crowd until they found Sean. Sean quickly herded them out ahead of the mob toward Artimé. Henry took Ava back onto his shoulders as they went.

"Thank you," Gunnar said, glancing behind him. They began to pick up speed to stay ahead of the others. "They weren't quite grasping the fact that things can't be restored without Claire going into Artimé." Then he looked at Henry. "What news do you have?"

"None," said Henry. "We can only assume Alex is dead."

Gunnar Haluki looked pained, and he closed his eyes momentarily, then shook his head. "Of course, we thought as much. But it's . . . It's hard to hear that."

"It's terrible," Claire said. Her face was smudged with soot, and her cheeks had tear tracks running down them. "No word from anyone?"

Henry shook his head.

"Do you have the robe?" asked Sean, looking anxious. Claire wasn't carrying it.

"Not yet. I don't keep it in our house in Quill, since it would disappear with the world the moment I'd need it."

"Well, that's brilliant of you," said Sean. "Where is it?"

"It's inside the gray shack along with the clue and the miniature model of the mansion. Those were the three items that Alex used to bring the world back the first time. If all goes as I planned, I'll find the things in the little cupboard in the kitchen." She hesitated. "I hope everything's still in place after all these years. I've been meaning to go to the gray shack in the Museum of Large to check on the items once Alex left, but I'm afraid I haven't done it."

"Hopefully everyone will have emptied out of there by the time we return," said Henry. "There were hundreds of people inside the mansion when it happened. It was a disaster, all of them falling on top of one another from all locations—the living spaces, theater, lounge, dining room. The upstairs on top of down, I imagine—all squished into that tiny space. They were breaking windows to get out."

"Oh dear," said Claire. "That's horrible."

"It was frightening," Sean said. He glanced at his daughter and son, but they appeared to be handling their fear. They rode quietly on his and Henry's shoulders, sometimes pointing and talking with each other about the strange sights they were seeing.

Their little group went faster, but the way became more difficult the closer they got. People began chanting "Bring back Quill!" as they converged into the area that, with magic, would expand into beautiful Artimé. Without magic, it was a small plot of land, and there was little room to move.

"Let us through!" Henry called out. "We can fix this, but we need to get to the shack!"

Sean began hollering too, though it was hard for anyone to be heard. They lost Gunnar Haluki somewhere along the way, but Claire pushed on with Henry and Sean. They had to squeeze and weave through the people who were packed all the way to the seashore.

Then Henry stopped and grabbed Sean's arm. He beckoned to Claire and then pointed to the gray shack . . . or what was left of it. Only one wall remained standing. The roof had collapsed. The rest of the little house had apparently exploded due to all the people inside.

"Oh no," Henry muttered, looking at the others in alarm. "It's in shambles. Now what'll we do?"

"Come on," said Sean. "Link arms so we don't get separated. Children, hold on tight!"

Sean led the way with one elbow, shoving roughly to clear a path to the shack. The others plowed after him, fearing the worst. Would people be crushed under the debris? When they finally reached the area, they could see that the exterior walls of the shack had collapsed outward and lay flat, so if anyone had been in the way, they would have been pulled to safety by now.

Henry spotted the nurse he'd spoken to earlier and saw Clementi and Ibrahim and the other four of his wards present with them. He breathed a sigh of relief, then turned to look at the mess before them.

The interior of the shack was almost completely torn apart. Shredded.

"This is not good," Claire muttered. She pushed her way

over to where the kitchen cupboards should have been, but there was nothing left except piles of splintered wood, broken shelves, and shattered glass.

"The robe has got to be here somewhere," she said as Henry and Sean caught up to her. She looked frantically around people's feet. "Maybe it's buried under the collapsed walls." Exasperated, she put her fingers in her mouth and emitted a sharp whistle, startling those nearby into silence. Then she put her hands in the air and shouted, "Attention, everyone! We need to clear this area. Now!"

A Fish and a Fire

Thisbe Stowe and Sky from Warbler, both bedraggled, stared at each other for a split second in the cave's firelight. Then they threw themselves together in a huge, long embrace.

"You came for me!" Thisbe exclaimed.

"You found me!" said Sky. They danced in front of the fire together, and then Sky pulled back to look at the girl. "How did you know I'd be here?"

"I should ask you the same question!" said Thisbe. She looked around. "Where's everybody else?" There were a few makeshift supplies, nothing more.

LISA McMANN

"I haven't seen them yet—did Alex come with you?"

Thisbe blinked, and her grin fell away. "What? Is he here?"

"I assume you'd know better than me," said Sky with an unsettled laugh. Something clearly was being misunderstood here, but she couldn't figure out what. She thought back to when she'd last seen Simber, Carina, and Thatcher at the Island of Fire, on their way to get Fifer, Thisbe, and Seth, who'd run off to help the dragons. But that was a long time ago, before she'd been sucked into the volcanic island. Surely Thisbe had been rescued by now. "Wait a minute—have you been in the land of the dragons this whole time? Since Simber and the others went chasing after you?"

Thisbe gave a confused look. "Of course. Where else would I be? I just escaped the catacombs this morning. I haven't seen anyone from home since before the Revinir captured me." She paused, still not quite understanding. "Is Fifer okay? Did she survive? Who else came with you?"

Sky's face wrinkled up. "I'm extremely confused."

"So am I," said Thisbe. "Didn't you come here to rescue me?"

"Me? To rescue you? No. I figured Simber and Thatcher

and Carina would have found you by now. They'd stopped to tell me they were going after you. . . . It was weeks and weeks ago, before the Island of Fire swallowed me up."

"Before . . ." Thisbe stared at Sky, the love of her brother Alex's life. She tried to understand the strange conversation, but she had no idea what Sky was talking about. "The Island of Fire . . . swallowed you up?"

"Yes," said Sky. "I arrived here all alone. I—I didn't know you'd been captured." She paused, looking consternated, then continued. "I wasn't even sure where I was, or the name of this land, until the other day when I ventured into the marketplace and listened to some of the townspeople who were speaking our language. I'd assumed you and Fifer had been rescued weeks ago. And that you and Alex and the others had figured out the volcano connection . . . and came looking for me."

"The volcano connection?" Thisbe asked, even more puzzled. "What are you talking about? You mean the one in the crater lake over there?" She pointed to the center of the lake.

"Yes, exactly!"

"I still don't get it."

Sky's expression became strained. Smelling food burning,

she looked at the fire to check her fish and saw that it was beginning to char. Quickly she removed it from the spit and set it aside. "It's a long story. Do you want to eat something first?" Suddenly Sky remembered how Thisbe had nearly stolen her fish. "And what was that lie about getting food for your sick mother? Your mother died when you were a baby!"

Thisbe's lips parted; then heat flooded her face. The lie had come so naturally. The Revinir must be right about her being more evil than good, no matter what Rohan had told her. "I've been through some tough times," Thisbe said in a soft voice. She grimaced as the memories of the Revinir forcing her to drink the broths flashed through her mind. The horror she'd felt as dragon scales erupted from her arms and legs after the dragon-bone broth. And the shock of the strange images that had blinded her after the ancestor broth. Absently Thisbe pulled her sleeves down over the scales—she didn't feel like explaining those quite yet.

The small movement made her groan in pain. Her limbs were weak, her muscles sore from escaping the catacombs. Her stomach ached with hunger. But she remembered Rohan back in their camp area and knew he'd be worried if she stayed away too long. "I have a friend who escaped with me. He's hiding over there in the brush. May I . . . invite him to eat something too?"

"Of course," said Sky, eyeing the girl with concern. "I was only teasing about your little fib. You can move your things into my cave. There's room for three, and the fire keeps the bugs away."

"Thanks." Thisbe didn't bother to explain that they didn't really have any "things" other than their bone harnesses and the clothes on their backs. She squeezed Sky's arm. "It's amazing to see you. You have no idea."

"And you," Sky said, heartfelt.

Thisbe ran off to get Rohan while Sky wiped the dust off two large pieces of bark, which she'd collected and used as plates over the past weeks. When she heard the two coming toward the cave, she broke into the fish with a stick and portioned it out onto the bark.

Thisbe introduced the two. "Rohan is from here in Grimere," she explained. "He was one of the black-eyed slaves with me inside the catacombs."

"I'm so sorry you were imprisoned," Sky said. "I'm glad you escaped."

"Thank you," said Rohan, bowing his head slightly. "I'm happy to meet you. And to learn more about how you got here." Thisbe had given Rohan a hurried explanation of who Sky was as they ran to the cave, but he was not quite sure he understood what she was doing here, if not to rescue Thisbe.

"I think we're all a little confused," said Sky. She handed Rohan and Thisbe plates of steaming fish.

As they ate, Thisbe explained that Simber had indeed arrived and had tried rescuing her and Fifer, but he'd hit the invisible glass and hurt Fifer. He'd managed to collect her, but before he could come back for Thisbe, the Revinir's soldiers had snatched her up. She'd been forced to work underground in the catacombs for the long-fingernailed woman all this time. "I thought Simber would come back for me," Thisbe said quietly. "Even once I heard that they'd left the land of the dragons and headed home to get Fifer to safety, I expected him to come back. But no one ever did." She paused as tears sprang to her eyes. "That's why I thought you were part of some sort of rescue team." She stared blearily into the fire for a moment, then set her bark plate down. "I thought you'd finally come for me. But that's not it at all, is it?"

"No. I'm sorry." Sky watched Thisbe, her compassion evident. "But at least we're together now," she said quietly.

Thisbe pulled her gaze away from the mesmerizing flames. "Yes. At least there's that. Though it sounds like we're still stuck here." She was quiet for a moment. She and Rohan accepted another serving of fish. Then Thisbe glanced at Sky. "What happened to you?"

Sky stoked the fire and sat down with a sigh. "About a week or so after Simber, Carina, and Thatcher stopped by, I was out working on the Island of Fire. Just minding my own business as usual, trying to figure out how and why the volcano rises and plunges the way it does." Like Thisbe had done, she stared into the fire as she spoke, her eyes reliving the experience. "With almost no warning, the island began to go down. I dove for the white boat but couldn't get it started in time. Scarlet was in the skiff a safe distance away—too far to help. The island sank, and the boat and I were sucked with the sea into the mouth of the volcano."

Thisbe and Rohan stared. "Then what happened?" Thisbe asked. "How did you not drown?"

"The water poured on top of me like a huge, heavy weight,"

LISA McMANN

said Sky. "I got separated from the boat. I thought I was going to die. I held my breath as long as I could, but when I finally had to gasp for air, I discovered I could breathe. Only shallowly, and it was very uncomfortable, but there was some sort of protection . . . a bubble or something around me. It was too difficult to move my chest because of the intense pressure. I felt like I was moving at an extremely high speed, but I didn't have any way to gauge that. Everything went black for a moment. Then I could see a circle of light in front of me. It was like a pinprick at first, but it grew larger the closer I got. So I sort of . . . *aimed* for it, I guess, by pointing my head toward the light. Seconds later I was shooting up through the circle and exploding out of that volcano right over there inside a giant ball of water."

"Are you serious?" Thisbe exclaimed, while Rohan remained dumbstruck. "Did the boat come out too?"

"No—that's one confusing part I still don't understand. The boat didn't come out with me. It . . . it kept going. I guess. I don't know. I didn't see it."

"How can that be? Where did it go?"

"I don't know," Sky said again. "But I've had a lot of time

to think about this out here all alone. And I wonder . . . ," said Sky, her voice measured, "I wonder if there might be other volcano islands out there, connected to this . . . network. Or whatever. So maybe the white boat ended up going through one of them into some other world."

"Some *other* world?" Thisbe asked, incredulous. "How many worlds do you think there are?"

Sky shrugged. "No idea. It's just a guess. But clearly there's a system that none of us knew about, though if we'd just thought a little more, we might have come up with it."

"How?" asked Thisbe.

"Do you remember that pirates from our world used to travel somewhere to sell the sea creatures they'd captured? That's why Pan wanted to send her young dragons away in the first place, because they were in grave danger. But we didn't know where she'd sent them, or how they'd gotten there. It's all starting to make sense."

Thisbe was silent, trying to understand.

"Pardon me," said Rohan, a puzzled look on his face. "You mentioned that you flew out of the mouth of the volcano when it surfaced. Were you thrown clear of the volcano itself?"

"Yes, luckily."

"You must have hit the water with tremendous force. How did you survive?"

"Well," said Sky with a shaky laugh, "that's another mystery. I managed a deep breath before hitting the surface of the lake, so I wasn't worried about drowning, but I landed so hard I knocked myself out."

"How did you swim to shore?" Thisbe asked.

Sky gave the two a solemn look. "I didn't. I think . . . something . . . helped me."

"Some . . . *thing*?" asked Thisbe. "Like what?"

"When I opened my eyes, I was lying on the shore, and there were large footprints in the wet sand next to me. They weren't human. They were webbed."

"Webbed?" said Thisbe. "Like a duck?"

"No-o-o," said Sky slowly. "Much bigger." She hesitated, like she couldn't believe what she was about to say. "They reminded me of the footprints that our own dear Issie the sea monster makes when she comes to Artimé for a visit."

A Familiar Face

Fifer Stowe and the others on the rescue team had failed to find Fifer's twin, Thisbe. Now they were in a strange forest far away from home, injured, exhausted, and digging a grave so they could bury Alex Stowe, their head mage. Their brother. Their friend. The evil Revinir, once known as Queen Eagala of Warbler, had surprised them in the catacombs and struck him down with a lethal spear of dragon fire through his heart.

While Talon, the bronze giant, took over the grave digging, Lani Haluki and her husband, Samheed Burkesh, clung to each other looking shell-shocked. Alex had been one of their dearest friends for more than half their lives, ever since they were first declared Unwanted and purged from Quill. They'd been through so much together. They'd fought together, found love together; they'd even lost their faithful friend Meghan Ranger together.

The remaining three had forged stronger bonds in adulthood. There were few people who'd understood Alex better than Lani and Samheed. There were few people Alex had trusted more than them. The friends were in the prime of their lives! They had so much ahead of them! But in one horrible instant, Alex was gone. It felt like a nightmare.

"I can't believe this is happening," Lani whispered. Samheed squeezed her hand like he was holding on for dear life. He couldn't speak. Tears streamed down his cheeks.

A step away from Lani, Fifer was numb and silent. Her relationship with her brother Alex had been rocky. But in the past days he'd become so much more than the stern, slightly distant, rule-enforcing figure she'd known all her life. He'd changed himself and in the process had come to see and accept Fifer as a full-fledged mage—and a good one, at that. He'd become her partner in this quest. Her teammate. Her friend. He'd found trust in her, and she in him. And their relationship had just begun to bloom. They'd worked well together—imagine that!—and had talked about the future. Fifer had grown to love him more than she could have expressed. And she'd wanted to start making up for all the years they'd butted heads.

But now he was dead, and Fifer didn't know what to do. There was a fresh new hole in her heart, right next to the one for Thisbe. Fifer wasn't sure if her heart had room for any more. She wasn't used to this—wasn't used to losing anyone. The jolt of these losses hit like a hurricane. Her life had been completely upended over the course of months, and she'd been thrust into a nightmare . . . arguably one of her own making. A wave of guilt washed over her. She closed her eyes for a moment to try to withstand it.

And the chances of rescuing Thisbe had just plummeted. She was still being held captive somewhere in the catacombs. But the rescue group's magical components were useless. Alex's death had broken Artimé's magical system. Without it, they were too vulnerable to go after Thisbe again. So they were stranded here until someone in Artimé restored things. Even then, what would they do without Alex? It was a helpless spot to be in. Fifer edged closer to Lani for comfort, and the woman reached out and gave Fifer's shoulder a gentle squeeze.

Fifer's gaze turned to Simber, who'd become a frozen statue when the magic disappeared. Letting Simber know what had happened . . . It would be impossible. Fifer glanced at Lani and said quietly. "Will you tell Simber when he wakes up?"

Lani nodded. "Of course," she whispered. "Don't worry about that anymore." She kept her arm around Fifer. They watched Talon continue to dig.

The legendary winged bronze giant from Karkinos, the Island of Legends, was unaffected by the Artiméan magical outage. He raked his hands deeper and deeper into the forest floor, pulling roots and rocks and dirt out of the way. Digging a grave for a hero in a land that wasn't theirs.

As Talon was finishing, trumpets sounded in the far-off distance. The Artiméans paid little attention. When the grave was ready, they removed Alex's robe. Crow folded it carefully. Then Samheed, Carina, Seth, Thatcher, and Kaylee lowered Alex's body into the grave, laying their head mage to rest forever. Those who wanted to speak about what he'd meant to them did so tearfully, quietly. Others stood by, unable to find the words, staring silently through wet eyes.

When it was over, they each put a fist to their chests and tapped, saying, "I am with you." It was a symbol of unity that Alex had created in a dark moment many years before. A symbol the Artiméans intended to continue using in Alex's honor. No matter where his body was buried, the people of Artimé would hold Alex in their hearts, just as he had held them all in his.

Fifer stood back as the rest of them pushed the dirt into the hole, on top of her brother. Slowly they dispersed, but Fifer remained, watching the fresh mound of brown dirt turn gray in the heat.

Seth stood with her. After a moment he put his hand on her shoulder, but he stayed quiet too. He was trying to remember every second of the funeral perfectly. Someone would have to recount it to Thisbe someday, and Seth wanted it to be right. It was the only thing he could think of to do for his friends in this terrible time.

At the campfire a short distance away, Crow, still holding Alex's robe, looked at the others. "Does anyone remember the spell to bring the world back? Perhaps it can be done from here."

"I know the spell," said Lani, sniffling and wiping away tears that wouldn't stop flowing. "But I don't think it'll work, because part of it requires standing on the back step of the gray shack. But I'll try it. I'll try anything."

Crow brought the robe to her because Lani's wheels weren't working well at all on this terrain. Now that the magic had been stripped from the contraption she'd been using ever since her lower body had become paralyzed in the final battle of the seven islands, she struggled to move. She slipped the robe over her shoulders and fastened it. It smelled burned, but it also smelled like Alex. She breathed deeply, trying to absorb any possible lingering greatness from the mage, knowing there would be no more opportunities to get it firsthand. No more talks, no more philosophical arguments, no more laughter or playing tricks on each other. The harshness of that realization was more than Lani could take right now. First Meghan, now Alex. She and Samheed were the only ones left of the original foursome. At barely twenty-eight years of age, it wasn't right or fair. Her heart ached for Alex and Sky and their future lives that would never be. The universe was altered. All hope seemed to drip away from her limbs and soak into this miserable place, and there was nothing Lani could do to collect it.

She opened her eyes. "I'll try over there," she said quietly, pointing to an open area. Samheed helped her across the rough ground to the space she indicated, then stepped out of the way.

Lani blew out a breath and closed her eyes. She concentrated for a long moment. Then she recited the magic spell that she'd memorized years before, just in case she might ever need it, for that was the kind of person Lani was.

Follow the dots as the traveling sun,

Magnify, focus, every one.

Stand enrobed where you first saw me,

Utter in order, repeat times three.

Then she concentrated even harder and said, "Imagine. Believe. Whisper. Breathe. Commence." Those five words had been revealed in the "dots" found in artwork in the head mage's office, which is what the spell referred to. Lani didn't need to see the art to remember the words. She repeated them three times, pausing in between each word to really think about it and what it meant, and its significance to bringing back the world.

They all waited. After the last words were uttered, Lani opened her eyes and looked down at her wheeled vehicle to see if it had taken on its usual magical sheen. But nothing had changed. "Is Simber still frozen?" she said.

"Still frozen," Samheed confirmed. "I'm sorry."

Lani muttered an oath under her breath, clearly disappointed. "I didn't think it would work," she said. "I suppose I should try it again, just in case."

Carina nodded. "It won't hurt."

Lani concentrated and went through the slow process again. But it was to no avail. "I'm not standing where I first saw Mr. Today," she lamented. "We've got to be in Artimé on the back stoop of the shack to do this."

"Claire Morning has got to be getting there soon," said Samheed. "It's been hours."

"I hope nothing's wrong," said Kaylee. Kaylee Jones was not magical, but she was a skilled swordswoman and sailor. Nor was she originally from the world of the seven islands.

She'd come to their world on her sailboat through what she called the Dragon's Triangle, which was a deadly area of the sea in her world.

"If we don't get our magic back soon," said Samheed, "something is definitely not right."

Fifer, who'd left the graveside and wandered over to watch Lani, sagged in disappointment after the failed spell. She moved away again, but not out of sight. Seth stayed with her. They sat down, resting their backs against a large tree trunk.

"Do you think you should try it?" Seth asked her.

Fifer looked sideways at him and was surprised by his earnest, compassionate expression. A sudden pang pierced through her numbness, and she drew in a breath. "Try what?"

"That spell."

"Me? Why? I don't know it."

"You're the best mage we've got," said Seth.

Fifer was quiet. Then: "It won't work if it's like Lani said—you have to be standing in a place we can't get to."

Seth shrugged. "Yeah, I suppose." He glanced at her carefully. "So . . . how are you feeling?" He wasn't quite sure how to talk about someone being dead, especially a person who'd been so close to Fifer. It wasn't something he'd ever had to do before. He glanced at her, a bit nervous to see if he'd upset her.

"I feel odd," Fifer said.

"Me too," said Seth.

"It's like everything that I can't reach inside me hurts," Fifer went on. "But my skin is numb. My mind is thick, like half-frozen mud. I just . . . I can't believe Alex is *dead*. I feel like I should be crying more, but I'm just . . . I'm stunned. Why . . . ? How . . . ?" She was quiet for a moment. They listened to the trees groan and the crackle of twigs and leaves as the others moved around camp. "I can't make sense of it. How did this happen? *Why* was the Revinir in that crypt?"

"I don't know," said Seth.

"I mean, like, did your team see her sneak in there or something? You were over there the whole time."

"Of course not," said Seth defensively, "or we wouldn't have just barged in without a plan—or without telling Alex and you. We thought Thisbe was in there. Alone, like the other prisoners were."

"I know. I know," muttered Fifer. She put a hand over her eyes and sighed. "I'm sorry. I don't know what I'm saying."

LISA McMANN

She glanced at Seth with a guilty look. She'd hurt him with that accusation, and she knew it wasn't fair, but she felt compelled to find someone to blame for this in order to make sense of it. But Seth was her closest friend now. Another sharp pain found its way in.

"It's okay," said Seth.

They were quiet again, and the trumpet call could be heard a third time that evening. Fifer continued to grapple with the events and how they'd occurred. "It just seems weird that the Revinir was in there. Like one of the prisoners. Why did Dev lie to us? Why did he purposely say Thisbe was in a room in that hallway? Did he do that to trick us? Did he know that the Revinir would be in there?"

There was a crackling sound of sticks behind them. Seth turned but saw nothing in the shadows. "Maybe. Probably, knowing him. I'll bet he told the Revinir to do it after he saw we were back in this world."

Fifer nodded, then grew puzzled as she thought through the timeline. "What—you mean after Princess Shanti was killed? Dev didn't stick around. He ran away from the catacombs, not toward them. He must have known the Revinir would be in

LISA McMANN

that crypt before then. And that's why he sent us there." It felt good to blame someone. "He's a terrible person."

"Yes," agreed Seth.

"No," came a voice, and Dev stepped into the patch of moonlight. "I wasn't lying. I sent you to Thisbe's crypt. I swear it." He looked around, straining to see in the darkness. "Where is she? Didn't you find her?"

Finding Some Answers

Dev!" exclaimed Fifer. She and Seth got to their feet. Princess Shanti's personal black-eyed slave, Dev, stood before them. He looked ragged and filthy.

"Didn't you find her?" Dev demanded again.

Pulses of heat and anger throbbed through Fifer's numb body. Hot tears sprang to her eyes. It was Dev's fault they'd opened those crypts. Dev's fault that they'd been surprised by the Revinir. *It's Dev's fault that Alex is dead.* Fifer felt her cheeks burn, her skull practically expanding inside her scalp.

"This is your fault!" Fifer said angrily. Her face screwed up, and she ran at Dev, slamming into him and sending him flying

LISA McMANN

so hard to the ground that he hardly knew what had hit him. Then Fifer jumped on top of him and started punching him as hard as she could.

"Help!" Dev cried, shielding his face with his arms and trying to roll out from under her.

Seth, realizing what was happening, leaped to grab Fifer and drag her off Dev. Fifer kicked and yelled, bringing Thatcher and Seth's mother, Carina Holiday, running over to them.

"What's happening?" cried Carina, ready to fight.

"It's Dev!" shouted Fifer. "He tricked us! He sent us right into the Revinir's trap so she could kill Alex!" Spit and tears flew from her. She tried wriggling out of Seth's grasp, then kicked backward at him, mad that he'd pulled her away. She landed a blow that sent Seth yowling, and he dropped her to the ground. Fifer clawed her way to her feet again and ran at Dev once more, slamming her head into his stomach as he tried to get up.

"Fifer, stop!" Thatcher said, going after her. He grabbed her around the waist and pulled her away. She kicked at Thatcher, too, but he held her fast and wrapped a thick arm around her legs to soften the blows. "Seth, help Dev up."

Seth obeyed. Fifer's yells turned to sobs. "You tricked us," she said. "Just like you did before. It's your fault my brother is dead!"

"What? Dead?" Dev, his chest heaving and his nose and lip dripping blood, pulled from Seth's grip and scooted backward like a crab away from them, a wild look on his face. Seth, limping, stayed with him, like he was worried Dev might try to make a run for it.

Kaylee came running up to the group, sword drawn. "What's going on?"

"I don't know what happened!" Dev shouted back at Fifer. "I promise I didn't do whatever it is you think I've done. I mean it!" He looked around fearfully, then lowered his voice and said in a harsh whisper, "The Revinir is my enemy too!"

Fifer's throat felt scorched. Between sobs she looked at Dev's face. It was blurry through her tears, but she could see he was afraid, and she didn't think he was faking it. She began to struggle again in Thatcher's grasp. "You can put me down," she muttered.

Thatcher set Fifer on her feet. "Don't go after him again," he warned. "This boy saved your life once, when you almost

LISA McMANN

bled to death. You owe him a chance to explain at the very least."

Fifer frowned and swiped at her tears. Her knuckles throbbed from where she'd punched Dev, but she hardly remembered doing it. What was going on? It was like an explosion had happened inside her. She took a deep breath and blew it out, trying to calm down. "Dev has double-crossed us before," she said. "I should have known not to trust him. He sent us straight down into the catacombs to get ambushed by the Revinir."

Thatcher looked at Dev. "Is this true?"

"No," said Dev, impassioned. "I mean . . . it's true I might have screwed up in the past. But the Revinir thing . . . I honestly don't know what you're talking about. From the elevator, Thisbe's crypt is the last one on the left. I would have been more specific if I'd had time to tell you more. It was a big risk for me to tell you that much." He touched his protruding lip tenderly.

Fifer and the others stayed quiet, letting him explain. Dev, relieved, straightened his shirt and sat up a bit straighter. "I was outside all day working in the market. There was no way I could have known the Revinir would be in Thisbe's crypt.

She doesn't exactly fill me in on her whereabouts." He wiped his nose on his sleeve and, lifting his arm to the moonlight, he examined the amount of blood soaking in. "Maybe if you tell me what happened, I can help you try to make sense of it."

Fifer couldn't answer. She folded her arms over her chest, squeezing her fists to increase the stiffening, throbbing pain in her knuckles. At least that pain was something that made sense. Something that penetrated her numbness.

Seth told Dev everything that had happened on their mission, from the time they'd enacted their rescue plan to the critical moments after they'd broken the door to Thisbe's crypt.

Dev's mouth slacked when he heard about how the Revinir had killed Fifer and Thisbe's brother. "I'm sorry," he said. "I . . . I didn't know any of this. Like I said, I hadn't been down there since early yesterday morning before I got sent to work at the market."

"Why would the Revinir be hiding in a crypt?" asked Thatcher. "Is that something she often does?"

"She never does that as far as I know," said Dev. "But I was only there for a short time, and she kept me busy working. I don't know why she would have been inside Thisbe's crypt.

LISA McMANN

And I don't know where Thisbe could have been this morning when you went to rescue her. The slaves start work early, but if the other children were still in their locked crypts like you said, that means Mangrel hadn't been by yet to let them out for the day." He hesitated, then explained, "Mangrel is the crypt keeper, not a soldier. He brings water in the morning and opens the crypt doors. Maybe Thisbe got called to go in early this morning and was already in the Revinir's kitchen working on bone broth by the time you came down into the catacombs. Unless . . ." He stared thoughtfully and didn't finish.

"Unless what?" asked Fifer.

"Nothing. I was just thinking she could've gotten into trouble for refusing to help the Revinir. She was already on the edge after everything else the Revinir made her do. And maybe she's been sent to the dungeon. But that wouldn't make much sense. . . . She's too valuable to the Revinir now." Dev slid his hand over his dragon scales thoughtfully and tugged at his ragged sleeve. Then he turned and looked at Fifer with true remorse in his eyes. "I'm sorry about your brother. I promise you—I'm not that evil. I've . . . I've lost my family too. I wouldn't wish it on anyone."

Dev's confession came as a surprise, just like many of Dev's statements or actions did. He said it without looking for pity, but to prove his innocence.

Kaylee studied Dev's face for a long moment, then put away her sword. "I'm sorry," she told him. She'd also lost her family, since there was no way for her to get back to America. In fact, almost everyone in their group had lost someone dear to them. Carina's first husband, who was Seth's father, had died in the first battle Artimé fought against Quill long ago. Seth didn't remember him, but it was a loss nonetheless. Thatcher was the only one whose entire family was still living, all of them having made their way to Artimé years ago after Queen Eagala—now the Revinir—had been overthrown.

Fifer eyed the boy, feeling suddenly exhausted. "All right," she said warily. "Come with me before you bleed all over everything." Blood kept dripping from his nose, and she went to her bag to get him a cloth so he could clean up by the river. Now both she and Thisbe had given Dev a nosebleed. Fifer wasn't exactly proud of it, but she thought it was an interesting fact. When she got to her things and dug through the bag in the firelight, she realized it was suspiciously empty. "Oh no," she

LISA McMANN

45 « Dragon Ghosts

lamented. "All the food from Artimé has disappeared!"

"I didn't take it!" Dev said hastily.

"I know you didn't," said Fifer, sounding devastated. "It's our magic. It's gone for the moment because . . ." She grimaced. "Well, it's gone until somebody in Artimé figures out how to bring it back. But all of the magically prepared meals brought along have disappeared." She sighed heavily and started crying again, though it was more for their situation and the reminder that Alex was dead than the fact that the food was gone.

Carina came over to Fifer. "Don't worry. You brought fishing gear, didn't you?"

Fifer nodded.

"I can help with that," said Dev, seeming desperate to make up for past transgressions. "I'm—I want to help in any way I can. I don't really have anything else . . . to do. Now."

"Yeah," said Fifer quietly. "Sorry." She knew he must be grieving for Princess Shanti. "But why are you acting so nice?" She gave him a suspicious look. "It's not like we're going to turn you in to the king or the Revinir or anyone. I'm the one who shouted at you to run yesterday in the market."

"I know." Dev looked at the ground. "I knew it was you. Thank you."

"Whoa." Fifer eyed him suspiciously. "Did you just say thank you? Now you're starting to worry me." She pulled a cloth from her bag and shoved it at him. "What do you want from us, anyway?"

"Fifer," Carina chided softly, since Alex was no longer there to insist that Fifer be kind.

Fifer narrowed her eyes at Carina and said quietly, "You don't know Dev like I do."

"Fair point," Carina conceded. "Continue."

"Well?" Fifer prompted Dev. "Answer me." She was starting to figure out what he was doing. But she wanted to hear what he would say. Perhaps she'd be surprised again.

Dev glanced around self-consciously, seeing all of Fifer's group except for the strangely frozen ones looking at him. He wiped his nose with the cloth and held it there for a moment. Then he winced, whether from pain or because of what he was about to say, Fifer wasn't sure.

"I've never . . . been alone . . . before."

Fifer tilted her head disbelievingly.

Seth made a disgusted face. "Lie. You were alone on the rock the morning you took our food."

"True." Dev closed his eyes for a moment. "I meant . . ." He stopped and blew out a breath. "Without Shanti or someone else controlling me. You know? I'm . . . I don't know what else to do. And I also thought maybe you'd have Thisbe here now. She's been . . ."

"She's been what?" asked Fifer.

"A friend." He sighed again and closed his eyes, defeated. "Never mind. A lot has happened."

Fifer and Seth glanced at each other, confused. Finally they took Dev aside, out of the spotlight. Everyone else stayed near the glow of the campfire.

Fifer had always thought it was easier to talk in the dark, and this was no exception. "First, I'm sorry that Shanti died. That must have been a big shock for you." She knew well enough now how it felt to go through that—she was still reeling.

"Thanks."

"But I want to make sure you know that Shanti was not your friend. She didn't treat you like a friend. She was horrible to you."

Dev was silent. His expression became pained.

"Fifer," said Seth, "maybe now's not quite the time to talk about that."

Fifer pressed her lips together and glanced at Dev.

"It's okay," said Dev. "I know. I mean . . . she was nice to me sometimes, but . . ."

"You were her slave, Dev," said Fifer, trying to be gentle. "That's not okay, even if she was nice to you sometimes. You shouldn't have to be anybody's slave! Not for any reason! If she had been a real friend, she wouldn't have kept making *you* get punished for the things *she* did wrong. And she would have given you those gold rocks all the time, whenever you did work. Not just as a bonus for making a zillion gold rocks for her, or whatever."

Dev closed his eyes.

"Fifer, he knows," said Seth. "He doesn't need a lesson right now. He just . . . He needs some real friends." Seth put a hand on Dev's shoulder, and the boy startled at the touch and jerked away. "Sorry," mumbled Seth, dropping his hand.

"It's all right." Dev kept his gaze on the forest floor and tugged his sleeves again. "I was wondering if I could stay with your camp for a while. Until I . . . figure some things out."

"Of course you can," said Seth.

Fifer hesitated, then nodded. "Sure."

"I might be able to help you find Thisbe," Dev said, as if he were still trying to convince them.

"Even if you don't, it's okay," said Fifer. "You can stay with us." She hadn't fully let go of her wariness of the boy, but when she'd started to look at life from his angle, she was a lot more willing to give him another chance. "Just don't be a jerk," she suggested.

"I'll try not to be." Dev's eyes darted restlessly toward the river. "I'll go catch some fish if you want."

"Sure," said Seth. "That would be great. I'm starving. You're planning to share this time, right?"

"Yes, of course," whispered Dev. He knew he deserved that.

"My fishing tackle is in my bag if you need it," said Fifer.

"I've got my hook." Dev looked like he wanted to get away from the intense conversation. Fifer had had enough of it by now too.

As they walked toward the riverbank, the three heard a flutter in the trees that grew louder and more intense as dozens of red-and-purple falcons landed on branches above them. When the noise quieted, Shimmer, the leader, dropped down and landed on Fifer's shoulder.

Fifer petted the falcon. "You found us," she murmured. The bird shimmered brightly, magically, in the dark forest.

"Birds?" said Dev. "Are they your pets?"

"Sort of," said Fifer.

"Does that shimmer mean the magic is back?" asked Seth.

They looked back toward the camp at Simber, who was still frozen. "I guess not," said Fifer, confused. "But the birds have brought the hammock with them. And since she's still shimmering, I don't think they've lost their magic."

"Wait a second—maybe you haven't lost yours, either," said Seth, growing excited. "Your automatic magic, I mean. That stuff you were just born with."

"Maybe," marveled Fifer.

"What else can you do?" asked Seth.

Fifer pointed her finger to test her abilities. "Glass." Dev scooted away and shielded his face, just in case. But no glass appeared.

"That's an Artimé spell that you learned," said Seth. "So

LISA McMANN

it wouldn't work. Try one of your shrieks. Wait—on second thought, we don't want any glass breaking around here. Someone could get hurt."

"If there even is any glass in the forest," said Fifer. She glanced at Shimmer and stopped abruptly. "Hey! If the birds are still magical, we can get a few of us home in the hammock if we want to."

"Wow, you're right!" said Seth. But then he shook his head. "Talon could take us too. But that's not how we do things. We all go down with the ship, remember? Like in Lani's books about the old days. We can't leave until we have Thisbe."

Fifer nodded, a lump in her throat and the familiar Thisbe hole in her heart aching. She couldn't help remembering that they'd left this world once before without Thisbe. Would they have a reason to do that again? After Alex's death, everything had turned upside down. Nothing was certain.

As the three of them resumed walking to the river, the trumpets sounded in the distance once more.

"What is that?" Fifer asked. "Dev, do you know?"

From his pocket Dev pulled out a little box, which held his fishing hook. "It's the king's call to arms," he said in a low

LISA McMANN

voice. "He's telling the world that he's about to get revenge on the Revinir for Princess Shanti's death. He's declaring war on her, and he is asking the people to join him."

"The villagers, you mean?" asked Fifer. "What are they supposed to do—drop everything and go to the castle to volunteer?"

"Yes. Exactly," said Dev. "There will be some training first, of course."

"Oh," said Seth, looking puzzled. "But whose side are we on, exactly? The king's, right? Even though he keeps slaves too? That doesn't seem okay. Are you going to, like, heed the call, or whatever, Dev?"

Dev snorted. "Not me. I'll never go back there."

"So, wait. Does that mean you're on the Revinir's side?" Seth asked slowly, as if fearing the answer.

Dev just glared at him, and Fifer shook her head slowly. "He's on neither side," she said.

"True," said Dev.

"Just like us," Fifer continued thoughtfully. "We're on our own. No—we're on the side of the black-eyed people and the dragons—the original rulers. They aren't represented by

LISA McMANN

either the king or the Revinir. In fact, they're mistreated by both sides." She hesitated. "It seems to me like maybe it's time to get rid of them all. And . . . and put the rightful rulers back in power."

"You mean us," said Dev, looking at her.

Fifer blinked. She caught his gaze, his black eyes mirror images of her own. "Yes," she said, almost breathless. The size of the challenge poured over her all at once like a bucket of freezing-cold water. "Us."

Seth crouched down by the river. "But how? And where do we find the dragons?" he asked, puzzled. "Arabis is in this world somewhere, but I'm guessing she can't fly right now. Her wings must have fallen off since they're magical." He scratched his head. "Besides, we need to find Thisbe. That should be our main goal right now. The last thing we need is a war."

"I agree," Fifer said, breaking the connection with Dev and turning to Seth. "We need to find her. Before . . ." She blinked hard. "Before something else terrible happens." The last thing Fifer needed was to lose somebody else she loved. Fear rippled through her at the thought.

Dev glanced at Seth. "I have an idea where at least some of the dragons are," he said with a glint in his eye. He slid his hand absently over his forearm, the scales still invisible in the dark. "Once we have Thisbe back, I can take you there."

The Plight of Arabis

Arabis the orange's wings had turned to vines, cloth, and flower petals, and they'd fallen off. She'd noticed it immediately because she'd been flying back to the rescue team in the forest after having delivered her message to the ghost dragons.

She plunged toward the desertlike ground following the wings, not far outside the cavelands where the ghost dragons dwelled. The forest, where the Artiméans were camped out, was a few flight hours away. At the last moment before striking the ground, Arabis twisted and coiled her tail below her like a spring in a desperate attempt to soften her landing. But her tail had nerves too, so there wasn't anything she could do to avoid devastating pain. When she hit, her coiled tail flattened beneath her weight, and her neck bent and snapped like a sapling branch, giving her whiplash. It was a wonder her spine was intact after that.

She flopped to her side, the wind knocked out of her, unable to breathe for several moments, and then cringing in pain when she was finally able to suck in some air. Any ordinary beast of that size would surely be dead after a fall from such a height. But Arabis was a dragon from the line of Pan, and Pan's dragons had mysterious powers. She lay on the hard dirt for many hours, eyes closed, and drew in the healing auras of the bright blue sky and the baked earth.

While she lay there, her mind extremely rattled and still sorting out what had happened to her, she opened an eye and discovered her wings nearby. They were bent but intact, and looked like they had before Alex had attached them to her body and cast his magical spell on them.

Arabis pondered why her wings had separated from her. Why had they lost their magic? She didn't understand what could have happened. Were these new wings defective? She'd had the old wings for more than ten years, and they'd never done anything like this. Something must have gone terribly wrong. Perhaps Alex had made the wings temporarily magical by mistake. But Alex didn't seem to be the type of human who would make a careless move like that.

In the back of her mind, Arabis recalled someone from Artimé mentioning something about their magic disappearing once before—it had happened a few years prior to the young dragons' birth. But the details of the story eluded her. She drifted off and slept restlessly.

Sleep brought healing, and her foggy brain began to clear. When she woke, she tried moving her legs one at a time. One of the front ones was mostly benumbed, but she could slide it over the ground with a bit of effort. Her tail and her neck throbbed.

The dragon rested for a few more hours, channeling all of her strength into fixing her bruised body. Eventually she pushed herself up on shaking limbs, testing to see if they'd hold her. She uncoiled her crushed tail gingerly, crying out in pain as she did so. It had likely saved her life and would take time to heal properly. What she desperately needed now was food and water.

Arabis took a few steps and looked around the deserted landscape to get an idea of where exactly she was. She was much nearer to the ghost dragons than to the rescue team. Could she reach the Artiméans on foot . . . limping all the way? Would it be safe to do so without her ability to fly? There was a wide-open space to cross before the forest began, which left her feeling uneasy and vulnerable.

In her state, going back to the dragons was the only good option. The Revinir or the king's soldiers probably wouldn't think twice about recapturing her if they learned of her wandering about, injured. And trying to walk all the way through the entire forest to get to the section where the people of Artimé had set up camp was going to be too much of a challenge, at least right away. If she couldn't fly over the trees, she'd have to knock them down to make a path. It would take many hours to reach the river there.

She hesitated. Knowing the Artiméans would be expecting her, and perhaps needing her to make an escape across the gorge, she almost set out that way against her best judgment. But she couldn't help them get home in this condition. Sure, they might be able to bring her magical wings back, but she wasn't in any shape to fly or carry passengers quite yet. She needed at least a few more hours, and perhaps even a day, to fully heal.

She looked back toward the cavelands. It might take her only an hour on foot to get to the river. Perhaps she'd feel better after a meal and a drink of water. Then she could continue healing and go to the Artiméans when she was up to the travel.

With these things in mind, Arabis eased over to her wings and picked them up in her mouth to carry them. Then she turned toward the cavelands. She went slowly at first across the barren landscape, and her movements grew a little easier over time. Her tail, normally curling and in motion, dragged behind her, straight and limp.

Before too long she stopped and stared at a shimmering heat oasis in front of her. She lifted her snout, still holding her wings in her mouth. Smoke curled from her nostrils, but no flames appeared—that could set her wings on fire. Arabis's eyes narrowed, then cleared, and she continued. A moment later two ghost dragons appeared from the mirage, flying slowly and unevenly, low to the ground, toward her. Perhaps they'd sensed her fall by now.

In the air, the two knocked together as if in a quarrel. Flames lit up the space between them, and they tussled and sparred, nearly crashing to the ground before righting themselves and continuing on.

Arabis was nonplussed. Dragons sparred, often more for play than anything. She focused as they drew closer.

The ghost dragons had a thick skeletal appearance that was ethereal, yet their bodies were solid to the touch. Their overlay was a bluish, silvery gray that varied, occasionally even verging on brown depending on their surroundings. This coloring allowed them to blend easily with the enormous rocks in the cavelands. Out here, in the flat desert area, they took on a taupe tinge that matched the dirt.

Their wings were tattered and appeared moth eaten, leaving them with gaping holes between the long ribs of each wing, yet the dragons were somehow able to soar on the unhindered breezes of the open land. When they reached Arabis, they landed. Small clouds of dust rose from their feet on impact. It wasn't clear whether the dust came from their ghostly bodies or the parched ground.

Arabis recognized them from the previous day. She set her

wings down so she could greet them. "Gorgrun, Quince, I'm Arabis," she reminded them. "Daughter of Pan." She'd noted during her first visit that the ghost dragons were an unusual and especially forgetful breed, and she didn't want them to think she was an enemy.

"Ah, yes, Arabis," said the one called Quince. "Strange name."

Arabis frowned but didn't argue, as they were very old.

"We felt the impact when you landed," said Gorgrun, the larger of the two. "Reminded me of the great quake, after . . ." He trailed off as if he'd forgotten that he was talking and stood slightly stooped on his massive back limbs. He held his front limbs close to his chest. They ended in four fingerlike talons that curled and released rhythmically.

Gorgrun gave a puzzled glance at Arabis's strange-looking wings on the ground. "Quince flew up to the lookout point and saw you," he said. "We assumed you'd be embarrassed for falling, so we didn't come immediately. . . . It happens to the best of us." He looked away, as if he were the one embarrassed on Arabis's behalf. "This morning Quince remembered your fall and went again to check on you. When you hadn't gotten up, we thought something more might have happened. Were you attacked? What . . . are those?" He indicated the detached wings.

"I wasn't attacked." Arabis's tail was feeling better now, so she used it gingerly to pick up the wings and lay them across the hollow on her back. "But my thirst is great."

"Of course. There's a stream around here somewhere," said Gorgrun.

"It's this way," said Quince.

They turned together and walked toward the cavelands. As they went along, Arabis explained what had happened. "I didn't want to travel all the way to my destination without resting up a little more," she concluded.

"Your wings . . . came off?" muttered Gorgrun, glancing back at his battered wings. "I feel like that could happen to me, actually. It's unsettling."

Quince squinted at Arabis. "I seem to recall a trail through the forest that runs close to where you wish to go. I can show you once you're ready. That will give you cover and safety until your friends can repair your wings."

"I'm grateful," said Arabis. "Thank you." She hoped the

forgetful dragon would be able to remember where it was.

Soon the flat desert terrain became rolling and flecked with slate. The land sloped downward, and rock formations jutted like giant fingers poking up through the ground. Beyond the finger formations, the rocks grew larger and became a vast land peppered with caves. A wisp of fog curled through the area, and more exoskeletal silvery-blue dragons roamed slowly and purposefully.

Arabis reached the riverbed and drank eagerly. Then she found some plants among the scrubby brush to eat. Her body was continuing to heal, and her mind was clearing rapidly now. After more polite chatting about surface things—for dragons respected other dragons' secrets—Arabis began feeling like her old self again. Soon guilt returned about not getting back to the forest, and it occurred to her that perhaps something had gone wrong with the Artiméans' magic too—not just her wings. That was cause for alarm.

She didn't spend much longer in the cavelands. Instead she thanked the ghost dragons for their hospitality and reminded them of her original message: to beware of the Revinir now that Pan's dragons had escaped. They in turn thanked Arabis for being thoughtful enough to risk her own well-being to warn them.

"Try not to forget what I told you about the Revinir," Arabis implored.

"I will think about it every morning upon waking," Quince promised. "And if our time comes to fight for Grimere, we will be ready. This is of grave importance."

Arabis wasn't quite sure what Quince meant about fighting, but before she could ask, he told her where he thought the path was and offered to accompany her part of the way to make sure she was truly recovered and feeling all right. "I seem to recall it's hard to see the path unless you know where it is, but it'll make your journey to the opposite side much easier."

The two set off, leaving Gorgrun behind to meander off to . . . somewhere he probably couldn't remember. As they walked, Arabis thought about the previous day's conversation and her worries about the ghost dragons' forgetfulness. And despite her secretive nature, she decided that if she explained a bit more about what was going on with the Revinir, Quince might actually remember to be careful with the woman. It felt urgent somehow. So she waded into a deeper conversation. She told Quince about how she and her siblings had come to the land of the dragons ten years ago, seeking safety. And she told of their capture by the Revinir and how they'd been kept as slaves in the Castle Grimere until their recent rescue at the hands of the young black-eyed Artiméan girls and their friend.

Quince perked up. He seemed to recall at least a little about the black-eyed slaves. "Were the girls free? Are the black-eyed children no longer kept as slaves in Grimere?"

"These two were free in our land of the seven islands," Arabis explained. "But when the children released my siblings and me and we flew home to our world, the girls, Thisbe and Fifer, were captured. The king of Grimere sent them to the auction in Dragonsmarche. One of them got away. The other was kidnapped by the Revinir and taken into the catacombs. That's why I came back—to help them find the missing girl."

"So danger remains in wandering about?"

"Yes, especially without wings," Arabis said, and pointed her snout at the useless wings laid across her back. "You are in danger now too, if the Revinir comes this way."

"Right, right," said Quince, as if he'd just remembered what Arabis had come to them for in the first place. "I won't . . . I'll

LISA McMANN

try not . . . to forget." Then he stopped suddenly and turned to Arabis. "You must forgive our forgetfulness. We have so many years of memories that we cannot store the new information very well."

Arabis looked at Quince. "And how did you come to have so many memories?"

Quince looked at Arabis as if he expected her to know. "From being alive for so long."

"I see," said Arabis. Then she added, "My siblings and I weren't told much about this land while we were in captivity. We only heard whispers of your existence somewhere near the cavelands. Knowing the Revinir is growing more powerful and expanding her territory, we wanted to warn you." She gave Quince a sideways look, wondering, not for the first time, if the ghost dragons were truly ghosts or if that was just their breed name. But it seemed clear that Quince believed himself to be living, so Arabis respected that. "How long have you been alive?"

"Too long," said Quince. "Unfortunately, we cannot truly die until the dragon-and-black-eyed-human ruling body is restored to this land." He hesitated. "We've always known we

67 « Dragon Ghosts

LISA McMANN

might need to fight to help make it happen. On our own we're no match for young dragons or mages or Revinirs. But we hope to be of some use when the time comes."

"You are noble," said Arabis thoughtfully. "And admirable."

The old dragon nodded, then said, "Perhaps now that you are free, you can begin the process of putting the order of the land back together. With the help of your young human rescuers, you could try, at least. There are more dragons around, waiting to return home if things change." He paused, then added, "You could make a fair young ruler."

"Me?" said Arabis. "I don't have any experience with that."

Quince sort of shrugged his shoulders as they neared the end of the desert and the beginning of the forest. He peered through the trees as he walked along its edge, searching for the dragon path. "Somebody has to do it. And so many of the others have gone away."

"What about you?" asked Arabis.

Quince shook his head. "None of the ghost dragons can do it. We've had our turn. Through good and bad times. Some very bad. Now . . . we just want to sleep." He clamped his jaw shut, like he might have said too much. Without warning, he stopped in front of a row of young trees not as large as the rest. He slammed his tail into them, felling them so that Arabis could get through without hindrance. The path lay beyond.

Arabis felt a chill shake her spine, which reminded her that she still ached from her fall. She didn't ask any more questions, bowing to the tradition of not digging too deep into other dragons' secrets. They'd both already shared more than they'd intended at the onset of their journey. Arabis readjusted her wings across the hollow spot between her shoulder blades so they wouldn't get knocked off and stoically prepared to use her teeth and tail to pull out any other new growth that might be in her way.

"Thank you for your kindness," said Arabis, and reminded Quince one last time to beware the Revinir. "I hope you find what you are looking for."

"I wish the same for you," said Quince. He turned slowly, tilted his head uncertainly as he tried to recall where he needed to go next, then spread his tattered wings, rose on the wind, and soared away.

The Magical Robe

I t took some time for the leaders in Artimé to regain control of the area around the gray shack. Sean asked Clementi and Ibrahim to keep an eye on Ava and Lukas so he could focus on helping. Then he, Claire, and Henry organized a large enough group of their friends to begin pushing the Quillens away from the collapsed walls and back into Quill so they could look for the robe and the spell.

Darkness hampered their efforts, forcing them to stall action until morning so they could see properly. They spent a long, uncomfortable night on the ground. By first light they were up and at it again, keeping the people away by enlisting more Artiméans to form a human fence. Others were assigned to lift the walls so that they could search under the rubble for the items.

By the time the roof and the outer walls had been lifted and moved aside, it was noon. The interior walls remained, some of them crushed, but at least the group was making progress. Once Claire inspected each piece being removed, looking for signs of the colorful fibers of the robe, the team carried the items over to the area where the Quillitary yard had once been. They stacked things there, being careful to preserve as much of it as possible. Little survived unscathed.

Finally they'd removed enough to reach things like furniture and cupboards. "Let's start with the kitchen area," Claire commanded. "If you see any multicolored cloth, yell for me and don't try to pull it out. We don't want to tear it."

More time passed, and the sun crept across the sky toward Warbler Island. It was impossible to tell which of the cabinets had been where in the kitchen. Claire sifted through the broken contents of each cupboard and shelf and drawer, looking for spots of color, before allowing them to be pulled from the area. Inside a toppled pantry closet they found the emergency stash of water jugs, miraculously intact, which they'd kept in the gray shack after what had happened last time. It was a relief to have them. Everyone stopped to take a drink and pass out water to the people of Quill, which quieted them for a time.

Taking advantage of the momentary calm, Claire climbed precariously onto a three-legged chair that had somehow escaped the fate of all the others. She waved to catch the attention of the complainers, wanting to make sure everyone could hear her. "We're making progress!" she announced. "Please remain patient!"

She went on to explain the process that had to happen in order to bring the magical world back, and assured the people of Quill that all of their belongings would return with the houses and other buildings.

"What happened to Alex Stowe?" one of them cried out from far away. "Why isn't he fixing this?"

"Yeah!" shouted another, and a few others joined in. "Why did this happen?"

Claire's lips parted. She glanced at Henry and Sean, and they looked just as surprised. Hadn't the people of Quill understood why the world had disappeared so suddenly? Hadn't they

LISA McMANN

heard the Artiméans talking in hushed tones about the fact that Alex must be dead?

Claire's eyes grew moist. She cleared her throat. "Let me be clear: There's only one reason for our world disappearing like this," she said. "Some of you will remember the last time this happened, when my father, Marcus Today, was killed. You see, when the head mage dies, the magic disappears."

"It was Aaron Stowe who killed him!" shouted one angry Artiméan woman not far from Claire.

Murmurs rippled through the crowd, but Claire pushed onward, ignoring her. "Back then, only Artimé was affected. But after the great fire of Quill, when we fought against Gondoleery Rattrapp, your land was magically re-created." She paused, trying to find the gentlest words. "We believe that Alexander Stowe, our beloved leader, has died on his mission to save his sister. And despite our broken hearts, we're trying our best to put the magic back into our world."

The people became silent, and Claire continued. "Once we're out of danger, we can all properly mourn for him. So we appreciate your help in giving us the space we need to uncover a few crucial items that will help us do that. I know it's not

LISA McMANN

comfortable standing or resting in the soot of Quill, and there's not enough room for all of us in Artimé at the moment. But I promise we're going as fast as we can."

The crowd from Quill remained quiet. They might never show emotion, but they understood death and respected it. And they had come to appreciate Alex Stowe over time, even though he'd been an Unwanted. The young man had improved their lives dramatically. It was shockingly evident now that everything had been taken away in an instant.

"Thank you all," said Claire. She got off the chair and turned back to the work at hand.

The Artiméans continued digging through the wreckage. Finally someone spied a scrap of red cloth poking out from under a pile of splinters and the broken kitchen countertop. "Claire, look!"

"Yes," Claire said, dropping everything and rushing over. "That's it! Oh, thank goodness! Well spotted." Together she, Henry, Sean, and Gunnar lifted the largest piece off and set it aside, revealing more of the robe. Claire knelt and quickly wiped smaller bits of rubble off it. The others pried up another piece of the counter, freeing the fabric. With care, Claire picked up the robe and shook the rest of the dirt away. "Okay," she said under her breath. People watching nearby cheered. "Step one is complete. Now we need to find the spell and locate where the back doorstep is. Though I've got little hope of finding that tiny scrap of paper the spell is written on. This is too much of a mess."

"What happens if we don't find the spell?" asked Gunnar.

"I know most of it by heart," said Claire. "Well, some of it, at least," she admitted guiltily. "I've been trying to remember. It's coming back to me bit by bit."

Henry looked up from his search. "Part of it has to do with the mini model of the mansion. I don't know what, exactly . . . but I remember Sky using it to point something out to Alex."

"Ah, right," said Claire. "There were individual words in addition to the spell. I'd forgotten that part." She moved a few more things around, then lifted the corner of a bank of cupboards. Underneath she spied bits and pieces of the miniature model of the mansion, crushed beyond repair. "Oh no," she said in despair. "That's not going to help us much."

The others moved the cupboards aside. Claire picked up a few of the pieces of the model and examined them, but shook her head. "It'll be impossible to put this back together."

"I'm sorry," said Sean. "At least we've got the robe. That's a big part."

Claire nodded grimly. But she knew that they had to have *all* the parts to bring the magic back. "If I'd had any clue this could've happened, I would never have kept the items in here. But in my mind, it was the most logical place to store them at the time."

"This situation would be much worse if you'd kept them in your house in Quill," Sean reminded her. "You'd never have been able to get to any of them there."

"Yes," said Henry. "This was the smartest thing you could have done. Nobody ever imagined the shack would explode like this."

Some of the workers continued crawling through the area where the kitchen had been, hoping to find the small scrap of paper that would have the written spell on it from Mr. Today. Others went to where they thought the back doorstep might be and cleared the mess from it.

Claire looked anxiously at the sky. In a few hours the sun would be setting again, and their world would be pitch black.

Not wanting to go another night without magic, she called off the search for the spell. Then she went over to the cleared spot where her father, Mr. Today, had welcomed Unwanteds every year after the Purge. She could see a faint mark on the broken cement—a curve made by the door's opening and closing— and she knew this was the right place.

With a heavy heart she stood on the spot, picturing her father there year after year. She slipped on the robe, causing another stir among the Quillens, who started pressing forward again to see what was happening. Claire paid little heed to them, wrapped up in her own thoughts now. She had never wanted to be head mage, but now it appeared she would be, at least until she could figure out how to assign the job to someone else who really wanted it and would do a good job. And then she closed her eyes, concentrating on the spell as she remembered it. Phrases of the clue kept spinning around in her mind, and she hoped she could put them together correctly.

Sean, Henry, and Gunnar pushed the crowd back once more to make room for the magical mansion to reappear, and others doled out the last of the water to the sweltering Quillens and Artiméans who had no place to seek shelter from the sun.

LISA McMANN

Claire took a nervous, cleansing breath. *Stand in the place you first saw me—check. Follow the dots as the rising sun—* She remembered the five dotted pictures that had hung in the head mage's office and knew she had to recite their hidden words starting from the easternmost one. As a young mage, she'd spent a multitude of hours in that office with her father. But she hadn't known there were hidden words in the pictures. Without the mini mansion to help with this part, she struggled to recall them. "Envision. Breathe. Imagine . . ." No. "Envision . . . Breathe . . . Utter . . . Believe . . ." Was that it? Perhaps there were only four. Claire's mind was fuzzy with hunger and exhaustion, and she began doubting herself. But she knew it wouldn't hurt to try. She said the words again as sweat dripped from her temples, trying to concentrate on them and really feel their meanings floating around her. She needed to take control of them.

As the people watched and waited, they began to sense that Claire was struggling. Henry and Sean teamed up with her to brainstorm word options, hoping they could trigger some sort of recognition. Minutes passed, then a quarter of an hour. People started to murmur and shift. "Imagine," Claire said, her voice cracking. "That's the first one. I'm sure of it." She'd tried every combination of the words they'd decided could be the right ones. Sometimes she used four and other times five, but nothing seemed to be working. She wiped her brow and shook out her hands, trying to refocus. Then she closed her eyes, breathed deep, and tried a new combination for the second. "Envision."

A sharp cry rose from the crowd, followed by a hundred gasps.

Claire's eyes popped open. Had she done it? It couldn't be.

But the people weren't gasping at her. They were turned away, looking at the water. Speeding across the waves toward them, on the back of a shimmering black water dragon named Pan, sat Aaron Stowe. Alex's identical twin.

Aaron held a package in his hand. As they drew up to the shore, everyone could see his face was stoic, his eyes etched with grief.

Commence

Aaron came ashore, leaving Pan, the ruler of the sea, to wait and watch at the water's edge. He eyed the wreckage of the gray shack as he strode toward Claire and the others. The crowd of Quillens finally did the right thing in making a path for him—he'd been their ruler once. But a few of the Artiméans narrowed their eyes and shifted uncomfortably at the sight of him, including the one who'd shouted earlier about him killing Mr. Today. Now that same woman lifted her chin and eyed the package under Aaron's arm. "Do you suppose he's done it again?" she muttered.

An older man next to her gasped and jabbed her with his elbow. "Have some respect."

The woman didn't respond, but she kept a suspicious eye on the former ruler of Quill.

"Our deepest condolences," Gunnar Haluki said in greeting, making no pretense of Aaron not knowing what must have happened to Alex. "This is such a shock. How are you?"

Aaron's jaw tightened, and he didn't answer. Instead, he pointed to the rubble. "What happened here?"

Henry explained.

Aaron listened intently. He glanced at Claire and realized she was wearing the robe. His face softened. "I'm sorry. I interrupted your procedure. Please continue. I came because—I wasn't sure if—"

Claire held up a hand. "You've merely interrupted my humiliation, Aaron. I can't seem to recall the spell correctly. The note it was written on is lost in the mess. I've been trying everything I can think of. Do you have the spell memorized?"

"I . . . yes."

"Thank goodness."

"Shall I tell it to you so you can proceed?"

Claire rested her hand on Aaron's arm and gave a sad half smile. Sweat shone on her face and neck, and her hair was tangled and filled with bits of splinters and dirt. "You know I don't want this job," she said quietly. "My life is helping to govern in Quill now. I'm only doing this because we didn't expect you to come so quickly. We thought it might take you some time to realize what had happened since you don't use much magic on your island. And I guess we forgot about Pan. We expected your journey to last days by ship."

"I knew the instant it happened," Aaron admitted, but he didn't say how he knew. "Pan came to my aid immediately when I called out to her—luckily she was nearby."

"That's lucky for all of us. Please go ahead, Aaron."

He hesitated, looking down at the package he was carrying. "Are you're sure?" he asked, turning his gaze back to Claire.

"I'm positive."

Aaron searched her expression and found it sincere. "All right," he said quietly. He opened the package and shook out the robe Alex had given him. "You should keep yours, of course," he said. "For future . . . emergencies."

"I will." Claire took her robe off and folded it up, keeping it

LISA McMANN

close. The angry woman's eyes widened, as did those of a few others, when Aaron slipped his robe on.

Aaron tapped his lips thoughtfully, turning his attention to the rubble. "But let's think this through. We want the remains of the gray shack to reappear inside the mansion so we can rebuild it in the Museum of Large," he mused. "So before I begin the spell, we must pile all the pieces of the shack back onto the foundation. That way it will appear in the correct spot." He frowned as if what he'd just said somehow didn't quite ring true, then added, "I hope."

"Good thinking," Sean said. He organized volunteers to carry the walls and doors and roof and other bits and pieces back onto the foundation. They made quick work of it.

Before sunset, all was ready.

But Aaron hesitated again, feeling waves of guilt over what was about to happen. And he knew not everyone in Artimé would be pleased about it. He'd been acutely aware of dissenters over the years. And he'd noticed the angry woman and the small group forming around her who were beginning to mutter at the proceedings.

Aaron glanced at them uneasily, then looked back at Claire.

LISA McMANN

"Are you absolutely certain you want *me* to do this?" he asked. "Even . . . after everything I've done? Have you thought this through?" This wasn't going to be a seamless transition.

Claire nodded, tight lipped. She knew what he was asking. "Ignore them. The past is forgotten. You and I will work well together, I think. Perhaps . . . perhaps like Gunnar and my father did."

"I'd like that." Aaron gave her a grim smile. She'd come far in forgiving him. Now, with darkness descending, he barely had time to comprehend the job he was taking on. He moved to the correct spot. The dissenters in the crowd grew louder. The angry woman shouted, "We want Claire Morning in charge! Not a mage killer!" But her voice was soon drowned out.

Aaron cringed but tried to focus. His mind was on the one who should be wearing the robe—his brother. How was this possible? How was Aaron standing here, doing this? A wave of grief broke his concentration, but he pushed it back and gripped the robe's placket tightly until the moment passed. He closed his eyes and took a few breaths to clear his mind.

Everyone grew quiet, even the dissenters, for despite their suspicions they all wanted the magical world back. They could

LISA McMANN

fight about who the leader was later, once comfort was restored.

Aaron recited the poetic spell. The lines, spoken softly, were lifted onto the wind and carried about. And though Aaron wasn't musically gifted, the words contained music of their own.

Then Aaron moved to the five crucial words. "Imagine," he said softly, picturing Artimé in all its glory. "Believe." He felt his heart swell in grief and certainty, knowing with all confidence that this would work. "Whisper." He whispered the word, hearing it echo through the land, giving strength to it and defining the boundaries of the magical world. "Breathe." He let his chest swell, his lungs taking in the hot, salty air, giving life to the magic. Then he let it out. "Commence," he said finally. He waited a moment, then began the words again.

"Repeat times three," Claire murmured to Gunnar. "I'd forgotten that part."

Gunnar nodded, watching intently.

When Aaron ended the spell a third time, he dropped his head and rested in place a moment. And then he lifted his chin and opened his eyes.

Colors began swirling around him, around the entire island.

Everything began to spin. The cracked cement and dirt and burned-out weeds turned into a lush lawn. A fountain sprang up, and trees sprouted from the ground and grew to maturity. Platyprots and owlbats and squirrelicorns and beavops populated the land and the trees. A jungle appeared in the distance. The pile of junk that had once been the gray shack became a beautiful mansion. And Quill's simple houses and ground cover and dirt paths and its cool, clean stream reappeared as before—just the way the people liked it.

Aaron breathed a huge sigh of relief as cheers went up for the new head mage. The people of Quill celebrated and immediately began streaming back to their part of the island.

The Artiméans were less vocal, deeply feeling the loss of Alex. Most of them headed for the mansion to check on their rooms and belongings and confirm everything was indeed back to normal. The dissenters lingered for a moment, but Aaron was surrounded by supporters. From the corner of his eye, he saw the angry group reluctantly disperse and hoped he'd heard the last of their complaints, but he doubted it. There would always be some who couldn't forgive him, no matter what he did or said now.

Henry and Sean gave Aaron a quick embrace, then excused themselves. "We're going to make sure the gray shack pieces are where they need to be in the Museum of Large," said Henry.

"And," added Sean, "we need to put Ol' Tater back to sleep in case he was revived with the world coming back." He remembered what had happened last time with the enormous mastodon statue.

"Thank you both so much." Aaron didn't smile. Seeing the magical world return was a wonder unto itself. Realizing his new role in it was breathtaking in a most horrifying way. Artimé's return by Aaron's hand had a far graver meaning to him than most people knew, because Aaron Stowe carried a deep secret within him—the secret of his potential immortality. Few were aware of it. Only the grandfathers, who'd administered it to him, and Alex and Simber had known. It was the only secret he'd kept from his wife, Kaylee, for telling her was just too painful to think about—she'd age normally and eventually die, but what would he do then? Without her? As for Artimé's magic, the chances of it ever disappearing again just became incredibly small. And Aaron had just agreed to take on a very difficult job . . . perhaps for eternity.

LISA McMANN

Despite the weight of that, so many other things fought to dominate Aaron's thoughts in this moment. He'd spent his journey with Pan in denial of Alex's death. It couldn't be! But the overwhelming truth had pounded him when he'd caught sight of the island. Now that he'd taken care of restoring the magic and was left alone, his mind returned to the reason for Artimé's disappearance. His insides still ached with a pain he'd never felt before. The pain of the severed connection to his twin. It had to be true.

"Oh, Alex," Aaron whispered. He sank to the back step of the mansion and covered his face with his hands, thinking about his fate and how it had changed so drastically. He'd possibly rule Artimé forever, if he weren't somehow ousted. But his termination as head mage didn't seem likely, unless the dissenters somehow gained support and traction. And starting now, for the rest of forever he'd be without Alex. Would this pain last that long too?

There was another question that had plagued him. And now it began to take over. What about the others who'd been with Alex? Everyone he cared most about was either on that mission or being rescued. Alex, Fifer, Thisbe, Kaylee . . . What were the chances that he'd lost *all* of them? And how long would he have to agonize before finding out if his wife, the mother of his son, was alive or dead? He didn't know if he could stand the infinite wondering. He buried his face in the crook of his elbow and let out a ragged, muffled sob.

Moments later, from the lawn, Aaron heard an old familiar whizzing sound. He lifted his head and wiped his eyes on the sleeve of his robe. Then he saw that Henry and Sean had returned to the lawn and had just cast seek spells, trailing light that soared away from Artimé heading west. The pressure threatening Aaron's chest lightened, and a thread of hope weaved through. "Brilliant," he murmured. He sniffed and got up and fumbled in his pockets, hoping he carried the exact things he needed.

Far away, in the land of the dragons, Simber, the winged-cheetah statue, stirred and looked around. The tiny kitten on his back stood and stretched. "Mewmewmew," she said.

"Good question," said Simber, looking with a puzzled expression at the rescue team, who had all turned at the sound and were staring at the cats. He was completely disoriented.

LISA McMANN

"When did you rrreturrrn frrrom the catacombs? Is Thisbe herrre? Is she okay?" Then the giant cat narrowed his eyes and looked harder at the faces of his friends, reading their expressions. Realizing who wasn't there, he faltered. "Wherrre is Alex?"

A Loyal Heart

The magic returned to Lani's wheels, and she took in a sharp breath. "Thank the gods," she whispered. Then she turned and quickly glided over the rough terrain to Simber's side to fulfill the promise she'd made to Fifer.

"Simber, Kitten," Lani began, trying not to falter, "I'm so sorry. You've been frozen. We lost our magic. It just happened yesterday." She spoke tentatively at first, then pushed forward to get the information out as fast as she could so the statues wouldn't have to be in suspenseful agony for long. "We were on the mission to rescue Thisbe, but we failed to find her. The

LISA McMANN

Revinir ambushed us. Alex was hit by her spear of lightning. It . . . It struck him in the chest, and . . . he died." She blinked hard and whispered, "He's dead."

Nearby, Fifer stared at Simber, watching him hear the news. And as his face changed, something happened inside her. It felt as if the words were finally starting to sink in. The numbness was beginning to wear off. And the pain grew. Tears flooded her eyes.

Simber and Kitten were silent, listening intently to the details. When Lani finished, Kitten ran down Simber and over to Crow for comfort. But Simber . . . Simber looked away. Then he knelt on the forest floor and rested his chin on the ground, placing his giant paws over his face. A low groan escaped him, making the forest floor vibrate.

No one knew what to do. Simber's closest companion for more than a dozen years was gone in the blink of an eye, without a good-bye. Clearly he didn't know where to go with his grief either.

Lani returned to Samheed and Fifer. "Give him a few moments," she said quietly. The enormous cat, frightening as he could be, had been sculpted from sand by the original mage of Artimé, Marcus Today. Despite that gruff exterior, he'd been given a tender heart. Simber had been Mr. Today's first living statue, brought to life for one sole purpose—to be a companion and confidant to the head mage. And Simber had done that with every ounce of life in him. Marcus had filled him with everything noble, brave, loyal, and wise that the man had been able to gather and instill. And the cheetah had lived every minute of every day for the pleasure and honor of serving the head mage.

When Mr. Today had been killed by Aaron Stowe and the magic had disappeared, Simber, who'd been flying above Alex and the white boat, had plunged to the bottom of the sea. And when Alex, still a young teen, had brought the world back with the help of Sky, Simber had awakened to find himself covered in water, unable to remember how he'd gotten there. When he'd risen from the depths and had come shooting up above the surface, Alex had been there waiting for him. Wearing Marcus Today's robe. It had been a terrible shock.

Simber's soft heart had torn in two that day. He'd spent decades dedicated to the aging man, protecting the mansion and fighting for the world of Artimé, listening to Marcus's

LISA McMANN

philosophical dilemmas time after time after time, offering advice whenever he was asked, and sometimes when he wasn't. It had been a fulfilling and mostly peaceful time, until Alex Stowe had come along.

Despite the boy's mistakes, Simber had grown to appreciate Alex by the time of Marcus's death, and he'd seen the potential in him. But he hadn't expected to become the new mage's right-hand cheetah so suddenly. He'd thought he had years left with Marcus. The transition had been hard at times, and there were more mistakes and many battles to come.

Simber and Alex had grown closer with each one, and as time passed, they often could communicate thoughts without needing to speak—a look was all it took sometimes. They'd understood one another deeply, and they rarely argued in their most recent years together. But it had been in the early days when Simber's love and devotion to Alex had grown exponentially. Especially as Alex had overcome challenge after challenge, and survived near miss after near miss.

So many close calls had made Alex seem like he'd survive anything, Simber realized now. A tumult of grief crashed over him, and his paws moved to cover his ears as if to block it out.

Marcus Today hadn't had nearly the scares that Alex had faced, yet the first attack on Marcus had done him in. But Alex . . . he'd been struck down and sent to the hospital ward more times than Simber could remember. He'd even suffered permanent injuries, but he'd survived. He'd always, always survived.

Until now.

The cat closed his eyes, squeezing out a tear. It was disorienting being thrust back into the world on a different day. He'd missed a full day of listening, smelling the smells of a forest, sensing things that weren't quite right and warning the others. And it was heartbreaking learning of it after waking, and knowing there was only one reason for the magic that gave him life to disappear.

Simber sampled the air, smelling danger and death on it. He searched it for signs of Alex, and they were everywhere, growing fainter by the moment, or so it seemed. Simber could feel his heart shredding inside. He pulled his paws away and pushed himself to his feet. The low groan began again from the depths of his chest and became a roar that exploded from him without permission or warning. It shook the leaves on the trees. Dev cowered behind Seth and Fifer.

"How many times must I go thrrrough this?" Simber moaned.

It was the only thing he said to the others before walking stiffly to the mound of dirt. He stood there for a long moment alone, unmoving.

Carina glanced at Fifer and Lani and the others. "I'm just going to stand nearby," she said. The others nodded. She went to be near Simber, staying a respectful distance but wanting to be there in case he needed anything.

Simber knelt and rested his head on the dirt that covered his fallen companion. He hadn't expected to be doing this again so soon. Alex should have had decades of life remaining. It wasn't fair.

Still bewildered, Simber tried to piece together the time that had passed without him in it. Losing the magic always made everything happen so abruptly for Artimé's statues and creatures. Simber would never get used to it because of what it meant for him, and him alone. The sudden losses that came with being the living-statue confidant of the head mage made his situation unique. He never wanted to have to do this again. Who would wear the ominous robe next?

There was guilt, too. Simber hadn't been there to protect Marcus. And he hadn't been there for Alex, either. How could he go on as a protector of Artimé when he couldn't even keep the head mage alive? What was he doing wrong? Perhaps he shouldn't have let the mission proceed without him. But his large proportions prohibited him from getting into human-size places. He cringed, knowing there was no easy solution. But also knowing that both mages had died by going into places Simber couldn't access.

Interspersed between waves of guilt were questions about who was the head mage now. No one here wore the garment of head mage. Should Simber return to Artimé to be there with whoever wore it now that the magic was restored? Did the new mage need him like Alex had so desperately needed him years ago? What was he supposed to do now? They were so far away.

And who would take Alex's place here, leading this mission? Alex had left him no clues on what to do or who to turn to. He considered the group of humans around him, wondering which of them would step up. Possibly Carina Holiday—a fierce fighter, one of Artimé's sharpest. Her son, Seth Holiday, was thirteen and just coming into his own, but he wasn't a natural

LISA McMANN

leader. Lani Haluki, Artimé's writing instructor, and her husband, Samheed Burkesh, the theater instructor, were also highly skilled. No doubt Lani would consider taking on the role. Thatcher, a former Warbleran, was a top-notch mage, and he knew this land of the dragons even better than Carina, who'd also been here before. But Thatcher wasn't originally from Artimé and would likely refuse the position as temporary leader, deferring to someone with more experience. Kaylee Jones was also from a foreign land. She was a strong swordswoman but not magical, which eliminated her from the running—or at least from taking the lead temporarily. Talon was another from a foreign place and, like Kaylee, didn't possess the magic of Artimé. Crow, averse to fighting in general, wouldn't have any desire to be in a position like that.

And then there was Fifer. One of the two most naturally gifted mages Artimé had ever seen. Not yet thirteen, she was younger than Alex had been when the job of head mage was thrust upon him. But as Simber knew all too well, years passed in an instant, especially for a magical statue like him, who had no expectation of ever expiring for good.

Simber closed his eyes, a sharp pain piercing through him.

Not even fifteen years after Alex had brought the world of Artimé back to life, he was gone. And Simber was still here. Would always be here. Forever. Or at least for as long as the magic lasted. For a moment he longed for the freedom from pain that being put to sleep would grant him. Ol' Tater, the mastodon statue who'd been put to sleep in the Museum of Large, certainly had some luck.

Simber's eyes flew open wide. Ol' Tater had come to life the last time the world had been restored. Would the people back home remember that in time to keep him from terrorizing everyone? There was nothing Simber could do about it from this great distance. It was terribly distressing. And what must they have been thinking over there?

The cheetah finally turned his head and noticed Carina sitting quietly nearby. "Who do you think rrrestorrred the worrrld?" he asked her.

"Our guess is Claire," said Carina. "But it could have been Aaron."

"That's what I thought." Simber grew quiet again. He was fond of Claire, but he knew she didn't want the position of head mage. He was also one of the few who knew the truth about

LISA McMANN

Aaron Stowe, for Alex had told him years before. Though many in Artimé had wondered aloud about the strange longevity of the scientists on the Island of Shipwrecks, no one knew that Aaron had been given the mysterious magical seaweed that had kept him from dying and would likely keep him from death forever. In a way, he was a lot like Simber.

The enormous cat hoped it was Aaron who'd taken rulership of the land for his friend Claire Morning's sake. But he also wanted it for a selfish reason. Not because Simber had any kind of affinity toward Aaron—he didn't even know him that well, so that could cause a few uncomfortable moments once he was back home. But that would work itself out. And even though Aaron had been the one to kill Marcus Today, that incident was behind them now, and Aaron had earned Simber's respect. The truth was with Aaron as head mage, it would mean less heartache for Simber in the future if Aaron truly was immortal. They could be together forever. They could share their loneliness and heartbreak together as the humans around them lived out their lives and left them for a spot under the dirt.

"Therrre was no way to get his body home?" Simber

murmured, more thinking aloud than asking the question, because he could imagine the many reasons why they'd chosen to bury Alex here.

"We didn't know how long it would be before we had you back," Carina explained. "We considered asking Talon to carry him, but it seemed like too much to ask for such a long journey, though I know Talon would have said yes. It just didn't seem feasible. We waited several hours for the magic to come back, and debated what to do once we got over the shock of . . . of everything. Ultimately we decided that with the length of the journey home, carrying his body, even waiting one day . . . It was too long."

Simber nodded. "Though I hate to leave his body herrre alone, it's forrr the best. Besides, I won't go home again without Thisbe." Simber surprised himself with the declaration, for the words came out before he'd thought them through. But it had been Alex's final quest, and Simber was going to carry it out no matter how long it took. A burning lump rose to his throat. He turned back to the mound of dirt, his heart aching for a word with the late head mage. *Alex*, thought the cat. *Tell me what to do.* He waited in the silence.

That is indeed what I want, Alex seemed to whisper in Simber's ear. *You know me well.*

It was true. Simber knew it without a doubt. Relief flooded the cheetah. *Therrre is no need to worry,* he replied, his heart aching. *I'll see to it.* Simber could picture the look in Alex's eye. The head mage could rest easy knowing Simber would carry out his wish.

Then, *Use Fifer.*

At first Simber wasn't sure why Alex would say that. Perhaps the grieving cat's mind was just playing tricks. Fifer was terribly young. But she'd proven herself. And there was one other factor that Alex had said many times: There's something special between twins. *Use Fifer?* Simber asked, hoping against hope for some confirmation from Alex. But there was only silence.

And then noises rose all around them.

Samheed and Lani whirled around to the west. Kaylee and Talon turned east. Carina, Seth, and Dev looked south, and Simber and Fifer to the north. A dozen green uniforms emerged from the trees.

The rescue team from Artimé was surrounded.

Fueled by Grief

The green-uniformed soldiers stared for a moment at the strange band of vagabonds, looking most fearfully at Simber and Talon. "Attack!" ordered their leader. They recklessly rushed forward, weapons drawn.

Not wanting to be recognized, Dev dove for cover. The magical Artimeans quickly reached for components while Kaylee and Talon drew their swords. Crisp clangs resounded as Kaylee advanced, slicing and jabbing at the enemy soldiers. Talon lunged at two of them and stuck them one after the other, dropping them alongside the one Kaylee had toppled.

Fifer felt uncontrollable fury rise up—how dare anyone

disturb their time of mourning? She whipped off three heart attack spells at her nearest attacker, felling him, then jumped onto Simber's back and threw another one, connecting with the next soldier, giving him a temporary heart attack. Teeth bared, Simber charged angrily toward three more soldiers as Fifer continued firing freeze spells. Two soldiers went down, and the third narrowly escaped. Lani snagged the woman with scatterclips, sending her flying backward and pinning her to a tree, then silenced her shouts with a freeze spell. Samheed, Carina, and Seth fired off multiple shackle and freeze spells at the remaining attackers. And even though this was the king's army, a totally different group than they'd fought before, there was no leniency in their counterattack. No one on the rescue team had patience for this nonsense. Not today. Not with their leader dead in the ground. Within moments, the entire green troop was overcome.

Fifer and the rest ended their attack, almost in shock, looking at the frozen and bloodied bodies strewn about. Carina dropped her gaze as a fleeting look of regret crossed her expression. But then she frowned at the ground, muttering, "You shouldn't have surprised us."

Dev lifted his head and took in the gruesome scene, dumbstruck. "Egads!" he exclaimed.

Carina reached out a hand and helped him up. Fifer slid off Simber's back, and she and Seth and a few others searched beyond the circle to make sure there weren't any more soldiers hiding under the cover of trees. If there were any, they'd run for their lives by now.

Samheed seemed disturbed. He put his remaining components in his vest. "Talon," he said quietly, "can you help me remove these soldiers from our camp? Let's put them by the road so they can be discovered and tended to."

"Of course," said Talon.

"I'll help," said Kaylee, sheathing her sword. Carina nodded and went to assist as well.

Simber, feeling more savage than he'd felt in a long time, had no sympathy for anyone attacking his people. He snorted and abruptly left the area before he could do something worse to them. Moving back to Alex's graveside, he dropped heavily next to it.

As Talon, Samheed, Kaylee, and Carina began dragging the soldiers out of sight, Dev looked fearfully at Seth and Fifer,

LISA McMANN

perhaps unsure if his own life was in danger. But Fifer beckoned the boys to sit by her.

"That was incredible," Dev began, eyes wide. "I mean . . . you sure know how to fight."

"Did you recognize them?" Seth demanded.

"A few. They weren't dungeon soldiers."

Seth narrowed his eyes. "Do you think they'll come back?"

"Are they . . . alive?"

"Some of the spells were temporary," said Seth. "They'll wear off in a while. I wonder if we should move camp."

"Oh," said Dev. "I doubt they'll come back after what you did." He looked admiringly at the other two. "How did you learn—"

Fifer shook her head impatiently, cutting him off. "That's not important. Do you think they recognized *you*? Or me? Or saw our eyes?"

"I hid as soon as I saw them," said Dev. "I don't think they recognized anyone. They didn't have time before you blasted them."

"Good," said Fifer, relaxing a little. She glanced at Simber, who seemed to have calmed down a bit. "Maybe we'll be able to stay here. I'd hate to move now."

The adults and Talon returned after removing the remaining fallen soldiers to the roadside. Fifer watched them go to the river to wash their hands. "I hope we haven't started something," Fifer murmured. "It couldn't be helped, though. There was nothing else we could do. They attacked us."

"They shouldn't have done that," said Seth solemnly, echoing his mother's statement.

"You're right," said Fifer. "They made a big mistake." She fell silent; then her tears welled up again as she suddenly remembered Alex, her fighting partner, with a sharpness that made her stomach hurt. Dev and Seth watched her helplessly and teared up too.

A moment later Simber got up and sighed deeply, lingering by the graveside, then coming over to where Seth, Fifer, and Dev were sitting. The three looked up when he approached.

"Oh, Simber," said Fifer, seeing his pain and getting up to give him a hug. She was terribly worried about him. "Thanks for protecting us from those attackers."

"Fiferrr," Simber said quietly. "May I have a worrrd?"

Fifer nodded. "Sure." She loosened her grip around his neck and went with him for a short walk outside of camp. As they

LISA McMANN

went, she laid her hand on his flank, feeling the stony muscle churn as they walked.

"I'm sorrry," Simber said.

"I'm sorry for you, too," said Fifer. "What a shock it must have been to wake up to all of us standing there without . . . him."

Simber nodded. "I've always hoped I'd have a last meaningful moment, orrr a special worrrd with the mages I've serrrved beforrre they died," he said. "I didn't have that with Alex. But I know he loved you and Thisbe verrry much. Even though he didn't always know what to do with you."

"I know."

"He would want me to tell you that. And he trrrusted you fully, especially at the end. He knew what a powerrrful mage you arrre. And will continue to be. I believe he saw you as an equal magical forrrce at the end. A parrrtner. He . . . He lit up. His face, his attitude . . . in a way I hadn't seen in a long time. That was parrrtly because of you."

Fifer nodded and swallowed hard. "But I didn't save him."

Simber stopped walking and turned his head sharply toward her. "You couldn't have. Lani said the grrroup was ambushed, and he died immediately. Therrre was nothing you could have done."

Fifer was silent.

"Do you hearrr me?"

"Yes, Simber. Thank you."

Simber hesitated. "I want you to know that I trrrust you too."

"You do?"

"Yes. And while we continue ourrr rrrescue of Thisbe, I'll take input frrrom everrryone. But it's yourrr voice I'll listen to above all. So if something feels off, you must tell me."

Fifer wasn't sure what to say. It was the biggest compliment she'd ever received at the worst of all possible times. Somehow it meant even more to her because of it. "I will tell you."

"That means you need to find and listen to yourrr innerrr voice, yourrr instinct, and be one with it. Believe it when it tells you something. Don't push it away."

Fifer nodded, unsure how to do that. But wanting badly to learn. "Why do you trust me?" she asked.

"Because you prrroved yourrrself. But also because I underrr-stand the connection you have with Thisbe. She's yourrr twin.

LISA McMANN

You will know what to do morrre than any of us when the time comes to go afterrr herrr again. Did you feel herrr prrresence in the catacombs when you werrre down therrre fighting? Was she nearrr?"

Fifer glanced away. "N-no," she said, growing concerned. "Not really. I didn't feel . . . much." Nothing at all was more like it. But had she missed something important? Was Fifer supposed to have some strong inner connection with Thisbe that would answer all of these questions? Because she hadn't felt anything like that the whole time. She'd felt more connected to Alex, in fact, than to Thisbe, while in the catacombs. "Is that bad?"

"No," said Simber. "I don't think so." But he seemed troubled. "Perrrhaps yourrr connection to Thisbe isn't as strrrong as Alex's was to Aarrron. Marrrcus and Justine werrren't close like that eitherrr."

Fifer's heart fell. She felt somehow terribly inadequate, like she'd failed some very important twin test. They turned back toward camp.

"Orrr," said Simber, glancing at her with sympathy, "maybe it simply tells us that she wasn't actually down wherrre you expected herrr to be."

"What do you mean?" Fifer asked. In her mind she went over the horrible surprise attack on Alex. Then, with a start, she remembered something that the Revinir had said. *Thisbe isn't here anymore.* Fifer turned to tell Simber, but out of nowhere, something else caught her attention. Speeding through the air toward them was an entire fleet of seek spells.

As the balls of light entered camp, they split up, and all but one came to a stop in front of Fifer, Kaylee, Carina, Kitten, Crow, Talon, Seth, Thatcher . . . and Alex's grave. The one that kept going continued through the forest and out toward the Dragonsmarche square.

The lone spell caught Simber's eye and puzzled him. But then he realized it was probably heading to the catacombs, to Thisbe. By the time he looked harder, the fiery ball was long gone, and the trail of light was fading fast.

A Fourth Opening

The barrage of seek spells reached the rescue team in the land of the dragons and exploded in front of the loved ones they were sent to, causing fresh chaos and much commotion. Carina immediately realized what the people of Artimé must be thinking. "They want to know if we're *all* dead," she said grimly. "Quickly—everyone respond with whatever seek spell items you've got so they know we're okay."

"I don't have anything—I can't respond," Kaylee lamented as a seek spell from Aaron faded in front of her. "How can I let him know I'm okay? Can anyone do it for me?"

"You don't have *anything* that Aaron created with you?" Lani asked.

"Aaron's creativity lies in making machines," Kaylee stressed. "Not exactly easy to travel with. Besides, I can't do the magic anyway. So it wouldn't have done me any good."

"Oh, you can do this spell," said Fifer, rejoining the group. "Even Kitten can do it, and she can't even say the word." Seth nodded in agreement as he and Carina sent seek spells to Sean. Thatcher sent one to Henry.

Kitten proved them right by pulling something tiny from inside her fur and saying "Mewmewmew!" A ball of light shot from her paws, nearly toppling her over backward.

"You think I can do it even if I don't have anything Aaron's created?" asked Kaylee.

Lani pursed her lips, like she couldn't believe Kaylee wouldn't carry with her something special to remind her of her husband on a trip like this. "Nothing at all? Not even a love note or a poem or . . . ?"

"I'm just not sentimental like that," said Kaylee.

Lani wasn't about to give up. "What about a belt or some jewelry he's made?"

"Your ring," said Samheed. "Aaron designed your wedding ring and gave it to you—that fits the rules of the spell. Try it!"

With shaking fingers Kaylee removed her wedding band and held it tightly in her palm.

"Now concentrate on the item and on the person who gave it to you," said Lani. "Picture the ball of light going to wherever Aaron is. When you've got a good solid feeling about it, say 'seek,' and it should work."

Anxious, and knowing that her husband must be tied in knots with worry, Kaylee closed her eyes and took a minute to concentrate and do what Lani told her to do.

"It helps to believe you can do it," Seth offered.

Kaylee let out a breath and nodded. She continued concentrating, picturing the seek spell flying toward Aaron, and believing in her ability to do it. The others remained quiet as they sent out whatever additional seek spells they were capable of casting based on the items they carried with them, and the silence was occasionally broken by a whisper of the word or the sound of the spell blasting out and away.

Finally Kaylee felt a calm come over her. With it came a sense of confidence. She seized the moment and whispered,

"Seek." A ball of light flew from her hand. When she opened her eyes, she could see its tail fading, the ball flying eastward. "Whew," she muttered, then turned to look at everyone. "I did it!"

The others congratulated her and breathed a sigh of relief on her behalf—it would've been awful for everyone but Aaron to get confirmation that they were okay. Him of all people.

"Has everyone else finished?" asked Kaylee.

As the others confirmed that they'd sent theirs off, Kaylee noticed Simber returning to Alex's grave. Above the mound hovered an unexploded seek spell. "Simber?" Kaylee said, walking over to him. "What's that?"

"This one . . . ," Simber said, looking at the spell and choking up. "It can't be deliverrred."

Kaylee reached Simber and stood looking at the hovering ball of light. "I wonder who it's from." As they stood there, two more seek spells flew in and hovered alongside the first. Then a fourth one came.

"Everyone's hoping for a response from him," said Kaylee, tearing up as she imagined what was happening back home. "They're praying it's all a big mistake."

LISA McMANN

"They'll learrrn soon enough when all of ourrr rrreturn spells arrrive without one frrrom Alex."

"How long does it take?"

"Not long." Simber looked up at the others. "Does anyone here have something that Thisbe crrreated?"

Several of them did—it had been a given, considering they'd be searching for her. But they hadn't been sending them to her for fear of tipping off the Revinir or other onlookers in the catacombs. They hadn't wanted to risk using the spell and putting her in danger unless it was absolutely necessary.

"Someone frrrom Arrrtimé sent a spell, and I saw it whiz by us, towarrrd the catacombs," Simber said. "I assume they werrrre sending it to Thisbe. I hope it doesn't put herrr in a bind."

"So she *is* still down there!" said Fifer. The Revinir had lied.

"Though it could have been meant for Arrrabis, I suppose," Simber added.

"I don't think that Arabis was tasked with creating anything for someone back home," said Carina, her voice doubtful. "But certainly Aaron would have something of Thisbe's."

"Thisbe doesn't have any items from any of us, though," Fifer reminded them. "I was carrying the page of a script from

Seth in my pocket when she got snatched up by the Revinir. Neither of us had any other created gifts. So she can't reply."

"We could send her a spell, but it's a big risk, especially now that we've failed to rescue her once already," said Thatcher. "If the Revinir sees it or hears about it, she'll know enough to suspect we're coming for her again."

Dev spoke up. "There are almost always guards around the slaves, and I bet the Revinir has put more on Thisbe now that you attempted to rescue her. They'd definitely get angry at Thisbe if they saw something like that. They'd tell the Revinir. They aren't very kind."

"I hope we haven't caused more trouble for poor Thisbe," said Lani. "I agree with Thatcher. We don't want to do anything to jeopardize her safety. It's too bad, though. It would've been helpful as we plan our next move."

"Perrrhaps we should discuss that now," said Simber, looking at Fifer. "Arrre we agrrreed that we won't leave herrre without Thisbe?"

"*I'm* not leaving without her," said Fifer decisively.

"Neither am I," said Seth.

The decision was unanimous.

"Should we move our camp?" asked Lani. "Now that the green-uniformed soldiers know where we are?"

Talon spoke up. "It's my fault they attacked us," he said.

"And mine," said Simber. "We werrre distrrracted. It won't happen again—I can assurrre you Talon and I will be watching forrr them. I think we should rrremain herrre at least until Arrrabis rrreturns, so she can find us. With luck, it won't be too long."

Fifer spoke up. "Dev doesn't think the soldiers will return after we decimated them." She looked around uneasily. "But I don't think I want to make it easy for them to find us if they ever decide to."

Talon nodded. "Perhaps a couple of you can scout out a location you'd like to move to once we're ready."

Samheed and Lani agreed to take on the task.

"But what about Thisbe?" asked Seth anxiously. "Do we have a plan?"

Fifer noticed Simber looking at her, a mixture of kindness and sorrow in his eyes. With a start she realized he was waiting for her to answer the question. "Oh," she said, not quite sure what else to say. "Well. Let's, uh, figure out how to find her."

Carina nodded. "I'm worried that if we try the same thing we did last time, they'll be ready for us. So we need a new approach."

"Maybe Dev can help," said Fifer. "He knows his way around inside there."

"Yes," said Lani, turning to the boy. "Can you shine some light on the conditions in the catacombs? Is there any other way out besides the three exits?"

Dev, who'd been mostly silent in the presence of the larger group, was still marveling over the magic he'd seen these people do so effortlessly. So destructively. He'd witnessed Thisbe doing a couple of things in the past, but if she'd had the ability to freeze everybody, or to use those clips to pin soldiers to the wall, they could have escaped the catacombs ages ago. He wanted to know more, but Fifer clearly didn't want to talk about it today. At the mention of his name, he looked up. "Sorry. What's that?"

"Is there any other way in and out of the catacombs?"

LISA McMANN

Dev shook his head. "Just the three exits you already know about: Castle dungeon, Dragonsmarche elevator, and the cave opening on the far side by the lake."

"Mewmewmew," suggested Kitten.

Everyone looked at Simber to translate.

"Thank you forrr the offerrr, Kitten," Simber replied. "We'll let you know if we need you to make that arrrduous jourrrney again. But I hate to put you thrrrough that. And I'm not surrre what good it would do, otherrr than confirrrm Thisbe is down therrre."

"Which we're already quite sure of," added Fifer, "since the seek spell went that way."

Kitten gave a tiny smile and nestled into the fabric on Crow's shoulder. The others contemplated quietly, hoping to come up with a solution.

After a moment, Lani spoke up. "It seems strange that there's no other access to air in such a sprawling system. No vents anywhere? What about for cooking—where does the smoke go?"

Dev lifted his head. "Oh," he said, his eyes lighting up. "The kitchen! That's right! There's a vent in the ceiling of the Revinir's kitchen where Thisbe and I worked. The smoke from the fires drifts up there. It didn't seem very big, though."

Lani raised an eyebrow and leaned forward eagerly. "So you're saying Thisbe might be in the room under the vent sometimes?"

"If she's still working for the Revinir, she would be." He tugged his shirtsleeves down over his scales as he remembered the tasks they'd done. So far no one had noticed the scales.

"How can we find the vent?" asked Lani. "Maybe there's a possibility for a rescue, or at least a way to communicate. Where does the vent come out, would you say?"

Dev frowned, thinking about where the kitchen was in relation to the elevator and then considering where that might be under the city. "It's hard to guess exactly because of how the catacombs are laid out," said Dev. "The passageways twist and turn a lot, and it's impossible to tell which direction you're facing down there. But the kitchen exhaust probably vents somewhere down one of the cobbled streets or alleyways."

There were many dozens of those.

"Which direction?" asked Fifer.

Dev closed an eye as he tried to figure it out. "It would be on this side of the square. Between it and the castle."

"Is it worth scouting for it?" asked Samheed, sounding doubtful. "Especially if the vent is so small no one can fit through it. We don't want to tear it up and accidentally cave in the ceiling on top of her."

Kitten's eyes glazed over. She sighed heavily.

Crow glanced at her and couldn't help smiling.

"Mew. Mew. Mew."

Everyone turned this time.

Hoping to Connect

Thisbe had been staring at the scales on her arms, lost in dark memories, when the seek spell reached her. She gasped as it exploded into a picture of a painted daisy on a pebble. She knew immediately the spell had come from Aaron, for she'd given him the pebble when she was five years old for this exact purpose. It was the first seek spell she'd received since the Revinir had taken her captive. She wasn't quite sure why, but it made her cry. Maybe because she wasn't able to send one in return. More likely it was because it finally seemed like someone was looking for her after all this time.

LISA McMANN

"Who is it from?" asked Sky frantically. "Can you send a response?"

Thisbe shook her head. "It was from Aaron. But I don't have any created items from anyone." She looked at the floor of the cave they now called home, regret filling her. "I didn't do a very good job of planning ahead when Fifer and Seth and I snuck away to save the dragons."

"Do you think Aaron is looking for you? Do you think he's in this world?"

"I don't know. It came from the direction of home."

Sky wasn't magical, but an idea dawned on her now that she was finally with someone who was. "If I have something that Alex gave me, can I give it to you and have you send a seek spell to him?"

Thisbe thought about that. "No," she said slowly, reasoning aloud. "It won't work because he didn't give it to me. If you give me an item that another person created . . . I don't think anything would happen. But it's an easy spell. Do you want to try it?"

Rohan looked on curiously, taking it in.

"You know I'm not very good at this stuff," said Sky. "All I know how to do magically is run the white boat."

"If you can run the boat, you can do a seek spell," Thisbe assured her. "Do you have an item from someone?"

"Yes. From Alex. Naturally."

"Well, then," said Thisbe, growing excited once she realized what it could mean for them. "That's great news—maybe we can find someone to come after us!" Thisbe taught Sky how to perform the spell, and then gave her some space so she could concentrate. She moved over to where Rohan sat, and they exchanged a hopeful glance.

Sky reached into her pocket and pulled out a piece of slate. She ran her finger over it. Its edges, once sharp and ragged, had been worn down after spending years in her various pockets. She'd never gone anywhere without it and had often held it as a source of comfort over the past few weeks. She turned it over and looked at it. Roughly etched in the stone was a silly poem that Alex had written.

> In the morning
> and when it's slate (ha!)
> my love for you
> will never

LISA McMANN

Sky smiled to read it. Alex had run out of space to write the last word but had given it to her anyway, making her guess what it was, and that had somehow made the gift more special. It showed Alex's goofy side, something she'd seen less frequently in recent years. "Abate," she murmured, finishing the poem. Then she clutched it and closed her eyes. Thisbe glanced at Rohan, who seemed enthralled by the way Sky had gazed so lovingly at the rock.

"She adores him," Rohan said quietly. "Look at her face."

Thisbe turned to look. For the first time she studied Sky from a stranger's perspective, and she saw what Rohan was talking about. It was pure and unabashed love glowing through her skin and in the slight curl of her parted lips. "My brother Alex isn't easy to love," Thisbe whispered. "But he adores her, too."

"It's beautiful to see," Rohan said. "My parents were in love like that."

"Now watch," Thisbe said, hearing him but preoccupied with what Sky was doing with the spell. "It'll shoot out that way." She pointed out the cave to the left, which she believed was east—it was the direction of home, which was where Aaron's seek spell had come from.

Sky was still for a long moment. Then, with a soft breath, she whispered, "Seek."

A ball of light shot from Sky's hands out of the cave, startling her. But it didn't go the way Thisbe had predicted. Instead it went out the other direction and disappeared.

"That's strange," said Thisbe, getting up to see where it had gone. "Do I have my directions mixed up?"

"The way you pointed is east," confirmed Rohan. "But the ball of light went west. Is there a rule on how it flies?"

"It takes the shortest path," said Thisbe, growing even more puzzled.

Sky followed Thisbe. "What's wrong? Did I mess it up?"

"Nothing's wrong, exactly," said Thisbe, peering out of the cave, "but I'm confused. Aaron's seek spell to me came from the direction of home. But the one you sent to Alex went the other way. Which means . . ." She looked at the faint trail of light that quickly diffused in the sunlight. "Hang on. I'm going to check it out." She ran after it. It wrapped around the rocky hill and along the lake, and went straight up, past the mouth of the cave that led to the catacombs.

As the light faded away, Thisbe squinted, trying to figure out where the seek spell could have gone. Rohan and Sky came up behind her, and she pointed to where the trail of light had been. "What's up there, beyond the rocky hill and the catacomb entrance? The spell curved around and up."

"Beyond the hill to the east is where Dragonsmarche is," said Sky. "There's a rough path that goes up this way—I stumbled across it when I was searching for a place to camp." She pointed away from the cave.

"But..." Thisbe hesitated. "We were in the Dragonsmarche square when the Revinir snatched me and took me down in the elevator." She was momentarily disoriented, trying to line up the outdoor locations to the maze of passageways underground and realizing that the tunnels must have twisted even more than she'd thought.

"Yes," Rohan confirmed. "We're nearest the southwest corner of the square. The elevator is quite a hike over that way, on the opposite end." He waved toward the north and east. "And the forest is beyond that."

"The forest?" Thisbe murmured. She remembered it. The other two gazed at the intimidating mountain wall while Thisbe got her bearings. Then she turned to Sky. "You said you went up to the market the other day, right? How long does it take to get up there?"

"An hour or more to climb up. Not as long coming down, obviously."

Thisbe checked the sun's location in the sky. "Should we venture out tonight to find Alex?" she asked.

"Why not go right now?" asked Sky, anxious.

"Because of our eyes." Thisbe told Sky the history of Grimere as it pertained to the former human and dragon rulers, and how the dragons had been banished or, like the black-eyed humans, driven out of power and sold as slaves. Rohan further explained how owning a black-eyed slave was a sort of status symbol among the higher class and current royalty.

"So that's why the pirates threatened you so long ago," Sky mused, looking at Thisbe. "They knew you were valuable back then already. I'd often wondered about that."

"I suppose." Thisbe explained to Rohan that the pirates they'd fought had threatened to sell her and Fifer many years before, when they were only two years old, but nobody knew why.

"We shouldn't go out right now because of our eyes," Rohan agreed, "but also because the Revinir's soldiers would recognize us if they're out and about."

"Right," said Thisbe. She turned back to Sky. "Plus, we don't want anyone to see us perform the seek spell if we can help it. It would draw too much attention to us in a nonmagical world." Thisbe had only been in the square for a short time, but it had been packed with people—it didn't seem safe.

"It would draw enormous curiosity," agreed Rohan. "There's no natural magic in Grimere at all. Except for the Revinir's, of course."

"You can go alone if you want to, Sky," said Thisbe. "I know you must be so anxious. We can wait here for you. Soon I expect Alex will send you a seek spell in return—once he gets over the shock of seeing yours." She smiled, imagining how surprised Alex must be, for surely they must have thought Sky had perished. "Does he have something of yours?"

"Oh, yes, I would imagine so," said Sky. "He's sentimental

enough. Though," she continued, thinking about it, "I don't know that I've ever created art for him, other than singing a song now and then, which he can't exactly keep in his pocket. I'm more creative with science and mathematics. I may have given him a chart or graph at some point. . . . Would that work?" She looked worried.

"Of course it would," said Thisbe.

Sky hesitated, glancing up the steep incline. Then she shook her head. "Now that we've found each other, I don't want to go anywhere without you. Especially with how dangerous it is for you two. We need to stick together. Our cave isn't exactly invisible, you know? I mean, I haven't seen anybody venture down there, but that doesn't mean they can't."

"I'm glad we'll stick together," Thisbe admitted. "Though I'm much better at aiming my explosions now than when you last saw me, so I can protect myself." She smiled, thinking of all the hours of practice she'd had inside her crypt. "Once we go up to the square and the coast is clear, you can send another seek spell to Alex in case he doesn't have anything you created with him. We'll be able to follow the light until it fades. Then we'll send another. If we do it late at night, the spell will be super bright, but hopefully there won't be anyone around to notice."

Sky nodded. Her anxious look didn't fade, though. As they started walking back to the cave, she asked, "Why wouldn't anyone have sent a seek spell to me when I got sucked into the Island of Fire? Not even Alex? Or Scarlet? She was right there. She saw me go down. Does that mean no one has anything from me?"

Thisbe contemplated the question. "They probably assumed you were dead," she said, as kindly as she could. "Especially with Scarlet witnessing it. So they wouldn't think it would do any good."

"Of course you're right," said Sky. "And it must have taken time for Alex to learn of my disappearance. Poor Alex." She shook her head. "Then again, it really could have been because nobody has anything I've ever created. I can't think of one single thing. That's just not me, you know?"

"Like I said," Thisbe responded patiently, "we'll find them one way or another." Thisbe wanted to find Alex as desperately as Sky did. She put a reassuring hand on Sky's back and glanced over her shoulder to make sure Rohan was following. He smiled and winked at her, and Thisbe felt her face get warm.

"All right," said Sky as they approached their sparse home. "Let's go catch some fish for dinner. I need to keep busy, or I'll go crazy waiting." She entered the cave to collect her makeshift fishing gear, then stopped and turned. "Sooo . . . are you sure that seek spell I sent didn't just go that direction because I messed up?"

"I don't know," Thisbe answered truthfully. "I've never actually made a mistake on that spell. But we'll find out more tonight."

"Yes," said Sky, her face clearing. "And who knows?" she added. "Maybe we'll be on our way home by morning. We can always dream."

"Home!" Thisbe grinned and let out a sigh, imagining it. "Wouldn't that be amazing?"

"It would." Sky turned and smiled at the girl, then grabbed her hand and squeezed. "Let's keep that hope alive."

Rohan watched Sky and Thisbe, seeing the excitement dance on their faces. He tried to smile too, but his lips wouldn't curl. And his empty expression didn't matter anyway—the two weren't looking. He glanced up at the cave entrance to the catacombs, knowing his enslaved friends were toiling away while he was free. And he began to wonder what exactly he was supposed to do all by himself once Thisbe was gone.

A Sigh of Relief

The return seek spells from the rescue team went whizzing back to Artimé, each one causing a shout of joy from the people who'd been desperately waiting. Aaron noted them with relief, but at the same time he cursed himself for not teaching Kaylee the spell and giving her something he created to use. But after years of peace and calm in their world, it had grown difficult to imagine people could suddenly and tragically die—important people in his life. In one abrupt moment, those days were gone.

How long would he be wondering if Kaylee had died along with Alex? Would their son, Daniel, grow up not remembering

LISA McMANN

his mother? It was unthinkable. Yet all too familiar. Even his sisters didn't remember their parents. Why had he let himself grow so complacent?

Around him, Sean, and Henry's fears were assuaged. Cheers erupted at proof that Carina, Seth, Lani, Samheed, and Thatcher were indeed alive. Aaron, grateful but growing more distressed, withdrew inside himself, remembering the muttering dissenters. Thinking about how he really didn't deserve someone as wonderful as Kaylee Jones to be in his life. Aaron had done some terrible things, even to family members like his father, a burier, who had been a quiet man. A Necessary. Aaron had been horrible to him back when he'd been so misguided by the errant ideals of the High Priest Justine. He wrestled with the memory of how he'd made his father work so hard, then sent him to the Ancients Sector. Luckily, Secretary, Eva Fathom—who was Carina's now-deceased mother—had gotten him out of that scrape. But Aaron hadn't made up for it. He deeply regretted that his parents had been killed by Quill's notorious wall coming down. A deed he'd orchestrated.

His mother had died protecting Thisbe and Fifer. It seemed fitting for her. She'd been quiet too, like their father. Like most

Necessaries. Her striking beauty had been downplayed and her features grayed by the desert land of Quill. But Aaron remembered her face every time he looked at his sisters. They had her eyes, her warm skin tone, her dark brown curls. As Fifer and Thisbe grew to look more like women every day, their resemblance to their mother became more evident. But their personalities were very different from their mother's quietness.

It made Aaron wonder if his mother had been more outspoken as a girl and a young woman. Had she been adventurous? Creative? Loud? What had she really been like? Had she even been born in Quill? Nobody wrote down such things or talked about them—it was too much like storytelling, which had been against the law in Quill for decades. Now the stories were slowly coming out from within that community, under Gunnar Haluki and Claire Morning's encouragement. Drips of history, for there remained a lot of fear of sharing. Still, it was happening. But as far as Aaron knew, his mother's story was buried with her.

Would his parents have been sad to learn of Alex's death? They'd sent him away to die once before with no outward emotion. They'd been trained so well. They'd probably always lived in fear of getting sent to the Ancients Sector. Both declared Necessaries, they must have been caught at least once doing something creative. That was the definition of a Necessary—caught once, but then reformed. Or at least never caught again. Aaron had made himself sick with worry about it as a child.

Aaron, a Wanted, had actually been caught once, drawing with a stick in the mud, but Alex had generously taken the blame for him since he'd already been given numerous infractions. Now Aaron wondered what his parents had done wrong to be deemed Necessaries. And he realized he had no idea. No inkling of what they would have been like if they'd lived in Artimé instead of Quill. No idea who they were as people. That haunting look that his father had given him when Aaron had so rashly sent the man to be put to death—Aaron would never forget it. What had his mother thought of him once she'd found out? Would she have cared? Aaron hadn't witnessed any sign of affection between his parents, not even in the privacy of their home. They'd spoken civilly with each other and never fought, at least not in front of Alex and Aaron. Who were they? Did they even know each other? Did they know themselves? Or did they just . . . exist with one another until death took their nothing lives away?

With the loss of Alex, and with Kaylee's status unknown, Aaron floundered in his memories and tried to push back the voices that said he deserved these heartaches. He'd been a terrible person. He'd killed the original mage of Artimé—and now he was wearing that man's robe and leading his people. Turning away from being a terrible dictator had been tremendously difficult, and even somewhat out of his control, at least at first. Ultimately it had been a rewarding shift for Aaron. And it was all thanks to the scientists Ishibashi, Ito, and Sato, also known as the grandfathers.

But now Aaron was left with a million questions. And as much as he tried to eliminate them, they pounded him from all sides. Would he move here, to Artimé, with Daniel? Live in the head mage's quarters, filled with constant reminders of Alex? What about the dissenting Artiméans who protested Aaron's leadership? How would he handle that conflict when he knew full well that they were justified in their feelings? And what about the scientists? They didn't want to leave their island, but

LISA McMANN

with all three of them well over one hundred years old now, they needed help with their experiments and with sailing their boat. Who would go to be with them?

The seek spell arrivals slowed. Aaron glanced at the water between Artimé and the Island of Legends and noticed Florence, the ebony-colored stone statue and Magical Warrior trainer, slowly rising from the sea and coming toward him. She'd no doubt walked from that island along the sea bottom. Her visit pulled Aaron from his morbid thoughts. He jogged to the edge of the water to greet her, feeling strange and self-conscious in the robe, and knowing that she likely had guessed by now what had happened. "Florence," he said, looking up and searching her face. "How are you? You've figured out the horrible news?"

"That's why I came," Florence said. As a magical statue, she'd awakened to Lhasa, the legendary snow lion on the Island of Legends, floating just above the ground as usual, circling her and exclaiming that Florence had been frozen for an entire day. Issie, the sea monster, had been there too, worrying over the statue. They'd never seen Artimé's Magical Warrior trainer like that before. "I knew right away what must've happened,"

Florence told Aaron. "My, but it's a jarring experience. I can't believe he's . . . gone. I'm—I'm so sorry, Aaron. I don't know of anything to say that would give you comfort. I'm heartbroken."

"Thank you," said Aaron quietly. He took in a steadying breath and let it out. "At least we're discovering that some of the others are okay. So far Carina, Seth, Thatcher, Lani, and Samheed have returned seek spells." Another seek spell was sighted in the distance, just a pinprick in the sky, and the people of Artimé pointed and waited to see who it would go to.

"How did you get here so quickly from the Island of Shipwrecks?" asked Florence. "And how did you know to come?"

"I felt it," said Aaron quietly. "Alex's life fading away. The moment it happened, I imagine. It was a searing cut to the heart," he said, tapping the spot. "I thought I might be dying myself, and then just as quickly the pain eased and left a . . . a dull aching emptiness, I suppose. It dawned on me that the unthinkable could have happened. I dashed to the tube on my island and discovered it was gone. That . . . That confirmed everything, though I didn't want to believe it." He eyed the sea where Pan appeared in the lagoon, having circled the island. She floated respectfully offshore in case she was needed. "I let out a cry, and with some luck Pan had been nearby, and she knew to come. Within moments she was there. I left Daniel with the grandfathers, gathered a few things, and came. By the time I got here, the place was utterly destroyed." He shook his head, remembering the sight. "Claire and Gunnar and the others were nearly to the point of restoring it." He looked down at the robe. "Claire asked me to do it," he said apologetically.

"She never wanted the job," Florence said. "She saw how hard it was, watching her father."

Aaron nodded. He was in for an eternity of difficulty. He pinched his eyes shut, then opened them again and scanned the western horizon. "Are you worried about Talon?"

"Not really," said Florence, though her expression betrayed her. "It's almost impossible for him to die. But I wish I'd taught him to do a seek spell. It just never seemed necessary. Now I'm kicking myself."

"I'm cursing myself for the same thing. It's not a hard spell to learn—why didn't I teach it to Kaylee? That was so stupid of me."

LISA McMANN

The ball of light grew larger and stopped in front of Florence. The two raised eyebrows at each other.

"Talon?" Aaron asked, incredulous.

"I hardly think so," said Florence. It exploded, bursting into a stick-drawn picture . . . of the Magical Warrior trainer herself. It took Florence less than a second to remember who she'd given that to. "Oh!" she said. "It's from Fifer!" She blew out a breath of relief. "Thank goodness she's okay."

"That's a huge load off my mind," said Aaron, clutching his robe in relief. "Though Fifer's so powerful—I was less worried about her than the others. Now . . . have they got Thisbe with them yet? I don't think we'll find out this way, since Fifer told me before she left that Thisbe doesn't have anything from any of us. I couldn't help but send one to Thiz, though."

"I don't blame you."

Another ball of light appeared, and everyone watched as it flew through the air and stopped in front of Fox, confirming Kitten's status. Fox melted into a puddle of sobs, even though Kitten would have to die a lot of times for her to be dead forever, so he need not have worried quite so much.

As the relieved loved ones celebrated the safety of their

LISA McMANN

rescue team members, one last ball of light appeared in the west. Aaron swallowed hard, his heart pounding. He knew it couldn't be Kaylee, unless . . . unless . . . someone there had taught her the spell. But did Kaylee carry anything with her that Aaron had created and given to her? He didn't think so. She wasn't a sentimental person.

The ball came to a stop in front of Aaron, and Florence gave him a hopeful glance. Others nearby watched to see who it could be from. When it exploded into an image of a wedding ring—the ring Aaron had designed and given to Kaylee five years ago—Aaron clutched Florence's arm, then sank to his knees. He covered his face with his hands. A sob let loose from his chest.

At least he hadn't lost her, too.

Revising the Plan

The rescue team, having alerted all the ones they could alert, broke for a meal at camp while Talon and Simber kept a careful lookout in case the green army was foolish enough to return. Afterward Samheed and Lani went scouting for a new camp location.

When the pair was out of hearing range of the others, Lani let out a deep sigh.

"You doing okay, love?" Samheed asked.

"Not really. You?"

"No."

They went in silence, Lani navigating the uneven ground

LISA McMANN

easily now that the magic was back, and Samheed walking beside her, holding her hand. "I don't want to let go of you," Samheed said after a while. "Ever. I'm scared."

Lani looked sidelong at him. "I'm afraid too. We're losing everyone."

"I just . . . I can't believe he's gone. It was so quick! I mean, with Meghan, I felt like things went in slow motion. Like maybe there was a chance to save her, you know? We rushed her to the hospital ward. Henry tried . . . but then he couldn't do anything. And she was gone."

Lani nodded. "But with Alex, it was instantaneous. One second changed everything." She moved around a tree. "He was supposed to be our invincible one."

Samheed swallowed hard. "I'm so angry."

"I know."

"I mean it. I haven't felt this angry in a long time. Not since early on in Artimé. It feels out of control."

Lani squeezed his hand and skirted around a clump of trees. "I wish Mr. Appleblossom were here to help you through it. He was such a rock for you." She hesitated. "What would he tell you now?"

Samheed was silent for a long moment, his lips pressed into a hard line. "He'd tell me to take my feelings and write them into a play."

Lani came to a stop and turned to face her husband. She looked into his troubled eyes. "Are you going to do that?"

Samheed looked down at her. With gentle fingers he pushed a lock of her hair off her face. His eyes brimmed. "I don't think I have any good words left inside me."

Back at camp, Fifer, feeling troubled and unsettled, wandered the area doing little that was productive. She couldn't stop thinking about Alex and how painful it felt to lose him. Being separated from Thisbe was overshadowed by this throbbing new wound. Fifer never wanted to go through something like this again—she couldn't. It made her sick just thinking about it. Fearing it. All she wanted to do was to collect everyone she knew and keep them safe in the mansion. But she couldn't do that. It was the most helpless feeling she'd ever known.

She glanced at Seth, who was collecting firewood, and imagined what it would be like to lose her best friend. The tears, always close now, surfaced again, and a sob escaped her before she could stop it. She wished she didn't care so much about him. Or any of them.

Seth dumped his armload of wood near the fire. "Ready to discuss a plan, Fifer?" he called out.

Fifer swallowed hard. "Almost," she squeaked. She wiped her tears and took in a few deep breaths, then joined her friends. Carina went to summon the rest of them. They trickled over. It was so strange to have to regroup and come up with a new rescue plan that didn't involve Alex.

"We should wait until dark to start our search for the smoke vent," Dev said, looking at Fifer as the other team members came over. "You and I don't want to be caught in daylight with our black eyes—the Revinir might have her soldiers out looking for me. And they'd recognize you once they saw you."

"Good point," said Carina. "Will the fires still be going then?"

"Yes," said Dev. "The catacomb kitchen fires stay lit all the time while the Revinir makes her disgusting broth, so the smoke should still be coming out, day or night." He glanced at his arms and crossed them, trying to hide them in his lap. Some of his dragon scales were evident despite his constant efforts to pull his tattered sleeves over them. No one had asked him about them yet. Perhaps they hadn't noticed or were too wrapped up in their grief to really focus on him. It seemed like too much to explain right now, but he knew he'd have to eventually. It wouldn't be fun telling them what the Revinir had done to Thisbe.

"Tonight sounds good," said Fifer, as Samheed and Lani returned from their scouting trip. "I don't want to go to auction ever again."

"I don't want that eitherrr," said Simber from across the clearing, where he was stationed. The cheetah statue's hearing remained impeccable, and he was angry at himself for not hearing the king's soldiers approach. He moved closer, repositioning himself to face the direction of the road and the square in case anyone ventured into the forest from that way. Talon remained just outside the camp, watching in the other direction.

Occasionally Simber glanced at Dev. He'd noticed the boy's scales but hadn't said anything. He was certain they were new—Dev hadn't had them the first time they'd met, back on the road when Fifer was bleeding profusely and Dev had helped

LISA McMANN

them save her. And Simber would have noticed, because along with the scales came a faint dragony odor.

It reminded Simber that Arabis still hadn't returned. "While you discuss yourrr searrrch plan forrr tonight, I'm going to have a look arrround frrrom above to see if I can find Arrrabis. I'm beginning to worrry."

"Oh good," said Fifer, feeling a bit guilty. She'd forgotten about the dragon. There were so many people and creatures to keep track of. If Simber was looking to her to step into some sort of leadership role, then she should at least remember everyone who was supposed to be with them.

Simber backed up to some trees to give himself the longest possible runway, then took off, clipping a few branches as he rose and scaring up Fifer's league of birds. As they resettled, Crow hopped up and collected the wreckage Simber had left. He began to break up the sticks and set them aside to dry for kindling in case they'd be here longer than they expected.

While the others talked through the plan and Samheed and Lani informed them about a potential spot for a new camp, Crow continued gathering firewood. As he did so, a lone seek spell came flying past him, coming from the direction of the square. It joined the others that hovered above Alex's grave. Crow noticed the fading stream of light that confirmed the direction it had come from. "That's strange," he murmured. All the other spells had come from the east, but this one came from the southwest. He turned toward the group planning the search and went back to them.

"But will Thisbe be in that kitchen at night?" Lani was asking Dev. "Didn't you say she gets locked in her crypt?"

Dev's mouth opened, and then his face fell. "Oh. Right." He thought a bit more. "We often worked really late into the evening, though. If we go right at nightfall, there's a good chance she'll still be there. We might see villagers out and about, but at least it'll be dark, and Fifer and I will be safer than in daylight."

"Plus, we don't know how long it'll take to find the smoke," said Fifer. "If it gets too late, we can always go back the next night."

Crow stopped at the edge of the circle around the fire. "I'm sorry to interrupt," he said, "but did any of you notice the seek spell that just came in for Alex?"

None of them had.

"It came from that way," Crow said, pointing. "That doesn't

seem like the right direction if someone from Artimé sent it."

"Are you sure?" asked Carina. She jumped to her feet, and Crow showed her the fading trail. She ran in that direction a few dozen yards and looked around, catching sight of the road in the distance, but soon came back. "You're right," she said. "That's really strange. Do you think Thisbe has something of Alex's after all?"

Fifer shook her head. "No way. Not possible. We talked about it a million times."

Seth agreed. "None of us had anything, and believe me, we checked *everywhere*."

"Maybe Alex dropped something meant for her in the catacombs that we didn't notice," said Lani, "and Thisbe found it. That's the direction it came from, isn't it?"

"Alex was the creator of the heart attack component," said Samheed slowly, "and we didn't stop to pick any of them up. So maybe Thisbe found them in her crypt? It's a stretch, though. He didn't exactly give them to her as a gift."

"Maybe Thisbe figured out how to use them," said Seth, growing animated, "and she killed everyone singlehandedly! And now she's trying to get out!"

"She's known how to kill people since she was two," Fifer pointed out matter-of-factly.

Dev's eyes bulged. "What?" he said, incredulous. "I mean, I saw her destroy that snake, but I didn't know she could kill *people*. Then why hasn't she done it already? She could have gotten us both out of there!"

Fifer shook her head. "First, she never wants to kill anyone or anything. So there's that. She feels terrible about the ability and doesn't even want it. But who knows why else she didn't use it? Maybe she wasn't desperate enough. And there were a lot of guards down there! I don't know that she could take out that many of them. They'd tackle her."

"That's true," said Dev. "Once she started, they would have taken her down in an instant."

"She's smart enough to figure that out," said Seth with a hint of pride for his friend. "She wouldn't risk getting killed herself."

"Okay, so anyway," Crow interrupted, "we're saying this seek spell could be from Thisbe? Shouldn't at least some of us go in that direction to see if we can find her? Or do we think it just came from inside the catacombs?"

"That's what I think," said Carina. "That's the direction it points to. I'll bet Samheed is right, and Thisbe found a heart attack component and used it for the seek spell."

"I don't know," said Lani, doubtful. "The spell works because the created item is given like a gift. Alex didn't 'give' it to Thisbe like that."

Thatcher looked troubled. "I agree, Lani. I don't think that's what happened. Maybe she just discovered she had something that you all overlooked before. A button on her shirt, or, like, maybe her shoes were a gift . . ." He didn't seem to be very confident of that, though.

Fifer shrugged. "I guess it's possible, but I don't think Alex was exactly making shoes in his spare time and giving them out as gifts. I'm just saying."

"I wonder if he gifted her something magically as he was dying, like Mr. Today did when he sent that spell note to Alex's pocket just before he died," Lani mused, thinking back. "That seems the most plausible, now that I think about it."

"I'd forgotten about that," said Samheed. "But that makes a lot of sense."

"I'll go with you to the square if you want to look around," Thatcher told Crow.

Crow nodded. "I'd feel better about it. I know we use the seek spell for a bunch of reasons now, but originally it was supposed to be a distress signal, right? It meant 'I need help.' I don't want to dismiss the possibility that Thisbe is using it that way."

"Should we send a seek spell to Thisbe to sort of let her know we're here and that we received hers?" asked Seth.

Dev looked immediately concerned. "Do you care if the soldiers see it?"

Carina shook her head. "Too risky. We don't want them to suspect anything is happening."

"I don't want to risk *anything*," said Fifer emphatically.

"But she sent one out," Seth argued.

"Maybe she had a moment when no one was around," said Dev. "Those times are rare—the soldiers are almost always patrolling the hallways."

"You're right," said Fifer. She thought for a moment, then remembered again what Simber had told her about taking charge.

And she knew they'd have to take *some* risks if they were ever going to find Thisbe. It was just . . . hard. "I agree . . . um . . . that Crow and Thatcher should check out the Dragonsmarche area as long as you can do it without any soldiers recognizing you. Be really careful."

Thatcher flashed Fifer a quizzical look—he was unused to her calling the shots. But Crow seemed okay with it. And really . . . who else was in charge now? He shrugged and picked up his rucksack.

"We'll be careful," said Crow. He and Thatcher set off in the direction the seek spell had come from.

In addition to her nerves, Fifer was still puzzled. Since the spell came from the Dragonsmarche area, it had to be from Thisbe. There simply wasn't anyone else, unless some other magical person from Artimé had somehow made it across the space between the worlds. But that didn't seem likely. There would have been no way for the other dragons to cross without their magical wings, and the magic had just been restored. It was physically impossible for them to have arrived so quickly.

The rest of the group confirmed that the best plan would be

to venture out at nightfall and go in search of the smoke vent. They dispersed to various tasks in the meantime.

Fifer stayed by the fire, her thoughts a jumbled mess. She wished she felt something in connection to Thisbe. Her heart ached for her siblings, but she didn't feel Thisbe trying to tell her anything. There was simply no connection there, no matter what Simber had said about twins. And despite what Lani had said earlier, the thought of Thisbe possibly being somewhere other than the catacombs returned to Fifer. What had the Revinir meant when she'd said that Thisbe wasn't there anymore? If the Revinir had done something awful to Thisbe, would Fifer ever know? Why wasn't their invisible bond stronger?

Fifer shook off the unsettling feeling. According to Dev, there was literally no way for Thisbe to escape from the catacombs. And since the seek spell came from that direction, it seemed to offer even more proof that Thisbe was still underground and the Revinir had lied. The only logical answer was what Lani had suggested. That in the seconds before death, Alex had magically sent Thisbe something special, which she was now trying to use to let them know she was alive.

Fifer sighed, feeling completely stressed out and near the

end of her rope. Her brother was dead, and her sister was missing. Could this possibly feel any worse? She never wanted to experience this horrible pain again—and it all came from loving people in the first place. Growing so close to people . . . *loving* them . . . Maybe it wasn't all Fifer had thought it was. The loss of someone like that was too much to bear. And now, on top of everything, Simber wanted *her* to be a leader. Great.

Fifer went to her bedroll and burrowed into it, exhausted. She couldn't take any more. At least for now.

Around dusk Simber returned with news that Arabis was in sight and should be arriving shortly with her wings ready to be reattached.

"I can do it," Seth offered, noting that Fifer was taking a nap. He was glad—she needed it. He began to prepare his mind for the magical task. He knew how hard this would be, but he was ready for it.

Before the dragon arrived, they heard the king's call to arms again. Fifer stirred and sat up.

Dev's skin prickled at the sound, making his dragon scales stand on end, but they weren't noticeable in the growing darkness. "Did you hear that?" he said to Fifer. "It's the trumpets again."

Fifer, a bit groggy, listened, and soon the mournful call came through, louder this time. "I hear it. Is it the same call as before?"

Dev closed his eyes for a moment, focusing intently. "It's getting louder," he said. "They must be moving toward us."

"Are they coming to fight us again?" Fifer asked, jumping to her feet, wild eyed. She looked at Talon, who rose above the trees to check.

"It's a procession," the bronze giant reported, settling back down to the ground. "They're not leaving the road. And there are wheeled vehicles with them—they certainly won't be able to get to us with those."

Dev looked perplexed. "It's probably the army with all the new volunteers. They're coming up the road to the city to show the rest of the people how much support the king has." He winced, imagining the scene. The last time he'd seen a procession was the parade that Shanti had led right before she'd been killed. He tried to block the images from his mind, but they'd been plaguing him. "The king is making sure everybody

LISA McMANN

hears and sees it," he said. "Even the Revinir and her soldiers. Maybe he thinks they'll surrender before the war even starts."

"That would be easier for everyone," said Carina. As the trumpet call grew louder, Thatcher and Crow came running back to the camp out of breath.

"What's going on?" asked Samheed.

"We didn't find Thisbe anywhere," said Crow, his chest heaving. "But the king is in that procession. Right up front. We saw him stick his head outside of a curtain and wave to some spectators along the road."

"The king? Himself?" asked Dev. "I suppose he wants the people to see he's not afraid. But that's really dangerous after what happened with Shanti."

"Yes," said Thatcher, "you're right on the mark, Dev. We saw a few blue-uniformed soldiers sneaking out of the catacombs through the elevator. They headed through the side streets toward the procession."

"Yes," said Crow gravely. "And it didn't seem like they were wanting to join the king's side, if you know what I mean. I'm afraid they're going to try to jump them. Assassinate the king while they have the chance. That would throw everything into mass chaos."

Just then the trumpets' song ended in cacophony, and the ground began to shake. Shouts rose. A few moments later Arabis came crashing through the trees into camp, nearly crushing Kaylee and Lani and Samheed, but narrowly missing them. The orange dragon, carrying her wings with her tail, came to a stop and looked at Simber. "I think they saw me," she said. "I'm sorry. They'll be after me." She looked around the group. "We need to relocate immediately."

Samheed jumped to his feet. "We have a new campsite in mind, west of the square."

"Okay, everybody," said Fifer, stooping to roll up her bed. "Let's pack up."

Dev's eyes widened. His scales flattened, and a strange low buzzing filled his ears. Without a word he started toward the road.

Fifer stared. "Dev, wait!" she said. "Where are you going? Didn't you hear Arabis? We need to move our camp!"

Dev turned, making Fifer gasp. His eyes were wild, and a wisp of smoke curled from his nostrils. "I'll find you," he said. "Don't worry. I . . . I've got to go save the king."

LISA McMANN

An Eventful Evening

What are you talking about?" Fifer cried. "Dev, why? The king never did anything nice for you. We're not on his side, remember? We need to stay hidden. We need you to help us find Thisbe! We need—" She looked closer, and an expression of horror crossed her face. "Is that *smoke* coming out of your nose?"

"What? *Is* it?" Dev crossed his eyes but was unable to see it. He turned around frantically, trying to catch sight of it, but then he stopped. "I can explain that later. But for now, all I know is if the Revinir's soldiers kill the king, she wins. She'll

LISA McMANN

Dragon Ghosts » 162

have no other barriers in taking over all of Grimere. She'll take his soldiers, his castle, his entire kingdom."

"And that means," said Seth, figuring it out, "that she won't need to focus on overcoming that enemy. She'll move on to take over the rest of the land of the dragons without having to fight anybody."

"Except us," said Fifer. "And then she'll head back to the seven islands to take that over." She started after Dev. "I'm coming with you."

"Wait!" roared Simber.

"Simber," said Fifer, ready to argue, "we have to! We need the king in place to keep the Revinir from advancing without a fight. We're not on the king's side or anything, but we'd rather *he* win than the Revinir, because she's so much more destructive to our black-eyed people and the dragons. Don't you get it? You said you'd listen to me."

"I was only trrrying to say that I'm coming with you," said Simber. "It's just a few blue-uniforrrmed soldierrrs, rrright?"

"Oh," said Fifer. She blinked. "Okay. But won't people see you? They'll freak out."

Simber's gaze turned hard. "They'rrre alrrready frrreaking

out with this call to arrrms. They know what a warrr means to them and theirrr families. Besides, it's inevitable that I'll be spotted eventually. So we'll let them . . . frrreak. I'm not staying behind anymorrre. Not forrr anything. I can't stand being stuck herrre. And I won't let anotherrr frrriend be killed without the enemy getting past me firrrst."

"All right," said Fifer. "Let's go, then! Come on, Dev—we'll climb on Simber's back. The rest of you can pack up and move to the new camp. Simber will help us find you." She hopped on Simber and called to Shimmer. A group of birds came without the hammock this time, so they could act as lookouts and attackers.

Seth started toward Simber. "Wait. I'm coming too."

Fifer turned to him, and a pang of fear went through her. He could get killed. "No! You should stay here."

Seth stared. "What? Why?"

Simber frowned but remained silent.

"I don't know," said Fifer, feeling anxiety bubble up in her chest. "They need you to help move camp. Let's go, Simber."

"They do not. I'm coming with you!" Seth hesitated a split second, still puzzled by Fifer's command, then continued to join Dev and Fifer on Simber's back. "Hey, Mom, can you help Arabis with her wings?" Seth called back over his shoulder. "I'm a little too busy right now."

"We've got you covered!" said Carina.

With Fifer's birds fluttering overhead, they set off toward the potential ambush on the road, hoping it wasn't too late to save the awful king.

Moments later, when the people in the procession spotted the flying statue coming out of the forest, they shrieked and scattered, leaving the king in his chariot and his protective guards alone in the road. Screams and shouts rose into the air and grew louder as Simber, with his three passengers, dove down and swept low to the ground. Dev gripped the stony cheetah, his face turning green.

"There they are!" said Fifer, spotting the blue uniforms. "Be careful!" She turned to look at Seth. "Don't do anything dangerous," she pleaded.

"Fifer, quit being so weird!"

"I'm not!"

"Whatever." Seth reached for his components, and when

LISA McMANN

Simber grew close enough, he and Fifer sent off a pair of freeze spells, hitting two of the blue soldiers and stopping them in their tracks.

At the same time Simber dipped to one side, nimbly avoiding the king's people. He plowed into a couple more of the Revinir's soldiers, catching them with his lowered wing, and knocked them senseless into a row of waste bins alongside a building. While Dev was busy hanging on to Simber for dear life, Fifer and Seth pelted the remaining soldiers with freeze spells. Then the winged cheetah rose and circled. He dropped again so Seth and Fifer could send off scatterclip spells, pinning the guards to the wall of a building.

Simber rose and circled again, searching for more sneaky Revinir soldiers. Dev, lying flat now, finally dared open his eyes and lift his head. Seth glanced at him to make sure he was okay, then turned back to the soldiers. He faintly recognized some of the people in green uniforms who'd stayed around the chariot, valiantly protecting the king. Seth realized this group had definitely seen Simber before, in the castle dungeon, leaving a trail of destruction as he'd searched for Thisbe down a hallway that was just slightly too narrow for the beast. He'd carved great long gouges in the walls along both sides of the passage, widening it so he could fit.

"There's one of the soldiers who guards the dungeon," Fifer said, pointing out a woman to Seth.

"I remember her," said Seth, eyes narrowed. "Can't we take them out too?"

"No," said Fifer. "Their time will come. We need them to fight the Revinir first."

"I know, I know," Seth mumbled.

Feeling better, Dev sat up a little and waved and shouted to the king's soldiers—he wanted them to see him. He pointed at the Revinir's soldiers up against the building. "Do you see them? They were about to assassinate the king!" he cried out accusingly. "We saved you. And your jobs!"

The captain whirled about at the sound of the familiar voice, then turned to see what Dev was pointing to. She recognized the boy, all right. He'd been the princess's slave before the spoiled girl gave him away to help pay back the Revinir for the dragons' escape. The captain looked closer and saw the blue-uniformed men somehow shackled to the bins. It didn't make sense to her, since no one had physically done the shackling. But she ordered her soldiers to take them captive, along with the frozen ones.

Dev, scales raised, kept his eye on the woman as Simber continued to circle. Mentally he willed the captain to acknowledge what Dev and his strange party had done. Almost as if she were being pulled by magnetic force, the captain, glaring, lifted her head. She reluctantly nodded her thanks to the former castle slave. "You're joining the king's army, aren't you?" she asked. She eyed Fifer and Seth, recognizing them now too. They'd been the ones responsible for letting the dragons loose. She was still furious about that. But maybe this helped make up for it.

"No," said Dev. "I'm free. Free from all of you. The Revinir, too."

The captain glared. "Not if we catch you. Bring back our dragons and I'll see to it you're truly free. Forever."

"That'll only be enforceable if you take down the Revinir," said Dev coolly. "But if you don't pay closer attention, she's going to beat you before the war even starts." He glanced at the Revinir's frozen soldiers, then told the captain, "We didn't have to save you. I hope the king can hear this so he knows you nearly got him killed with this stupid stunt."

The captain glanced uneasily at the chariot. The thick curtain was drawn, partially enclosing the king inside. Chances were good he was listening to everything.

"Like I said," the captain went on, ignoring Dev, "bring back the dragons. I know they're hiding around here somewhere. I saw the orange one. Her days are numbered if the Revinir catches her—you might want to deliver my warning. But if the dragons choose to work for the king . . . well. Maybe a better outcome can be arranged."

"Her name is Arabis!" shouted Fifer angrily. "And you'll never keep the dragons in your horrible dungeon again."

Simber, tired of circling, veered away toward the forest. The captain snarled at Fifer and shook her fist in the air. "You— just stay away. We have too much work on our hands to go after you. We don't have time for your destructive antics."

Fifer turned her head and made a face at Seth. "She's still awful," she said.

"Yep," agreed Seth.

LISA McMANN

"No kidding," Dev muttered, tentatively sitting up a little more as he got used to the ride. "Okay. We did what we needed to do. Now the king's soldiers are indebted to us. You can tell Simber we can go now."

"I can hearrr you," said Simber. "We'rrre going. I'm taking a cirrrcuitous rrroute so they won't be able to follow us back to ourrr new camp."

"Oh, good," said Dev. He was still nervous about Simber—the statue was gruff and frightening, and he hadn't quite figured him out. He glanced over his shoulder as the procession began to form again. "I hope the captain realizes what she's in for and keeps a better eye on the king. At least for now. It's good she noticed us."

Dev sat back, a gleam in his eye as he thought about what had just transpired. His dragon scales flattened. He assumed the smoke from his nose was long gone—no one had mentioned it again, and he wondered if it would be possible to explain away the dragon features once this was all over. No doubt Fifer would remember and ask again soon. Should he tell them about Thisbe? Or would that only make them worry more?

Simber and his passengers stopped at the old now-deserted camp to pay their final respects at Alex's grave, for they didn't know when, if ever, they'd be back. They stayed several minutes, giving Fifer and Simber some time by themselves while Seth and Dev hung back, trying to be respectful.

The tears flowed freely. When Fifer was ready, Simber followed the scent of the rest of the rescue team down one of the multiple paths marked by trampled bushes and trees, thanks to Arabis. Painstakingly, Simber and the young riders covered up the trail behind them so it wouldn't be quite so obvious. After a while they made it to the new camp location on the far side of the square.

The others had set up by the meandering river, equidistant from the square as before but on the west side of it now, farther away from the castle and nearer to the desert and the desolate cavelands beyond. If anyone were truly looking for them, it wouldn't be too hard to find them. But perhaps, as the king's captain had said, the impending war really did have everyone a little bit too busy to worry about the eclectic group of strangers in the forest . . . especially since the strangers had already beaten the king's soldiers once.

LISA McMANN

While they waited for things to settle down in the square, Arabis, her wings properly reattached, recounted her visit with the ghost dragons and her talks with Gorgrun and Quince. She told them that the dragons seemed relatively strong despite their condition, and perhaps could help if there ever were a battle against the Revinir. But she also warned that they were very old and in desperate need of a leader to remind them to stay on task. "In short," said Arabis, "I'm not sure they're much help without someone to guide them. Perhaps when the time comes, I could help with that."

"Arrre you saying you'll stay with us?" asked Simber. "What about Pan? She's expecting all of us back, especially you."

"This is my land," Arabis said simply. "My family's land. It's my duty to take it back. If that is your goal too, I will remain with you."

"It is," said Fifer earnestly, surprising herself a little. But the land belonged to her, as well, in a way. And Dev.

Arabis caught Fifer's eye and nodded, an understanding passing between them. Almost certainly she was reassessing the girl, rechecking her levels of good and evil. The dragon

LISA McMANN

remained quiet and brooding, thinking about what the ghost dragons had said about not being able to die until the land had been restored to the proper ruling bodies. It had seemed too intimate a detail to share with the others, at least for now. Perhaps the time would come for telling them. If it came to that, Arabis knew exactly whom she trusted the most out of all the humans. It was easy enough for her to tell which ones had just the right levels. But until that time, Arabis would continue to brood about what her role should be in fulfilling the wishes of the ghost dragons and allowing them to finally die. When she really thought about it, the job seemed tougher than at first glance.

The king's call to arms grew faint again. When darkness fell, Lani, Samheed, Kitten, Fifer, Seth, and Dev ventured out to look for the fourth opening to the catacombs.

Flashes of the Past

Thisbe, Rohan, and Sky climbed the steep path up the rock wall. They went mostly in silence, concentrating on their footwork so they wouldn't plunge to their deaths. As they progressed, Thisbe's dragon scales glinted in the setting sun. She'd showed Sky and told her all about them and about how she'd gotten them. But she hadn't mentioned the effects of the ancestor broth—all those images were so stark and unsettling. Thisbe wasn't sure what to make of them. Why did that happen? What did the images mean? For a few seconds a strange feeling came over her, almost making her dizzy. The lake below them wavered, its edges blurred. It felt like she'd been here before. Doing this. She gripped a rock and took a few steadying breaths until the dizziness went away. But the memory of the images remained.

She recalled a few of the scenes: Meteors slamming into the ground. An earthquake. A girl being dragged away by soldiers. A weyr of fearsome silvery dragons in flight. A rogue group of stealthy bandits sneaking through the forest. Armies clashing and people dying. The scenes were disturbing. The only explanation that made sense to Thisbe was that the ancestor broth she'd drunk had brought these specific pictures to her mind because they were things the ancestors had witnessed or experienced. If that was true, they'd had horrible lives.

To clear her thoughts, Thisbe glanced down over the lake again. Now that it wasn't wavering, she took in its beauty. The sunset reflected orange on the surface and lit up the canyon walls. Thisbe studied them and noted the smooth grooves of the canyon all around the shore, as if something had forcefully carved space for the lake. Thinking of the image, she wondered if a meteor could have done it. Could there be a giant stony

LISA McMANN

mass embedded below the water? She smiled ruefully—if that were so, it would have to have a volcano attached to it, she supposed. One that submerged and emerged randomly. And led to other worlds. She chuckled at the absurdity.

Rohan heard her and glanced her way. "What's funny?"

Thisbe shook her head. It was too ridiculous to share. "Nothing. Just . . . thinking about meteors."

Rohan gave her a quizzical look. "Meteors are funny?"

"No. I didn't mean . . ." She laughed again. "Never mind."

Rohan continued climbing. "A pair of meteors hit our world a long time ago. Some have said that one of them formed this lake. Others say the impact caused a major earthquake that split off our world from yours. I'm not sure where the other meteor landed."

Thisbe stopped. "Are you serious?"

"Of course. It was a long time ago."

Sky looked over her shoulder. "That's fascinating. What else do you know about it?" she asked.

Rohan thought for a moment. "That's about it. I didn't have a chance to learn more before I was taken captive."

"But . . . But what about the volcano? Is it somehow

attached to the meteor?" Thisbe was very confused. "Or did the meteor somehow break through to the network? And the impact created the volcano?"

"Perhaps the volcano built itself over time," Sky mused. "Yes, that's my question too. Any ideas, Rohan?"

"I don't know," said Rohan. "That's the biggest mystery."

Thisbe fell silent as their climb became more arduous in the growing shadows. As they neared the top, they heard some commotion and music coming from the square, but it quieted before the three could see what was going on. Finally, at dusk, they crested the hill and came down. They crossed the vast square, reaching the side of Dragonsmarche nearest the castle after dark.

They strolled casually, trying not to be noticed, while other pedestrians moved along carrying baguettes or flowers or baskets of laundered items. Once the three continued beyond the square, the pedestrian traffic became minimal. An occasional cart or other vehicle passed. They ventured down the main road over which Thisbe and Fifer had been driven on their way to the auction. On one side were narrow roads, small shops, and neighborhoods. On the other was the forest.

Rohan looked around curiously. He knew the area, though he said it had changed in the years since he'd last been free to roam. "The houses and storefronts look tired," he remarked, pointing at fading and peeling paint. A cracked window here, a broken carriage there. "Like the king has forgotten to care for his people."

Thisbe tipped her head up. "Did you live around here?"

She saw him swallow. "No." He hesitated, then changed his mind and said, "Yes. If you could call it that. Not for long, though." He tucked his chin, shoved his hands into his pockets, and kept moving.

Thisbe and Sky exchanged a glance. It was clear Rohan didn't want to talk about his past life. At least not right now.

When no one was nearby, Thisbe stopped the others and led them off the road to the edge of the forest, where there appeared to be a narrow, overgrown path. "Try the seek spell here, Sky, so we can see what direction Alex is in."

Sky reached into her pocket and glanced around. All was quiet. She cautiously lifted the piece of slate in front of her and concentrated, then whispered, "Seek." A bright ball of light shot from the slate and went due north, directly into

LISA McMANN

the forest. Definitely not toward the seven islands.

Sky and Thisbe gasped. "Alex *is* here!" Thisbe said in a harsh whisper. "Or, at least, he's not in Artimé." She hadn't dared to believe it. It was troubling, though. How long had he been here? Why hadn't he come for her? So many thoughts like that threatened Thisbe's self-confidence, and she had to shake them off. She was sure that once she saw him, he'd explain, and she could forgive everything.

"That is a remarkable bit of sorcery," Rohan remarked as they tromped into the woods following the spell. The light was already fading away.

"Would you like to try it sometime? It's not hard."

"I would," said Rohan, giving her a half smile. "But, unfortunately, I have no possessions but this harness from the Revinir, and I've no desire to send *her* a seek spell. And no family left, other than some distant black-eyed cousins back in the catacombs. I wouldn't want to get them in trouble. So alas, I don't have anyone to send a seek spell to."

"The other black-eyed slaves are your cousins?" asked Thisbe.

"Some are bound to be," said Rohan lightly. "There are

only two lines of black-eyed royal families. I don't actually know which of the other slaves might be related to me. Never had the chance to get close to any of them. So I guess I'm pretty much on my own."

Thisbe didn't know what to say to that. As lonely as she'd felt lately, she'd never had a problem like that. She caught his eye and regarded him for a long moment. "Maybe they should have blasted a tunnel to your crypt like I did." She smiled warmly at him.

Rohan tripped over a vine, and they both laughed uneasily.

"Well," said Thisbe, "I'll make you something you can use for a seek spell. For when we leave. Then . . . if you need . . ." She frowned and didn't finish.

Rohan gave a sharp nod and looked away. "That's very kind of you."

Sky pursed her lips, determined to keep things as light and cheery as possible under the circumstances. "This way," she instructed. "As long as we keep going straight, we'll be fine. But I'm afraid we won't be able to see our way there."

"I can help with that." Thisbe stopped abruptly. She reached around the forest floor and picked up a thick, dry stick with dead leaves all at one end. "Here we are," she said. "A torch." She stared at the dead leaves and concentrated. Seconds later sparks flew from her eyes and lit the leaves on fire. She held the stick at an angle so the flames would light the end of the thick branch as well. Rohan and Sky stomped out the wayward sparks. When the flame went out, Thisbe tried again, holding her concentration until a solid orange flame remained steady at the end of the stick.

"There," Thisbe said when she was satisfied with the task. "Now we can see."

"Well, you certainly have improved," said Sky admiringly. "You've got so much control now."

"I've been practicing my magic on dragon bones for weeks," said Thisbe. The dragon scales awakened and shifted at the mention of the bones. Thisbe grabbed Sky's elbow in preparation for the images to blind her like they had before, but that didn't happen. It hadn't—not since the first time.

"Are you okay?" Sky asked, taking the torch from her. "What's wrong?"

Thisbe shook her head. "Nothing," she said shakily. The moment passed. They walked on as straight as they could,

LISA McMANN

with Thisbe taking back the torch and leading the way.

Eventually Thisbe called for Sky to send another seek spell so they could see where it went and make sure they were still going in the right direction. Once the spell flew out, they adjusted their course slightly, running after the streak of light to gain as much ground as possible while they could still see it. Of course it faded fast, and they continued on as best they could. After a quarter of an hour, they emerged into a clearing. Sky touched Thisbe's arm and stopped. Thisbe stopped too, and Rohan did as well behind them.

"What is it?" asked Thisbe, holding the torch to one side and peering out into the darkness. Lights danced in front of her, and she blinked hard, thinking it was the brightness of the torch affecting her sight.

"Look," said Sky, pointing in the distance to where several orbs of light hovered together, shimmering but not moving. She frowned. "Are those my seek spells? They seem strange just sitting there. I've never seen them do that before."

"I don't know what they are," said Thisbe.

The three ventured forward, looking carefully around as they pressed on, until they reached a large area that looked like it had been thoroughly trampled. Thisbe held up the torch. "What happened here?" she breathed. There was a place where a fire had been, and off to one side were the glowing seek spells.

"Perhaps we've found Alex's campsite," Rohan suggested.

But Sky wasn't interested in the landscape, or in trying to figure out how everything had been trampled down. Instead she stumbled toward the seek spells. Thisbe, sensing something ominous, turned to watch her, and Rohan did too. Something was off. It didn't feel right.

Sky reached the spheres of light and looked down at the mound of dirt below them. "It's . . . a grave," she said, horror building in her voice. She clutched her throat. "Dear gods! No! It can't be!"

Thisbe came running as Sky hurried to pull the piece of slate from her pocket. She held it with trembling hands. Then she took a deep breath and hesitated, as if she wasn't quite sure she wanted to send it, because then she'd find out the answer to the biggest fear she'd ever had. "I can't do this," she muttered, dropping her arms; then just as quickly she lifted the stone again and held it to her lips. She swallowed hard and

LISA McMANN

closed her eyes. Then she pulled the slate away and whispered, "Seek."

The ball of light shot out and went a few short feet, then stopped abruptly to join the others hovering there.

Sky didn't need to see it. She knew. With a ragged cry she dropped to her knees beside the grave and put a hand on the ground to steady herself.

Thisbe, realizing what it all meant, let out a gasp. She couldn't believe it. There was no way . . . no way that Alex could be *down* there. *Buried* there. "This can't be happening," she whispered. She began to wail.

"Oh, Thisbe," whispered Rohan, coming over to Thisbe and putting his arm around her shoulders. He looked like he might weep with her. "I'm so sorry."

Thisbe turned to him, eyes wide in horror, tears blurring everything. "My brother," she said, and broke down again. Rohan, helpless, took the torch from her so she wouldn't have to hold it anymore.

Sky pivoted on her knees, and then stumbled to her feet and went to comfort Thisbe.

Neither of them could say out loud that Alex was dead. But as they held each other, they both knew in that instant that their lives had changed drastically. Nothing would ever feel the same again.

Searching for Smoke

While Thisbe, Sky, and Rohan were discovering Alex's graveside, Fifer, Seth, Dev, Lani, and Samheed, with Kitten asleep in his pocket, crossed the square from the opposite side. Dev led the way, purposefully steering around the area of the square where Shanti had been killed. Her blood likely still stained the pavers, for it hadn't rained since then, and he didn't want to see it.

The group entered the nearest neighborhood, searching diligently for the vent from the Revinir's catacomb kitchen. They weren't sure what to look for other than smoke or steam from the broths. Perhaps it would come from a pipe in an alley or through a grate in the road.

They entered a quiet street, and Fifer whirled around, her heart in her throat. "Did you hear something?" she whispered.

Everyone looked. There was nothing. They continued on.

Fifer thought she heard another noise and grabbed Seth's arm, making him wince. Again, there was nothing. Seth peeled his arm out of her iron grip.

Samheed and Lani exchanged a worried look.

Fifer noticed it. She took a deep breath and let it out. "I'm just a little nervous," she explained.

"We can certainly understand why," said Lani.

"We're safe up here in the dark," Dev muttered. "The only danger is under our feet." He kept a sharp eye out for smoke as he led them down the street, but his mind wandered back to Shanti and the events of the past few weeks. The internal wound in Dev's chest was still fresh when he let it be. Most of the time he covered it or pushed it aside. They were all reeling from recent deaths, which was almost comforting in a strange way. But he couldn't just sit around and dwell on it. Like the team from Artimé, he had work to do. And Dev wanted to find

LISA McMANN

187 « Dragon Ghosts

Thisbe as much as the others did. After their week together in the Revinir's kitchen, Thisbe knew more about Dev than Shanti ever had. And she'd cared about him. It was . . . a new feeling.

Dev slipped his hand inside his jacket pocket where he kept his treasures. His gold rock that Shanti had paid him used to be the only thing there, but now he also had the money belt he'd been wearing when he'd run away from the Revinir's Dragonsmarche booth. He was richer than he'd ever been.

And that wasn't all. He moved the thin belt aside and touched the small glass bottles of dragon-bone broth he'd managed to steal before his escape from the marketplace. He wasn't sure why he'd grabbed them; to him, stealing was more instinct than anything. And his instinct had felt sharper than usual in the days since the Revinir had forced him to drink the dragon-bone broth. Sometimes he wondered if he was just imagining it. Other times he was sure his perception was deeper than before. He felt almost . . . intuitive. He hoped these improved traits would somehow help them find Thisbe. He'd drink more broth if he thought that would sharpen his wits further, but doing that made him feel uneasy, like it would be

LISA McMANN

too much of a good thing. More likely he would keep them to sell. Or share them with Fifer in case it could help her in some way find her sister.

He missed Thisbe. A lot.

Dev knew the village well, including the back alleyways. He'd helped Shanti sneak away from the palace to this area on many occasions when she'd been bored. And he'd suffered the punishments for both of them, he remembered ruefully. He'd take another punishment if it meant she'd come back, he thought. Then he narrowed his eyes. Would he really, though? Obviously he didn't wish her to remain dead, so in that respect he might. But did he want to go back to that? To being her slave? Sure, the only life he'd ever known had been with the princess, but Fifer and Seth were right. She'd treated him horribly most of the time. He was still processing that, for he hadn't experienced anything different before. And so far, this new life had been chaotic. He hadn't had much of a chance to evaluate or compare.

When he thought about Thisbe stuck in the catacombs, probably being punished severely after the people from Artimé had come in and fought against the Revinir's soldiers, a strange

LISA McMANN

buzzing seemed to appear around him. It wasn't a sound, though—that was the oddest part. It was more like a buzzing *feeling* on his arms. As if his dragon scales were more alert when he thought about her—or maybe it was the thought of the catacombs that triggered it. He couldn't quite pinpoint it. And he couldn't tell the others about it. They didn't even know about his scales, and the longer he waited to tell them, the more he didn't want to. They might think he was strange or dangerous and make him leave. And then what would he do? Being alone was frightening. He felt . . . He felt braver when he was with these people. And he wanted to find Thisbe more than anything.

Fifer seemed to have forgotten about the smoke that had come from Dev's nose earlier. She hadn't asked again, anyway, after the attack on the Revinir's soldiers. She'd certainly remember it eventually, though. Part of Dev felt like he should just get it over with and offer an explanation before she asked. Maybe doing that would somehow make her trust him more. But it seemed awkward to just bring it up. *So, about that smoke pouring out of my nose . . .* Nope. And he didn't want the passersby to overhear anything about it.

Although Dev had assured Fifer that the only danger was underground, he was secretly worried about the soldier presence in the square and surrounding neighborhoods ever since the king's procession and call to arms. He vaguely recognized a few faces from the castle—some had been part of the attack on the rescue team too. He was glad to see they'd been assigned to other tasks, since that meant they wouldn't be chasing down the strangers in their new camp. That made Dev rest a bit easier. The Revinir's soldiers were often out and about, especially at night when they could more easily use the elevator in the square. Surely the king would focus his soldiers on tracking them from now on.

They traveled in silence for a long time, all of them thinking about gravely important things. At one point, upon hearing the trumpets in the distance again, Fifer turned to the others with a quizzical look. "Has the war actually started now because of that attack? Or is the king still doing that call-to-arms thing to continue building his army?" She'd read in Lani's first book about how Mr. Today had originally organized his Artiméans to prepare for battle some time before the battle happened, and she wondered if things worked the same way everywhere.

"I'm not sure," Dev admitted. There hadn't been a war here in his lifetime. He'd only heard the soldiers doing drills a few times a year on the castle lawn outside the moat. It had been fascinating to watch. At one point he'd wanted to be like them. But that had changed the older he got and the more horribly they'd treated him.

"I think the king is still recruiting a larger army," said Samheed. "He's already got enough soldiers for peacetime, but now he needs more. And he's doing it publicly because he wants the Revinir to know how much support he has. People are clearly flocking to him. He's trying to frighten her, or to make her surrender. But no one knows how many people are flocking to her side."

"There's no way she's going to surrender," Lani said. "Not her—she practically came back from the dead! She'll definitely respond in some way. Whether she does the same by parading her soldiers around or has a different method remains to be seen. But she'll have to increase the strength of her army somehow if she's going to compete with the king's."

Dev's eyes widened as a thought came into his head. Would the Revinir think to use the dragon-bone broth to strengthen

LISA McMANN

her existing soldiers and make them more like her? He bit his lip, then glanced back at the others and saw his moment to confess. "You know she's got dark magical powers," he said quietly. "But there's something else I haven't told you. She has also been making broth out of the bones of the dragons and . . . and other bones." He slid his sleeve up and moved under a streetlamp. The dragon scales sparkled in the light. "She made me test it, and this is what happened. The Revinir forced me to drink it."

The others gathered around and gasped at the sight of the scales catching the light. "That's horrifying!" said Samheed. "What a monster!"

"Indeed, she is," said Lani gravely. "I'm sorry, Dev. Are you okay?"

Dev wasn't used to having people ask about his well-being, and he was momentarily taken aback. "Yes, I'm okay." His face grew warm from the attention. "That's why there was smoke coming from my nose, Fifer. Apparently I am a fraction of a dragon now."

Fifer inspected the scales, knowing better than to fully trust Dev at his word. She lifted one and tugged at it. Her expression betrayed how repulsed she was by it.

Dev jerked his arm away like she'd hurt him. "It's no joke. They are really attached." Hastily he turned and pulled his sleeve down, having had enough of the gawking. "So, yes. You saw smoke coming from my nose. That was the first time it happened as far as I know. I'm not sure what triggered it."

"Do you have special dragon powers now or something?" Fifer asked, incredulous and still staring at the boy. She almost couldn't believe him, but the scales had felt real, like they were stuck as tightly to him as if they'd grown there. It was horrifying . . . but fascinating, too.

"I don't know." Dev clamped his mouth shut, annoyed, and moved into the shadows. Then he glanced sidelong at Fifer. "There's one more thing."

"What is it?" Fifer narrowed her eyes.

"Thisbe . . . has them too."

"What?" cried Fifer and Seth together.

"It's true. The Revinir made her drink the broth."

"Wait a second," said Fifer, grabbing Dev's shoulder and turning him roughly. "You're saying Thisbe has dragon scales? Like yours? Are you joking?" Her stomach churned at the thought.

Samheed muttered furiously under his breath and started pacing.

"I'm not joking." Dev yanked away from Fifer and began looking for smoke again, while Fifer just shook her head and the others murmured in shock. A moment later they followed him.

"It's horrible," said Fifer, catching up to him. "You should have told us before."

"Well, I'm sorry," said Dev. "It's a little complicated. Besides, I thought you had enough on your mind." That last part was a fib, but it sounded good. Then, feeling like he owed them more of an explanation, he added, "But maybe it's not so bad. Sometimes I feel like I can ... I don't know ... *sense* things better than I used to be able to do. Like that attack on the king. Once Crow told us what was happening with the Revinir's soldiers, my scales stood up and the smoke came out and I just knew—inside me—that we had to go save the king. I wasn't sure where that came from. I just had this urgency. And once we all talked it through, it made sense."

"Wow," said Fifer, still eyeing him. He seemed sincere.

"Well, Dev," said Lani, "there's a silver lining in that you have greater intuition now. Perhaps Thisbe does too."

Dev nodded. "She does," he said. "And . . . and she's handling the scales okay too. Or at least she was the last time I saw her."

"That's nice to know," said Seth with relief in his voice. "Thank you."

"Sure." Dev frowned and continued searching.

They came upon a small, weathered house where a few neighbors had gathered and were sitting on the steps, eating and drinking and talking quietly. Dev nodded politely to the people. He asked them something in another language, but they shook their heads. One of them pointed behind them and said something with a noncommittal shrug.

"*Tat*," said Dev. He continued walking with the others behind him.

A block farther and out of the neighbors' hearing distance, Fifer stepped up to walk next to Dev. "Did you ask them about the vent?"

"Yes."

"What does *tat* mean?"

"It means 'thank you.'"

LISA McMANN

Fifer nearly mentioned that she didn't think he knew how to say thanks, but that no longer seemed accurate. That trait had belonged to the old Dev, but the boy had changed. Not drastically. He still annoyed Fifer for what he'd done to them when they'd first met. But in the time between the dungeon when she and Seth had freed the dragons and Dev's arrival at their old camp on their return visit, something had happened to his personality.

Maybe it was the dragon-bone broth. Or Shanti's death. Or perhaps it was his time in captivity with the Revinir. The woman was clearly very awful to her slaves, and it sent a fresh pain to Fifer's heart to imagine what Thisbe was going through. In a way, Fifer wanted to know exactly how bad it had been down there. But in another way she didn't. It would only make her feel more helpless to her twin at a time when Fifer was already feeling so vulnerable. And while Alex's shocking death had overrun everyone's thoughts lately, Fifer was struggling with the separation from Thisbe even more than before— what if she lost Thisbe, too? Or Seth or Lani or Kaylee or any of them? The thought took her breath away.

They *had* to be close to her. Perhaps she was directly below them right at this moment. But Fifer had no inkling of it. Nothing! No twin sense at all like Alex and Aaron had felt for each other. What was wrong with her?

And what might Thisbe be thinking of them after all this time? Had the Revinir told Thisbe that she'd killed Alex? How awful for Thisbe to find that out and have no one to go to. Or was Thisbe really gone, like the Revinir had suggested? Was this search completely fruitless? Were they just wasting time? Fifer's anxiety grew, and her heart ached anew. Why did she have to care so much? Life would be easier if she didn't.

She frowned and pushed that thought aside. "If Thisbe *isn't* in the catacombs . . . ," Fifer said quietly to Dev. "Like, if the Revinir did something else with her, where do you think she'd be?"

Dev thought for a long moment. "The only thing I can think of is that the Revinir might have given her to the king to make up for her soldiers killing Princess Shanti. But that's a stretch. They used to trade slaves regularly when one wronged the other, but now, with this war looming and the tensions rising . . . I'm not so sure the Revinir would even offer."

It was unsettling. "*Tat*," Fifer whispered, not realizing at

LISA McMANN

first that she'd said it out loud. She glanced sheepishly at Dev, who turned his head and nodded. "That's right," he said with a hint of a smile.

She started to smile back, then stopped herself. She didn't need to start caring about Dev, of all people—she had plenty of others to worry about already.

As they went slowly up and down the streets for hours, sniffing the air and looking for wisps of smoke curling up from cracks or holes or pipes in the ground, Fifer kept most of her agonizing thoughts about her loved ones to herself. Eventually she grew exhausted by them, and her mind turned to the common language that Dev had spoken to the people on the house steps. And she felt a strange yearning inside her to learn it. Perhaps that would keep her occupied with things less painful.

When they gave up for the night, they crossed over the square again. This time it was almost deserted, except for a party of three in the distance. Their heads were down as they went toward the hill and the cliff that dropped sharply down to the crater lake. Dev and Fifer veered northwest, in the direction of the forest and their camp, with the others behind.

"Will you teach me more words of the common language sometime?" Fifer asked Dev. "I'd like to learn."

"Sure," said Dev. "There are a lot more neighborhoods to search. We can do it to pass the time while we're looking."

Fifer smiled. *"Tat."* Behind them, Lani poked Samheed in the arm and gave him a sly grin. But Seth, breathing heavily from all the walking, frowned at Dev's back.

Trying to Make Sense of It

Âfter seeing Alex's grave, Thisbe had felt physically ill with all the unanswered questions. How had it happened? Who or what had killed him? Had there been a battle? Wild animals? A tragic accident? Who else had been with him, and where were they now? How long ago had it happened? Was he the only one who'd died? What about Fifer? The questions pounded in her ears, and she couldn't turn them off.

After they'd absorbed some of the shock, Rohan had suggested trying to figure out which way the party had gone so they could follow. But despite the torch, their efforts had

LISA McMANN

been fruitless in the dark. There were several trampled paths branching off the flattened camp area, and they couldn't tell who'd made them or when. It was overwhelming. Had they been made by the Artiméans? Or by soldiers? Or perhaps something else that had attacked and killed Alex? Were they coming or going? Were there other graves they didn't know about? Was Fifer alive? Or Seth? Or anybody? The fact that there were no answers was debilitating. They'd ventured back to the cave with no information.

Over the next few days, Thisbe, Sky, and Rohan stayed in their cave, trying to deal with this terrible blow and put the pieces of the story together. Sky spent endless hours staring into the fire. Occasionally silent tears would slip down her cheeks, and she'd bury her face in her hands.

Thisbe felt strange most of the time. It seemed so weird and terrible and foreign that she didn't know how to feel, how to react. This death was so . . . complicated. Alex and Fifer and everyone from Artimé had been distant for so long, they almost didn't seem real to Thisbe anymore. And she and Alex hadn't exactly been very friendly toward one another the last time she'd seen him. She felt terrible about it now, and guilty.

She'd loved Alex—she just hadn't liked him very much, and now that felt wrong. She longed for a chance to change it. To be a better sister to him. Sometimes at night, when she heard Sky sniffling, Thisbe would start crying too. Those were the moments when the girl felt the most human. The least frozen.

While Sky and Thisbe mourned, Rohan took care of the camp. He felt terrible for the two—especially that they had to find out about Alex this way, with no explanation. It left so many questions. He listened when they felt like talking, fished and cooked when they needed to eat, fetched water and firewood and cleaned the makeshift plates after the meals. And he tried now and then to make them smile when it seemed appropriate. They appreciated him more than they could express.

A few days later, Sky felt recovered enough from the shock to venture out on her own. She needed some time alone, outside of the depressing cave. And she wanted to go back to the grave and the forest area during daylight to see if she could find traces of any Artiméans remaining in this world. For as she and Thisbe adjusted to the idea of Alex being dead, they'd begun to imagine that any remaining Artiméans might have gone home once their magic was restored. The loss of the

LISA McMANN

head mage might have been so great that they'd need to return home to regroup and help people there cope. But what if some of them had stayed? Sky needed to find out.

Leaving Thisbe and Rohan to the safety of the cave, Sky set out in the morning and retraced their steps. At the old campsite she stood for a moment at Alex's grave. Nothing had changed. The seek spells still hovered.

Sky knelt and talked to him quietly. "I have Thisbe with me," she said through tears. "Everything is going to be okay. I just . . . I miss you. I can't believe you're gone." She cried harder and collapsed on the dirt that covered him. "This just isn't fair! I'd give anything," she sobbed. "Anything to have you back."

She lingered, draped over the grave, wishing for a sign from him to indicate he'd heard her. But there was nothing. After a while she sat up and wiped her eyes. Then she rummaged through the brush for a large piece of bark and something sharp, and painstakingly carved the words "Sky/Thisbe together/alive by lake" on the bark. She laid it on top of the grave in hopes that someone from Artimé would come to Alex's grave and notice it.

Then, with a start, she picked it up again. What if the Revinir's soldiers discovered it while looking for Thisbe and read it? She'd just given away her location. That would've been a terrible mistake. She debated what to do—cross out the names? Or just Thisbe's? She settled on scraping off several words, leaving "Sky by lake," thinking anyone other than Artiméans would confuse her name for the actual sky above and wouldn't think anything of the strange words. She set the bark down again. It would be difficult to notice even for someone looking for a message. But it would have to do.

Eventually Sky got up and chose a wide, trampled path to the west that seemed recent. She went down it for several hours until the forest ended and a desert landscape began. In the far-off distance were slate-colored rocks jutting up with some hills. Everything in that direction looked dead, like nothing could possibly live there. She could no longer see the river. Sky knew she had to turn back for water, if not food. She didn't think the Artiméans would continue in this direction, especially if they thought they knew where Thisbe was. The trail she'd followed must have been made by someone or something else. She returned the way she'd come.

LISA McMANN

By the time she got back to the abandoned campsite and gravesite, it was afternoon. She refreshed herself at the river, then stopped, thinking. The group would no doubt stay along the river—there was no other source of water except for the lake near her cave, and they definitely weren't there. The second path she chose went to the east, toward the world of the seven islands, and it followed the river most of the time. Occasionally Sky could see the main road that connected Dragonsmarche to the castle. There were green-uniformed soldiers stationed along it. She wasn't sure if that was a new thing since the call to arms, or if they'd always done it. It seemed like a waste of time, but who was she to say? Again Sky walked a couple of hours, but there was no sign of her friends this way either. There was also no sign of an end to this path, so she kept going.

Eventually the forest thinned, and she caught sight of a breathtaking castle set on top of a needle-shaped cliff with a great waterfall and a wall of mist billowing up beyond it. According to Thisbe, the seven islands were just past the great gorge that the water fell into. It was so close, yet impossible for her to cross.

In that moment Sky's heart constricted. She thought about

life in Artimé without Alex. Could she go back there? Would she? Or would it be too painful? Perhaps she'd go to her mother on Warbler Island . . . or just stay here to tend Alex's grave. She laughed ruefully for the first time in days. Perhaps she was arrogant thinking she'd have a choice.

Putting up a hand to shield her eyes, Sky focused on the castle. It would take half a day to get there on foot, she reckoned, but the path she was following didn't lead to it. Not that she wanted to go there. She knew that castle had to be the one where Thisbe had been imprisoned—the one where the Revinir had kept the young dragons captive. It was strange to think that there were underground crypts and tunnels running all the way from the castle westward to the Dragonsmarche square, and beyond it to the lakeside cliff and cave exit from which Thisbe and Rohan had escaped.

Sky turned and looked down the path ahead of her. With less and less growth and more dirt and stones underfoot, the path was harder to see, but it seemed to open up and continue over rocky terrain toward the cliff's edge. Toward home.

"Perhaps they really have given up," Sky murmured. "Gone home." After all, it had been a huge loss for them. Maybe others had been hurt or killed too. They would have lost their magic for a while, Sky remembered, and she knew how awful that would be for the mages, especially if they were in the midst of battle like last time. Her soul groaned at the memory of bringing Artimé back with Alex so many years ago. Clearly the provisions Alex had put in place for the occasion of his untimely death had been easier to decipher than the hint Mr. Today had left for Alex, for Sky had been able to send the seek spell recently—they couldn't have been without magic for too long.

She pulled the piece of slate from her pocket, and it blurred in front of her. Her trembling lips formed a smile as she tried to read the words through her tears—though she knew the silly poem by heart.

With a slight shake of her head, she turned and started walking toward the road so she could take the easier terrain back to her cave.

As she went, a song played in her mind from a musical that Samheed had written. The young Unwanted students had performed it a few years ago. The story was about a kingdom reeling after the tragic death of the crown princess. The song was called "Alone and Away," and it had been sung onstage by a tearless, defiant young woman who'd loved the princess wholeheartedly. They'd planned so many things together. In the song the woman was making a decision to do those things alone.

Sky had felt a strong pull to that character back then, and she'd loved that musical more than any other she'd ever seen—Samheed's creative ability was truly majestic. The story and song had moved her tremendously. But she'd never imagined that she'd lose Alex like this young woman had lost her princess.

Sky hummed a few bars, remembering the lilting, mournful notes. She hesitated, then haltingly began to sing:

This song is from the crushed part of my heart.

Sky's voice, permanently scarred by the thornament she'd been forced to wear on Warbler Island as a child, was husky and pleasant, though it faltered with emotion now. She continued, half in a whisper as she trudged to the beat.

The part that thrums reminders that you're gone.

I don't regret a moment of our days.

But I won't fall. I'll be okay, you know.

I've always been that way.

As much as I wish you back with me,

I'm still the same. My dreams remain.

I don't need a soul to know my name.

And I'll get on just fine—I always do.

Alone and away.

Alone and away.

As the last words slipped from Sky's lips, the sun began to sink, lighting up rainbows in the mist that rose between the worlds.

Moments later came the king's call to arms from the castle. It was a sharp reminder that all was not well in the land of the dragons. And things were about to get worse.

Back at the cave, Thisbe and Rohan were cleaning up after a meal. "Tell me more about the meteors," said Thisbe. "They caused an earthquake?"

"That's what the books say," said Rohan. "They hit, and there was a huge impact. Some accounts called it an earthquake. Everyone panicked, and an uprising of militants that had been slowly growing over the years seized the moment of fear and vulnerability to try to oust the black-eyed rulers. Some of the rulers sent their children away to try to save them—east toward your seven islands and west, just there." He pointed across the lake to the land beyond. "Several of the rulers were killed or taken captive, though I'm not sure how—there was only a small mention of it in the book I was reading."

"Then what?"

"Then the ghost dragons drove off the uprisers. But they'd already done quite a lot of harm. A few days later, as a result of the earthquake, our world split from yours and formed that chasm near the castle. The theory is that a crack had formed unnoticed under the sea from the meteors' impact. Without warning, it gave way. Now the sea plunges into nothing on your side of the chasm. The sea's basin was much smaller on our side, and eventually it dried up."

"Wow," said Thisbe. "That's . . . a lot of awful stuff all at once." She thought about the images she'd seen when she'd

LISA McMANN

taken the ancestor broth. The meteors, the earthquake . . . even the uprising and the fleet of dragons seemed to fit into Rohan's story. Perhaps the screaming girl being taken away too.

They grabbed their fishing gear and headed out of the cave to catch something for Sky, who would surely be hungry by the time she got back.

"How long ago was that?" asked Thisbe.

"What?"

"The meteors and stuff."

Rohan thought as they made their way to the shore. "I don't recall the exact date. Forty or fifty years ago, I think." He sighed. "I miss books."

"Where are all your books now?" Thisbe asked.

"Who knows? They could be anywhere." He turned away. "Destroyed, probably."

"That's horrible." Thisbe hesitated, feeling as though she'd stepped too close again. She turned the conversation back. "Did the uprisers get taken down by the dragons?"

"Most of them," said Rohan. "But one group managed to seize the realm."

Thisbe looked in the direction of the castle. She couldn't quite see it from down here by the lake, but she knew well where it was. "The man who is king now?" she asked.

"He was one of them," said Rohan.

"And now he keeps black-eyed children as slaves."

"Yes."

Thisbe cast her line, and they fished in brooding silence until they heard footsteps on the path near the cave.

"Sky must be back," said Rohan. "We'd better catch something quickly, or she'll think we've been slacking off."

"We're at the lake!" Thisbe called out to Sky.

But Sky didn't answer. Instead they heard two familiar male voices, followed by the *zing* of a sword being drawn. Thisbe caught a flash of a blue uniform and froze. Then she and Rohan dove for the bushes.

But it was too late.

A New Direction

The two blue-uniformed soldiers came charging toward Thisbe and Rohan. Thisbe swore under her breath and flexed her fingers. She'd been so stupid to call out, assuming any noise would belong to Sky. Rohan bent and grabbed the dagger from around his ankle.

One of the soldiers barked out a question in the common language of Grimere. Rohan hesitated, then answered. The man said something more. Rohan's eyes widened, and he put his lips to Thisbe's ear. "They're looking for us," he whispered. "But they haven't yet figured out they've *found* us."

Thisbe's heart pounded.

The soldiers trampled through the brush, talking more in the common language. Then one, who'd guarded the river, pulled the brush aside and caught sight of the two former slaves. "It's them!" They continued to converse in the common language as they advanced on Thisbe and Rohan.

With their backs against the cavern walls, there was nowhere for Rohan and Thisbe to hide. Before they could decide to jump into the lake and try to escape that way, the men had their swords in the two friends' chests, pinning them. One shouted triumphantly.

The other responded in kind. The cold blade slid upward to Thisbe's throat. What were they saying? Was she about to die? She recognized the second one from the catacombs too. He'd been the one to burn the back of her neck with the Revinir's branding tool. Wild with anger and fright, her childhood instincts kicked in. She knocked the sword away and pointed at the soldiers. "Boom!" she yelled, stumbling backward. She grimaced, clutched her chest, and said it again. "Boom!"

Huge sparks slammed into them. Their swords went flying. They flew backward, shrieking. When they hit the ground, they broke into dozens of pieces, which scattered over the shore and into the water.

Thisbe sucked in a gasp and fell forward. Blood dripped from her neck. Her limbs shook.

Bewildered, Rohan let out a ragged breath. "What just happened?" He jumped forward to look all around. The coast was clear. He examined the toylike pieces of soldiers, then noticed Thisbe was still on all fours. He reached out to help her up. "Are you okay, Thisbe? You're shaking. And bleeding. How did you make *that* happen?"

Thisbe got to her feet and dabbed the cut with her shirt collar. "I think I'm okay." She felt weak, drained by the intense magic. But she'd done what she'd had to do. She was not going back to the catacombs. Ever. Not if she could help it. "I used an old spell I learned as a toddler. I hate using it." She pursed her lips and brushed herself off. "But it was necessary, and since there were only two of them, I was pretty sure I could get them both before my strength ran out." She wiped the sweat off her forehead. "What were they saying?"

"One said they'd get reward money from the Revinir. They said she was desperate to have her test subject back again."

Rohan picked up the soldiers' unharmed swords.

"Test subject? That's me."

"I'm pretty sure you're who they meant, yes," said Rohan, giving her a side-eye glance. "They also said she wants us both for her new army."

"Oh." Thisbe swallowed hard. *Her new army?* "Do you think there are any more soldiers coming?"

"I don't know. The second one said nobody wanted to search down here because it was too difficult. So I'm hoping nobody else will come."

"When these two don't return, somebody else will come looking for them," said Thisbe grimly. "I'm glad they can't tell anybody they found us."

"I don't know, Thiz—I see a pair of lips over there on the shore."

"Rohan, no. Gross." But she gave him a shaky grin.

"Speaking of gross, let's clean your wound before you leave a trail of blood for the next group of soldiers to follow," said Rohan, only partly joking. He helped her back to the cave.

When Sky returned, Rohan and Thisbe filled her in on what had happened. They discussed relocating, but ultimately they decided to remain in their cave. With such a big bounty on their heads, they were safer here than anywhere else. And Sky refused to leave the lakeside—there was still a small chance that the volcano could bring rescuers from Artimé, and she wasn't going to miss it if it happened.

Over the next few days Sky went back to the forest to search the other trampled paths, but none of them led to any of the kinds of clues she was looking for. And her bark note remained untouched. She began to lose heart.

Confined to the cave area but always on edge after what had happened, Thisbe grew restless. She was starting to come to terms with Alex's death. At least she could function again, and she spent most mornings at the lake catching fish with Rohan. When Sky finally decided to abandon her searches, she returned to camp and found them there.

"Did you discover any other graves today?" asked Thisbe.

"No," said Sky.

"Good." But then Thisbe's voice tightened. "They've gone home, haven't they?" She tossed the wormy hook end of her string into the water. She hadn't said those words aloud so definitively before, but she'd thought them many times. What would anyone do if their leader fell? They'd retreat. Even if it meant leaving someone behind.

Sky gave Thisbe a long look, as if deciding to reveal what she really feared. "I believe they've gone, yes."

Rohan, standing between them, dropped his gaze and cast his line too. He got down on his haunches and stared at the smooth water.

"So they've abandoned me for good." Thisbe flinched, but she took a deep breath and blew it out. "Okay. Well, it feels better to say that out loud. After all, it was only me they were looking for. I doubt anyone expected they could've found you here too."

"Thisbe," said Sky softly.

But Thisbe didn't want to be told anything different. It was the truth. Alex had died. Maybe others were hurt or killed—who knew? Would they come back eventually? No one knew that, either. "We can't sit here forever waiting for them."

"We could go to the edge of the gorge and camp there," suggested Sky. "Then we'd see them coming across."

"There's no drinking water there," said Thisbe mechanically, staring at the volcano. If there was one thing she'd learned, it was to always know where the water was. The most important thing in the world was water, it seemed.

"Right, I forgot," murmured Sky. "But there's that waterfall near the castle."

"Neither Rohan nor I are safe there," said Thisbe. "Or anywhere out in the open. We need to stay hidden from the soldiers on both sides. And from the people of Grimere. We can't trust anybody. But I'm going crazy being stuck in that cave."

"Tell me about it," Sky admitted. "I've been there for months. At least we're a little safer there."

"True." Thisbe felt a tug on her line, and she tensed. The volcano in the lake belched out a puff of smoke, and the water rippled all around it. "It's going to blow in a few minutes," said Thisbe.

"Yes," said Sky, who'd been keeping track of its movements since she arrived. "It'll pop its top in about six minutes, spewing fire and lava, followed by a big rush of water that'll shoot up and outward. It'll stay up while its core cools, about twenty or thirty minutes, and then it'll sink, taking all the water around it down into its giant crater."

"You sound like a scientist," said Rohan.

"I've studied the one in our world for years," said Sky. "And, to be truthful, I think about giving the volcano network a try again. But . . ." She trailed off as another, larger puff of smoke came out of the top. "I don't know."

Thisbe yanked on her line like Sky had taught her to do, and she pulled a fish out of the water. She held it up as it wriggled and dripped. Then she laid it on the shore and took the hook out, and used one of their newly acquired swords to quickly put the fish out of its misery.

"Nice catch," said Rohan.

"It's a little small for breakfast," said Thisbe. "One more should do it, though."

They felt the ground shiver and looked at the volcano. It began rumbling, and then fire shot from it as predicted. Molten lava streamed down the sides, and then a burst of water flew out. It arced like a fountain, and most of the liquid went just beyond the boundaries of the volcano. There was a loud clap when it hit the surface of the lake.

"I still don't get how you survived getting shot out of that thing like a cannon," said Rohan, glancing at Sky. "Was it hot being so close to that lava?"

"Not really. Maybe the bubble protected me from the heat. All I remember is that somehow I made it to shore, and I saw those strange footprints near me."

"Do you think," said Thisbe, pausing to put a bit of a worm on her hook, "that any of the water creatures from our world ever come through the volcano? I know Pan doesn't. She didn't seem to know about this passage when Fifer and Seth and I snuck off. I remember she told Hux to let her know if they find the other way to get there."

"I don't know," said Sky. "Maybe Issie does. She often disappears for a few days when she's out looking for her baby."

"Issie is a . . . a sea monster, you said?" asked Rohan.

"Yes," said Thisbe. "She's been looking for her baby for more than seven hundred years." She turned back to Sky. "Maybe she was here and she helped you?"

"I suppose stranger things have happened," said Sky with a shrug.

"I just hope the eels don't travel through there," said Thisbe, remembering the stories from Lani's books.

"You can say that again." Sky had witnessed them in action.

They went silent for a time. Then Rohan looked up and

LISA McMANN

tilted his head, straining to listen. "Do you hear something?"

They looked around, but no one was in sight. Thisbe looked up at the open entrance to the catacombs, wondering if the sound was coming from inside it. She knew no one there could see them since the River Taveer flowed across the passageway, stopping anyone from getting across. Well, anyone but Thisbe and Rohan, who'd gotten out using Thisbe's magic.

Thisbe's scales on her arms and legs tingled.

"It's coming from the square," said Sky.

"Drums," said Rohan, pivoting toward Dragonsmarche. "Is it market day? I've lost track. Maybe another procession?"

"Yes, I think it's several drums," said Sky. "But I've never heard ones like that before. It sounds . . . ominous. Not like a parade."

The beat grew louder, and then they heard a faint voice, like someone speaking into a bullhorn very far away. They couldn't make out the words.

"Something's happening," said Sky, looking concerned.

"The war," said Rohan. "Do you think it's beginning? Are they trying to draw the Revinir out?"

"What should we do?" said Thisbe.

Sky thought for a moment. "We're safest where we are. They probably won't bring the fight down here because of its inaccessibility. And there's not much land to fight on."

They went back to fishing, but the developments made them uneasy. Just as Rohan was feeling a tug at his line, the lake shivered and the volcano plunged down loudly, causing the fish to dart away.

Sky and Thisbe stared at the spot where the volcano had been and watched the waves ripple, then settle. Both were thinking the same thing. Before, when they'd thought someone from Artimé would be looking for them, they hadn't wanted to risk death or even just getting lost in some other frightening place. But now that they feared they were stuck here, perhaps forever, they began to wonder what they had to lose by giving the magical transportation volcano a try. Besides their lives, that is.

Brimming Over

O n the day the ominous drumbeat sounded, Fifer heard it from the safety of their new camp on the west side of the square. She sat up from playing an idle game to pass the time with Dev and looked around, alarmed. "What's going on?"

"I don't know," said Dev. He flicked a small stone like a marble at another pile of stones, hitting a few of them.

"I hope they haven't followed us." Fifer got up and peered through the trees, but of course the camp was too deep in the woods for her to see anything.

LISA McMANN

"It's coming from the square," Talon informed them. "No one is approaching."

"Oh. Well, that's good," said Fifer. She plopped back down next to Dev and stretched out. Surprisingly, she was the tiniest bit disappointed by the report. She was getting extraordinarily restless after being cooped up in camp all day, every day, with Dev and Arabis because of their wanted status. Plus, they'd just ended their evening searches for smoke after scouring every side street twice. Either the Revinir wasn't cooking broth anymore, or Dev had the location completely wrong in his mind. Nobody blamed him. It was clear Dev was making a huge effort to be a better person, and they believed he was trying his hardest to help them. Besides, it was difficult to fathom how he could get the location right in the first place—they'd all seen how the passageways weaved around like a labyrinth.

Simber stayed in camp too, keeping a close watch in the opposite direction from Talon, and Arabis was there to help. "All clearrr frrrom this dirrrection," Simber reported. He wasn't about to let another surprise attack happen.

Everyone else had ventured to the market like locals. Even Lani, who wore a long coat to hide her magical wheeled machine. But Fifer didn't have her dark stage glasses anymore, and she and Dev couldn't hide their eye color. Before they left, Carina promised she and Seth would look for items in the market that would help, but even if they found something, the Artiméans didn't have any money.

Dev had money. He had the piece of gold that Shanti had given him for turning in Fifer and Thisbe to be sold as slaves, and the belt from the market, which held all the money he'd collected from selling the dragon-bone broth that day. And he'd sold quite a lot. He wondered idly about the people who'd bought it. Had they drunk it by now? Had it done anything to them?

Dev didn't mention his sudden wealth to his new friends, though it burned on his conscience. Maybe he'd never spend it. Then again, it technically belonged to the Revinir, so maybe he would. He had no idea what to buy with it.

Fifer rolled over and propped herself up, her elbows sinking into the soft ground. "What do you think the Revinir meant when she said Thisbe wasn't there anymore?" Fifer asked Dev.

"I've already told you," said Dev. "Are you still thinking about that?" He automatically plucked a dried leaf from her

LISA McMANN

sleeve, like he'd have done for Shanti, then flushed as he realized it. It seemed a little too intimate, somehow.

Fifer didn't notice. "I think it's important. It feels like a clue." Once she'd gotten over some of her initial fears, stepping into being a leader had come pretty easily. And naturally. She'd always had strong opinions and liked to be heard, so that felt like a good fit. But now the pressure was growing to figure out a solution, and the theory of the fourth entrance seemed to be a dud. Fifer was trying to listen to her instincts like Simber had told her to do. And this was one thought that kept popping up and making her feel uneasy.

Dev gathered the stones that had been knocked loose from the pile and brought them back. "The Revinir was probably lying. Are you even sure you heard her right? She has an accent."

"She has *our* accent," said Fifer, popping Dev over the head with a stick full of leaves. "I'm pretty sure that's what she said."

Dev recoiled at first, having been struck more times in his life than he could count, then relaxed and laughed a little when he realized it was a playful gesture. "Well, maybe she meant that Thisbe wasn't in her crypt anymore because she was in the kitchen."

Fifer blinked. "Oh," she said. "I guess that makes sense."

"There are only a couple other places to go besides the kitchen. The extracting room—maybe she got sent there to work. That's by the river and the cave entrance." He paused. "She might have tried escaping that way—I'm pretty sure every slave down there has eyed that river and thought about the risk of trying to cross it." He took a stick and drew a crude map in the carpet of brown pine needles on the forest floor, pointing out the places. "The only other one is the castle dungeon."

"She'd never make it through the dungeon without getting captured," muttered Fifer, who knew the area all too well. "I'm sure there are even more guards there now after what we did. Thisbe might try the river. She can hold her breath really well." She cringed, thinking about Thisbe trying to swim across the river and getting swept away. It made her stomach ache. She tried to shake the image from her mind—she couldn't be thinking like that if she was going to be a good leader. She needed to tamp down her feelings, or it could cost her. She had to make cool, collected decisions and not care so much about her loved ones. But the image of Thisbe being swept down that rapid river continued to torture her. What if Thisbe was dead?

Why didn't Fifer feel anything? Could that be the reason?

Dev put the stick down. He turned back to his game, tossing another stone and knocking loose three others in the pile. "Excellent," he said under his breath, pleased with himself. He gathered them up and glanced at Fifer. "Honestly, I don't know. Like I said before, maybe she got sent to the castle dungeon in a trade and she's chained up." He paused, thinking harder about what he'd just said. "You know, that's actually starting to make sense."

"The dungeon?" asked Fifer, horrified. "Oh, I hope not."

Dev frowned and tapped his lips. "If the Revinir was mad after your attack, who else would she take it out on?"

"There is no one else," said Fifer.

"Exactly. Maybe she's punishing Thisbe."

"But—but the Revinir said that Thisbe wasn't there anymore while we were there fighting her! So she wouldn't have had time to punish Thisbe for us attacking."

Dev glanced at Fifer. "How long had you been down there before you got to Thisbe's crypt? The Revinir could have seen you coming and . . . and, I don't know, maybe hidden her or something."

LISA McMANN

"We were fighting for a while," Fifer admitted. "All over the place. We didn't see the Revinir until the end, when . . . well, you know." She didn't want to talk again about what had happened with Alex.

"The Revinir is pretty smart," said Dev. "I'll bet she got wind of what was happening, grabbed Thisbe, and hid her somewhere so she could use her crypt to ambush you. Then she told you Thisbe wasn't there just to mess with your head."

Arabis, who'd been keeping watch nearby, turned her head. "I think the boy is right," she said. "The Revinir is devious. I imagine she intended to throw you off with that remark—perhaps even to keep you from coming back again to look for Thisbe."

That made a lot of sense to Fifer.

Simber turned sharply. "Hmm." It made sense to him, too. He caught Fifer's eye and nodded. "Thank you forrr that insight, Arrrabis," he growled.

Arabis tipped her head in response, then turned back to scanning the forest for intruders.

"This constant rehashing is driving me crazy," muttered Fifer. "And I keep doing it to myself." The unanswered questions were getting harder to withstand, and the feeling was sure to get worse before it got better. She looked to Simber for guidance. "How are we going to find out for sure where Thisbe is without being caught?"

Simber was quiet for a long moment, deep in thought. "It seems like we can use the impending warrr in ourrr favorrr," he said. "I'm not surrre how. But warrrs can be a big distrrraction."

"Especially if the Revinir needs all her soldiers to fight the king's people," said Fifer thoughtfully. "That'll make it easier to get inside without having to fight so many of them. Maybe we wait until the war starts before we go after her."

"That still doesn't help us know where Thisbe is," said Dev. "Unless . . ." He looked sideways at Fifer. "Unless we send a spy down before we go in after her."

"Ahh," said Fifer. "Good idea, Dev." The time had come again for their tiniest member to act. "Where's Kitten?"

A Rocky Start to Forever

Once Artimé was back to running normally, Aaron took the tube to the Island of Shipwrecks. There he explained to Ishibashi, Ito, and Sato what had happened, and told them he'd be taking over Artimé. He promised to return to see if the scientists needed anything.

The scientists took the news hard. They mourned their friend Alex's passing and assured Aaron they'd be fine on their island, like always. Aaron promised them that Henry would continue to visit, as he often did, to check in and collect some of the scientists' unusual plants from the greenhouse. Aaron

LISA McMANN

said a reluctant good-bye to the three men who had taken him under their wing during his rocky coming-of-age years and taught him how to change his life and be a better person. He collected Daniel and returned to Artimé to fulfill his duties.

Unfortunately the few grumblers hadn't stopped just because their magical comforts were restored. Instead their numbers seemed to be growing. Aaron soon discovered the leader's name when he returned to find a letter from her.

Aaron Stowe,

You were the one who exposed our secret world to Quill years ago. You worked with the High Priest Justine against Artimé in the first battle. Then you killed Marcus Today and plotted to take over Artimé again.

You didn't succeed. But now here you are.

I'm not the only one wondering what sort of plotting you've been doing all these years and what you plan to do now that you are in power. We demand answers.

Frieda Stubbs and the Dissenters

Aaron troubled over the harsh letter. All these years? He'd been helping Artimé and falling in love with Kaylee and taking care of Ishibashi and Ito and Sato and having a child. And now mourning his brother, worrying over his sisters, and trying to lead a world he didn't feel totally comfortable leading. But he certainly wasn't *plotting* anything. Those days were long gone. He'd changed. Period.

Apparently Frieda Stubbs still saw something sinister in him.

He didn't answer the letter. But Frieda and the dissenters found him on the lawn one day playing with Daniel. Aaron saw the small, angry-looking group coming and gathered Daniel into his lap. The woman who'd heckled him his first day back led the charge.

"You should give up your position as mage," the leader announced without greeting. "Your presence soils this great world. There's no forgiving what you've done."

Aaron held his seat on the lawn, but his heart began to race. "You must be Frieda Stubbs," he said. "I received your letter."

"That's right. I am," said Frieda, her eyes like slits. "It figures you wouldn't know who I was." She seemed offended that he hadn't recognized her, which could only add to the weight of her grievances.

Aaron got to his feet and held Daniel close. He scanned the group warily as the others caught up to her and crowded around him, nearly enclosing him in a circle. "I understand that there are people who will never forgive me for . . . what happened with Mr. Today."

"You've got that right," said a man with her. "It's not just a 'what happened with Mr. Today' thing. Say the words! Say what you did!"

The group inched closer. Aaron swallowed hard. "I accidentally killed Marcus Today with heart attack spells," said Aaron. "I didn't know there was a lethal dose. I'm terribly sorry for what I did. If I could take it back, I would. In an instant."

"Well, you can't take it back!" shouted another from behind the first two. "How do you expect us to follow a leader who killed the man who created this world? It's madness!"

Frieda leaned in menacingly. "Did you kill your own brother, too, so you could finally take over? That's what I want to know! People everywhere are saying it."

Aaron stared. "What?" he exclaimed, incredulous. "That's

preposterous!" He couldn't even begin to understand where such a claim had come from.

"You did it, didn't you!" snarled Frieda. "So you could take over once and for all. You've been plotting it for years."

"My God," whispered Aaron, feeling sick to his stomach. He didn't know how to respond. To not only lose his soul-mate twin, but to be accused of killing him? "How could you . . . ?" he whispered.

As the group inched even closer, Daniel started to cry. Shaken, Aaron took several steps back, breaking through the circle, and soothed the boy while glancing quickly around the lawn for allies. But no one seemed to have noticed what was happening. Aaron looked back at Frieda, his expression hard. "Perhaps you could take a meeting with Claire Morning to sort through what is truth and what is not."

"Claire Morning should be our head mage!" cried Frieda.

"Yes!" said the man next to her. The group circled the mage again.

Daniel's cries turned to wails. Aaron's stomach churned as he looked for a way to escape. He held the baby close and whispered calming things in the boy's ear as the accusations

LISA McMANN

continued around him. But when Frieda stepped too close, within reach of Daniel, Aaron's face darkened with anger. "Step back!" he said.

"Make me!" said the woman.

"Frieda Stubbs," said Aaron, his free hand moving to his pocket full of spell components, "you are threatening my child. Please. Step. Away."

The woman faltered but remained scowling. The man next to her put his hand on her shoulder.

A few of the others snapped to their senses and moved back, and finally Frieda did too. "I feel sorry for your boy, having a murderer for a father."

Aaron stared; the blood drained from his face. His fist was balled up and aching inside the sleeve of his robe, clutching components. But he retained some sense and held back.

Frieda sneered, then spat on Aaron's shoes and stormed away. Her companions followed, a few of them looking a bit dazed, as if they hadn't expected things to go quite like they'd gone.

When they disappeared around the fountain, Aaron let a wild breath escape and dropped to his knees. He closed his eyes for a moment, cradling his precious crying boy, then kissed him on the top of his head and shakily started to sing him a lullaby to quiet him.

All the while his mind raced. What kind of fringe lunatic was this Frieda Stubbs to accuse him of such a thing? And with people like that around, how would Aaron ever be an effective leader? He'd never succeed without the full support and love of Artimé, like Alex had had. Could Aaron possibly last with such rancor surrounding him? Even after this generation of Artiméans passed on, the stories would remain. Who knows what other wild accusations could be next? It seemed controversy would never stop plaguing Aaron, not through all eternity.

Perhaps he really wasn't the right person for this job.

Filled with Doubts

Weeks passed in Artimé. Aaron spent his days figuring out the ins and outs of the mansion while having deep conversations with friends about what to do next regarding the rescue team, for whom concern was growing. In between talks Aaron survived a few more confrontations with Frieda Stubbs and her band of conspiracy theorists.

He shared the situation with a few trusted friends. They promised to keep an eye out and try to reason with the concerned citizens. Henry came to Aaron's aid once in the dining hall, and Claire broke up another group on the lawn . . . at least temporarily.

Also during that chaotic time the four young dragons—Hux the ice blue, Drock the dark purple, Yarbeck the purple and gold, and Ivis the green—came to Artimé with their detached wings. Aaron reattached them magically, and they returned to their island.

And of course Daniel was there and needed to be cared for. With everything going on, Aaron was disoriented and still grieving and trying to figure out what else he was supposed to be doing as Artimé's new leader.

But the false accusations were hurtful, and Aaron couldn't forget them. Was there any way to convince the dissenters that he had changed? Or should he just write them off as a lost cause? Aaron couldn't stand the thought of Daniel growing up hearing and understanding the horrible rumors. How could he protect his child from such vitriolic people?

Life with the scientists seemed so much more peaceful. Aaron longed for it. But he had responsibilities, too. For his wife. His sisters. All of the rescue team, really. He had to continue to do what he could to stabilize the home front so he could focus on getting them back safely. If only he could hear from one of them so he would know what to do! But there was no explanation. No guidance. So they waited, hoping to see a familiar sight on the western horizon. He knew he'd have to make a move soon.

Aaron hadn't been able to bear moving into the head mage's quarters—just going into Alex's apartment felt horrible, like an invasion of space and privacy. It was too soon for that. So he'd settled in an empty room in the family hallway with Daniel, keeping the boy with him most of the time. It was comforting to have him there, a constant reminder of Kaylee, which in turn reminded him that she was alive. Reckless though it might be, he began sending a daily seek spell to her, as had Sean and Henry to their loved ones. He needed her and wished for her to come back every day. Things would be better when she came home. Maybe the dissenters would listen to her.

No one had heard from Thisbe. Or Sky, of course, but no one expected to, since she was likely dead too. Aaron had the tiniest amount of bittersweet comfort in knowing he didn't have to break the news of Alex's death to Sky. That would have been the most difficult task of his life. But he would gladly do it if it meant she was somehow, somewhere, alive and well.

Every day, despite chancing a confrontation, Aaron and Daniel took a stroll along the shore. Aaron wouldn't hide. He refused to be intimidated, and he needed to be present and available for the people of Artimé. Daniel, who couldn't quite walk yet, rode on Aaron's back in a little knapsacklike holster that Ms. Octavia, the octogator art instructor, had sewn for him.

Daniel seemed to be the one person who could keep the confrontations from getting violent. And while Aaron didn't trust Frieda, the members of Frieda's group had clearly drawn a line at harming the child, and they held their leader back. It showed Aaron that they had at least a little compassion in them. But Aaron didn't want to use Daniel as a shield. He debated daily about handing over the robe and going back to hiding on the Island of Shipwrecks, where things were, frankly, much easier. Once the situations here were resolved and Kaylee was home in his arms, he just might have to do it.

LISA McMANN

As they walked, Aaron scanned the western sky for signs of Simber or Arabis or Talon returning. The longer they stayed away, the more worried Aaron became. Their magic was restored—why weren't they coming home? Were they still trying to find Thisbe? Or had they been captured? Had something happened to their fliers that was keeping them from returning? Knowing they were alive was wonderful. But not knowing anything else was agonizing. How was Aaron supposed to guess what to do? Did they need help? Did they need him to come? The seek spell, which traditionally had signaled a need for help, no longer meant that—or did it? Its meaning was muddled.

Aaron wasn't sure if he could leave Artimé right now—things were in such a fragile state. There were the dissenters, obviously, but the rest of the people were upset over Alex's death too, and they wanted answers. Was Artimé in danger because of this? What did it mean for them? Would there be a war, like after Mr. Today's death, only with this far-off land of the dragons? Would they have to attack whoever had killed Alex?

The thought of that made Aaron even more uneasy. Frieda

LISA McMANN

and the dissenters would certainly point out that no one had attacked *him* after he'd killed Mr. Today.

Not that anyone wanted to go to war. Could Artimé trust their new leader to keep them out of it? Could they trust him not to turn against them? To take care of them after his sordid past? Would the dissenting fringe continue to grow and spread even more rumors?

Most Artiméans had forgiven Aaron for everything long ago, and they would support him in whatever they had to do. But old questions had resurfaced, and people were whispering. What if some of them just couldn't feel at ease with the current situation? What if the suspicion planted seeds of doubt in his acquaintances? His friends?

Artimé was in crisis. If Aaron messed up in any way, the dissenters would jump on him like wild dogs, and they wouldn't hold back. Hopefully, no more lives would be lost, or Aaron might be blamed for them, too. And, hopefully, he wouldn't land them in another years-long war. There were so many things to get perfect. Maybe that was partly why Aaron was hesitating to make a move. The pressure was so high.

Aaron knew there was no way he'd get everything

LISA McMANN

right—the odds were impossible. Heightened confrontations were inevitable. He was smart enough to know that. And he'd become wiser during his time with the scientists. He knew he could be a strong leader for Artimé. But he also knew that his past rode along with him on his back, kind of like Daniel was doing right now, except much more of a burden. He'd have to tread very carefully. At least until he could hand over the reins. But in the meantime, his name was being slandered. All the things he'd worked for over the past many years were being questioned. Leader or not, Aaron couldn't bear that.

"I must prove my trustworthiness to Artimé every day," Aaron muttered as he walked along. "Or the arguments will never go away." Perhaps they wouldn't anyway, no matter what he did. He tended toward thinking the latter. But he had to do everything he could to let his true self shine in the face of the lies.

"And I'm going to have to make a move soon," he added grimly. He was becoming more and more convinced that something wasn't right with the rescue team. He'd talked to Florence about it several times, and together they'd decided to wait and see, but every day made Aaron more uneasy. Sure, the group was highly capable, even without Alex. They were the A team, with many years of combined experience. But Florence and Aaron didn't want to be foolish.

A few days passed with no sign of the fliers returning, and finally Aaron had had enough. One morning, after Florence finished leading the more advanced mages in brushing up on their old skills, Aaron pulled her aside along with Henry and Sean, who were participating in the training group.

"Can you meet me on the lawn this evening after dinner?" he asked them. They agreed on a time.

Then Aaron set out to the lagoon and called out for Pan, who'd circled the island daily since the incident, ready to assist in case she was needed. He invited her to attend the meeting as well.

When Aaron went on his daily walk along the shore-line with Daniel on his back, he deftly dodged a heckler and focused on planning out what he'd say that evening. Trying to trust his instincts despite all the doubts that flooded his mind, he turned to gaze over the water as if questioning the sea for guidance. He noticed a spot of color on the waves

LISA McMANN

approaching Artimé, and his heart leaped—was it them? He lifted his hand to shade his eyes and saw an approaching vessel. It was small—a skiff—and the spot of color that he saw appeared to be a single person in a red shirt. Definitely not the team returning. Perhaps it was someone from Warbler. Aaron quickly unhooked Daniel from his back and cradled him in his arms securely, then moved swiftly toward the mansion.

The skiff arrived a while later, and by the time it reached the shore, Aaron had figured out who its bright blond occupant was. He waded out to help pull the boat closer and cast an anchor spell to hold it in place. "Scarlet," he said warmly. "It's good to see you." Then he turned somber. "You've heard the news about Alex?"

"Yes. Pan stopped by the island. We're all flabbergasted. What a year of losses." Scarlet climbed out of the boat. Like Thatcher, she was a Warbleran who'd been catapulted onto Artimé's shore as a child. Now she was an accomplished mage who had gone back to Warbler recently with Sky to figure out how to stabilize and repopulate the volcanic Island of Fire nearby.

She'd stayed on after the tragic loss of Sky to comfort

Copper, Sky's mother. "Also," Scarlet went on, "I ran across Spike Furious on my journey here—she'd heard the news from Pan as well. And Karkinos has been telling all the other sea creatures whenever they've come by. Spike said she'd had a feeling something had happened to Alex when her heart felt cold." The young woman smiled sadly. "She was already so sad about Sky, never stopping her search for her, and now this. Poor thing."

"Oh, Spike," said Aaron, his heart sinking. He'd nearly forgotten all about Alex's intuitive whale. "Thank you. It's been a bit chaotic around here. I haven't seen her since it happened. Is she okay?"

"She seems to be quite downcast and said she wants to be alone."

"I see." Aaron dropped his gaze. He wasn't sure what to do about Spike, but he was grateful that Pan was checking in with her.

"How are you holding up?" asked Scarlet, examining Aaron carefully. "You look like you could use a nap."

Aaron let a small laugh escape. "I've had a lot on my mind. And you?"

"I came to see if I could help. And to find out if, um, if everyone else . . . is okay. The ones on the rescue team, I mean. Or anyone else . . ." She blushed and became flustered.

"Crow is alive," said Aaron kindly. Everybody knew that Scarlet and Crow were in the slowest-moving relationship anyone had ever witnessed. "We've heard from everyone except Thisbe, who doesn't have anything to send a seek spell with." He hesitated. "No sign of Sky or the white boat out your way, I presume?"

"No. Not a trace."

"That's what I thought you'd say."

Scarlet looked curiously at Daniel, who was in the rucksack carrier again. "He's getting big." She held out a finger to the boy, and he grabbed it and tried to put it in his mouth. Scarlet laughed and pulled her hand away.

"He's teething," said Aaron as Daniel began to fuss. "And it's nap time." He turned, and they walked together toward the mansion. "Once you get settled, would you be willing to meet with me and a few others on the lawn? Tonight after dinner. We're going to discuss what to do next."

"Of course. I'd be happy to." Scarlet glanced at Florence,

who was training a group of new thirteen-year-old Unwanteds how to throw scatterclips. She recognized Clementi Okafor and Ibrahim Quereshi and a few others of Henry and Thatcher's adopted Unwanteds in the group. "Ah," she said, "the good old days. I should join in and see if I still know how to do magic."

"There's a daily Advanced Magical Warrior Training class in the mornings. You're welcome to participate. You're one of our best fighters—I'm sure you haven't lost your touch."

"Thanks," said Scarlet. "Maybe I'll stay a few days and see. And . . ." She flushed pink. "Thanks for the update on Crow. I'll find you tonight for the meeting."

Aaron smiled and waved off her thanks. Weary, he turned toward the kitchen so he could warm a bottle of milk for Daniel. Maybe he'd nap alongside the boy today.

LISA McMANN

Delicate Decisions

That evening Florence, Scarlet, Sean, and Henry converged on the lawn, meeting Pan and Aaron, who were already there and waiting. Other Artiméans wandered about, as it was a beautiful night. Aaron kept an eye on the group of dissenters lurking nearby, but Pan's looming presence kept them from venturing too close.

Aaron and Sean had easily found childcare for the evening—Clementi and Ibrahim were keeping Daniel, Ava, and Lukas entertained in the lounge. They were listening to a mournful saxophone solo concert by the one and only Fox, who was in a deep funk these days without Kitten. Daniel seemed to be a fan of the blues. He also seemed to enjoy the tiny tastes of orange creams that Ibrahim gave him.

"Thanks for coming," Aaron said to the group on the lawn.

"This is an unusual gathering," remarked Sean, looking around at the others and up at Florence and Pan.

"I feel privileged to be included," said Henry.

"We all do," said Pan, and Scarlet nodded.

Aaron smiled distractedly. "It's been a hard few weeks. Discouraging, too, at times. I hope you've been coping all right."

"Obviously we're worried," Sean said. "Why is it taking so long for them to return? Something's not right."

"Are they captured?" asked Henry. "That's my biggest fear. That they're chained up in that awful castle dungeon Thatcher told us about. Or worse."

Others chimed in with their concerns, including Pan. "It's difficult to hide a dragon for long," she said. "Arabis isn't safe in that world. We never intended for this to be a long-term mission, and I want her back here."

Aaron nodded, listening carefully and acknowledging their concerns. "I agree with you, and I have the same questions and worries. The problem is, what do we do about it? If we go after them, we leave Artimé vulnerable. Leadership here on the island is already sparse." He didn't mention how apprehensive he felt about what the dissenters could do to sow unrest in his absence.

"And," Aaron continued, "we don't know what kind of situation we'll stumble on. We could unwittingly foil their rescue of Thisbe. But we also can't wait endlessly, not knowing what's happening. What if something even worse occurs, and others die too? That would be on our heads—on *my* head—if I didn't do something about it. Not to mention I care very much about everyone involved."

Florence listened carefully to what Aaron was saying. After a moment, she spoke. "Do you have any reason to think Artimé will be attacked in the near future?"

Aaron thought about it. "No. Though there's that group that wants to take me out."

Florence smiled sympathetically. "That's a different matter, which that I hope will dissolve on its own. As for an attack by a foreign group, I agree that we're in no imminent danger."

"So we should take a team and go after them?"

LISA McMANN

"I believe so. Those of us here, if you're willing. Plus, we should take a few extra sharpshooters with us." Florence glanced at Henry. "Clementi and Ibrahim are ready if you'll allow them. Clementi's a natural and could be very helpful, and Ibrahim is very close behind her in talent. They remind me of you, Scarlet, and Thatcher, back when you were first learning. Very strong."

"I'd definitely trust them, then," said Scarlet with a grin.

"I think you're right," said Henry with pride. "I've been watching them in training, and they're both excelling."

Sean nodded in agreement. "They're great."

Scarlet turned to Aaron, her face turning troubled. "Not to be rude, Aaron, but will you be going? What happens if you get killed? Do you think it's wise to put the people of Artimé through that again?"

Aaron looked at the grass, hating to lie about his life status. He dodged the question. "I don't know yet who should go. I also don't know how we'll get there. If only Simber would come back . . ."

"I do miss his words of wisdom at a time like this," Florence admitted. She glanced to the west, as many of them often did, but as usual there was no sign of him.

LISA McMANN

"What about the young dragons? They can carry us there." Scarlet turned to Pan, who was wingless. "What do you think, Pan?"

Pan sniffed.

"It's not safe there for *any* dragons," Sean explained to Scarlet, who hadn't heard all the details of the original trip while she'd been in Warbler.

"Oh, I see," said Scarlet.

"I was thinking if we had a way to contact Simber," said Aaron, "we could pelt him with seek spells so he knows we need just him. Then perhaps he'd come, and we could send a few people over to help."

"But that would put their party at risk to be without him," Henry pointed out.

"Hmm," said Aaron. "Right."

Sean sat up. "I think Simber gave Alex something once for the emergency seek spell. A dew claw—he broke it off and declared that growing it was the same as creating it." He chuckled softly, remembering.

Florence smiled. "That's right. He did. But Alex carried it with him. I imagine he had it with him in his pocket when he died."

"Oh." Sean slumped again. "I guess it wouldn't help us anyway, would it."

"No," said Florence. "Simber didn't give it to any of us."

"So," Aaron summarized, "we're in agreement that we should send at least a few people to the land of the dragons, but we have no way to get there at this time." He, too, looked long at Pan. But the dragon looked back, stone faced. Smoke curled from her nostrils.

"Pan," said Henry, "aren't you worried about Arabis?"

"Of course I am," said the dragon. "I didn't want her to go in the first place. Who knows if she is even with the others— she had plans to go to the cavelands to warn the other dragons there about the Revinir. She might have gotten stuck somewhere, or captured. She would have lost her wings too, and could be anywhere. Perhaps we'll never know what happened to her. I'm sick about it."

"At least Fifer and Seth are there to fix her wings," Sean pointed out.

"If Arabis is anywhere near them," Pan said coolly.

Florence tapped her lips, making a clunking sound. "Pan," she said, "maybe there's another, safer way. Are you opposed

257 « Dragon Ghosts

LISA McMANN

to having one of your other young flying a few of us across the gorge and dropping us off? Then turning around and returning to our world immediately?"

Pan frowned and snorted. Henry and Scarlet deftly dodged the boiling-liquid discharge.

But Aaron nodded thoughtfully. "That might work," he said. "The team should be able to figure out a way to get everyone home again without too much trouble, what with Fifer's birds, and Simber, Arabis, and Talon." They would be coming home presumably with one fewer passenger too, which freed up a spot, though no one mentioned that.

Pan frowned harder. She didn't seem to appreciate the pressure they were putting on her.

Aaron saw it in her face. He reached out to touch her shimmering neck. "Pan, I see that you are conflicted. Let's keep thinking about this. Perhaps there's something else we can try. We don't wish to endanger your young ever again. You've done so much for us already."

Pan bowed her regal head slightly, acknowledging Aaron's diplomacy. "Thank you. I'll consider the options."

Sean nearly butted in to point out that there really was only one option on the table, but the dragon suddenly got up. "I'll check in with you again soon, Aaron," she said a bit stiffly. "But I have enough to consider for now." She lumbered off to the water, leaving the rest of them.

With the dragon moving away, the nearby group of dissenters started walking toward the meeting. Aaron spotted them coming and sighed. The size of the group looked larger today. "Watch out," he warned the others quietly.

Frieda Stubbs strode boldly up to them and crossed her arms, staring at Aaron.

Aaron smiled stiffly. "How can I be of service today?"

Frieda narrowed her eyes. "You can stop with that patronizing tone," she said. "I know you hate us."

"I don't hate you," said Aaron patiently.

Florence bristled, ready to step in. She slipped the bow off her shoulder and pulled an arrow from her quiver, then pretended to examine the point. "Aaron is one of the sincerest people I know."

Aaron touched Florence's arm, holding her back. "They have a right to speak their concerns."

"You know what our concerns are," said Frieda. "We want

a murderer out of power. Especially one who would kill his own brother."

Sean, Henry, and Scarlet exploded in anger at the accusation.

"I'm just saying it looks suspicious!" shouted Frieda.

"Where was he when we lost the magic?" asked her male friend accusingly. "What's his alibi?"

Soon everyone was shouting. Aaron just sat there, defeated. Eventually he threw his hands in the air and got up, then went down to the shore, letting his friends fight for him. It was nice to know they would.

After a while Florence broke up the fight with a threat and sent the dissenting group fleeing. She and Henry, Scarlet, and Sean joined Aaron by the shore.

"I'm sorry you're dealing with those people," Florence said. "I didn't realize how awful they were. At least it's a small group."

"But it's growing." Aaron continued gazing out to sea, where Pan was still visible. "Anyway, about our new plans, I'm not sure what we can do without Pan's assistance."

Henry watched the dragon too. "Do you think she's going to agree?"

Scarlet nodded. "I think she might."

"I don't know," said Sean. "She got out of here in a hurry."

Aaron glanced out over the water. "I'm fifty-fifty on the chances," he said. "I really don't know what she's thinking. But then again, with Pan, no one ever does."

Mother of All Dragons

Deep underground, the Revinir was quietly and quickly gaining power. The army she was building was very different from the king's—one that couldn't be defeated. She paid little attention to the concerns of her blue-uniformed soldiers, who were often muttering and worrying about how they'd be able to fight against the green military's increasing numbers. She ignored their pleas to build her army in the same way by recruiting people from the outside. "It's not necessary," she told them. "Numbers aren't important." But they had a hard time believing her. When one grumbled too much, she silenced him by shooting a fiery lightning spear into his chest, like she'd done with Alex Stowe. It was deeply satisfying.

She didn't care about losing a few soldiers. Her need for them was dwindling. The truth was that the Revinir could take over the land almost single-handedly. She required only a handful of key players to help her out. Sure, she still needed the soldiers around to threaten the slaves and keep them in line until she had them fully under her power, but that was about all the soldiers were good for these days—they'd proven to be pretty useless when the Artiméans had attacked. And when they'd tried to ambush the king in his silly parade, they'd wound up being taken out in mere moments. They were severely outnumbered by the green army, which was making them uneasy. The more insecure they got, the more annoying they got. Frankly, the Revinir couldn't wait to get rid of them.

As the woman sipped dragon-bone broth and grew stronger, she spent a little time thinking about the three escapees—Dev, Thisbe, and Rohan. Now, *they* were actually important to her. She was furious about what they'd done. But she knew she could get her two test subjects back for sure. The third, Rohan, would be a little harder, but not impossible. They'd return to the catacombs soon enough.

She'd determined by now that the ancestor broth had been a waste of time. Even after she'd taken in gallons of the nasty stuff, it hadn't affected her in the least, other than to give her a sour stomach. So she sent her soldiers out to sell it at the market and stuck to the dragon-bone broth, which continued to strengthen her.

Now she entered her throne room and opened a glass bottle of the liquid. She chugged it down, barely grimacing. She was almost growing to like it. Moments later a few more scales burst from her skin. She was covered now—thinly in some places, like around her eyes and throat, and thicker in others, like her arms and legs and torso. The scales acted like armor. She peered at her reflection in the golden sheen of her throne and noted with satisfaction that two large lumps on her back were decidedly growing.

She dabbed her speckled forehead with a cloth to wipe away the sweat. Her inner body temperature seemed be rising, keeping her core's fire going strong. The heat had intensified her dragon-fire spears, and she could now control their size, from thin and sharp to full and all-encompassing flames, like real dragon fire. She took a few moments to practice the new feature, training herself to feel the flames curl and flicker just below her throat so they'd be immediately accessible the instant she needed them. Then she opened her mouth and blew, forcing out a thick burst of fire that slammed into her throne and singed the velvet fabric. She tamped it out, not fussing over the damage she'd caused. She'd have a new throne soon.

The time for all-out war was coming, and the Revinir was impatient. She burst into the kitchen to check on the latest batch of dragon-bone broth. Her new black-eyed kitchen slaves scrambled to their feet when she came in. Reza, a boy of twelve, and Prindi, a girl of thirteen, were speckled with scales on their arms and legs. They cowered by the back wall as if they expected the woman to do something terrible to them again, but the Revinir stayed near the doorway.

"Prepare the next dosage," the woman growled at them. She moved to the hall and listened at the door. She could hear footsteps echoing in the passageway. "Time for your medicine," she whispered, pleased.

Reza and Prindi sprang to obey, filling bottles with the hot broth and trying not to spill any with their trembling hands.

Then the Revinir turned to the soldiers who guarded the area. "Bring in the first two," she said.

The blue-uniformed soldiers did so, dragging two bewildered slaves into the kitchen and demanding they drink the dragon-bone broth. The children obeyed. The Revinir observed the scales as they popped out of their skin, then gave them a second dose. When she was satisfied that the two had enough scales, she ordered them to be let go.

"Bring in the next two!" she said to her guards.

They did. Over and over, until one of the soldiers said, "That was the last of them."

The Revinir smiled. A trail of smoke curled up from her left nostril. "Excellent. Prindi and Reza, bottle the rest of the broth and start a new batch. Then deliver the bottles to my throne room. Once you're finished, you're free to go back to your crypts." She turned to the soldier. "Tell Mangrel to leave all the doors unlocked until I give the word."

"Yes, Revinir," said the soldier. He went in search of the crypt keeper, and the Revinir returned to her throne room. She lit all the candles in the room with her flaming breath so that she could admire the way her scales sparkled in the firelight.

Then she drank one more bottle of dragon-bone broth and sat down to wait for Prindi and Reza to finish their work. From the table next to her, she picked up a yellowing scroll she'd found years before in a dragon crypt. Though she knew the look of the drawing by heart, she didn't understand what all the things meant on it. She studied the strange words and sketches. There was one main drawing of an army of ghost dragons flying together over the land where the forest met the desert near the cavelands. The dragons' silvery-gray wings were tattered, and their huge bodies were bony and ghostlike. They looked frightening. But the Revinir smiled. She knew better than to fear them.

Next to the picture of the dragons was a map showing the rolling hills of the cavelands, hours to the northwest, and the land beyond the crater lake to the southwest of the catacombs. Without transportation the Revinir would have trouble getting to either place. But she didn't need the map. If all went as she expected, the dragons would come to her. All the dragons, she thought. Not just the ghost dragons. Every last one of them.

Prindi and Reza brought armloads of bottles into the throne room and arranged them on a long table that was already holding dozens of others. "We've finished," said Prindi. "The new broth is heating on the fires."

The Revinir waved them away, and the two left to go back to their crypts.

The woman continued to wait, drinking one bottle of broth per hour, resting her hands on her bulging stomach in between. Feeling the heat increase.

In the depths of the night the Revinir's eyes popped opened and glowed yellow in the darkness. The bumps on her back felt bigger. They ached and pulled at her skin. Her fingers and toes ached too, like they were being stretched beyond their lengths. She rose from her throne. Clutching her belly, embracing the burgeoning flames within, she closed her eyes. Taking a deep breath, she held it. Then she let out a bloodcurdling roar. Flames shot out, stopping short of the wall. The sound echoed throughout the cavernous room and far beyond.

The soldiers stationed nearby came running in to see what the noise was, but the woman shot lightninglike spears at them. The ones who weren't struck ran away. A few minutes later the first of the black-eyed, dragon-scaled slaves appeared, looking bewildered and sleepy.

A slow smile spread across the Revinir's lips as a second slave appeared. Two more, then a small group of them walking together, all having been pulled from sleep by the Revinir's roar. All of them leaving their crypts at a time when ordinarily they wouldn't be able to get their doors open.

The Revinir looked over the group as the last of them arrived. "Why did you come here?" she asked them. Testing them.

Reza, whose eyes were glassy, stepped forward. "Because you summoned us," he whispered. As he said the words, a wisp of smoke slipped from his nostril and floated to the ceiling.

In the Night

Arabis's eyes popped open, and she looked around camp. Everyone seemed to be asleep except for Simber and Talon, who were keeping watch as usual. She got up, feeling her scales tingling. "Did you hear something?" she asked Simber.

Dev jerked awake too. He sat up, looking confused.

"No," said Simber. "Nothing." He looked at Talon. Talon shook his head.

Arabis rose and stood uncertainly for a moment. Then she began walking toward the road. "I . . . I think I heard something."

Simber narrowed his eyes. He had the best hearing of all of them. He shrugged but didn't try to stop the dragon. She could handle herself.

"I heard it," said Dev softly. He stood up and watched Arabis.

Simber ignored the boy. It was impossible for a human to have heard anything better than the cheetah statue. But he and Talon got up anyway and swept the perimeter of the camp just to be safe. When the two were on the opposite end, Dev stole away after Arabis, leaving what little he owned behind.

Arabis felt a distinct dragon call tugging inside her. What was causing it? And how was it that Simber hadn't heard anything? Had the calling been silent? Perhaps it was the ghost dragons. Or could it be her mother, Pan, all the way from their world? Arabis didn't think that was possible. Dragons were powerful, but that seemed too much of a stretch. Still, her mind buzzed, and her eyes glazed over. A dragon call this compelling was rare. There was no refusing it unless one was physically restrained. What other dragons could there be in this land that Arabis didn't know about?

She began to trot down the trampled path, making the

ground shake. When she reached the road, she unfurled her wings and rose into the air to fly to the call.

Dev ran along after her, following it too. He soon fell far behind, but he continued, dazed but determined, to the square, his scales raised.

In the cave by the crater lake, Thisbe startled awake. A dragon's roar pounded in her ears, but she was almost certain it had come from inside her, not through the air. It shivered through the rocky mountain and the cave walls, calling her. She sat up, bewildered, her scales standing sharply.

Just as abruptly as the roar, the stark images she'd seen after she'd drunk the ancestor broth flashed in front of her in a random pattern. Ghostly dragons on the move. A girl being taken away. Meteors slamming into the ground. An earthquake.

There were new images there too—or perhaps they'd scrolled through so quickly the first time that she'd forgotten them. A band of rebels fighting an army of soldiers. A castle on fire. People fleeing. Chaos and screaming. Groups of people clearing stones and rubble. Then the dragons again.

Blinded by the images, Thisbe felt the dragon call inside her, compelling her to follow it. To go to its source. She didn't understand why—it was beyond logic and completely out of her control. She got to her hands and knees and crawled out of the cave, feeling her way to the narrow path that wound around the base of the mountain, hundreds of feet below the catacombs.

But the images continued flashing brighter as she moved, as if they were fighting against the pull of the dragon's roar. The brightness began to burn inside Thisbe's head, sending pain shooting through her body. Her limbs faltered and gave out, forcing her to stop moving. She cried and rolled to her side along the path as the flashing images continued, stronger than the dragon's call. The roar inside her begged her to go on. But the blinding images kept her imprisoned near the rocky wall by the crater lake. The random pattern of scenes landed on the girl being taken away, and it seemed to stick there. Then, dreamlike, an additional scene played out. Soldiers dragging the girl to the water's edge, tossing her onto a pirate ship as she fought and cried out. A woman silently screaming in the background. Swords clashing. A pirate chaining the girl to the deck. Then the ship being violently pulled down raging waters, sailing out of control.

Thisbe blacked out.

Across the land of Grimere, in the dungeon below the king's castle, the last of the black-eyed rulers who'd survived in the land of the dragons opened her eyes. She stared at the ceiling in the pitch darkness, her heart pounding. Aching.

She'd had the nightmare again: The girl struggling, being taken away. Water. A ship. Pirates. Then darkness.

A Surprise Meeting

Thisbe lay limp for hours, half asleep. It felt like she'd lost all her stamina. She could hear animals rustling nearby, but they weren't loud enough to fully rouse her. Finally the sun and the birds' morning songs woke her. She opened her eyes with a start, finding herself on the shore of the volcano lake. She stared at the water, puzzling over the nightmare that had brought her out here.

Another noise nearby made her sit up in fear and look around the bend. When she saw a large, flippered sea creature lounging on the shore, she gasped and scrambled to her feet, pointing her

LISA McMANN

finger at it and ready to hit it with a boom spell if necessary.

It didn't charge at her.

Thisbe stared, then wiped her eyes to make sure she was seeing what she thought she was seeing. It was a deep-purple-and-charcoal-spotted sea monster, a lot like Issie from the Island of Legends, but . . . smaller. And less wrinkled. It stared at Thisbe with big brown eyes, then blinked. Its long lashes dusted freckled cheeks. Then it made its mouth into an O and let out a sad mooing noise.

It sounded eerily like the sound Issie made when she was calling for her baby. Thisbe's pulse quickened. Her dragon scales rose. She dropped her hand to her side and took a cautious step toward the creature, studying the spotted pattern on its back. She remembered the sea creatures that had been in the giant aquarium in the square when she and Fifer had been brought to the stage to be sold. This looked suspiciously like the one in the aquarium.

"Are you . . . ? Are you Issie's baby?" Thisbe asked the creature. She almost felt silly saying it. But the resemblance was uncanny. Could it be that this was the baby who'd been missing for seven hundred years?

The creature didn't indicate that it understood or had even heard the girl. It just stared back. Then it mooed again.

"Moo-ooo," said Thisbe, trying to sound like the thing.

The creature walked on its stumpy flippered legs toward Thisbe. Its long neck arched, and its head came up to Thisbe's shoulder. Its body was thick and looked very heavy. A fat, short tail rested on the ground and ended in a rounded-off point.

When Thisbe tried to touch the creature, it skittered away and went splashing into the lake. It swam out several yards. It swiveled in the water and seemed to wave a flipper.

Thisbe laughed and waved back. The creature bobbed and swam side to side, then headed out toward the volcano. It looked back every now and then, as if it expected Thisbe to follow. The girl frowned and watched as the creature swam farther and farther away. Was it going to accidentally get sucked into the volcano the next time it sank? Or . . . perhaps that's what it was intending to do. "I'm sure you can take care of yourself," Thisbe said. "You probably know more about that volcano network than anybody."

After a while Thisbe couldn't see the creature anymore. As she turned away, the ground trembled, and it reminded

LISA McMANN

her of the earthquake in her very realistic nightmare. Had it been more than a dream? Fearfully she crouched and braced herself for the images to come and blind her again, but that didn't happen. She quickly realized the trembling was the volcano. It rumbled and spit out smoke and fire, then a giant ball of water.

She stood again and watched the display for a minute or two, then turned and continued to the cave, the nightmare still on her mind. She touched her fingers to her chest, to where the dragon's call had seemed to originate. It had been so real. It was distressing that she'd felt so compelled to leave the cave, which could've been dangerous. And those images blinding her—that was troublesome. What if it happened again? What if it happened when she really needed to see?

At the cave, Thisbe turned for one last look at the lake. She could make out a plump blob on the base of the volcano. Was it the sea creature? It had to be. After a while the volcano plunged underwater, dragging the monster with it.

Would it ever return? Or was it lost forever? Thisbe placed a bet with herself that the sea monster was off to somewhere better than this world. The thought of getting out of here was growing more and more tempting after what they'd learned about Alex and whoever else might have come and gone.

Maybe next time, if there ever was one, Thisbe would try tagging along with the sea monster. It was starting to seem like the only way to get home.

Without a Trace

Fifer woke up with the sun's rays warming her face. She rolled over and curled up under her blanket, feeling unusually tired. She'd had a terrible nightmare—a dream that her body was completely paralyzed and someone was shining a painfully bright light in her eyes. And while she'd felt aware that it had been a dream, she couldn't pull herself awake, no matter how hard she tried. It had been exhausting and scary.

Thankfully it hadn't lasted all night, but Fifer was in no mood for niceties today. She wasn't looking forward to another tedious day of waiting for the real battles to start so they could

LISA McMANN

sneak into the catacombs. Fifer had just about had it with that, and she was glad they'd decided to send Kitten into the catacombs again to scout around and see if Thisbe was truly down there.

Once again, Fifer teetered on the conflicting evidence: The Revinir had said Thisbe wasn't there anymore. But the seek spell they presumed to be for Thisbe had soared straight toward the elevator in Dragonsmarche. To Fifer, the spell seemed much more reliable than the lying Revinir. But the Artiméans hadn't technically seen where the spell had come to a stop, and of course they couldn't send any more to test them without arousing suspicion.

It was frustrating. Why couldn't Fifer's inner-twin radar kick in and just tell her where Thisbe was so they could go straight to her? Fifer was feeling more anxious than ever to take another trip to the cave entrance with the birds and risk being spotted by guards just to see if there was any sign of Thisbe.

Today Fifer decided her twin had to be down there. According to Dev and their own experiences, there was really no way out unless you could fly or get past a mountain of soldiers outside the elevator. And it didn't make sense for the

Revinir to send Thisbe to the king's dungeon when the guy was about to declare war on her—wouldn't he just say thank you very much and take Thisbe for his own slave or sell her since she was valuable? But every now and then Fifer had an uneasy feeling that she couldn't quite shake. It was like a tiny itch somewhere that couldn't be scratched. Or the bother she felt when she was trying to remember just the right word to use but she couldn't think of it.

She pushed her blanket aside and sat up, seeing only Samheed awake, his back against a tree. He was frowning at his little notebook and holding his pencil poised, but not writing anything. Fifer knew better than to bother the theater instructor when he was like that.

Instead she stretched and yawned, noticing that the fire was out. Arabis wasn't around to light it, so she grabbed an origami fire-breathing dragon from her vest pocket and moved to the fire pit to rekindle the flames and get breakfast started. She passed by the spot where Dev usually slept. His blanket was rumpled and his jacket was balled up, but he wasn't there.

Fifer squinted, trying to remember if something was supposed to be happening today and feeling a little groggy still from her long night of bad dreams. She went over to Simber and Talon, who were talking quietly away from the sleepers. "Where are Dev and Arabis?" she asked.

Simber regarded her. "We'rrre not exactly surrre."

Fifer frowned. "What do you mean?"

"He means they wandered off during the night," said Talon. "At daybreak I flew around the area to see if I could find them."

"They said they hearrrd something," said Simber. "I didn't believe them."

Fifer's eyes widened. "What kind of something?"

"They didn't say."

"So you just let Dev take off in the middle of the night?"

"I'm not in charrrge of him," Simber said a bit defensively, as if he felt like he'd failed at something important. "Besides, I didn't notice he'd gone too. Not until daylight. He must have snuck away when Talon and I werrre doing ourrr perrrimeterrr check."

"You didn't see them this morning, either?" Fifer asked, turning to Talon. "Not even Arabis? She's kind of hard to miss."

"No," said Talon. "She's gone." He looked incredibly

bothered. The two nonsleepers had huge nighttime responsibilities to watch over things, which were not to be taken lightly. "I apologize for failing my duties."

Fifer softened. "Oh, Talon. I'm sorry I was sharp. You didn't fail," she said. "Not at all. It's not like they're prisoners—they're free to come and go. It just seems strange that they'd go off together in the middle of the night. Dev didn't even take any food or his jacket or a blanket with him . . . and trust me, that's not like him to leave without his things, much less without stealing something as well."

"I agrrree," said Simber. "It's unsettling."

"I'm going to have a look," Fifer said decisively. "I was planning to go for a ride anyway. I'm so sick of sitting around here all day. Don't bother telling me not to."

Talon and Simber exchanged a concerned look but said nothing to stop the young mage. They were sick of it too, and frankly, everyone had been wondering how much longer they'd go on like this before they'd just have to recklessly go after Thisbe, or give up and go home without her.

Fifer shoved the origami dragon back into her vest pocket, deciding to let the next person start the fire. She had more important things to do. She grabbed the canvas hammock, dragged it to the clearing, and spread it out. Then she let out a soft whistle.

Shimmer flew down, and a few dozen other birds appeared soon after. Fifer sat in the middle of the hammock, and the birds picked up the ropes in their beaks. At Fifer's command, they began flapping and lifting the hammock. Soon they cleared the treetops.

Like Simber, Fifer decided a bit recklessly that it couldn't be helped if she got spotted flying over the townspeople. By now they no doubt knew the strange crew was in the area, but with all the volunteering and training and the threats from the Revinir and the king being on their minds, they hadn't pursued the strangers since they'd moved camps. Besides, word had spread that the flying cheetah and his riders had saved the king's life, so the majority of people and the green army in Grimere no longer considered the group a threat, and many assumed they were allies.

Still, the sight of Fifer flying over the square while the locals were setting up their booths for Dragonsmarche was notable, and there were a few fingers pointing her way. Fifer ignored them and trained her eye on the marketplace, trying to get a good look at the salespeople. Had Dev rejoined the Revinir so he could sell that awful broth again? And if so, why in the world would he do that?

"Because you're a double-crossing traitor, that's why," she mumbled. It was actually a relief to be mad at him rather than to continue growing closer. He was one less friend to lose. Her heart twinged, but she shoved her feelings down. She knew the truth now: The only way not to suffer hurt from someone dying was to not love them so much.

She scanned the booths in the marketplace, but there was no sign of Dev. That was good news, though she still wanted to know where he'd gone. She gave up on the square and decided that since she was already halfway to the cave opening, she might as well continue toward it to have a peek inside.

The birds flew her there, and they made a pass nice and close to the opening. Fifer hung over the side of the hammock, eyes trained on the passageway. But all she saw were three blue-uniformed soldiers on the other side of the river, standing together and talking with their backs to her. She thought she recognized them. They'd been there at the end when Alex was killed. They'd been frozen by spells, sure, and hadn't been aware of Alex being killed. But the thought of them back up and working their jobs when her brother was dead made Fifer's skin burn. It wouldn't take much to take them out right now. For good.

She considered it for a long moment as the birds circled around. But ultimately she couldn't go through with it. She made another pass, then sighed and turned the birds away. It wasn't right. And it would tip off the Revinir that they were still here. "Bad idea," Fifer said. Then to Shimmer she called out, "Let's go back."

As she guided the ravens up over the treetops, something sparkly glinting in the sun caught her eye. She turned and saw an orange creature flying in the distance. It was Arabis, heading away from Fifer, toward the castle. And there was someone sitting on her back.

A Pressing Need

I n the world of the seven islands, Pan heard the Revinir's call too, though she didn't understand who it was coming from. It was distant but pressing, and it stirred inside her and wouldn't settle. She knew instinctively there was no way to reach it—not for her. But her young had noticed it as well, and they were growing more and more restless, fighting the urge to go to it. With wings, they could make it. But Pan never wanted her remaining young to cross that gorge again. She wouldn't risk losing any more of them.

"But what if it's Arabis calling us?" asked Hux the ice blue, agitated. "She needs us."

Drock, who rarely spoke, snorted restlessly in the water as they swam around the cylindrical Island of Dragons, just one island east of Artimé. The dark purple dragon was the most temperamental of all of them. If it weren't for his sisters, Ivis the green and his lookalike, Yarbeck the purple and gold, he'd have set off alone. They were always holding him back, keeping him close. They didn't trust him. He didn't like to follow the ancient dragon rules.

"It can't be Arabis," Pan muttered. "I would know her voice." But even as she batted down every argument from the young dragons, she doubted herself. She feared Hux was right and that the call meant Arabis was in trouble.

The ruler of the sea looked long and hard at her young. Could she risk losing more of them by letting them follow the call? Or should she just give up on Arabis and consider her gone forever? It was an impossible dilemma.

"We must go back inside the island," Pan said with less enthusiasm than usual. Her young sensed it, and they didn't go. Instead they swam uneasily, looking always to the west, just like the people of Artimé did, as if doing so would bring Arabis and the Artiméans into view. But even their astounding

LISA McMANN

dragon vision wasn't magical enough to conjure them out of nothing.

"Do you think Arabis delivered the message to the other dragons in the land?" asked Ivis. "Perhaps they're the ones who've attacked her."

"Or maybe they are the ones who called for help," said Hux. "Could it be coming from one of the ghost dragons?"

Pan's enormous jaw was set firm. She had no wisdom to offer, which was unsettling. She didn't like not knowing. The ruler of the sea had very few vulnerabilities, but this was one of them—without wings, she couldn't go rescue her child. And poor Arabis was alone out there without her siblings. Vulnerable. In danger. Had her wings been repaired now that Alex was no longer with the living? She remembered that Fifer and Seth had done it before, and found some comfort in that. But if Arabis did have wings again, why hadn't she returned?

Drock, who couldn't handle the tense situation any longer, broke away from the others and dove completely underwater. A few moments later he burst through the surface and jumped at Yarbeck, grabbing her by the neck and dragging her under with him. Yarbeck recovered from the surprise and clamped down on Drock, then rolled him over and attacked. The two tussled for several minutes, working out their frustrations through rough play.

Pan didn't stop them—they were still young children who'd been forced to grow up all too soon. They needed to play, and fighting was part of a dragon's life. It helped them become stronger, quicker, and abler to defend themselves. Barely a blip of their lives had gone by as far as the longevity of a dragon. They needed plenty of exercise, especially the temperamental ones like Drock.

Besides, Pan was distracted by the sense of need stirred by the dragon call. It seemed to be growing. Patiently she swam around the ruckus and thought about the meeting she'd had with Aaron Stowe and the others. She'd told him she wouldn't send any more young dragons to be potentially captured and enslaved again. And she'd meant it.

But that was before the call.

Pan's neck arched as a pang of longing for Arabis shot through her. All she'd wanted was for her family to be together and safe, and for the worlds to be at peace. Why did that seem like such a tremendous thing to ask of the universe? She'd ruled

LISA McMANN

the sea to her best ability. She'd done her good deeds—many of them. She'd helped when Alex had asked her to help. The people of Artimé were her allies, and they'd come to her aid more than once in the most sacrificial ways. But she'd repaid the debts and offered her support time and again. She wished all the problems would drop away and she could continue to rule the sea in peace.

She swam away from her children, who were all in on the play fighting now, and looked to the east, then to the west. Water everywhere. Her kingdom. It had been a good home for her for many years. She'd been lonely at times, no doubt, especially after the great earthquake that had rent the world in two, leaving an impassible gorge between this land and the land of the dragons. She'd never expected that she wouldn't have a way back to her dragon roots. The world split had rocked her. But she'd recovered.

She'd had visitors of the flying variety over the years. Dragon friends who'd come for a few weeks or months. They'd stayed hidden from the other islands, traveling unnoticed in the dark. If anyone in this world knew of Pan's visitors, it might be Simber, but he never brought it up. He wouldn't, unless Pan spoke of it first. Simber was becoming a good friend, and Pan felt like she could trust him to keep her secrets whenever she'd felt forced to reveal them. That was the best kind of friend for a dragon to have. Too bad the cheetah was gone to the other world now. She could use his advice.

The old dragon sighed. She hadn't had a visitor in quite some time. That call had reawakened the loneliness inside her.

Late that night the roar came again, startling awake the five dragons in the land of the seven islands. Their insides yearned to go to it. It seemed stronger than before. By morning, Pan was so disturbed she could hardly control her reactions. Feeling oddly distant from her herself, she climbed up and out of her hollow cylindrical island. Leaving Ivis the green to stop the others from following, the ruler of the seas set off to the west at top speed. Hours later, as she neared Artimé, she scanned the lawn for Aaron. When she saw him, she approached the shore.

Feeling light-headed, almost dizzy, Pan approached the new head mage. "Aaron, we must talk," she said.

"Hello, Pan," said Aaron, who'd hurried out of the mansion

upon first sighting her. "You don't seem yourself. What's wrong? Can I do something?"

"I've decided I want to help you," said Pan. To her it sounded like her voice was coming from some other place. She wasn't sure what she was about to say next. This felt reckless for someone so cautious, yet she couldn't stop herself. "Aaron Stowe, *I* will take you to the land of the dragons. But first you'll need to make me some wings."

Preparing to Go

Aaron took a step back in surprise. "You?" he said incredulously to Pan. "You want to go? But who will rule the sea while you're gone?"

Pan, her eyes still glazed, frowned slightly, as if she hadn't thought it through. "We won't be away long," she said, her voice wispy with air. "Spike and Karkinos will take care of things until . . . until I return."

Aaron studied the dragon's expression, though he couldn't see her face very well from his position on the ground. Something seemed off, but the new mage wasn't sure if he was

LISA McMANN

imagining it. He didn't know Pan as well as Alex had known her. Perhaps this was just one of her mysterious ways. "Are you sure?" he asked. "We can make wings for you if you really want us to."

"Yes. How long will it take?" asked Pan anxiously.

Aaron sized up the dragon. She was at least double the size of one of her children. Her wings would have to be that much bigger in order to carry her. "It'll take a few days. Are you sure we can't just borrow one of your young dragons? That way we'd be able to leave right away."

Pan snorted her displeasure, and flames shot through the air above Aaron's head, singeing some leaves on a tree. She swung her head around to look out to the west, in the direction of the dragon's call, but saw no one coming their way. Her taut skin sang with energy; her insides ached with yearning to go to the land of the dragons. To that voice.

She couldn't explain it. What Aaron had said made sense, yet Pan couldn't agree to it. Deep down she knew her other children wouldn't be able to resist the call. The best way to protect them would be for her to accompany them. She . . . She *bad* to. There was no other way. In fact, *yes*—perhaps they all would go together. As soon as possible. It would be terribly hard for Ivis to hold back Drock for long.

"Please make the wings," Pan said, turning her gaze back to Aaron. "As quickly as you can. I'm not sure how much time we have."

Aaron looked alarmed. "What do you mean?"

But Pan acted as if she hadn't heard him. She turned and lumbered into the water, and with a tremendous shove of her tail she was off, straining her eyes to the west, but beginning to travel east. Back to her island.

"Pan!" shouted Aaron. "Are our people in danger?"

Pan turned, startled, and gave the question some thought. "I . . . I would assume so," she said. "Or they'd have come home by now. Wouldn't you agree? That's why we must make haste with the wings. I'll be back." With that, she shot over the waves, not giving Aaron a chance to ask for more clarification.

Aaron stared after her. "Wait!" he yelled. "I need to measure you!"

LISA McMANN

But the dragon kept going.

After a few moments Aaron shook his head slightly, unable to make sense of Pan's odd change of mind. But he was anxious to get started on the wings. Whether he understood her motivation or not, he and his team finally had a way to get to the land of the dragons. He hoped Pan wouldn't change her mind. He was fairly certain he could estimate the size of the wings they needed.

He called to Florence and Scarlet and told them what had happened. "Scarlet, will you and Henry and Sean and the children start gathering as many flower petals as you can, and put them in Ms. Octavia's classroom? Florence, I'm going to need your help in the jungle. We have to collect more vines than I can carry on my own."

As the people of Artimé got to work, Aaron jogged toward the mansion so he could grab his tools and prepare for the trip. As he did so, his stomach flipped. He hadn't gone on a mission like this in a very long time. And now, for the first time, *he* was the one in charge.

He hoped he wouldn't mess up everything even worse than

it already was. If he did, his adversaries would never let him hear the end of it.

The only thing Pan's request solidified for Aaron was that no matter what the dissenters said or did, Aaron was in this leadership thing too deep to turn back now.

Fifer Gets Restless

Before the sun rose, Talon dropped Kitten off in the castle tower, and she started her journey downward, sneaking past the soldiers all the way to the entrance to the catacombs. If necessary, she'd go through the entire maze, looking specifically for the kitchen and returning to the crypt that supposedly belonged to Thisbe.

Knowing Kitten's quest could take a few days, Fifer and the rest of the crew took to the skies and searched through the forest looking for signs of Arabis and Dev. Every now and then they'd spot the orange dragon flying in the distance with someone riding, sometimes near the cave entrance to the catacombs, other times near the castle. The Artiméans assumed the passenger was Dev, but there was no way to be sure from such a distance.

At one point Simber raced after them, but the dragon was too fast, and Simber couldn't catch up. It was troubling wondering what they were up to and why they had left so abruptly without a word. Had they been planning it? Had they turned against them? It seemed out of character for Arabis, if not for Dev. Even more troubling for the new young leader was trying to figure out what to do if Arabis had indeed switched sides. They wouldn't be able to leave all together without her.

Regarding Dev, Fifer and Seth felt the most sting, though Fifer continued to try to push it away. After all they'd been through with Dev, they'd come to consider him a friend. He'd been teaching Fifer the common language of the land. But friends don't leave in the middle of the night without a word. Something seemed terribly wrong about it, and Fifer couldn't help but wonder if something more nefarious had occurred. Had he just gone to see where Arabis was off to, and had both been abducted by soldiers? The king's green-uniformed army was becoming more and more of a presence on the road and in

LISA McMANN

the square. But without her muzzle, Arabis was very power-ful and could easily fight off a few soldiers. Not to mention Arabis was responsible—the most responsible of all the young dragons—and she hadn't come back. She didn't even seem to be friends with Dev, so everything just seemed so strange. And for Dev to leave without his jacket and his treasures . . . That was something Fifer would have never imagined happening.

"Something's definitely wrong," Fifer muttered as she folded Dev's things and put them in her bag for safekeeping. She and Seth finished straightening up camp and started out to gather firewood. Every day they had to go farther outside their new camp to find loose branches.

"Did you say something?" said Seth crossly. He was cranky in general lately. Nothing specific had set him off, other than the fact that he preferred living indoors, where there weren't any bugs and there was a kitchen full of food that *wasn't* fish. If only Fifer's magically prepared meals had reappeared inside her bag when the magic had come back . . . but alas, for some unknown reason they hadn't. He kicked at a root and hurt a toe that was already tender because his shoes were getting too small.

"I said something's definitely wrong," Fifer told him. "It just doesn't make sense."

"You mean with Dev and Arabis?"

Fifer nodded. "Arabis is too loyal to leave us without explanation."

"Dev isn't, though," said Seth. He frowned. "You trusted him too much."

"I did not." Now Fifer was testy. If anything, she was pulling away from people. Not trusting them more. "Besides, he left his money. Even his gold nugget. Something weird happened."

Seth was quiet. Then: "Are you going out for a ride today again?"

"Probably."

Seth glanced sidelong at her, waiting to be invited along, but Fifer didn't ask him. "Can I come?" he said, even more crossly since he had to ask. He sounded like his younger siblings. It made him feel like a baby.

Fifer shrugged. "Sure, I guess."

"Maybe just never mind." Seth rolled his eyes and picked up some small sticks for kindling. Fifer had been acting so

303 « Dragon Ghosts

weird lately. He wasn't sure what he'd done, but she seemed to be taking something out on him. He'd tried to be patient and kind because of everything she was going through, but it was hard. Was it okay to be mad at someone whose brother had just died? His patience was starting to wear thin.

Drums started up in the distance and then the trumpet's wail. "Ugh, not this again." Seth was tired of the constant recurring call to arms. He stood up straight and sighed, exasperated. "Seems like everybody would've heard by now, King!" he called out.

"Yeah, King," said Fifer, picking up one end of a long branch and stomping on the middle of it to break it in half. "You're not going to convince more people to join you by being annoying."

Seth snickered. "Hey, King, do you know any other songs? I can tell you about a place where you could learn some."

"King, you could be so much more than a one-hit wonder," said Fifer, half grinning now. She turned to Seth. "I learned that term from Kaylee. It means you're only—"

"Famous for one song," said Seth. "Yeah, I know. She told me."

"Oh." They both grew silent again, the game over. Things were bleak once more.

On the other side of the mountain and down by the crater lake, Thisbe was fishing. Again. It seemed like that was all they did, but at least it was something to pass the time while wondering what in the world they were going to do.

She'd had a rough time of it lately. That awful dragon call that Rohan and Sky didn't seem to hear had occurred once more, and the accompanying urge to go climb the mountainside to get to it had nearly done her in. But then the images had blinded and paralyzed her like they'd done before, stopping her in her tracks. It sapped her energy. Rohan had found her by the shore again that morning, lying on her side. He'd helped her back to the cave. She knew he had questions—she could see them in his eyes. But she wasn't ready to answer them. Somehow he sensed that and refrained from asking.

What did the images mean? Who was the girl being dragged away? And why was Thisbe getting that uncontrollable yearning feeling to climb the mountain and go somewhere deep inside the earth? The sound seemed to be coming from the heart of the catacombs. Thisbe never wanted to go back there. She just wanted to pretend this thing wasn't happening. But

LISA McMANN

she knew it had something to do with the ancestor broth—the images had originally appeared right after she'd drunk it the first time.

Rohan came up to her and touched her shoulder. Thisbe turned and looked up. Seeing his face made her feel calm, like things would be okay again someday. In fact, his friendship was the one bright spot in all of this. Well, finding Sky was pretty great too.

"What are you thinking about?" Rohan asked. He dropped his hand and moved down to his haunches next to her, gazing out over the calm lake. The volcano was down, and they could see the line of the land on the opposite shore, shrouded in mist.

Thisbe didn't want to talk about the disturbing things that were going on inside her. She wasn't sure she could describe them properly, and she knew her story would be hard to believe for someone who wasn't experiencing it too. Instead she pointed to the opposite shore. "Is that part of Grimere too?"

"No," said Rohan, picking up a stiff piece of bark. He began to dig for worms to use as bait. "That's where some of the black-eyed people were exiled after they escaped or were driven out of here. The land extends to the west and north and borders the cavelands, where the ghost dragons live. But the human side is mostly deserted now." He didn't explain why, but his lips made a tight line.

"Mostly?" asked Thisbe.

Rohan nodded. "There might be a few of our people left. Kept as slaves by a beastly old curmudgeon named Ashguard who lives in an old stone fortress. Some say the former queen is in hiding there too, but I don't know. Nobody's seen her in years. She's probably dead too."

Thisbe pulled in her empty line and checked the hook. Her worm was still there. She tossed it back in. "Anyone you know live over there?" she asked lightly.

"Not anymore."

They were quiet. Thisbe had gathered from what little Rohan offered up in conversation that he had no family left. She wasn't sure what had happened to them. He didn't seem open to discussing it. They both had secrets they didn't want to share—Thisbe could respect that.

LISA McMANN

After a moment she lifted her head and looked around. "Where's Sky?"

"She went to Dragonsmarche."

"What for?"

"She's going to try to barter for some vegetables. She took the big fish we were going to have for lunch with her, so . . ." Rohan looked sideways at Thisbe, his eyes crinkling.

It reminded Thisbe of their talks in the tunnel. She grinned. "So I'd better get on with it?"

Rohan nodded.

"Vegetables sound delicious. Roasted over the fire . . ." Thisbe's mouth watered. It was food like they ate back home. She'd never missed Artimé's cooks so much before.

Rohan deposited the worms he'd collected into their bait cup, a dirty old vessel they'd found washed up along the river. He wiped his hands and pulled out his string and hook too, and began fishing alongside Thisbe.

"You were talking earlier," Rohan said. "When . . . whatever it was happened again."

Thisbe swallowed hard and kept her gaze on her line. She hadn't known that.

"You mentioned the River Taveer, I think. You said something else with it, but I didn't catch it. Haven, maybe? Like it was a safe place, which seemed odd after what we went through to cross it."

"Haven?" Thisbe murmured, and she knew it wasn't quite right. "Taveer." Then she suddenly made the connection to the familiar river name. Perhaps it was *Maiven* she'd said, not haven. Maiven Taveer, her old cell mate in the castle dungeon. But why would she have said Maiven's name? She had no idea, but haven didn't make sense. The River Taveer wasn't a safe place—she knew that well enough. At least the part of it that rushed through the mountain and blocked the opening to the catacombs, where she and Rohan had escaped. Thisbe felt uncomfortable that he'd overheard her saying something that she didn't remember saying. She didn't like that she'd spoken and had no memory of it. It felt like she'd been out of control. Embarrassing. Like when someone catches you talking in your sleep. Maybe if she didn't respond further, Rohan would stop talking about it.

He picked up on her discomfort and didn't say any more. After a while Thisbe caught a fish, and by the time Sky returned with fresh vegetables and a loaf of bread, they had the fish browning nicely on the spit.

"How did you get the food?" Thisbe asked, delighted.

"I tried trading for it, but the vendor told me I had to sell my fish first, then come back with gold stones to buy his vegetables. So I stood there with my fish and held it up for people to see. After a few minutes someone offered me a couple gold pebbles for it, so I took them, though that didn't seem like a fair deal. I was skeptical and worried I'd just given away our lunch. But when I showed the rocks to the produce guy, he seemed happy. He let me take all I could carry and gave me the baguette, too." She pulled the loaf of bread out of its thin paper wrapping and ripped a hunk off it, then passed it around.

"It seems like a waste of time," Thisbe remarked. "Trade for stones, then trade the stones for food. Why not just trade the fish for the vegetables?"

Rohan observed the conversation with interest. "Because maybe the vegetable seller doesn't want a fish. He wants the gold because it can buy anything, not just the thing you're selling."

"Hmm. I guess that makes sense," said Thisbe. She turned back to Sky. "What was it like in the market?"

"Different," said Sky. "Armed soldiers everywhere. People moving about uneasily. Not very busy today. I think the towns-people must be scared."

"On the verge of war," mused Rohan. "But people must eat and make their wages. Life goes on. It feels surreal."

"This bread is very real, though." Thisbe chewed on the soft insides of the crusty loaf, letting the piece melt in her mouth. She hadn't eaten something so fresh in months. "Almost as good as our chefs make back home."

Sky nodded in agreement. Thinking of home, the two glanced at each other, then looked out to the lake, where the volcano was still down. Trying to get home through the vol-cano was on their minds constantly, each of them weighing the risks that were all too scary. They were relatively safe here, which was a factor in the decision. And maybe soon a rescue team would return to find Thisbe. Unless they'd given up.

Thisbe pushed that thought away and tried to enjoy the food. As they finished the bread, muffled shouts echoed against the mountain and bounced across the lake. The three turned and looked up. Thisbe gasped as she caught a glimpse of something orange flying high above the catacombs. "Hey! That's Arabis!"

A bevy of arrows soared through the air, striking the dragon, most of them bouncing off. Arabis roared in indignation.

Thisbe jumped to her feet. "What is she doing here? I thought Dev said all the dragons escaped and went home." She cupped her hands around her mouth. "Arabis!"

"Maybe she's come back for you?" said Sky, and she called the dragon too. "Arabis!"

All three shouted and waved at the creature, who disappeared behind the mountain. They ran down the path continuing to call out, but the dragon was gone.

"Should we climb up after her?" asked Thisbe. "Or just hope she'll circle back around? She'll be long gone by the time we get up there." Thisbe and Rohan didn't want to be reckless without a good reason, going out in the open market in broad daylight.

They abandoned the impossible chase. "Maybe she'll come back," said Thisbe, holding her hand to shield her eyes from the sun and breathing hard. "Oh, please, Arabis," she pleaded, tears springing to her eyes. "Please come back."

They stayed awhile at the edge of the mountain, peering at the sky in a desperate search for another spot of orange, but there was none.

"Was she alone?" Sky asked.

"I thought I saw someone riding on her back," said Thisbe. "But she went right over us and I couldn't tell for sure. I wonder what she's doing. She must be looking for us, right?"

"You, anyway," said Sky. "But why would she be alone?"

"Maybe no one else is left alive," said Thisbe, thinking of Alex's grave and imagining a massacre. Her heart dropped. "Maybe she's the only one."

"That can't be true," said Rohan firmly. "Not with your kind of magic to fight with."

"Besides," said Sky, "I've been all over the forest—I would have seen graves. Or at least more signs of a fight."

"Not if they all died in the catacombs," said Thisbe.

"Please stop doing that to yourself," Sky said softly.

"Perhaps we're misinterpreting everything," said Rohan. "Was Arabis wearing a muzzle? What if she didn't make it out safely with the others and she's still being held captive?"

"That's not a good scenario either," said Thisbe, dropping her head and rubbing her neck, which was stiff from straining it. "Besides, Dev would have known about that. He said they all got away."

Sky kept looking, willing the dragon to return. After a while they gave up and walked back to their cave, but remained outside it so they could see.

An hour later, Sky caught a flash of orange out of the corner of her eye. "There she is again!" she said, pointing to the dragon far above them, heading toward the castle. This time there definitely was a rider on her back. "Arabis!" Sky shouted and waved.

Thisbe gasped and jumped up. "No, Sky!" she said in a harsh whisper. "Look who it is!" She grabbed Rohan's wrist and dove into the cave, pulling him in with her.

Sky whirled around, confused. From the floor of the cave, Thisbe pointed to the rider on Arabis's back, her heart sinking. It wasn't anyone from Artimé.

"Who is that scaly monster-person?" whispered Sky, stepping into the shadows as Arabis dipped down. The sun

Dragon Ghosts » 314

glinted off the dragon-woman on her back as Arabis glided out of view toward the market, letting out a roar and a spray of flames as she went.

"That," Thisbe said grimly, "is the Revinir."

It Begins

Arabis just breathed fire!" Sky exclaimed.

Thisbe peered out from her hiding spot in the cave. "Are you sure? I can't believe she'd do that so close to where people are."

"She's obviously not wearing a muzzle, then," Rohan noted. "And she's allowing the Revinir to ride on her back—has she changed sides?" It was puzzling to imagine Arabis willingly working with the Revinir, but it seemed to be so. He started down the path to get another look. Adrenaline pumping, Thisbe and Sky followed. They ducked into the brush alongside the lake, though there wasn't too much risk of them being noticed from this distance if they stayed still. A few arrows flew over the cliff and fell among the rocks.

"Who's shooting at them?" asked Rohan. "I don't think the townspeople generally carry weapons around—not that I've ever noticed, anyway." They could see Arabis occasionally when she flew high enough, but they couldn't see the unknown dragon attackers.

"It's got to be the king's soldiers," said Sky. "There were so many out there today."

"I think . . ." Rohan's expression grew strained. "I think this is it. The war must be starting. And Arabis and the Revinir started it."

"The Revinir can't be ready," Thisbe mused. "Does she have an army?"

"Perhaps the Revinir is going it alone at first," Sky said. "And she's trying to catch the king's army flat footed before they're fully trained." Sky had been in more than her fair share of battles.

"But the king's soldiers aren't being caught flat footed," Rohan said, pointing as another arrow came flying over the cliff. "They're letting the Revinir know they're serious too."

Thisbe was conflicted. "Something strange is happening. Our dragons would never do what Arabis just did on her own. The dragons *hate* the Revinir. I'm worried. Why doesn't Arabis just fly away and dump the old bag off her back?"

"That's what's got me completely puzzled," said Rohan. "Perhaps the Revinir is using the same threatening techniques she used before with the young dragons."

"What techniques?" said Thisbe.

"Didn't you tell me that she would threaten to kill the other dragons when she needed to use one of them to transport goods, so they wouldn't try to escape? Or wait—no, it was the guards between the dungeon and the catacombs who told me that."

"Oh, yes," said Thisbe, remembering what Hux had shared with her and Fifer and Seth. "If that's the case, though, she must have other dragons captive somewhere too—to use as leverage to get Arabis to work for her. But . . ." Thisbe frowned. "But the Revinir always muzzled them before to keep them from turning on her. And Arabis isn't muzzled. Why isn't she taking over the situation? I don't get it."

"Maybe the Revinir does have another dragon," said Sky.

She was just as disturbed and puzzled. It was useless to speculate. When there were no more flying arrows, she crept out of the brush and strained to see. But their angle from this depth below the action gave them only a glimpse of the sky above the market, and Arabis wasn't in sight. "I wish there were a quicker way up the mountain so we could tell what's going on," she said.

Just then Arabis appeared once more, high in the sky, flying wildly. The Revinir held on with one hand and whipped the dragon with the other. The dragon-woman blew a breath of fire as Arabis dipped low, then out of sight. Sky gaped.

"What a frightening monster," said Rohan. "She seems much more scaly and fiery than usual."

Trumpets sounded, then the striking of some sort of gong, which echoed through the canyon.

"Wow!" said Sky, startled by the noise. "What was that for?"

"The king's army is trying to organize." Rohan frowned. Arabis soared above the catacombs once more with the Revinir. Then a roar shook the earth, but it didn't come from Arabis.

Thisbe shuddered. She felt the strange roar through her

LISA McMANN

skin and bones, all the way to her core, like the feeling she'd had twice before in recent days. She groaned and gripped her head, stumbling forward toward the noise as if she were being yanked by a rope. She cried out, and at the same time flashes of images pounded with light behind her eyes, blinding her. Her limbs grew numb. She flew forward and lost her balance, tripping over the uneven shoreline at the lake, and plunged sideways into the water.

"What in the—" muttered Sky, incredulous and shocked by Thisbe's strange actions. "Thisbe! What are you doing?"

Thisbe didn't surface. Rohan sprang in after her. He grabbed her around the waist and yanked her back onto the shore.

Thisbe sputtered and flailed. "Taveer!" she cried out between coughs and gasps. The series of images pounded inside her head like an ever-worsening migraine, one after the other. Meteors slamming into the earth, breaking into pieces. Soldiers sparring. Bandits sneaking around a burning castle. The girl being taken away and chained onto the pirate ship, then sailing out of control. Silvery-gray dragons like ghosts, marching and flying across a barren land. Then an earthquake, separating the worlds and leaving water plunging into the chasm between.

While the images flashed and became longer scenes, Thisbe couldn't think of anything else. She could barely breathe. The numbness enveloped her, and she stopped flailing. Finally there was darkness. Thisbe lay with her head in one companion's lap, her feet propped up by the other one, waiting for her vision and strength to return.

Eventually her body began to ache, and she could hear again—Sky and Rohan talking quietly about her. Rohan explaining that their harrowing journey in the catacombs had been across the River Taveer and speculating that Thisbe might be experiencing some sort of trauma related to that. When Thisbe opened her eyes and daylight slowly seeped back in, she looked up into Rohan's concerned face.

He gave her a shaky smile and pushed her bangs out of her eyes. "You okay?" he asked.

Thisbe nodded and struggled to sit up, embarrassed. "Sorry that happened again," she said. "I . . . I'm not sure what's going on." Her lip quivered, though she tried to stop it. She didn't want to cry right now, even though this was scary.

"Are you sick?" asked Sky.

"I don't think so."

"Please don't be sorry," said Sky. "You obviously can't help it. Do you know if it just happens randomly?"

Thisbe stared at the ground. Things were still wavering a bit, and she was more scared than anything that the blinding visions would come back again. Or the urge to run toward . . . toward that recurring roaring sound. She looked up. That was it—the trigger for these episodes happening. "I know what it is now," she said grimly, though not all the pieces had fully come together yet.

"What is it?" asked Rohan, who looked terribly worried still.

"That dragon roar. It wasn't Arabis; it was the Revinir. She has more magical power than ever before. She's . . . She's using it to call to me. To try to get me to rejoin her. She's . . ." Thisbe clamped her mouth shut as more truths came together.

"She's what?" asked Sky, leaning forward with alarm.

"She's trying to control me. Like she's controlling Arabis. That's . . . That's what drinking all of that dragon-bone broth did for her." Thisbe pressed her lips in a firm line. "She has become the leader."

Sky stared. "The leader of what?"

"The leader of all dragons." She pushed up her sleeve and stared at her scaly arms. "Including me."

Restless and
Reckless

The time waiting for Kitten to return went by slowly for Fifer and her team. Fifer became more and more reclusive as she tried to distance herself from loving her friends too much, in case someone else died in their next attempt. It hurt her stomach so much to imagine losing any of them. These thoughts became more frequent and made her head spin with growing worries. Being a leader was difficult—she finally understood Alex's old attitude and serious temperament a lot better now.

And thinking about all the mistakes she could make was

overwhelming. Sure, she hadn't made any major ones yet. But that day was certain to come, and Fifer could hardly stand knowing it. On top of the worries, she still had so many questions. Would she ever know the answers?

She dodged Seth, painful though it felt, especially when she saw the hurt in his eyes. Better to have a little pain now than a lot later. She stuck with her birds. With them, she could wonder aloud as many times as she wanted. Why did Arabis and Dev abandon them? Where in that giant maze of crypts was Thisbe? And Fifer's most desperate question: How could they get to her without losing someone else in the process?

Multiple times a day Fifer took to the skies with her birds. She was wary of the soldiers, but more than ready to fight back if they shot at her. They never did. Obviously they were foolish to think a twelve-year-old girl and a bunch of birds weren't threatening, but Fifer appreciated being left in peace. She explored the forest and Grimere in ever-widening circles around their base, looking for a variety of things: Dev, Arabis, and smoke from the vent.

Simber watched her carefully. He knew she could take care

LISA McMANN

of herself and that she never landed anywhere, so she was relatively safe and out of reach. But he still worried about her like he'd worried about Alex. He could tell she'd been struggling. And if there was anything he'd learned from supporting Alex, it was to let the leader struggle and make some mistakes. As hard as it was to watch it happen, he knew it was the way humans learned.

The cheetah trolled the skies too, but mostly at night. He didn't want the sight of him to cause too much alarm with the townspeople now that they had so much to worry about, like who's side they were on. From the conversations Simber's sharp hearing picked up as he flew overhead, not all of them had made their decisions yet, and it caused quite a bit of friction among neighbors.

After the Revinir and Arabis had done their fly-by attack of Dragonsmarche, skirmishes broke out frequently in the square. Polite and careful discussions about who the vendors supported turned into table-tipping brawls and severed friendships. The ancient baker woman who'd been selling baguettes for forty-five years next to the florist man had spat in his face and demanded he find a new booth, for she could no longer stand to be around the Revinir-supporting idiot. More and more women and men began to show up in green military garb, having decided to fight for the king, while members of their own families waved blue flags to declare their support for the Revinir.

"Therrre's no way this turrrns out well," Simber remarked to Fifer as the two of them stood at the edge of the forest overlooking the square. They hadn't seen the attack that had started things escalating, but they'd heard about it and had witnessed others since. "It's a civil warrr. These families will neverrr be the same again."

Fifer glanced at the stone beast. "Then they'll understand how I feel," she said. "I know my family isn't in a civil war, but everything is broken. And it can never be fixed. Even if we find Thisbe, we've still lost Sky and Alex. I can't bear it. I can't stand to think about losing anyone else."

Simber nodded and was silent. After a while he sniffed the air. His eyes narrowed, and he sniffed again. He shook his head.

"What is it, Sim?"

"I thought I picked up Kitten's scent, but it's gone now."

LISA McMANN

"I hope she's found Thisbe." A pang of longing tore through Fifer's heart, ripping open the wound again.

"So do I," said Simber. "We need to hearrr frrrom herrr soon. This waiting is drrriving me crrrazy."

"Me too." Fifer placed her hand on Simber's side. "If only we could find Thisbe and get out of here before this war gets worse. . . . That's my wish, anyway."

"We can hope forrr that," said Simber, eyeing another skirmish just starting in Dragonsmarche. "But I don't think we'll be so lucky."

Within the hour Simber was proven correct. They heard a rumbling, and soon the king's army rolled into town. They swarmed and descended on the shop owners and vendors in Dragonsmarche who had declared their loyalty to the Revinir, and captured them.

While Fifer and Simber watched in shock from their hiding place, the fists and the weapons began to fly, and soon all of the merchants and shoppers were either running for their lives or partaking in the battle. It was messy and disastrous. Before long, the king's army took control. They gathered up the Revinir supporters and chained them, then forced them to walk back down the main road toward the castle, where they would be imprisoned.

Hours later, as things settled down, Fifer and Simber looked over the near-deserted square. "Do you think the war is over already?" Fifer asked. "Did the king win? I hardly saw any of the Revinir's soldiers—just the ordinary people who support her. She wasn't around either."

"It's not overrr," said Simber wisely. "It's just the beginning. And we're stuck in the middle of it. It makes me wonderrr . . . ," he said, but he didn't finish.

"Wonder what?" asked Fifer suspiciously. She was worried that he'd suggest they all go home to get away from this war.

Simber glanced at her and shook his head. "Neverrr mind." He frowned at the few skirmishes still going on, then turned away. "I've had enough of this forrr today."

Just then a chilling roar—the second one that day—echoed in the canyon on the far side of the square, causing those who remained to pause and look up. Fifer and Simber looked up too and saw Arabis rising from the canyon. The Revinir was on her back.

"What's going on?" Fifer exclaimed. "What is Arabis doing?"

"Nothing good," said Simber. They crept closer to get a better look.

"I can't believe this," whispered Fifer. "Arabis is working for the Revinir. Is she being forced?"

"She's not muzzled," said Simber. Then he pointed a claw toward the center of the square. "Look therrre."

The catacomb's elevator was rising. Everyone stopped to look as a dozen blue-uniformed soldiers emptied out. With them was one tiny Kitten, whom no one noticed.

Another thing no one noticed was that these soldiers were not the usual ones. They were much younger. Black-eyed children with dragon scales beneath their clothing. And they were prepared to fight.

Many miles away in the cavelands, an army of ghost dragons, led by Quince and Gorgrun, had assembled. Shoulder to shoulder, dust rising around them, they began their long journey trudging and flying slowly toward the Revinir's roar. Not to heed it, for in their ghostly state they were unaffected by the call. Instead, they planned to fight against it with all their worth.

If only they could remember that once they reached their destination.

A Tough Decision

Thisbe, Sky, and Rohan heard the Revinir's latest roar directly above their cave.

"Not again." Thisbe moaned as she felt the symptoms come on strong. She resisted the urge to follow the roar and soon lay helpless once more as the images flashed in her mind and her body became paralyzed. Sky and Rohan helped her the best they could while two equal parts of her fought against each other in their own little war. Everyone could hear the distant echo of weapons clashing. But there was nothing they could do.

By the time Thisbe opened her eyes, Sky and Rohan were

exchanging somber looks above her. These unpredictable instances caused by the Revinir's roar were increasing, leaving Thisbe vulnerable more often. Added to that, the threat of war loomed greater than before. If any of the fighters ever strayed down to their lakeside level, they'd be trapped in the midst of battle. And if the Revinir decided to roar during it, they could be in big trouble.

"We need to get out of here," Thisbe whispered. She barely had the strength to get the words out, but she said exactly what the other two were thinking.

"Yes," Sky said grimly. "I know it's dangerous, but we're going to have to try the volcano. We don't have any other choice."

"What about the forest?" asked Rohan. "We could try escaping to there, or perhaps to the land across the lake. Though there's not much left there," he admitted. "I'm not sure how far the Revinir's roaring range is, but at least we'd be away from the fighting."

Sky considered his idea, then shook her head. "I've stayed in sight of the volcano for a reason, always hoping that someone from home will figure out how it works and make their way to this shore. I didn't want to miss them if they did. And anyone coming for Thisbe will search the area above us, near the catacombs entrance in the square. If we go elsewhere in this world, our people will never find us. I think it's time we take a frightening journey through the volcano."

"Of course." Rohan dropped his gaze. "That makes the most sense for you two. Forgive me—I wasn't thinking."

Thisbe looked at him. "You're . . . not coming with us." She'd meant it as a question, but felt suddenly self-conscious and ended it like a statement. What if he'd never planned to go with them? How arrogant was she to assume he'd want to?

"No?" said Rohan, glancing up quickly to read her expression. "I mean, no." He seemed as flustered as Thisbe, if not more so. Then he added weakly, "I worry about the volcano. I . . . I mean for *me*, as a weak swimmer. Not for you." He turned sharply to avert his gaze and stared at the spot in the lake where the volcano would eventually surface. "Aren't you afraid of drowning? Or of ending up somewhere completely foreign?"

Thisbe and Sky exchanged a glance. Of course they'd thought about it. Then Sky spoke up. "I'm not afraid of

LISA McMANN

drowning now that I know it's possible to breathe a little when traveling through the volcanic tunnels—even if it's difficult to do so. And . . . well, I ended up somewhere completely foreign once already, and found you. So. I'm game to have a go if you are, Thisbe." She searched Thisbe's face. "Considering what the Revinir is doing to you, and the war that's beginning, I think our safest move is to leave here as soon as possible and try to get back to Artimé so she no longer affects you."

Thisbe stared off into the distance, lost in thought. She felt certain there was a way back to the seven islands through the volcano network. The pirates had gone back and forth for years. Hux the ice blue had told Pan that there had to be another way—and this was it. And Issie's baby seemed to know something about it. The volcanos were a transportation system between the two worlds . . . and maybe other places too. It was frightening to think about being swallowed up by the volcano and spat out into another world, possibly painfully so. And who knew if they'd land in water? Just because the two volcanos they knew about were in water didn't mean others would be.

Thisbe cringed. What other option was there? It wasn't

LISA McMANN

safe here anymore, and the Revinir's roar was having a worsening effect on her. The fact that the woman was trying so hard to make Thisbe join her meant that her life was in even more danger than they'd realized. Thisbe knew this had to be the right move, as scary as it was. "We'll do it, Sky," she said, her heart seizing up. "Once the volcano comes back up, we'll head out there. Then we'll have to wait for it to go back down again. And then . . . well, that's it. We'll go down with it."

"It just went under this morning, so it'll probably resurface sometime this afternoon," said Sky.

"Maybe Issie's baby will be around to guide us," Thisbe said with a shaky laugh. She felt relieved that they'd made a decision, but now the fear began in earnest. And what about Rohan? She turned to him and clutched his arm, but the lump in her throat rendered her momentarily unable to speak.

"Would you like help building a small raft?" asked Rohan quietly, not looking at Thisbe. "So you can swim out holding on to something while you wait for it to go down?"

Thisbe studied his profile as a thousand feelings swirled around her. "Yes," she said. "That's a great idea." Next to the fear inside her was a growing ache. She realized it was because she would miss Rohan. She'd miss him desperately. More than she'd ever expected. They'd been through so much together. "Thank you."

"Of course." Rohan got up abruptly. "I'll start gathering branches and leave you two to . . . figure things out."

When he was gone, Sky glanced at Thisbe. "Don't you want him to come with us?" she asked. "He's in danger here too."

"I—I think he doesn't want to come with us. This is his homeland. I don't know."

Sky was silent. Her heart ached too. This risky decision to try the volcano was easier for her, she knew. Sure, she had her brother and mother, but they likely thought she was dead already. And Alex . . . well. That made this decision easier. She got up. "Maybe you should go help Rohan while I pack a few things," she said. "We don't have much time."

"Okay." Thisbe rose numbly and started down the path to the wooded area next to the lake. She followed the sounds of crackling underbrush to where she caught sight of Rohan.

He had begun piling a small pyramid of long, thick sticks in a clearing. He heard her coming and flashed a crooked grin that somehow seemed incredibly sad. "Hi," he said.

"Rohan?" said Thisbe.

"Yes?"

"Where will you go? Will you stay here?"

Rohan straightened and threw another stick on his pile, not daring to look at her. "I haven't given that any thought yet."

"You know you can come with us, right?" Thisbe felt her face grow hot, and it only made her flustered. "If you want to."

"That's very generous, Thisbe," said Rohan. "Thank you for your kind offer. Like I said, I'm not a good swimmer. I'm afraid to do it. And . . ."

"And?" Thisbe prompted.

"And I don't know if I should leave here, even if I dared."

"But why?" Thisbe demanded, casting aside her early feelings of discomfort. She wanted him to come with them. She knew that now.

"This might sound strange, but I think . . . I think I'm supposed to stay. Stay and fight for our people and my friends in the catacombs. And our land. Somehow. Perhaps I'll go back

LISA McMANN

to try to free the other slaves or something. I just . . . I feel like I'm supposed to do that."

Tears sprang to Thisbe's eyes. Wrapped up in herself, she'd all but forgotten about the other slaves. And she'd forgotten that Rohan considered her to be one of *them*, the rightful ruling people of Grimere. "What good can one person do?" she asked, all the while feeling guilt creep into the pit of her stomach.

"Maybe I won't accomplish anything," said Rohan. "But I have to try."

"Of course. I'm sorry." Should Thisbe be staying too? Fighting for her people? But what if she didn't feel like these people were hers? What if she felt like she needed to go home and be with *those* people? The Artiméans were her people—the ones she knew best, anyway. "But . . . will I ever see you again?" Thisbe cried. Her voice cracked. "I wasn't planning on leaving you behind. I'm not sure . . . not sure . . ."

Rohan dropped the sticks he was holding and went over to her, and she reached out and took his hand. Startled, his hand remained limp at first, and then he gently squeezed her cool fingers. He swallowed hard. "Thisbe, if I never see you again, my heart would break. I admit I'm tempted to go with you. But there's a stronger calling inside me that has nailed me to this land. It's something even stronger than the friendship I feel for you. Perhaps . . . Perhaps one day you'll find your way back here."

Thisbe looked up and saw his eyes glistening, which made her feel even sadder. "How will I find you?" Her ribs felt like they were tightening around her. She couldn't breathe.

"I can't say," said Rohan. "I've no idea where my path will lead me. But our connection is strong." He wiped a tear from her cheek. "I feel certain we'll find ourselves in one another's company again one day."

"What if I don't come back here?"

"Then I'll learn to swim and hold my breath like you and your people. And I'll dare to scour all the worlds to find you."

A sob escaped Thisbe, and she looked away, overcome with the intensity of the moment. She took a step back but didn't let go of Rohan's hand. He was right. Their connection *was* special. Stronger than anything Thisbe had ever felt before—from their nights in the tunnel between their crypts to their perilous escape, they had shared a lifetime's worth of events in the span

LISA McMANN

of months. She felt like she should give him something, a gift to remember her by, though it was clear he, like she, would never forget their time together. She went to her pocket to see if there was any token she could offer, and her fingers landed on one of the tiny bottles of ancestor-bone broth that she'd stolen in hopes of being able to sell it in the marketplace.

Her breath caught. The ancestor-bone broth was the thing that was helping her resist the Revinir's dragon call. She was certain of that. But it also gave her something she couldn't explain. A connection to the history of the people of Grimere. A closeness . . . almost as if she could read their minds if they'd been alive today.

She pulled out the bottle and looked at it, then held it out to Rohan. "Here," she said. "It's the ancestor-bone broth. I swiped a few bottles as we were leaving, thinking I could sell them in Dragonsmarche if we needed those gold stones to buy food. This broth is harmless to people without black eyes if the Revinir is any proof—she drank it and it didn't affect her. But to us . . . Well, this broth opens a whole world of history and wisdom through the images. I know I haven't told you much about it. But now that we're leaving so suddenly, well, I just wanted to tell you more. Maybe it'll help you in your quest to save the others. And . . . I don't know. Maybe it'll also keep us connected somehow."

Rohan hesitated. "Broth made from human bones is not something I've ever thought I'd be interested in," he said.

"You don't have to drink it unless you want to," Thisbe hastened to say. "If not, you could sell it someday if you need the money. Or . . . keep it. To remember me by."

Rohan took the bottle and slid it into his pocket. "I have nothing to give you," he murmured. And then he remembered. "Wait." He bent down and lifted his pant leg, then pulled out the knife he'd stolen from one of the guards. It rested in a worn leather sheath. Eyeing Thisbe, he touched the handle to his lips, then held it out to her.

"Don't you need it?" Thisbe asked, worried. "What if you're attacked?"

"I'll keep one of the swords." Rohan dropped his gaze. "Besides, I need the memory of this moment more."

Thisbe's heart fluttered. "Then you'll have it." She took the knife.

He smiled and dipped his head. Impulsively Thisbe rose to

her tiptoes and placed a tiny kiss on his lowered cheek, catching him by surprise. But he couldn't dwell on that action, for the lake waters began to shiver.

Rohan turned. "Is that . . . ?" he said, noticing the ripples.

Thisbe nodded and clutched Rohan's hand as she watched and waited. A few moments later the volcano in the lake came torpedoing up, spewing water everywhere. There was no time to waste.

On the Move

As Arabis and the Revinir flew out of sight and the skirmishes in the Dragonsmarche square began to ramp up again, Kitten returned to camp with much to report. She relayed the story of the past few days to Simber, who listened intently without translating. Kitten mewed for many minutes before stopping. The others gathered around and waited impatiently to hear what Kitten had learned.

When she finished, Simber looked up at the others.

"What's happening?" asked Fifer. "Did she find Thisbe?"

Simber shook his head, looking a bit puzzled. "Kitten says

Thisbe is not in the catacombs. She looked everrrywherrre. She's cerrrtain of it."

"What?" said Carina. "How could that be?"

"I knew it," said Fifer under her breath. She'd had a feeling nagging at her all this time, but she believed the stupid seek spell. She frowned to herself—why hadn't she listened to her instincts?

Simber went on. "But Kitten did find someone else."

"Who?" asked Lani.

"Dev." Simber looked puzzled. "She says she trrried to talk to him, but he just looked at herrr with a strrrange, glazed exprrression, like he didn't know who she was. She said all the otherrr slaves had that same look too. And they all had drrragon scales on theirrr arrrms like Dev."

"Oh my goodness," said Fifer. "How could he not recognize Kitten?"

"That's frightening," said Kaylee, sitting up straight. "What's going on with the glazed expressions? And I still don't understand what the deal is with the Revinir riding Arabis around like that. Arabis might have decided to leave us, but I can't imagine a single scenario in which she would willingly rejoin the Revinir after all that's happened in the past. After all we know about Arabis and the Revinir." She paused, thinking it through. "Does anybody else suspect she has some sort of mind-control thing happening?"

"I've been wondering that too," said Crow. "Maybe the Revinir's control of Dev and Arabis and the others has something to do with the dragon scales. It makes sense if everyone with the glazed look had the scales. And Arabis has them too, of course."

Kitten began mewing again, and Simber paused to listen, then translate. "She says that when the Rrrevinirrr rrroarrrs, all the slaves go to herrr. And that Arrrabis is kept chained up in some cave at the top of the mountain when the Rrrevinirrr isn't flying arrround on herrr back."

"What?" said Samheed, incredulous. "What's going on? This is some kind of strange magic. I don't understand it."

"And where is Thisbe?" demanded Fifer. She was beginning to panic, but she didn't want to let on how scared she was for her sister. "Kitten, are you absolutely sure she's not down there?"

"Mewmewmew!" said Kitten.

"She's surrre. She checked everrry crrrypt and everrry hall-way. The kitchen and the extrrracting rrroom. She looked at each slave when they all came togetherrr at the Rrrevinirrr's call. Thisbe isn't in the catacombs."

Fifer put her palm to her forehead and started pacing. Her heart filled with dread. "Where could she be? Do you think she's . . . *dead* and buried down there? I mean, the seek spells went toward the square. Maybe they're in some empty crypt . . . hovering . . . like . . ." *Like Alex's.*

No one jumped to respond, for they were all picturing it too.

"We can't think that," said Carina firmly after a moment. "She must have escaped."

"Kitten *searrrched*—" Simber began.

"Or she's back in the dungeon like Dev told us," said Thatcher, cutting him off. "That's my guess. The Revinir put her back there after we tried to rescue her."

"But the seek spell!" said Fifer, growing impatient.

Seth nodded grimly. "She sent Thisbe to the dungeon after the seek spell was sent."

"None of this makes sense," muttered Fifer. "Why would

the Revinir give a black-eyed slave to the king when they are so valuable? And when they are fighting each other?"

Lani spoke up. "Maybe she knows about the seek spells and she understands how they work. Remember, Samheed—we were able to send a few when she held us captive back when we were Fifer's age. She certainly knows about our other magic after the great battle. She's smart enough to have figured out the seek spell just by seeing one."

Samheed slowly nodded. "I'll bet she moved Thisbe to the dungeon after the seek spell in hopes of us sending more and tracking her down over there instead of at the catacombs."

"So," said Seth, trying to follow the conversation, "she expects that we'll attack the castle instead of the catacombs?"

"Ohhh," said Fifer. "She wants us to attack the *castle*, not her. The king is her enemy. She's getting us to help her without meaning to. Is that what you're saying?"

Lani nodded. "Something like that."

The group fell silent, trying to poke holes in this new theory. Fifer had to admit parts of it made sense. The Revinir was trying to draw them to the castle to fight the king for her. *That would definitely be a clever move,* she thought begrudgingly.

LISA McMANN

There was no telling for sure, unless maybe they could get the information from someone outside of the catacombs. Like Arabis. "Kitten," Fifer said, "where is Arabis's cave?"

Kitten shrugged. "Mewmewmew."

"Kitten says she only overrrhearrrrd the Rrrevinirrr talking about it being on a mountain. She didn't say wherrre exactly it was."

"Well," said Fifer, "I'm going to find her and make her tell us what's going on. And then we'll track down Thisbe, wherever she is, and get out of here before this stupid war gets any worse." She got up and called to her birds.

"Mewmewmew," said Kitten, impassioned.

"Wait, please," said Simber. "Therrre's morrre."

He listened as Kitten gave a lengthy explanation of something.

Then he turned to the group. "The black-eyed slaves, who now apparrrently have some minorrr drrragonlike powerrrs, arrre drrressing like the Rrrevinirrr's soldierrrs. They came out of the elevatorrr with Kitten and arrre on the marrrch to the king's castle. They'rrre going to attack and attempt to overrrthrrrow him."

The revelation was met with stunned silence.

"What? You mean right now?" said Seth. "What will happen to Thisbe if she's in the dungeon?"

"I doubt they'd go down there," said Carina. "The king didn't seem to spend any time below the main floor, right? And that's who they're after."

Fifer and Seth agreed—they hadn't seen him anywhere near the gross dungeon.

"And why would he?" said Thatcher. "He wouldn't bother with the prisoners. I agree, Carina."

"But what are we going to *do*?" said Fifer, her voice pitching higher. Was she, as a leader, supposed to know? Was she supposed to be answering the questions instead of asking them? She took a deep breath and blew it out in frustration. "We need to find Thisbe and get her out of there. Can we make it to the castle before the Revinir's soldiers?"

"Mewmewmew," said Kitten.

"They have a prrretty good starrrt on us," translated Simber.

"But we have you," said Carina to Simber.

"And the birds," said Fifer.

"And me," said Talon.

They all looked at one another, silently counting the number of passengers.

"We'll plan everything on the way," said Kaylee, grabbing her sword and shoving it into the sheath on her belt. "Come on."

"But we can't attack the black-eyed slave soldiers," said Fifer. "They're not the enemy. They might be under the Revinir's dragon-magic control, but they're . . . they're MY people."

Carina frowned. "If someone attacks me, I'll fight back," she said without apology. "But I hear what you're saying. According to what Dev told us and what we know about them being slaves, they're obviously not on the Revinir's side—at least when they have control of themselves."

"This argument is meaningless if we just sit around here speculating about things," said Samheed impatiently. "Simber, do you want to fly up and get an idea of what's happening out there while we gather our supplies?"

"Great idea," said Lani, who was also eager to get moving.

Simber didn't wait for anyone else to chime in. While the rest of the team prepared a hasty collection of their camp so they could move to the castle area, the great cat rose above the treetops and began flying in ever-growing circles, trying to assess everything from the skirmishes in Dragonsmarche to the easternmost point of Grimere, where the castle stood.

From the sky Simber could see the battle still going on in Dragonsmarche. And he could see the small army of a dozen or so blue-suited soldiers that Kitten had mentioned. They were making quick time walking up the main road toward the castle without being challenged—so far. Simber could barely make out a much larger army of green-uniformed soldiers assembling at the road outside the castle miles away. There seemed to be many more of them than he'd seen in one place before. The king's call to arms had worked. His army was far larger than the Revinir's. But where were all her other soldiers? Had they deserted her?

As Simber headed back toward camp to rejoin the team, something caught his eye in the direction of the cavelands, where Arabis had been visiting. He could just make out a faint cloud of dust rising, as if there was a wild stampede in the desert. Simber narrowed his gaze. Instead of heading for the clearing in the forest where the others were, he continued beyond it, toward the dust. In a few minutes he could make out dark blobs within the cloud. And a few minutes after that, he could see the distinct shapes of dragons.

Some were flying slowly, and others were marching, causing the storm of dust. All were enormous, many times larger than Simber. They were heading toward Grimere. Had these dragons been summoned by the Revinir's call too, like Arabis? If so, the Artiméans were in big trouble. Maybe that was why the Revinir's army was so small. She didn't need humans when she had dragons.

Simber circled back and soared at top speed to camp, where the others were packed up and waiting for him. He told them about what he'd seen.

The Artiméans were mystified about the ghost dragons and scared, too. Arabis had told them that the ghost dragons would fight for the land when they needed to. But if those dragons

LISA McMANN

were under the Revinir's spell, would they instead turn on the Artiméans?

"I'm so confused," Seth lamented as he climbed into the bird hammock with Fifer. "Who are we fighting again?"

Fifer signaled to Shimmer to lift off and gave Seth a grim look. "Everyone, I think."

No Time to Lose

Thisbe!" Sky called. "The volcano!"

Thisbe and Rohan jerked their hands apart. "I see it!" Thisbe replied. "We're coming now!"

They quickly gathered up the sticks and yanked some stringy vines down as well to help secure them together to make a raft. As they did, Thisbe's stomach felt like lead. "This is really happening," she murmured. "I'm going to get sucked down the volcano. And I might never make it out." She paused, thinking about it. "I might die."

Rohan looked away, his face pained. "I want to tell you not to go," he said. "But it's no safer for you here."

LISA McMANN

That was the grim reality. If Thisbe stayed, she might get overpowered by the Revinir's dragon call. Or kidnapped by someone seeking to cash in on her value as a slave. Or caught in the middle of a war between two parties she disagreed with. The black-eyed slaves had no one fighting for them. And now Thisbe was leaving Rohan to do the fighting alone.

It didn't feel right. But she couldn't stay here and be vulnerable. The way she reacted to the Revinir's roars was not just debilitating for her, but it made everyone with her vulnerable too. And it put them in danger when they had to tend to her.

"This is the hardest choice of my life," Thisbe said. "If I could tear myself in two, I might just do it."

This brought a small smile to Rohan's face. "I'm not sure that'll help things," he said, his familiar teasing tone seeping into his voice. "I'd have to help you walk . . . unless the bottom half of you stayed here. . . ."

"I was thinking I'd be split the other way, top to bottom," Thisbe said with a grin, straining hard to keep from crying. "So I might still need help." The tears came anyway.

Rohan nodded, unable to choke out a laugh or even a single word.

They reached Sky, who'd packed up a few things and was ready with more vines. Sky had made rafts before; one had been strong enough to get her and Crow from Warbler to Artimé. Now she began expertly tying the sticks together and weaving extra vines around them to secure them. "This isn't going to be a very big raft," she said after a while, "but it'll hold us. We won't need it for long."

"I feel sick," said Thisbe.

Sky glanced at her. "We don't have to do this."

"No . . . it's okay. We need to get back. With Alex gone . . . We just need to give Artimé some good news."

Sky teared up and nodded, swallowing hard. She turned back to the raft.

When they finished the last of the knots, they brought it to the shallow part of the lake to test it near the shore. Sky climbed aboard while Thisbe and Rohan looked on, numb and silent. Thisbe stared at the volcano, which had quieted by now. Once it cooled off enough it would sink again.

There was something making a ripple in the water a long way off, and Thisbe hoped it was Issie's baby ready to guide them. But to where? If Issie had been lost for seven hundred years, that meant that she'd never been back to the water surrounding the seven islands. Or if she had returned, she'd never been discovered by any of the sea creatures there. Not by Karkinos, the giant crab island, nor the squid who lived under him. Not Issie herself, who'd been searching constantly, or Spike Furious or Pan or any of the other creatures. Despite knowing that the pirates had somehow found a way to get back and forth, Thisbe began to worry that the journey back to the seven islands through this route wasn't going to be easy.

"It's time," said Sky gently, getting off the raft and preparing to push it out to deep water. "I don't think we should wait any longer."

Thisbe sucked in a deep breath. "Okay."

Sky hugged Rohan, thanking him and saying a quick good-bye. Then she pushed the raft out a bit farther to give the two friends a chance to bid farewell. Thisbe turned, her eyes burning, and hugged Rohan good-bye. He held her tightly for a moment, his face anguished. And then they let go. "Good-bye, *pria*," Rohan whispered.

Thisbe didn't know what "pria" meant, but she was too choked up to respond. With a hard swallow she broke away and followed Sky to the raft. They began wading out with it.

Thisbe couldn't look at Rohan standing alone on the shore. She couldn't think about the sacrifices he'd be making to help the other slaves while she returned to the comforts of Artimé. Their short time together had become the most important thing in Thisbe's life, and now it was ending. Perhaps for good. The empty feeling left by that thought seemed bottomless.

When the water got too deep, Sky and Thisbe pulled themselves halfway onto the raft, leaving their legs in the water to propel them toward the center of the lake. Eventually Thisbe glanced over her shoulder, half hoping Rohan had left. But he was still standing there. He saw her turn and raised his hand to her, which made Thisbe tear up again. She waved back, then continued with her task, vowing not to look again. It was too hard.

All was going according to plan until the beastly roar of the Revinir split the sky. Immediately Thisbe felt herself losing her sight, and the images began flashing. She stopped kicking and tried to cling to the raft, but the paralyzing effects of the ancestor broth left her hands numb. She couldn't hang on.

When Sky heard the roar, she realized immediately what

LISA McMANN

was happening. Quickly she hoisted Thisbe fully onto the raft so she wouldn't slip off, then carefully climbed aboard after her. She worried over the girl, holding her and eyeing the volcano as they drew close. What would happen if Thisbe got sucked down in this state? Would she be able to hold her breath? Would she be able to steer through the tunnels? Sky didn't think so. She'd have to hang on to her and hope she recovered in time.

The snapshots and scenes of history flashed one by one in front of Thisbe. Meteors slamming into the ground, leaving huge craters. The dragons marching. Soldiers and rebels fighting in battle. The earthquake, and the world splitting and separating. The girl on the deck of the ship that went spiraling out of control. And now something new. The river. The River Taveer. Somehow connected to Maiven with the same surname.

This time, instead of just images and short scenes, Thisbe could hear sounds that went with them. The roaring of the dragons. The crack of the earth breaking. Water spurting up from where a meteor struck. Screams and shouts. The snapping of trees and the castle walls as flames engulfed them.

LISA McMANN

The struggling girl came to the forefront again, closer up. Water poured over the ship's rails, then over her. Her screams intermingled with the rush of pounding waves. Someone in the background was turned away from the girl and shouting the same thing over and over again, beckoning to someone Thisbe couldn't see.

Then the sound stopped abruptly. Thisbe gasped, the silence more horrifying than the noises. What had happened? She couldn't understand.

The images and scenes subsided. Thisbe's vision slowly returned. But echoes of the scream rang in her head, and she had no problems understanding it now. Over and over it continued with the same words. *Maiven Taveer! Maiven Taveer! Maiven Taveer!*

A Different Course

Thisbe slowly focused on Sky, who was leaning over her. There was a splash nearby—a fish, or maybe Issie's baby.

"Are you okay, Thisbe?" Sky asked, her face worried. "Can you see?"

Thisbe nodded. "I'm okay." She sat up weakly, then squinted at the volcano a short distance away. There was no doubt they'd go down with it when it plunged underwater. It could happen any moment—there was no telling for sure. Thisbe hoped she'd have at least a few minutes to recover. She flexed her hands, trying to get full feeling into her fingers again.

LISA McMANN

The scream from the images still echoed in Thisbe's ears. Where was the ship going, and what was causing it to move so out of control like that? The poor girl was chained to the deck with no shelter from the waves. Thisbe was sure someone was shouting "Maiven Taveer" before everything went silent. But what did that mean? And why did the river bear the same name as Maiven? She should have asked Rohan where the river's name had come from.

"Oh!" Thisbe said weakly, realizing Rohan would be worried about her after hearing the Revinir's roar. With effort she turned and waved her arm wide at him so he'd know she was okay.

He waved back, a tiny spot of movement on the shore. Behind him to the north the sheer mountain wall that contained the catacombs rose hundreds of feet. She scanned the skies, taking in scenery that she might never see again. Grimere was a beautiful place despite all the agony it had caused Thisbe. She felt at home here—in the cave, that is, not the catacombs.

"What's going on over there?" Sky said. She pointed to the east, where the castle lay. They couldn't quite see it from this distance, but the sky above it was charcoal.

Thisbe squinted. "Those aren't rain clouds," she said, sitting up. "That's . . ."

"Smoke," said Sky, worry in her voice.

"That's where the castle is," Thisbe told her. "Do you think the Revinir has gone there?" She thought about the Revinir being so much like a dragon now. "Has she . . . Has she set the place on fire?"

It seemed the only logical answer. Thisbe lifted herself onto her knees on the small raft and waved wildly at Rohan. "Smoke!" she yelled, and pointed toward the castle. "The castle!"

But they were too far away for him to hear her or understand her gestures. He waved back, oblivious.

"This is terrible," Thisbe said, her mind whirling. "If the Revinir, or Arabis, or her soldiers or whoever set fire to the castle, it's just . . . It's going to be a horrible tragedy. The place is absolutely *huge*." She quickly described the vast entryway and the white tigers adorned with jewels, and then she stopped abruptly as the scream from the images pierced through her again. Her eyes widened. "Oh no," she said softly as the dreadful truth came upon her. "The prisoners. So many of them!"

"What?" asked Sky. "You mean in the castle?"

Before Thisbe could answer, they felt a shiver in the water, and the calm surface rippled.

"The dungeon," Thisbe whispered, then sat up alarmed. "*Maiven Taveer.* Oh, Sky—Maiven Taveer is shackled in the dungeon of the castle along with hundreds of others!"

But Sky was looking at the surface of the water. It continued to tremble around them. "Do you feel that?" she said, gripping the raft. "That was the first warning ripple. It won't be long now. Are you ready for this?"

Thisbe stared blindly as a wave of horror washed through her. "Maiven Taveer," she muttered, thinking hard about the images. The girl being taken away. The screams. But what was the connection? Was Maiven . . . Could she possibly be someone . . . important? All Thisbe knew was that Maiven was a crucial link in finding out the history of the black-eyed people.

The water trembled again. "Thisbe, are you all right?" Sky asked anxiously. "Why do you keep saying that name?"

Thisbe turned sharply to face Sky, her expression deathly serious. "I have to go back," she said. "I have to save one of the prisoners. There's no time for me to explain—I know it sounds crazy, but I must get to the castle now. We'll have to try this next time." Thisbe jumped into the water and started paddling, pulling the raft with her.

"What? There's no time! The volcano is going down any second!"

"I have to try!"

"I'll help you, then—come on!" Sky dove off the platform, then surfaced and began pushing the raft in front of her.

"Let's ditch the raft and go for it!" cried Thisbe. "It'll be faster!"

"Oh, Thisbe—I can't. It's too far for me. There's no way I'll make it all the way to shore without the raft."

Thisbe let out a huff of frustration and swam back to help push. The two kicked with all their might, and they moved slowly toward the shore.

The surface of the water around them shivered again. "Faster!" cried Thisbe. "Are you sure we can't leave the raft behind?"

"I'm not a good enough swimmer!" Sky was already panting, and arguing about it wasn't going to make her any stronger. She could hold her breath for several minutes like the other

Artiméans, but she'd never loved the water, and she hadn't grown up swimming like Fifer and Thisbe had. Unfortunately, at this rate, they weren't going to make it. "Let go, Thisbe," said Sky. "Go ahead of me. I mean it!"

"I can't leave you behind!"

"You need to go!" Sky shouted. "Do it! It's an order! You know I'll be fine. I'll meet you back at the cave once you've saved Maiven."

Continuing to push the raft, Thisbe stared at Sky. The volcano behind them was shaking. It was starting to descend. She didn't know what to do. What if Sky didn't make it?

"DO IT!" Sky shouted in a horrible voice.

Thisbe cringed. Then she took a huge breath, dove under, and propelled herself through the water toward the shore, kicking and stroking faster than she'd ever done before, knowing that was the best way.

After a moment or two she felt the suction tugging at her, at her clothes and shoes, and she pushed onward. Could Sky withstand it too? She had to! For a long moment Thisbe struggled against the pull, sure she was making no headway. It grew stronger, and she started feeling herself being dragged

LISA McMANN

backward. A huge wave rolled over her, nearly flipping her in the water. Lungs straining, Thisbe kept going with every bit of strength she could gather until the suction began to ease. Soon she was making progress again, and when her lungs could stand it no longer, she rose to the surface, gasping for air, and whirled around. The volcano was gone.

And so was Sky.

To the Castle!

Simber sampled the air as he carried Carina, Thatcher, Lani, and Samheed to the castle. He sniffed again and stiffened. "Firrre!" he shouted as he and the team soared eastward. "Dead ahead. See the smoke? It's therrre." He pointed a claw to the east.

"Is it the castle?" Fifer asked, standing up in her hammock and hanging out over the edge. Seth and Crow peered over the edge from their knees next to her, and Kitten stayed in Crow's pocket. Behind them was Talon with Kaylee.

"It's nearrr it," said Simber, sounding unsure. He strained his eyes. "I can't tell quite yet."

"Oh, Thisbe," Fifer murmured, a terrible fear striking her. If Thisbe was in the dungeon and chained up, and if the castle was on fire, she'd die. Fifer would lose her—the most important person in her life. She couldn't bear to think about it, but she couldn't stop, either. That was a lot of ifs, and Fifer told herself to stay calm until they knew the truth about the situation. They all remained alert, trying to see where the smoke was coming from even though they knew Simber would be able to tell what was happening long before the others.

They flew in a triangle formation, soaring over the treetops. On the road to their right were hundreds of people, more in blue uniforms now, marching toward the castle at a fast pace. A group of the king's green-uniformed soldiers who'd been fighting blue soldiers in the square chased after them. The people didn't pay much attention to the flying group, and no one fired their weapons, so the Artiméans left the marchers alone too. They had more concerning things on their minds— like Thisbe and the fire and getting ahead of as many of these soldiers as possible.

After many agonizing moments, they drew close enough to the castle to see Arabis and her shiny passenger, the Revinir, flying around the front of it. "It's the drrrawbrrridge that's burrrning," Simber announced. "The Rrrevinirrr is therrre."

Fifer blew out a breath. It was a tiny bit of relief—at least it wasn't the castle in full-on flames. Yet.

"Why would she light the drawbridge on fire?" asked Carina. "Doesn't she want her soldiers to join her? They're all still coming up the road."

"I don't know," replied Simber. "It doesn't make sense. Perrrhaps she's powerrrful enough without them now, and she wants to keep the king's soldierrrs out."

"And the king inside?" mused Fifer.

"Maybe," said Simber.

"What about Thisbe?" Seth asked. "How are we going to get past the Revinir? She's going to see us trying to fly in."

"Maybe she'll be distracted by everything," Fifer said, "and we can go in from the tower like Kitten did."

"That's a lot of castle to get thrrrough," said Simber. "Besides, she'll see us no matterrr how we apprrroach. It's a rrrisk, but enterrring thrrrough the rrregularrr way is the simplest. And it's closest to the dungeon." He hesitated. "I wish we could convince Arrrabis to help us."

"And Dev," said Fifer. "Do you see him?"

"The humans on the grrround arrre too farrr away forrr me to make out."

They continued flying in tense silence. The winds shifted and began to pick up from the east over the enormous gorge, causing the smoke to blow in their direction. When the forest ended, they began to angle toward the castle, flying over the rocky land that Fifer, Seth, and Thisbe had spent days trudging over with Dev.

Then they circled around the fortress, hoping there was an off chance that the Revinir wouldn't notice them. But that hope was soon dashed when Arabis rose and the old dragon-woman began shooting fiery spears of lightning from her mouth directly at them—the same kind that had killed Alex, only thicker.

"Look out!" cried Seth, diving to the bottom of the hammock.

Fifer ducked to avoid a spear, but it knocked out two of her birds, sending them in a free fall to the ground, dead. Fifer gasped. Carina, Samheed, Seth, and Lani all retaliated with a variety of spells, including several handfuls of heart attack

LISA McMANN

components and lethal scatterclips. The components soared straight and true, pelting the dragon woman. But they all bounced off her. None of them seemed to affect her at all.

"What?" cried Seth, trying another, and Fifer joined him. Again the components bounced off, doing nothing. For a panicky moment everyone feared the worst had happened again—that whoever was mage now had been killed. Quickly Lani glanced at her wheeled device. It was unchanged—still magically engaged. As an extra precaution she tested an origami fire-breathing dragon. It lit up as it should and soared around them.

They all breathed a sigh of relief. The magic was still there—but there was something about the Revinir that repelled the effects.

Unlike in Thisbe's crypt when they'd last fired on her, the woman didn't seem surprised that the magic wasn't working on her. She laughed and sent another fiery spear at them. It slammed into Simber's side, leaving a divot and throwing him off balance, nearly tossing his riders off, but they managed to hang on. Simber veered and righted himself as the others retreated out of range.

"It's the dragon scales, I bet," Lani said as she pulled herself

LISA McMANN

solidly back onto Simber's back. "She's got so many now. She's protected from our spells like a dragon would be." She frowned. "That's really not good for us at all." The origami dragon she'd sent out circled and, not having any directive, came back to her. Lani caught it, then licked her fingers and doused the fire with a quick pinch of its mouth and made sure it was fully extinguished.

"What'll we do now?" asked Fifer, trying to direct her frightened birds after their scare. "We can't get past her. Everybody, come together! We need to figure this out."

The smoke from the burning drawbridge was growing thicker, and they could see flames licking at the entrance to the castle. Those inside, especially on the back half of the castle, would likely stay safe if someone extinguished the fire. But the Artiméans could see castle workers gathering and looking out over the balconies high above the ground. Someone threw a bucket of water at the fire from a window, but it was too little to make a difference.

As Simber, Talon, and the birds retreated down the hill and out of the Revinir's range, the dragon-woman turned her attention back to the approaching army of people. Soldiers and townspeople supporting both sides intermingled in a jumbled mass, no one quite sure what to do. Fifer looked back at the road, noting in awe the hundreds, perhaps thousands of people ascending the hill to the castle. "The fire is growing," Kaylee said worriedly. "We have to get to Thisbe before it's too late."

Simber and Talon circled around, while Fifer commanded Shimmer and the rest of the birds to ride on the wind in place so they could all talk together. Fifer, who'd been thinking hard about what to do, cringed and spoke first, not sure if her idea was a wise one. "I know you won't like this, Simber, but I say we split up. Half of us stay here and watch for the Revinir to leave her post at the main entrance. The other half should sneak around to the back of the castle and try to get in that way. There's got to be another way in, right? Like a servants' entrance or an open balcony or something."

Simber growled. "You'rrre rrright, I don't like it. But I think it's ourrr only option."

"If there's not a back opening," Seth suggested, "we'll just have to go through the top of the castle after all."

"Mewmewmew," Kitten said, muffled, from inside Crow's pocket.

"I agrrree, Kitten," said Simber. He looked at Fifer. "Kitten should be a parrrt of the firrrst team to go since she knows herrr way arrround that parrrt of the castle."

"Mewmewmew."

"Ah, okay. She says Talon and I arrre too larrrge to fit thrrrough some passageways, so we'll stay back and watch forrr a chance to get past the Rrrevinirrr." Simber's face was serious as he eyed the fire. It was his one natural enemy, but only if the flames grew hot enough. Red and orange flames like these he could survive. Blue and white? Not so much. "If we see an opening, we'rrre taking it."

"But how are we going to find Thisbe once we get to the dungeon?" Seth asked. "It's a huge maze down there."

"At this point," said Thatcher, "with everything that's going on, it probably won't do any harm to send seek spells. We just have to hope the rest of the castle doesn't catch on fire."

Several of them cast glances at the fortress. The flames were climbing up the actual doorway to the structure now. Would the Revinir put it out? Surely she wouldn't want the whole castle to burn down if she was trying to take it over.

"Who's on the first team?" asked Carina, looking at Fifer.

Fifer's eyes widened. "Um, I think the ones who've been there before should go, don't you?" she asked. "Carina and Thatcher. And Seth and me. Simber knows the way to the dungeon, so if there's an opportunity, he can take the lead with the group that stays on the ground."

"We can't all fit in the hammock, though, can we?" asked Seth.

"I can deliver one or two of you to whatever entrance you find," said Talon, "and stay nearby until you either return or make it out some other way."

"Great—that works." Fifer looked at Kaylee. "In that case, Kaylee should come with us too. She can help keep soldiers back." She eyed those remaining. "Samheed, Lani, Crow: You stay out here and be ready to go in on Simber's back the second the Revinir moves far enough away. Take down anybody in your path . . . except the black-eyed slaves, if you can help it. Stick to the nonlethal stuff on them."

They nodded, though Crow did so reluctantly.

"Okay, let's land and regroup," said Fifer.

Everyone landed so they could take their new places. Crow began searching the dirt for stones to load up his pockets for his slingshot while the rest of them reorganized and stood with their teams.

"Are we ready?" asked Fifer. Her team nodded.

"Please be carrreful," said Simber. "I . . . I can't bearrr to lose anotherrr of you."

"I know the feeling," Fifer muttered. "We'll be careful. I promise." She gave Simber a hug around the neck and a kiss on the jowl, then climbed back into the hammock with Seth and Carina. Thatcher and Kaylee went over to Talon, who picked them up and tested his wings with the heavier-than-usual load.

"Are we too much for you?" asked Thatcher.

"Not for a short distance," Talon said.

"We'll fly around back first to see if there's an obvious entrance," said Fifer, "but if we don't see anything, we're going straight to the top. We mustn't waste any time."

She emitted a sharp whistle, and the bird hammock rose and took to the sky. The bronze man followed closely behind. Simber stayed back with the others, his sharp eyes on the entrance to the castle and the scaly, fire-breathing woman who guarded it. They weren't going to get past her without some sort of fight. And there was no guarantee they would all make it out alive.

An Impossible Mission

In the crater lake, looking back toward the volcano that was no longer there, Thisbe knew her kind of magic wasn't any use in this situation. Sky and the raft were nowhere to be seen, swept down without her. And Thisbe could do nothing but tread water and panic. She could hardly catch her breath after her extensive swim away from the tug of the descending volcano. And she was still far from shore. "Sky!" she screamed when she could. "Sky!" She scanned the waves, which were still coming from the volcano's turbulent plunge. But her efforts to spot her friend were fruitless.

LISA McMANN

"Thisbe!" shouted Rohan from the shore. "What happened? Are you okay?"

Thisbe didn't have the strength to keep shouting. She waved, then took a few breaths and dove under again. She shot like a bullet through the water, everything muted. *Oh dear Sky,* she thought, like a little prayer. *Please be okay. Please make it back to Artimé.* She surfaced and flipped on her back and did the backstroke for a while.

While she swam, she thought about what had just happened. She'd made a wild, reckless decision—she knew that. And it was one that might cause rippling disasters for years to come. Would they ever find Sky? But no—Thisbe couldn't allow herself to think like that. If Sky wasn't back in the land of the seven islands soon, she'd be . . . somewhere else. Safe, no doubt. She had to be.

"Ugh," Thisbe said, and took a moment to cover her face and wipe the water from her eyes. "What have I done?" Guilt flooded her.

But the ancestor broth and the Revinir's call and the ensuing images, once a jumbled mess in Thisbe's mind, were finally becoming clear. At least a few of them were. And the one that

LISA McMANN

included Maiven Taveer's name seemed like an obvious calling to stay here and rescue the woman, if nothing else. But Thisbe had a gnawing sense of obligation to figure out what the rest of the scenes meant. Perhaps she was even more important to this land because of the images in her mind. She was a link to the history of the black-eyed people and their rule with the dragons. If she left, the young black-eyed slaves would have to figure it out alone.

And now she knew what one of the pictures meant, or she *thought* she did. The girl being taken away—was it Maiven Taveer, whose name was being shouted? Like Thisbe, Maiven was a crucial link. She didn't know why or how. All she knew was that she had to get to Maiven before the old woman died in the castle. The stakes just got much higher now that smoke was coming from it.

Finally Thisbe drew close enough to shore to reach the bottom. Rohan met her in the water and helped her slosh the rest of the way to dry land. When she could speak, she told Rohan what had happened with Sky. Then she pointed to the smoke, which was growing thicker now above the ridge.

"How long will it take us to get to the castle?" she asked, still breathing hard. "It took you fifteen hours to walk it through the catacombs, right?"

"Yes," said Rohan, still trying to comprehend what they were doing. "But there are many twists and turns underground. It's faster aboveground." He hesitated, looking at the smoke. "But still a long time. Whatever it is that's burning might be complete ash by the time we get there. And . . . it'll be dangerous for us in daylight."

"We have to try," said Thisbe. "Let's get our things and go."

She ran to the cave to grab whatever she could find—the harnesses and some dried fish were all that was worth taking with her. Rohan quickly buckled one of the sword belts around his waist. Thisbe considered taking the other sword but found it to be bulky and heavy—her magic was all the defense she needed. Perhaps she'd leave the sword here in case Sky came back and needed it.

As Thisbe turned to leave, something charcoal colored on the floor of the cave caught her eye. She stopped to pick it up and saw it was the piece of slate that Sky had kept with her, a gift from Alex. It must have fallen out of her pocket when she was scrambling to pack up so they could go.

LISA McMANN

"Now she's got absolutely nothing," Thisbe lamented. Her stomach hurt at the thought of Sky being swept through the volcano network without her. There was no way to communicate, which was the most upsetting part. But she knew that Sky wanted her to be strong. She'd ordered Thisbe to go back. That's how Sky was—unselfish and brave. She wasn't perfect. She had a stubborn streak, but that seemed to make her even more capable of survival on her own. And she'd made it just fine here. "Please be okay," Thisbe whispered, tears springing to her eyes.

Rohan came up behind her and knelt by the lake to take a long drink—they had no vessels for carrying more water with them. "Are you ready?" he asked.

Thisbe nodded, and the two set out as quickly as they could along the lake to the steep path up the mountainside that would take them to the square.

By the time they neared the top, they could hear a commotion in the square, but they couldn't see it yet. The ground had begun to vibrate. Screams and shouts rang out. Thisbe and Rohan exchanged a worried glance. What was happening?

"It must be fighting," Rohan surmised. "War has broken out at last, and we're heading into the middle of it. It isn't going to be easy to get through this."

"Is there another way around?"

"It would take days."

"Then we're going to have to go through the battle," said Thisbe, tight lipped. This was important. She could feel it. "I know it sounds reckless, but I can't explain why we need to do this. It's like the images are leading the way, telling me the clue I need to go after. If that makes sense."

"I believe you," Rohan assured her. "I'm not trying to talk you out of doing anything. I learned that lesson a long time ago. And I'm safer with you than without. Just because I have a sword doesn't mean I know how to use it."

Thisbe smiled. "With any luck you won't have to." She started climbing the few remaining feet to the top. "I'll see what things look like up there, and then we can decide our best route through this mess."

When she peered over the top and looked directly into Dragonsmarche, she grew puzzled. People were running, not fighting. And they were all running in the same direction, toward the castle.

"They're running for their lives." Thisbe glanced at Rohan, below her. "I'm not sure what's going on, but I think it's safe enough to run right along with everyone else. They seem preoccupied enough not to notice our eyes. Come on, let's go."

Rohan nodded. Thisbe pulled herself up and reached behind to help Rohan clear the summit. Then down to the square they went, turning to look at what everyone was running away from.

Both of them gasped. Just yards away was a silvery ghost dragon. Its giant clawed foot came down with an earth-shuddering stomp, and its bony tail slammed into the Dragonsmarche aquarium, smashing it to bits, sending the remaining sea monsters scattering.

Rulers Reunited

Thisbe screamed and pointed at the dragon. Sparks shot from her eyes and her fingertips. They bored deep into the ghost dragon's side but didn't seem to harm him.

Rohan ran back up the hill and struggled to take out his sword. He held it with both hands and pointed it at the dragon, but was clearly no match for the frightening beast. There were more dragons on foot behind the first, all about to pass through the square.

Several others flew overhead, their tattered wings somehow magically holding them up. One of them stopped and stared at the two. Thisbe felt her heart in her throat. Before she could attempt to fight off the beast with her magic, one of the images flashed through her mind. Silvery dragons marching to battle—just as they were lined up now. The vividness of that image was an identical match to this scene before her. The realization took her breath away. How could it be? She'd thought she'd been seeing the past. But this was happening now.

She felt a surge of energy and stopped firing at the dragons. Something about them was positive, despite how scary they seemed. The dragon stooped low and picked up Thisbe, his huge claws encircling her torso like a series of belts. She screamed as he lifted her into the air to examine her—had her intuition been off? His grasp was firm but not too tight. It felt like she was enveloped in his pillowy, ethereal grip. Thisbe began to panic, and more sparks flew from her eyes, one of them going straight up the beast's nostril. The dragon reared its head and snorted, blowing hot dragon mucus and smoke back at her.

"Help!" she cried, swiping at a glob that landed on her face. "Stop! Put me down. I . . . I promise I won't hurt you." She realized how ridiculous that sounded.

"I can't be hurt," retorted the dragon. He looked long and hard at the girl and then said more quietly, "Ah. I see you are one of us."

"I'm not a dragon!" Thisbe insisted, thinking the dragon must be stupid to think she was. "I only have a few scales. The Revinir—"

"I mean you are a descendant of the black-eyed rulers," said the dragon. "We are allies still, are we not? We've been in hiding for some time, and we're quite forgetful, but as far as I know that hasn't changed."

"Well, yes," Thisbe admitted, though it felt odd to say it. "I am."

The dragon set her on the hill. "My name is Gorgrun, and I am one of the leaders of the ghost dragons. I wasn't sure if there were any humans like you left. Though Arabis spoke of them."

"Arabis? You know her?" Thisbe backed away quickly, glancing around for Rohan. She extended her hands toward the dragon, ready to fire spells whether they hurt the beast or not. But Gorgrun didn't come after her again.

Rohan sidestepped over and stood next to Thisbe. With

shaking hands, he put down his sword. "These are the ghost dragons I was telling you about," he said in awe. "Rulers of this land. I've studied them. My mother once told me they lived in the cavelands. Waiting."

"Waiting for what?" whispered Thisbe, looking sideways at Rohan.

"Waiting for the reckoning," interrupted the dragon. "Waiting for the call, I suppose. I can't remember."

"The call?" Thisbe exclaimed fearfully. "You mean the call from the Revinir? Are you drawn to her too? Is that why you're traveling this way? Because you're compelled to follow when she roars?"

The dragon seemed confused. "When she roars?" he asked. "No. It isn't she who calls us. We've heard the Revinir's roar, but she doesn't control us. We heed the silent inner call of something greater. Something we've been waiting many years for."

"Something greater?" asked Thisbe, puzzled. She still didn't know whether it was safe to trust these dragons or not, despite Rohan's willingness to do so.

"Oh, yes." The dragon nodded thoughtfully. "I remember clearly now. We are heeding a different call. It's something that's coming from inside . . . you." He looked sharply at Thisbe.

Rohan did too. "What?" he whispered.

"Me?" Thisbe blinked. "That's ridiculous." But almost as if she'd called it up, the image of the ghost dragons on the run flashed in her mind again, making the statement seem less crazy.

It was still confusing. Could that image really have been a scene from the past if it had just been replicated before her eyes? Or had it somehow been an image . . . of the future? She was growing more puzzled than ever.

"Yes, it's you," said Gorgrun with certainty. "The call is centered inside you."

"I don't know how this could be happening," said Thisbe. Perhaps the bone broths had had even more mysterious effects on Thisbe than she'd realized. Suddenly she turned sharply toward the castle and remembered the smoke, and Maiven Taveer and her desperate need. They were still many hours away on foot.

She stared up at Gorgrun, fearful but also in awe, studying

his ghostlike body. "I'm not sure what's going on here," she said to the dragon as an idea grew in her mind. "But if you're responding to an inner call coming from me, and you're seeking to help in some way, Rohan and I could definitely use it." She hesitated, then asked, "Can you possibly take us to the castle? We're in a bit of a hurry."

Chasing Fire

What's happening out here?" Thisbe asked Gorgrun from atop his back. His strange body was almost cloudlike to the touch, and she sank into it. It felt good to rest. Rohan sat beside her, eyes wide. While Thisbe had ridden on dragons before, this moment was surreal for Rohan. Never in his wildest dreams had he imagined this scene. He'd rarely even seen a live dragon, much less gotten close enough to touch one.

Despite the moth-eaten-like holes in his wings, Gorgrun took flight and soared just above the heads of all the people running for their lives. It seemed like the dragons barely noticed the disturbance they were creating, or perhaps they didn't care.

"I am called Gorgrun," said the dragon.

Thisbe and Rohan exchanged a look. "We know," Thisbe said. "You already told us."

"Ah yes. I forgot. As I may have mentioned—"

"You're very forgetful," said Rohan. "That's all right. We understand. You've lived a very long time."

"Indeed."

"My name is Thisbe Stowe," said Thisbe. "This is my friend Rohan."

"Thank you," said the dragon. "Thisbe. That sounds familiar."

"I can't imagine why," said Thisbe. They fell into silence and watched the world go by. As they passed the path into the forest that would take them to Alex's grave, Thisbe glanced down it. A pang went through her. But they flew quickly past it.

"Thisbe," Gorgrun said again in a very deep voice, testing out the word, as if that might jog his memory.

Thisbe and Rohan exchanged a glance. In better times they might have started laughing.

Presently Gorgrun asked, "Do you know the orange dragon called Arabis? I haven't seen her in some time."

"Yes, I do!" said Thisbe, sitting forward. "You mentioned her before too. She is a friend of the people in my land. Or, at least, she used to be, before she joined up with the Revinir. How do you know her?"

Gorgrun didn't appear to hear Thisbe. "Arabis the orange warned us of the Revinir's recent actions and her plans to take over the land of the dragons. We ghost dragons have been waiting many years for this. When we felt your call, Thisbe, we knew it was time to fight. If we can restore the throne to Arabis and to you, we will have fulfilled our purpose, and we can go home to die."

"Whoa," said Thisbe quietly to Rohan. "That's a lot to take in." To Gorgrun she said, "I'm not sure I'm the right person for that, but the black-eyed people of this land would definitely do a better job than the current rulers."

"And Arabis," said Gorgrun.

"Of course," said Thisbe tepidly. "But she's being controlled by the Revinir at the moment."

Rohan leaned forward. "Yes, Gorgrun. Arabis is fighting for her now."

That didn't seem to matter to the dragon.

"I don't fully understand why Arabis joined her," Thisbe added. "But I can guess she is responding to the same urge I have whenever the Revinir roars. But Arabis doesn't have the power of the ancestors to fight it like I have."

Again Gorgrun remained silent. His two riders glanced at each other and shrugged.

"Perhaps I should drink the broth you gave me," said Rohan. "So I can see the images too."

"I'm not sure it's a good idea for both of us to be blinded by these images at the same time," Thisbe pointed out.

Rohan looked pained. "Good thought. We'd be useless together. I suppose I'll wait until you're gone. Though . . . I wouldn't want to experience the effects alone. That could put me in danger. Hmm."

Thisbe glanced sidelong at him. "Since you haven't taken in the dragon-bone broth," she pointed out, "it might not affect you in the same way."

"I don't really want to risk finding out," said Rohan.

Thisbe held his gaze, and they shared a grin. Even in the most stressful times, the two of them seemed to find a way to calm each other. "There's something weird about these images," she said. Then she told him how she'd thought they were all part of the history of Grimere until the ghost dragon scene unfolded before her eyes. "I can't tell if I'm seeing visions of the past or of the future."

It all seemed very puzzling to Rohan as well. "Time will tell, I suppose," he said. He pulled the bottle of broth from his pocket and studied it, but didn't drink it. "Are the ancestors telling their stories? Or ours?"

It was a mystery.

The miles flew by, and soon the castle and the burning drawbridge were in sight, bringing to Thisbe's mind another of the scenes. A stream of people stretched along the length of the road—thousands of them—and the rest of the ghost dragons rose into the air now to keep from trampling them. They all looked up in fright when the giant shadows passed over them. Many dove for cover in the forest until the dragons passed. No one on the ground seemed to notice the two humans riding along, as they were mostly hidden from the view of onlookers.

"The smoke is getting thicker," said Rohan, sounding worried. "And the wind is picking up."

Thisbe knew that meant the fire could be growing worse. Were they too late? As they got closer, she sat up and strained to see what else was going on. "Is that Arabis?" she asked, pointing. "Right in front?"

"I think so. I hope the smoke isn't hurting her."

"Even though she's working for the Revinir, I suppose we don't want her to be hurt. She'll come back to our side eventually, won't she? She *has* to." After all Thisbe, Fifer, and Seth had sacrificed to free Arabis and her siblings, it was hard to imagine that they would turn on them permanently.

"I don't know," said Rohan. "I'm not sure what has to happen to break the Revinir's spell. Perhaps . . . Perhaps she has to die for it to be broken."

Thisbe tapped on the ghost dragon's back. "Excuse me, please, Gorgrun, but will you be attacking the Revinir? Is that what your mission is?"

"Our mission is to serve your most pressing needs until the day comes when we are allowed to die."

"What if I need you to kill the Revinir?"

Gorgrun was silent for a while. Then he said, "It is not for our generation to defeat this generation's evil. We wish only to fulfill our duties until we are allowed to die. We can come to your aid, but we cannot defeat the ruler—that is something your people and the young dragons must do."

"Oh." Thisbe nodded and was silent, thinking that through as they drew closer to the castle. "Well, that stinks." The only young dragon here was Arabis, and she was against them.

The two passengers watched the fire and smoke and urged Gorgrun to go faster if he could. "I hope the smoke isn't getting inside the castle too much," Thisbe said, concern growing by the minute for Maiven. "The prisoners don't stand a chance chained in the dungeon."

"I'm worried too," said Rohan. "For us. We have to go down there."

"You can stay back if you like," said Thisbe.

"Please," Rohan said as if she'd offended him. "And miss this excitement? Besides, I want to see inside this grand castle, which is supposed to belong to our people." He looked down

LISA McMANN

at his ragged clothing and gave a sharp, sarcastic laugh. It was too hard to imagine after the life he'd been dealt.

Finally the spectacular line of ghost dragons curved to the north of the castle. Thisbe strained, trying to get a better view of it that wasn't obscured by smoke. "Look," said Thisbe with an air of relief. She pointed. "It's mostly the drawbridge that's burning, though the entryway is scorched too. Not too much of the castle has caught yet. I think there's hope."

"Is that the Revinir there with Arabis?" Rohan peered over Thisbe's shoulder as the dragon tilted into the turn. Arabis moved to the air above the moat.

"I saw a flash of light when she turned," said Thisbe. Through the smoke she could make out the Revinir on Arabis's back. "Yes, she's there." Thisbe leaned forward to speak to the dragon again. "Gorgrun, can your friends cause some commotion so you can drop us on the side of the castle without anyone noticing? I know a spot where we can sneak into the dungeon. There's a window in the section where the dragons used to be kept."

The ancient dragon roared with pleasure, sending forth a blast of fire. He was clearly delighted with the suggestion after so many years of aimlessly roaming the cavelands. "Yes, of course," said Gorgrun. He spoke to the others nearby, and they formed a plan. The other ghost dragons also seemed to be on the verge of celebration over the prospect of causing a ruckus. Thisbe wondered how long it had been for them since they'd ventured out of hiding and done anything dragonlike.

"I don't know what we'd have done without you," Thisbe said. "Thank you. Will you help us escape again if we need you?"

"If we remember," promised Gorgrun. "But if we forget and leave, you can just call us back. However you were doing it before."

"I'm not sure how I called you in the first place," Thisbe admitted. The situation was a bit unsettling to Thisbe and Rohan, but it would have to suffice.

They reached the castle. The other dragons began circling above the Revinir, too high for her lightning spears to reach them, not that it would matter if she fired at the ghostly beings. But she seemed excited to see them and tried to fly up and welcome them. They circled her and Arabis in random patterns, accidentally slamming into the castle and sending blocks flying or dipping too low to the ground and sending the troops of soldiers running for their lives.

As they distracted the Revinir, Gorgrun went to the north side of the castle and dropped low, then touched down just long enough for Thisbe and Rohan to slide through a battered hole in his wing to the ground.

With a silent wave, Thisbe and Rohan ran toward the castle. Gorgrun flew off to join the other ghost dragons in the commotion making. Scaring the green-uniformed soldiers sounded especially satisfying to him.

LISA McMANN

The Quest for Maiven

While Fifer and her team were flying around the back of the castle looking for an opening large enough for them to sneak into, and the silvery dragons were wreaking havoc with the Revinir and the soldiers near the front of the castle, Thisbe and Rohan set off for a particular dungeon window. It was in the dragon stables area, which Thisbe remembered having seen the last time she was down there, before she'd been captured and put in a cell.

They soon reached it and peered through the pane, over-looking several soldiers who were glancing around uneasily as a layer of smoke hung at the ceiling above their heads.

Thisbe silently removed the glass with a spell. Then she and Rohan crouched low and slid through the window. One after the other they dropped several feet to the floor below. Green-uniformed soldiers whirled around at the sound and charged at them, weapons drawn.

But Thisbe was ready. Feeling her dragon scales standing up on her arms and legs, she fired sparks from her eyes and from her fingertips, taking down the first two with one move. A thin curl of smoke rose from her nostrils, unnoticed. "Stay behind me!" she told Rohan.

Rohan pulled out his sword as Thisbe went after the next two soldiers, using her magic.

She knocked them flat as well. By the time the third duo of soldiers came upon the scene and saw the others piled on the floor, they backpedaled, wide-eyed and fearful. Thisbe quickly sent glass spells behind them so they slammed backward into them, then she neatly boxed them into a small space with more glass walls. "We don't need them running off and telling any-one we're here," Thisbe muttered.

"Good move, Thisbe," said Rohan, relieved once again not

to have to use the unfamiliar sword. He peered around her, seeing all the soldiers rendered motionless. Thisbe pressed forward, going past the five giant dragon stables. She could smell smoke. As they went past the wide ramp that led up to the entryway of the castle, they could hear some significant commotion happening.

"The ghost dragons have come to destroy us!" cried one.

"The fire'll get us first!" someone else yelled. "We need water! Hurry!"

A third shouted, "The Revinir is threatening to set the whole place ablaze if we don't produce the king!"

"Where is he? Who's got him?" called out the first.

Thisbe and Rohan exchanged a glance. It sounded disastrous. Had they somehow lost the king in his own castle? Or did they just not know where he was or who was in charge of handling him? And were all these servants and soldiers trapped, unable to escape?

"Unless they can swim across the moat, I think they're all stuck here," Thisbe whispered.

"How are *we* going to get out of here?" Rohan muttered,

glancing back at the window that was too high for them to reach.

"We'll worry about that later." Thisbe continued past the ramp to the narrow dungeon corridor that led to the prisoner cells. The dank, musty smells immediately brought Thisbe back to when she'd been imprisoned here, chained to the wall and sitting in a small stream of cold water inside Maiven Taveer's cell. Only now there was smoke as well. They crouched as they moved along.

The walls of the corridor had large, distinct gouges carved along them that looked fresh—they were a lighter color than the rest of the grimy wall. Thisbe wondered what had caused them. She hadn't remembered it being like this the last time she was dragged down here.

Thinking back, she knew for sure that Thatcher had escaped since she'd seen him on Simber's back when they'd crashed into the glass and injured Fifer. But Carina hadn't been there. Was she still imprisoned down here somewhere? Maybe that was how Alex had died—coming to save her.

Thisbe frowned. The constant speculation about the people of Artimé and their whereabouts only made her upset. Aaron had sent her a seek spell ages ago, but even he hadn't shown up or continued to send them. She'd been abandoned. There was no other way to see it.

"Do you know where you're going?" asked Rohan, interrupting her thoughts. He followed close behind as they went past cell after cell. The prisoners were beginning to shout and call for help.

Thisbe saw a guard far ahead coming toward them at a brisk pace. She shot the woman with sparks, knocking her flat, then answered, "I'm pretty sure I know the way. It's a maze, though, and we've got a long way to go."

"The smoke is getting thicker," said Rohan. "The prisoners are realizing what's happening outside with the fire. They're starting to panic. Is there anything we can we do for them?" He stopped short of suggesting they should try to free them all. They both knew that would be impossible.

"Once we get Maiven out, we'll try to help more of them," Thisbe said.

Just then a guard stepped out from a cell in front of Thisbe, his sword raised. He pressed the flat side against Thisbe's chest and stopped her. Thisbe didn't have time to react, and in a few swift moves, she and Rohan were side by side, backs against the wall and a blade at their throats. Rohan's sword dropped to the floor.

"Who are you?" the soldier demanded. "What are you doing down here?"

"We're . . . we're new servants," said Rohan, thinking fast. "Coming to tell you—all the soldiers, I mean—to flee. The castle is on fire! You need to get the other guards and escape now, before it's too late!"

Thisbe closed her eyes to hold back her sparks—if they could fool the guards rather than injure them, all the better. She still didn't like hurting people if she didn't have to. Though it was getting easier.

The soldier seemed suspicious of the story, but there was no doubt that smoke was in the air, even if he couldn't see it in the poor lighting. "Why did they send you and not the other soldiers?" the man asked.

"Because the other soldiers have already escaped and left you to die," said Rohan, his voice dead calm. "But we knew there had to be some of you down here. You should go tell the others. We'll help you. The Revinir is taking over the castle. She's burning everything."

LISA McMANN

The soldier seemed angry that his comrades had left him and the others who roamed the dark smelly passageways to die. He coughed from the smoke, then lowered his sword. "Cowards," he said. "We have families too!" Thisbe and Rohan weren't sure if he was talking about them or the other soldiers, but it didn't matter The soldier turned and started running deeper into the dungeon, shouting at the other guards to get out, essentially clearing the way for Thisbe and Rohan to find Maiven faster.

"That was really smart," said Thisbe.

"Thanks," said Rohan, picking up his sword and following her.

"I was about to strike him down." Remembering what he'd said about having a family, Thisbe added, "I'm glad I didn't have to." She thought again about how it was getting easier to hurt people, and her mind flashed to the Revinir saying she was more evil than good. She frowned and pushed on.

The soldier sped out of sight, though the two could still hear his voice ringing out for a few moments. But eventually that sound was drowned out by the hysterics of the other prisoners.

Thisbe went faster. "Come on!" She felt a new burst of energy even as the smoke grew thicker. She looked out one of the high windows and saw flames. "We're directly below the castle entrance now." As they twisted and turned, Thisbe began to fear she was getting horribly lost. But she kept her eye on the wall. "If we stay along this path, we can find our way back out because of this," she said, running her hand along the indent. When her fingertips touched the grooves, the image of the girl being taken away by soldiers flashed in front of her eyes. "Whoa," she said, pulling her hand away. She explained to Rohan what had happened. "That was strange. I think . . . I hope that means we're on the right track." She put her hand back on the wall, but nothing happened until she started moving forward. Then the image flashed again.

"We must be doing something right," Thisbe said, excitement growing. Perhaps all was not lost in this seemingly impossible quest. But the air quality was getting worse.

Rohan was bending down farther now to keep his head out of the smoke. Thisbe did too, and they ran as fast as they could down the passageway. Every few moments Thisbe touched the wall to confirm they were still making progress.

Soon they came to an area where the smoke was significantly thicker. Thisbe looked around, trying to figure out where it was coming from, and saw that one of the windows near them, at the ceiling, was missing its glass. Smoke poured in through it.

"That's the window I broke," Thisbe said, her eyes stinging. She pulled her shirt up to her face to cover it. "We're getting close." She cast a glass spell in front of the window to seal it, hoping to slow the smoke's progress, and continued.

When the grooves on the wall stopped, so did Thisbe. She peered into the cell across from the grooves' end. Could the grooves possibly lead her directly to the woman she sought?

"Maiven?" she called. She darted inside, but the chains hung loose on the walls. The cell was empty. "Maiven!" she yelled at the top of her voice. Her throat was aching, and she started coughing. Where was Maiven? Had the ancestor broth led her on a wild-goose chase? Why wasn't she here? She turned to Rohan, a heartbreaking look on her face, but he wasn't behind her. He'd vanished.

"Rohan!" Thisbe yelled. "Where are you?" Coughing, she ran back into the hallway and saw him sprawled on the floor in front of the next cell. He wasn't moving.

Thisbe ran to Rohan and knelt next to him. His eyes were closed. Before she could gather her wits and figure out how to revive him and get him out of here, she heard the faintest of cries somehow ascending all the others. "Thisbe Stowe! Is it you? I'm here!"

Fifer Connects

Finally, after scouring every curve and corner of every floor in the massive castle's exterior, Fifer and her team, made up of Seth, Carina, Thatcher, and Kaylee, found a safe way in through a set of balcony doors on an upper floor. Talon and the birds took off, vowing to stay in close range despite the ghost dragons circling the place.

Fifer knew there was no time to look around and marvel at the richness of the decor. "Downstairs!" she shouted. They ran for the nearest staircase and wound themselves down. As they did so, palace servants and soldiers tried to stop them. But Fifer and the others were prepared. They fired off rounds of scatterclips, sending the palace workers flying through the air and stacking up until they hit a wall, leaving them dangling.

The smoke wasn't bad here at the back of the castle. But as they reached the main floor and had to run toward the grand entryway, it thickened noticeably. People down here were running around in a panic, frightened and unable to go out the main entrance because of the flames and the smoke pouring in. Shanti's twin white tigers, adorned with jewels, tugged restlessly at their chains.

"There's no escape this way!" some of the panicked workers and soldiers cried out. "Up to the ballroom," shouted someone else. "The air is clear up there!" They dashed up the staircase that Fifer and the others had just come down.

"This way!" Fifer said, with Seth right behind. She led the team across the vast, open main floor, giving the tigers a wide berth and dodging those who were fleeing. They dashed toward the familiar sloped hallway that led to the dungeon.

Behind them shouts rose up. "The king!" screamed someone. "Help! The Revinir's soldiers are coming to capture him!"

Fifer turned wildly and saw the disheveled king, robes flying as he raced up the stairs with the others, trying to get away

LISA McMANN

from a dozen blue-uniformed soldiers who had somehow just entered the palace. She saw a flash of orange.

"It's the black-eyed slaves!" Fifer said, holding everyone back until the young soldiers passed. "Arabis must have brought them across the moat."

"And they've got dragon properties," said Seth as they dodged the soldiers and headed down the wide, sloping hallway. "I wonder if the fire and smoke doesn't get to them like it would for us."

"I'm just glad the king caused a distraction for us. Let's go!"

They curved down and around and reached the bottom of the ramp, near where the dragons had been captive. "This . . . brings back . . . the most terrible memories," said Seth between gasps for air. The smoke wasn't as bad down here as it was at the entrance, but it was thickening.

Kaylee spied a pump that had provided water for the dragons and prisoners. "Douse yourselves, everyone," she said. "In case we have to go near flames."

"And cover your faces," said Thatcher. They quickly splashed water on their hair and clothing to keep it from burning, then pulled their shirts up to protect their noses and mouths.

LISA McMANN

As they did so, Fifer turned to Carina and Thatcher. "Any ideas?"

"I think we just go in and start calling for her," said Thatcher.

Carina nodded. "Many of the empty cells are closer to the heart of the dungeon, so that's probably where they put new people. That's where they put us, and Thisbe was right next door."

Fifer nodded. "So it makes sense to head in the way you came out last time?"

Carina nodded.

"Lead the way," said Fifer.

Carina and Thatcher rounded the corner to the dungeon hallway and came to an abrupt stop. Fifer, Seth, and Kaylee slammed into them. In front of them was a line of prison guards running straight for them.

"Look out!" said Thatcher. He and Carina shoved the others out of the way, and they took cover, ready to send off a multitude of spell components as the guards reached them, but Carina held up her hand to stop them. "They're escaping. We don't need to hurt anyone."

Fifer nodded, happy that Carina had made the call and hadn't looked to her to decide. It was a relief not having to make such quick decisions for once.

Soon the guards were rushing up the ramp, leaving the Artiméans free to enter the dungeon unhindered. Except, of course, by the threat of a raging fire creeping ever closer, just outside the prison cell walls.

Too Little, Too Late

A seek spell flew straight to Thisbe, but she didn't see it in the smoke and panic of the moment. She turned sharply. "Maiven Taveer!" Thisbe's voice rasped as the spell exploded behind her. She left Rohan's side and rushed into the hallway and listened, hearing the woman calling again. Seeing a figure in the smoky shadows of the cell next door, she went in. "You're here! Are you okay?" She peered at the woman.

Maiven was holding her tattered shirt over her face, and Thisbe could see that it was dripping water. The woman nodded, then pointed to Rohan's still figure, barely visible in the

LISA McMANN

hallway. "Is that your friend?" she asked, her voice muffled by the fabric.

"Yes! The smoke was too much for him. What should I do?"

"Is he breathing?" said Maiven.

"Yes. Thank the gods."

"Good." Maiven mimicked dipping her shirt into the water that ran along the floor. "Roll around on the floor," she said, pulling the cloth off her face. "Take his shirt off and rip it into strips, then wet them and tie one around your face. Do the same for him and drag him in here. Lay him down so that his nose and mouth are near the opening at the floor where the water runs through."

Thisbe did what Maiven said, pulling Rohan inside the cell and facing him toward the opening at the spot where the floor met the wall. Then she crawled over to Maiven and examined the iron shackles around her wrists and ankles.

"Oh no." Her heart pounded—in their hurry to get here, she hadn't thought about *how* she was going to free Maiven. "I'm going to try my magic to break these, okay? Don't be afraid if you see sparks."

"I'm not afraid, child," said Maiven.

Thisbe stood back as far as she could so that she'd have the best chance of accuracy. Then she pointed at the top of the chains where they hooked into the wall and thought about how much she hated the Revinir. Her blood began to boil, and a wisp of smoke trickled from her nose, though, again, it was hard to tell that from the rest of the smoke in the area. Sparks shot out from her fingers and eyes. They slammed into the metal and ricocheted off. One of them hit Thisbe in the cheek before she could duck, leaving a blistering burn. She swore under her breath. She lifted her wet cloth to cool it as she ran over to the chains, expecting them to have split. But they remained intact.

Panic welled up. She tried again, shielding her face this time, with similar results. Thisbe hadn't planned for this problem—her sparks were powerful enough to kill a person. Why couldn't they break these old chains?

She tried a third time with no success. As the smoke descended, she was forced to stay low, and she utilized her breathing techniques to hold her breath for as long as possible. "It's not working," Thisbe said, panicked. Images flashed

LISA McMANN

before her. A castle on fire. Rogue bandits sneaking in. And the girl being taken away, chained to the ship's deck. Someone screaming Maiven's name. "I don't know what to do."

"Go, Thisbe," said Maiven. "Get out of here. You must! Save your friend if you can."

"I won't go!" said Thisbe, dropping to all fours and coughing for several seconds. "I can't. I'm supposed to be here. I have to save you! I can't explain it now. I just . . ." She wiped her eyes and looked around anxiously, and then remembered the guards. "I'm going to go find keys! I'll be back." She hurried out of the cell on her hands and knees, the wet strip of Rohan's shirt tied around her face.

She crawled through the dungeon. The screams and shouts from the prisoners inside were growing fainter, and the coughing was increasing. Some of them were bound to be unconscious soon. Thisbe cringed, heartsick, knowing what they were going through but helpless to do anything. And the thought of Rohan unconscious—she had to get him out of here. But the images that flashed before her eyes were spurring her on. She could hardly control her actions.

Soon her hands and knees were sore and bloody, and she

hadn't yet found a single soldier—they'd all escaped by now, no doubt. She didn't know what she was going to do, besides go all the way back to where she'd encased some of them in glass. Hopefully those spells hadn't worn off.

The farther she went, the more smoke there was. Heat filled the dungeon. Surely by now the grand castle entryway above her was in flames too. This couldn't all be coming from the drawbridge. Why the Revinir would burn up this incredible structure and everyone in it was beyond Thisbe's comprehension of evil—and it seemed like such a waste, too. And now she was beginning to doubt if *she* was going to make it out alive, much less Rohan and Maiven Taveer.

Finding no one, Thisbe finally gave up and turned back toward the cell, desperate, deciding to try her magic one more time. There was no other way to succeed. She'd just have to try harder. If she didn't, they'd all die.

Her mind was fuzzy with lack of oxygen. Coughing and choking, she crawled as fast as she could, ignoring the pain from her shredded knees. When she finally neared the cell, she heard a commotion. People running. Her heart leaped—had some of the guards come back to help the prisoners? Thisbe scrambled to her feet and started running, staying low. Her throat ached, and she couldn't stop coughing. She held her fingers pointed in front of her, ready to take down a guard and steal their keys if necessary.

Her eyesight dimmed, and she dropped to her hands and knees again. Then she saw the silhouettes of several people through the haze. She crept toward them, waving smoke away and trying to get their attention before she passed out. "Help," she whispered. Her lungs and throat burned, and she began to regret everything she'd done over the past several hours— leaving Sky and coming here, running into a burning castle. It had been a series of grave mistakes, and now Rohan's life was on the line as well as her own.

Her limbs grew weak, and she stopped to cough, placing her cheek on the stone floor for the best chance of a clean breath of air. As she did so, the Revinir's mighty roar could be heard echoing through the dungeon. On cue the series of images pummeled Thisbe, beginning to paralyze her. She felt like she was melting into the floor. Her life was slipping away.

But through some incredible unknown force, the image of the girl urged her onward. Blindly she continued, trying to feel the edges of the passageway with numb fingers. She could no longer afford to expend a single breath begging for help, and no one could hear her anyway. She just continued, hoping the soldiers would still be there when she arrived. Hoping they'd at least save Maiven and Rohan, if not her.

As the temperature rose, she could hear windows exploding all around her, one after another, and after a few moments, a hint of a breeze swept over her, but it wasn't enough. When at last she reached Maiven's cell, she collapsed in the doorway at the feet of one of the soldiers, knocking into him.

Thisbe's eyes closed, and she thought about how Alex had died, and now she was dying too. Poor Fifer would lose her twin like Aaron had lost his. It was a travesty. As she grew faint, she didn't notice that the soldier she'd fallen upon wasn't wearing a uniform or combat boots. This soldier wore the handcrafted shoes of an Artiméan mage. The exact shoes that Thisbe was wearing. In the exact size. "Fifer." She groaned. "I'm sorry."

The groan reverberated through Thisbe's twin. It felt like a jolt of energy. Like a connection stronger than anything Fifer had ever felt before. She turned to see the outline of the crumpled girl through the thickening smoke. "It's Thisbe!"

Fifer cried, dropping to the floor. "Thisbe!" Fifer screamed. "Wake up!"

Delirious, imagining she was dreaming that Fifer was really there, Thisbe coughed and pleaded, "Save . . . Rohan." It was the very best she could do.

In the whirling of Thisbe's fading consciousness, she thought could hear Carina's voice. "Dissipate," the woman said. Four times she said it.

Maiven Taveer was free.

Captive in the Smoke

L et's get her out of here!" Fifer cried. How much longer would Thisbe survive the smoke? She and Seth each hooked Thisbe under the arms and dragged her into the passageway.

"Magic carpet!" said Seth. He pulled out a magic carpet component, and Fifer did the same. They both cast the spells, and Seth helped Fifer lift Thisbe onto one of the carpets. Fifer got on it with her and commanded it to stay low and go. Seth got on the other and followed.

Behind them, Thatcher hoisted Rohan up over his shoulder, and Kaylee and Carina carried Maiven Taveer into the passageway. They did as the others had done, saving their breath and using the magic carpet spells for as long as they would carry them. When the spells eventually ran out and everyone coasted to the floor, they cast more and did it again, all the way out to the area where the dragon stables had been.

The place was deserted. The glass cages Thisbe had cast on her way in had faded, and the four soldiers were gone as well. The smoke was less intense here, but still lethal. "Where now?" Seth asked Fifer, lowering his shirt to speak.

"Up the ramp. Hurry!" said Fifer, heading that way with Thisbe, who was still unconscious.

"But the entry is on fire!" said Seth. "We can't get out that way."

"We'll keep going up then, to where we came in."

"I only have a couple of magic carpet spells left. Do you want to call the birds in to help?"

"Not yet. I'm worried they'll die in here with their tiny lungs. They can't hold their breath like we can." Fifer coughed violently and readjusted her shirt to cover her face better.

Seth nodded and lifted his shirt over his face too. He followed Fifer, glancing behind him and seeing that Thatcher was coming with the strange boy. Seth pointed out their route up the stairs, and Thatcher signaled back that he understood. Fresh air was crucial—they could always get help down to the ground from Talon and the birds if they ran out of components.

On the magic carpets they zipped quickly through the castle, Fifer leading them back the way they'd come. The smoke was noticeably less heavy the farther toward the back of the castle they went.

Another loud roar came from the Revinir outside, shaking all the chandeliers and making them rattle. Thisbe shuddered and convulsed, never opening her eyes.

Fifer worried over her sister as she navigated their way to the balcony exit. Thisbe was moving—did that mean she was breathing? It was hard for Fifer to keep an eye on her when they were dodging people and furniture and other castle-y things. Then the magic carpet they were riding on began to fade—it would be gone soon. "Let's stop for a minute!" she called back to the others.

They glided into a huge sitting room with high ceilings and only a little smoke, and ignored the dozens of servants and soldiers who had found temporary respite there as well. If the fire didn't get put out, these people would be stuck far above the ground with no way to escape except to continue upstairs to the ballroom and hope for the best from there . . . or succumb to the smoke. Seth immediately went to one of the vast windows and whispered a few words, and the glass disappeared, letting in a huge blast of air.

The palace workers eyed him warily but were grateful for the fresh breeze. Some of them looked out the window, judging the distance to the moat below, and moved away again. It was too far.

Fifer's carpet vanished. She pulled Thisbe to a lying position on the floor and tried resuscitating her, like Henry had taught them. Thatcher arrived with Rohan, and Carina and Kaylee came with Maiven, who hadn't lost consciousness. Carina helped Fifer, and Kaylee worked on Rohan while Thatcher dashed up the stairs alone without explanation.

Soon Thisbe was coughing and breathing better. Finally she opened her eyes and blinked a few times. She was disoriented, and she couldn't believe what she was seeing. Seth and Fifer? Were these new scenes from the ancestor broth, only of familiar people this time? Or were they real? She reached out to Fifer and touched her cheek. "Fifer!" she croaked. "Seth!" Tears soothed her burning eyes. She struggled to sit up.

"Shh," said Fifer, hugging her tight and starting to cry. "Don't try to speak."

"But—" She coughed harshly, then tried again. "Where's Rohan? And Maiven?"

"We've got them," said Seth. He pointed to the unconscious boy and the elderly woman. "That's who you mean, right?"

Thisbe had never seen Maiven in the light before. She was hardly able to take it all in, but she felt fear welling up inside her when her eyes landed on her friend. "Is Rohan okay?"

"He will be," Seth assured her. "Kaylee's working on him."

Overwhelmed, Thisbe nodded and sank against the wall in relief. Fifer pulled her canteen out of her rucksack and handed it to her twin. Thisbe drank greedily.

A few moments later Rohan was awake too, and Maiven, who'd survived an entire lifetime in the damp dungeon, was gingerly sitting up, giving the others their first real look at the old woman.

Her hair was starkly white, and she wore it in a loose, tangled braid. Her face was light brown with a gray tinge and bore a few deep wrinkles. Thisbe caught her eye and smiled, feeling suddenly self-conscious to see Maiven so clearly. The woman, squinting from the brightness, smiled back and nodded once, studying the girl as thoroughly as Thisbe was studying her. They would have time to talk later. Now they needed to get out of here alive.

Thatcher returned to the group, out of breath.

"Are we ready?" asked Seth, glancing around anxiously. A few soldiers recovering nearby continued watching them suspiciously. "These people aren't exactly our friends, you know. I don't want anybody trying to stop us. I think that guy recognizes us."

"Yeah," said Fifer, "but we saved the king once, remember? I think that's why they're not sure what to do." She glanced at the window. "Should we try to summon Talon and the birds to the open window or go up to the ballroom?"

Thatcher shook his head. "Too many people in here and not enough room for the birds to get in and out with the hammock. While you were resuscitating these two, I ran up to the ballroom. Unfortunately, it's packed up there as well. Soldiers and servants everywhere. They've gathered by the balcony to get some fresh air and hope for rescue. But the ghost dragons are circling and

LISA McMANN

breathing fire and bumping up against the castle. They keep diving at the people on the balcony and scaring them back inside. It's pretty chaotic." Just then the castle shook. Thisbe cringed, but the roar didn't come. The movement stopped.

"Let's get to the towers, then," said Carina. "Kitten can guide us. We'll have Fifer call the birds once we're up there, and she can send some of them to alert Talon to where we are."

"Birds?" croaked Thisbe in alarm. "What birds?"

Carina glanced over and saw Thisbe attempting to get up. She went quickly over to her and hugged the girl tightly. "I'm so glad you're okay. How are you, precious girl?"

Thisbe felt terrible physically, but she was thrilled to be alive. "I'm really glad to see you," she said. Her eyes burned with more tears. "You . . . came for me. After all."

Before anyone could explain anything, shouts rang out in the hallways leading to the sitting room. Everyone turned to see a line of the Revinir's glazed-eyed young soldiers marching in, carrying weapons and breathing smoke. The Artiméans whirled around, prepared to escape or fight. Then Fifer, Seth, Rohan, and Thisbe all gasped at the same time. The last soldier in the lineup was Dev.

Thisbe's scales rose on her arms and legs, and her stomach flipped in shock and fear. *What is he doing wearing a blue uniform? Working for the Revinir?* "Dev," she said weakly. She and Dev had been through so much together. She thought she'd finally understood him, at least a little. But the last thing Thisbe and Rohan had heard was that he'd escaped. This was so confusing! And the others with him—all black-eyed slaves that had been working in the catacombs with her. They didn't seem to recognize her or Rohan. She called out louder: "Dev!"

He turned sharply, but the dull look in his gaze remained. His lips parted as if he were trying to come up with a response, but then he closed them again and stared blankly away.

"The broth," Thisbe muttered. She could guess what was going on. The Revinir had gotten control of them like she'd gotten control of Arabis. Like she was trying to do with Thisbe.

Then came another roar, frightfully close and incredibly more powerful than before. Where was the Revinir? Clearly she was nearby and coming this way. Thisbe clutched her ears and dropped to the floor, letting out a bloodcurdling scream as the images took over all of her sensibilities.

A Race to the Top

Thisbe, blinded by the images and still affected by the smoke, struggled to find her voice before it was too late. "Dev, what are you doing? Come with us! Don't listen to her!" She writhed, hands still covering her ears as if to drown out the call of the Revinir. She struggled to get up. All the black-eyed slaves turned sharply to go toward the roar.

"What's happening to Thisbe?" asked Fifer, rushing to her sister's aid.

Kaylee lifted her sword, and Carina and Thatcher drew components from their vests, ready to blast the Revinir if she appeared—or anyone who threatened them.

LISA McMANN

Rohan struggled to get up and went to Thisbe too. "She's affected by the Revinir's roar, like Arabis and Dev. And like these other black-eyed slaves, apparently, based on their reactions." He helped Fifer get Thisbe to her feet and draped one of her arms over his shoulder. "Unlike the others, though, Thisbe has another element fighting it off. It leaves her blinded and unable to move, but she'll be all right in a little while. Let's get out of here before the Revinir shows up and does something worse."

As if heeding some unheard command, the Revinir's soldiers turned sharply and lifted their swords, coming at the rescue party. Kaylee charged and began fighting them off.

The soldiers roared and breathed fire, forcing Kaylee back and igniting the curtains. Carina, Seth, and Thatcher all fired freeze spells, stopping the first two soldiers in their tracks. A few of the servants rushed to put the fire out.

"Go!" shouted Kaylee to Fifer as Thatcher fired another freeze spell. The king's remaining servants and green-uniformed soldiers took Kaylee's command as an excuse to escape as well and scattered.

Fifer slipped Thisbe's other arm over her shoulders.

Thatcher paused in his attack and fished Kitten out of his pocket, tossing her to Fifer. Kitten mewed and pointed the way to their escape.

"Come on, everybody," Fifer said in a low voice. "Follow me." She and Rohan started toward the exit carrying Thisbe. Thatcher, Carina, Seth, and Kaylee held off the Revinir's black-eyed soldiers; then two of them helped Maiven to her feet.

Just then another roar shook the room, making Thisbe twist and cry out. Before the Artimeans and their friends could escape, the Revinir thundered into the room, blocking the exit. Only she was no longer the scaly human Revinir that Thisbe and Rohan had come to know so well. The woman had grown twice her size. Her body shape had changed too and looked more dragonlike, though she retained her human arms and legs instead of taking on dragon ones. The two bumps on her back stood out prominently. As they all stood watching, the Revinir cried out sharply in pain, and fire shot from her mouth. The bumps on her back exploded into dragon wings.

Everyone gasped as the wings unfurled. The Revinir groaned again in pain, then turned her head sharply to see them.

"What's she doing?" cried Seth.

"She's finally taken in so much dragon-bone broth that she's *transformed into* a dragon," Rohan said, horrified. "She's a . . . a monster!"

Thatcher urged the group to change course and continue out a side door. But the Revinir, looking around the room, saw the flurry of bodies sneaking away.

She almost didn't recognize them at first.

And then she did.

A slow smile spread across her face, revealing sharp dragon teeth. "Stop!" she yelled.

Fifer turned. Her heart pounded, and her eyes widened even more. Hatred welled up in her throat. The Revinir was . . . inexplicable. And she, this horrible monster, had killed Alex.

With a surge of anger, Fifer slipped out from under Thisbe's arm, leaving Rohan to support her. She pulled components from her vest and shouted, "Attack!" She whipped a handful of heart attack spells at the dragon-woman. Thatcher whirled around and followed with a lethal scatterclip, yelling, "Die a thousand deaths!" Carina and Seth followed with more of the same. Kaylee darted out of the way of the spells, swinging and slamming her sword into anyone in her way. Then, before the

Revinir could come after them, she ran to Maiven. Together they went to the front of the group, near Rohan and Thisbe.

"Let's move," Kaylee shouted. "Stay close." She turned to Rohan. "Have you got Thisbe all right?"

Rohan nodded. The boy scooped up Thisbe, who was still blinded by the images and barely able to move, and limped after Kaylee and Maiven to the narrow staircase that would lead them up to the turret. Sword drawn, Kaylee sent Rohan up first and followed with Maiven to protect them.

The others kept fighting. Like before, the spell components bounced off the Revinir as if they were toys. She was somehow protected from everything they flung at her. But the spell casters weren't giving up.

The Revinir was furious to see the Artiméans. She turned to her slave soldiers, some of whom were frozen. "Go, you idiots!" the dragon-woman yelled. "Attack them!"

"Fire away!" commanded Fifer in a low voice to her remaining team. She and the others sent one last round of freeze spells and ran for the exit. The team pounded up the winding steps as fast as their tired legs could carry them. Their lungs still burned with smoke.

The Revinir's unfrozen soldiers clattered after them. But in their dazed state, they could move only so fast. Back in the ballroom, some of the original spells wore off the soldiers. They followed the others.

After a few minutes Fifer's team caught up with Rohan and Kaylee and the ones they carried. "Faster!" Fifer urged, trying to help.

Around and up the spiral staircase the rescue team went. Fifer and Seth bounded past the others and helped with Thisbe and Maiven. Carina, Samheed, and Lani sent more nonlethal spells over the railings, trying to slow down the slaves without hurting them and stop the Revinir from making her way up.

By the time the Artiméans neared the top, it was clear the Revinir was still figuring out how to maneuver her new dragon body, for she was far behind her first group of soldiers. Finally Fifer reached the threshold and found a set of door handles. She opened one and burst outside through the doorway, finding herself in a large open area at the top of the tallest tower. She moved out of the way so the others could get out as well and, when she caught her breath, whistled sharply for her birds.

Seth followed and looked all around, then placed his hands

at the sides of his mouth and yelled. "Talon! Talon! Up here!"

The bronze man, who'd been flying around the castle waiting to be summoned, started toward them immediately. The rest of the party limped and crawled through the door of the tower and spread out, exhausted. Kaylee stayed near the doors to fight off any pursuers at the top of the stairs. Then, when the coast was clear, she slammed the door shut. She slid her blade through the door handles to keep the Revinir's slaves from opening them. The doors bulged and shouts rang out, but the lock held. Everybody breathed a sigh of relief. They were almost free.

Talon swooped in and landed. Quickly he assessed the group, his eyes widening triumphantly at the sight of Thisbe. But he didn't waste time asking questions. He pointed to her and Maiven. "Quickly. You two should come with me. All right, Fifer? You take two others with the birds, and I'll signal Simber to come fetch the last load."

"Yes, that's perfect," said Fifer. "Thank you." She gave Thisbe a quick kiss on the cheek. "I'm so glad we found you."

"Me too," said Thisbe, feeling better now that she could see again after the last roar, but of course her fear of heights flared

LISA McMANN

up in its place. She glanced at Rohan, worried about leaving him, but he urged her onward.

"I'll take the next, um, vehicle," he said with a half grin.

"Don't be afraid," Thisbe told him, though she cringed just looking out over the ground far below. At least she wasn't being flown around by that flock of birds Fifer was calling for—what was that all about, anyway? Talon secured her and Maiven under his arms for the flight to the meeting place across from the castle, where Simber's team waited.

The birds arrived shortly after with the hammock. They took Carina, Fifer, and Rohan. Soon only Thatcher, Seth, and Kaylee remained in the tower to hold off the pursuers and wait for Simber.

As they waited, they watched the ghost dragons. Some, on the ground outside the moat, chased after groups of soldiers, their heavy steps making the castle tremble. Others flew around the castle, peering into windows. Giant nostrils flaring, they sniffed for the Revinir and scared the people inside half to death. One flew near to see who the people in the tower were. Seth, Thatcher, and Kaylee pressed their backs against the tower wall, fearing for their lives. The enormous dragon switched its tail, hitting a nearby turret and taking down part of its ramparts. Stone blocks rained down on the soldiers below. Sharp cries rose from those on the ground. A second ghost dragon approached.

"We're going to die!" Seth whispered harshly.

"Just stay still," said Thatcher. "It's not after us. I don't think so, anyway."

Kaylee eyed her sword, still in the door. It wouldn't be much use against a dragon, but she felt vulnerable without it. "The other soldiers you froze will have awakened by now," she said. "If they show up before Simber gets here we're in trouble."

Luckily another roar from the Revinir distracted the dragons. They turned sharply and darted around the tower, then dove toward the ground. Seth let out a sigh of relief.

The three inched back toward the doors. The noise behind them had quieted by now. It sounded like the soldiers had given up on them. When they sighted Simber in the distance, coming swiftly toward them, Kaylee put her ear to the doors and listened carefully. Still hearing nothing, she slowly and quietly pulled her sword out of the handles. She signaled to the others to go to the open area where Simber would land.

As Kaylee slid her sword into its sheath, there was a loud cracking and creaking noise behind them. The three turned sharply to see the doors bowing and straining at their seams. One of them burst off its hinges and flew at the three.

"Look out!" cried Seth, diving into Thatcher and Kaylee and pushing them out of the way. The door skidded past, barely missing them.

The young, blue-uniformed soldiers poured out to attack, waving weapons and shooting small bursts of dragon fire from their mouths. Even Dev came at them.

"Dang it, Dev. Stop!" said Seth, shooting components and freezing a pair of the Revinir's slaves. He fished around in his vest for more components, but he was starting to run low. Frustrated, he ran up to their former friend, gripped the boy's arms, and peered into his eyes. "What's happened to you? Why are you doing this?" He slapped Dev's cheek a couple of times.

Dev blinked, but his eyes remained glazed. He didn't seem to recognize Seth. Then his face turned cold, stony-looking. He let out a small rumbling sound. Then he reared back and spit flames at Seth's face.

"Yow!" cried Seth. He struck out in pain, then dropped to the floor, writhing. His hair and eyebrows were singed, and his cheeks were red with welts.

Thatcher muttered an oath under his breath, frustrated by Fifer's order to try not to hurt any of the black-eyed soldiers. He fired off a backward bobbly head spell at Dev, knowing it would render the boy useless for about fifteen minutes. Dev's head began to bob and spin around. Then Thatcher ran to check on Seth while Kaylee fought off the rest of the soldiers.

"I'm okay," Seth grumbled, gingerly touching the red splotches on his face. He scowled at Dev but didn't do anything more to him—his head spinning around ridiculously was at least a little bit satisfying.

"The burns don't look too bad," said Thatcher. He batted out the smoking bits of Seth's hair and helped him up, and together they used their remaining freeze spells on the rest of the slave soldiers.

Once all the soldiers were frozen, Kaylee ran to the door and peered down the narrow stairs. The Revinir was nowhere to be seen. Perhaps, with her new large body and wings, she'd gotten stuck and gone back. Kaylee returned to where Thatcher

LISA McMANN

and Seth stood. Simber was fast approaching. "I didn't see the Revinir," Kaylee said.

"Good," said Seth, clearing a spot for the cheetah. "I hope none of us ever see her again."

Simber landed and urged the three to hurry aboard—he'd seen them fighting the soldiers and didn't want to wait for any more to arrive.

They hopped onto Simber's back, ready to make a hasty retreat, when the Revinir's horrible roar came again, piercing their ears and rattling their chests. They looked back at the door, but she wasn't there. Seconds later she swooped in from around the tower, using her own new wings to soar at them.

Alongside her was Arabis the orange, looking anything but friendly. The two split up and crowded around Simber and his riders, forcing him tight against the tower so he wouldn't have room to take off without running into one of them.

While Simber tried to talk sense into Arabis, Seth and Thatcher quickly launched spell components at the Revinir, but as usual they only bounced off her scales and did no harm. "We can't keep wasting components like this," Seth muttered. "I'm almost out."

"Same here," whispered Thatcher. "Kaylee, I wonder if you can do better with your sword than we can with our spells."

"We can't get close enough to find out," Kaylee said. "Not without getting torched." She sat back, feeling terribly vulnerable.

Simber gave up and roared in frustration. There was no way for him to move without jeopardizing his riders, and Arabis wasn't listening to him.

"Arabis!" shouted Kaylee, her hand ready on the hilt of her sword but not drawing it. "Arabis the orange, look at me! Don't you know who we are? Seth"—she pointed at him—"Seth saved your brother Drock's life! Don't you remember? Why are you attacking us?"

"So it was him," the Revinir said with an angry laugh, which sent showers of sparks at the mages. She peered at Seth. "Blue eyes?" she sneered. "Practically useless. But give him to me anyway and return my slaves, Thisbe and Rohan, and I'll let the rest of you go."

"No!" shouted Thatcher.

"You know I'll capture them eventually," said the Revinir. "You won't be able to keep them away from me forever."

"I'm never going anywhere with you," muttered Seth, his eyes blazing. "And neither is Thisbe."

"Arrrabis," Simber pleaded again, ignoring the Revinir's threats.

But Arabis was unable or unwilling to recognize them. The orange dragon didn't respond and continued to hover menacingly with the Revinir in front of Simber.

"Where are those ghost dragons?" Thatcher muttered under his breath. "We could use a distraction right about now." Simber's three riders stayed low, trying to take cover behind the stone cheetah's head, but they remained cornered and vulnerable. One burst of fire could end them all in an instant.

Frustrated and with his backside scraping against the tower, Simber finally couldn't stand it any longer. When the Revinir poked her head forward, he lurched at her and let out a forceful roar of his own in her face. Startled, she reared back just enough to allow for a short runway. "Hang on!" Simber cried. He ran and leaped over the tower's smashed ramparts, away from the castle, and flapped his wings.

Arabis roared after him, spewing fire. Simber veered. Thatcher, Kaylee, and Seth hung on for dear life.

"Get back here!" The Revinir sent a lightninglike bolt of fire at the three riders, narrowly missing Thatcher. She veered in front of the stone beast.

Simber cringed and kept going straight at her. As he drew frighteningly close to the dragon-woman, Kaylee saw her opportunity. She pulled her sword and got to her knees, then wound up and swung hard at the Revinir's elongated neck. The dragon-woman spat out another bolt of fire, trying to stop them. Simber tipped sideways to dodge it as Kaylee swung and missed her mark. With a yell of surprise, Kaylee lost her balance. She slid off the slick statue's back. Her sword went flying, and she raked the air, catching hold of nothing. Falling.

"Kaylee!" screamed Seth. He and Thatcher watched in horror, frozen as they realized what had happened. Simber plowed into the Revinir's side, then turned sharply downward as he sped to reach Kaylee before she hit the ground.

Reunited

Simber wasn't fast enough. But luck was with Kaylee, for Talon was there, on his way back to assist Simber after dropping off Thisbe and Maiven. He'd watched the scene unfold, and before Kaylee hit the ground, Talon darted in and caught her, saving her from certain death. But her sword wasn't so lucky. It hit the moat's murky water with a splash and disappeared under it.

Simber saw that Kaylee was okay. He curved away, drawing the Revinir and Arabis after them so Talon could escape.

"Thank you," Kaylee told Talon when she regained her ability to speak.

"You're welcome." Talon headed toward the meeting place. "I'm sorry I wasn't able to reach your sword."

Kaylee patted the bronze giant's muscular arm. "No problem. Though I'm not very useful without it." She hesitated, looking over Talon's shoulder at Simber and seeing what he was doing. "I suppose we should get out of here."

Simber flew back toward the tower, growling and dodging the Revinir's bolts of fire. He curved around the tower, trying to use it as a shield between him and his pursuers. "Hold on!" he growled to Thatcher and Seth.

They didn't need the reminder. "What are you doing?" Thatcher asked, gripping the cat's neck.

"I'm drrrawing theirrr attention away frrrom the rrrest of ourrr parrrty," Simber said quietly. "I want Talon and Kaylee to get to the otherrrs safely. I'm going to cirrrcle the turrret until I can think of something else to do. Hopefully I can keep the towerrr between them and us." The cat growled angrily under his breath, then glanced over his shoulder at Thatcher and Seth, who were hanging on tightly. "Arrre you okay?"

Thatcher was staying low against the cat's back. "I'm fine," he said. "I'm just glad we didn't lose Kaylee."

LISA McMANN

"Me too," said Seth, gripping Thatcher around the waist. His legs were shaking from trying to hang on to the slick stone beast. His normally pale cheeks held a greenish tinge from the rough ride. The red splotches from Dev's fiery blast stood out even more.

"I'm sorry," said Simber, facing the enemy again. "I've nev-errr lost a rrrider like that beforrre. I hope she can forrrgive me." The great cat caught sight of Talon and Kaylee growing small in the distance, and he soared close to Arabis to draw her attention away. Arabis spit fire at Simber when he got too near, then chased after him, her wing slamming into the turret and making it shiver and shake.

Seth ducked, then checked his hair to make sure it wasn't on fire again. He didn't know how long they'd survive if this kept up. Just then, with his burning cheek pressed against Simber's cool back, some broad movements in the distance caught Seth's eye. The gray-and-black smoke floating up from the front of the castle seemed to waver. A moment later, large shapes—the outlines of ghost dragons—pressed out. Seth sat up. "Oh no," he said, pointing. "They're coming back."

"And they brought all their friends," Thatcher said.

"Simber, we need to get out of here. Fast. They came up to us earlier. If they're heeding the Revinir's call like Arabis is, we're dead."

Simber dodged more fire from the Revinir and circled again, eyeing Talon's progress with Kaylee. "I need to keep the Rrrevinirrr's attention focused this way beforrre we can make any moves," he said, sounding frustrated. He glanced at the army of ghost dragons warily but didn't heed Thatcher's warning. Instead he kept the tower between him and the Revinir and Arabis the best he could, switching directions like they were playing a dangerous game of tag. "I was watching the ghost drrragons," he said in a low voice, "while you werrre inside the castle. They seem to be unaffected by herrr."

The Revinir caught sight of the ghost dragons returning. She seemed skeptical but let out another bloodcurdling roar and watched as they came toward her. Seeming satisfied that they were heeding her call, she flew to welcome them. "Aha!" she announced triumphantly, loud enough for Simber and his passengers to hear. "My call is working perfectly!"

"Are you sure they're not affected?" whispered Seth anxiously.

LISA McMANN

"We'll find out soon enough," said Thatcher.

Simber circled cautiously, taking care to keep his eyes on all potential enemies and backing away a little from the growing circle of beasts around the high tower. "We can't hold them all off. We may have to make ourrr escape and take a rrround-about way back to the otherrrs," said Simber. "Let's hope they don't all follow."

Seth felt a chill go down his spine. What if all these dragons came at them at once? It would be a very quick end to them, he was sure. Not even Simber could fight off so many enemies.

The army of ghost dragons drew closer, coming up behind Simber and his riders. Two of them, out in front of the others, were talking, but not even Simber could pick up what they were saying.

As the ghost dragons flew into the widening circle and Simber attempted to move safely out of it, the Revinir soared out from behind the tower and sent another lightning spear at Simber and his riders.

"Watch it!" Simber said, dodging. Thatcher and Seth ducked. The spear skimmed over the end of Simber's tail and continued on toward the lead ghost dragon.

LISA McMANN

Seth turned with a gasp. The spear went right through Gorgrun's ethereal body. He didn't seem to notice. In fact, the dragon ignored it completely and approached them.

"Hello, strange flying creature," Gorgrun called out to Simber. "Are you the ones Thisbe is seeking? Friends of Arabis?"

Simber glanced over his shoulder at his passengers. "Yes," he said hesitantly.

"Oh boy," Seth muttered. He started to shake, wondering what would come next.

"I am Gorgrun. We are here to help you."

Simber's eyes narrowed.

"I am Quince," said the other leader. He let out a roar in the direction of their army behind them, then continued. "Just leave this to us. You may go."

"Hmmm," growled Simber, sounding unsure.

"You heard them," Seth whispered anxiously. "We can go."

From behind the tower, the Revinir shouted to the ghost dragons. "Attack the flying cheetah!" Clearly she still believed they were there to help her.

Seth looked from one dragon to the next, not sure who was

right, but wanting desperately to believe the ghost dragons. "Please," he muttered to Simber. "Let's get out of here."

"I'm trrrying," said Simber. "Therrre's no easy path." He edged farther from the tower, worried that if he turned away fully to flee he wouldn't be able to see the Revinir or the others if they attacked. Besides, he wasn't used to turning tail and running away from anything.

Luckily, Gorgrun and Quince ignored the Revinir's order. They and the other dragons split up, taking different sides of the tower, and turned on her and Arabis instead. Sensing his chance, Simber spun out of the way.

The Revinir released more fiery spears at the Artiméans. Simber dodged. Thatcher and Seth fought back with their useless magic. The Revinir laughed, then fired more. One sliced into Thatcher's shoulder, knocking him off balance. He screamed. Seth grabbed his wrist as blood spurted from the wound. Thatcher dangled from Seth's loosening grip. Seth clapped his other hand around the first, trying desperately to hang on.

Simber twisted, nearly bending in half in an attempt to reach Thatcher with his teeth.

"Simber, do something!" Seth screamed as he started to slip off too.

Simber, still in flight, flipped upside down and folded one wing, catching Thatcher and Seth in the crook of it. Seth nearly passed out from fear, but he managed to grip the edge of Simber's wing. He hung on for dear life. Thatcher used his good arm to pull himself up next to Seth. But Simber couldn't fly with them on his wing. Or upside down. They started to spiral downward.

Suddenly Quince appeared, flying beneath Simber. "You can let them go!" the ghost dragon shouted to Simber. "I will catch them."

Simber didn't have a choice—Seth and Thatcher couldn't hang on, and they slipped off him. Quince caught them nimbly on his pillowy back. Simber righted himself and stopped free-falling. He circled around, then rode alongside Quince so Seth and Thatcher could climb aboard again.

"Now I must be going," said Quince. "The Revinir is looking for a fight. Keep your distance."

Simber agreed. He checked on his riders, who were in various states of shock after their acrobatic moves. The flying cheetah carried them out of range as Quince rejoined his fellow ghost dragons.

The Revinir seemed flustered by what was happening. "*Fight* them," she shouted. "Don't *help* them!"

Quince and Gorgrun signaled to their fellow dragons, and the entire group moved purposefully toward the Revinir and Arabis.

Arabis and the Revinir stood their ground for a moment, still confused. "What are you doing?" the Revinir said. "I'm the one who sent the call. Obey me!"

The ghost dragons circled them. The Revinir shot her spears at them, and Arabis breathed fire, but their weapons had no effect. Quince and Gorgrun and the others charged and began chasing the Revinir all around the top points of the castle. They rammed into the tower where the Artiméans had been and exploded more ramparts onto the townspeople below. A few of the young black-eyed soldiers who'd remained up there after their spells wore off went sailing over the side and disappeared into the smoke.

Seth gasped. His stomach twisted. Had Dev been among them? He couldn't tell from their distance. There was no way anyone could survive that kind of fall.

The Revinir became furious, but the ghost dragons kept up their chase, wearing her down. They roared and lunged through the air, trying to drive her away. A few of them tussled with Arabis, rolling about and flopping onto the top of the castle, breaking through the roof over the ballroom. Glass and rubble flew everywhere, raising even more dust and smoke.

Simber, Thatcher, and Seth could no longer see what was happening because of the destruction. "Hold on," Simber warned them. "Herrre we go." Carefully, to keep his riders from enduring yet another tragic fall, he circled and turned toward Dragonsmarche, taking a different route back to where the others waited across from the castle just to be sure he wasn't being tracked. As they exited the clouds of smoke and dust, Simber could just barely see that Talon was leading the rest of the Artiméans and their friends from the meeting place to the edge of the forest for protection. They'd no doubt be making a new camp there so they could prepare themselves for the long journey back home. Not a moment too soon.

Catching Up

With Seth and Thatcher on his back, Simber circled around Dragonsmarche and flew over the forest, eventually arriving at the east end of it, where the rest of the team had set up a new temporary camp. There they found food and water waiting, and everyone resting comfortably. The burning castle was still in sight, though the rescue team was hidden from the Revinir's view by the cover of trees.

Carina and Crow jumped up and attended to Thatcher's and Seth's wounds, while the giant cheetah went immediately to find Kaylee, who was cleaning up at the river. "I'm so sorrry

I lost you," he said to her. "I feel terrrible about it."

"It wasn't your fault, Simber," said Kaylee, drying her hands on her pants and giving him a big hug around the neck. "If you hadn't twisted away from the spear, you'd have been hit, and all four of us could've gone down. Besides, I wasn't hanging on like I should have been." She stepped back. "The Revinir was just . . . wow. Those wings. Right? Can you believe what she has become? That was a bit of a shock."

"Definitely shocking," growled the cheetah. "And worrse, she seems completely unaffected by ourrr magic."

"I don't know how to fight her," Kaylee admitted. "Nothing affects her. It's like with the saber-toothed gorillas on the Island of Graves. Your magic is almost useless against that kind of monster." They turned and walked together to the larger gathering near the fire.

"I'll be verrry glad to leave this prrroblem to the locals."

Kaylee nodded solemnly.

Simber moved to the edge of camp, where Talon was looking out toward the castle. The sky was an ugly gray. "Thank you, Talon," Simber said gravely. "You've neverrr let us down."

"I am always happy to be of service," said Talon. "Spending

time with the people of Artimé has given me a more interesting life than I've had in centuries."

Nearby, Carina overheard Talon and smiled. She finished bandaging up Thatcher's shoulder and put some salve on Seth's burns, then sent them to join Thisbe and Fifer by the fire to get food.

"Are you doing okay, Thiz?" Seth asked as he and Thatcher found spots near the girls. Fifer's arms were draped around her twin's neck.

"I'm okay," Thisbe said. "I'm alive. We're alive." She glanced at Rohan and Maiven and introduced them, telling a little about how they'd met and what they'd been through. Of course Thatcher remembered Maiven, and he greeted Rohan warmly.

Seth echoed the greeting, but he couldn't keep his eyes off Thisbe—she looked different. And seemed different too. Almost like a stranger. It felt odd having her with them again. She looked tougher. Older. Like he didn't really know her anymore. Her short hair had grown even more unruly in the time she'd been away, and she was more muscular, yet wiry—like she'd been doing hard labor without having enough to eat for a while. He had so many questions for her, but Fifer interrupted.

"Speaking of Thisbe," said Fifer, loud enough for everyone to hear, "and now that everyone is together, we have some . . . some news . . . to deliver to her." Her expression was pained. "Horrible as it is, I don't think we should wait another second."

The others froze and went silent—they'd been thinking it too. There was so much to tell, and most of it bad. Terrible. This wasn't going to be an enjoyable time. "You're right," said Lani softly. She cringed and took Samheed's hand.

Fifer felt overwhelmed trying to recount all of the things that Thisbe had missed since her capture. "Okay," she said, taking a breath. "Where do I start?" She pinched the bridge of her nose, trying to press the tears back. "Obviously you don't see Alex here," she said, turning to Thisbe. "But he . . . It's not because he stayed home. He didn't. He—"

"Oh dear . . . wait." Thisbe turned in Fifer's arms. She lifted her hand as if trying to stop the waves of pain that rushed back into their lives. "I . . . I know about Alex," she said quietly. "I know he's dead." She swallowed hard. "How did it happen?"

When they got over their surprise, Fifer and the others

recounted the horrible battle with the Revinir in the catacombs where they'd tried to find and rescue Thisbe. And Seth filled her in on everything that had occurred before and after that fateful moment in Thisbe's own crypt.

The story left Thisbe shocked and speechless. They'd been there after all—for a long time. And Fifer had come back to Grimere all on her own. To look for her. Her brother, the head mage of Artimé, had died trying to find *her*.

Thisbe took some time to process everything she'd heard. So much had happened—it was overwhelming. But the thing she heard over and over from the rescue team was that there wasn't a single moment when the people of Artimé had considered abandoning her. She might have felt like they'd given up, but they hadn't. It was comforting to know. She glanced at Rohan, whose face wore a curiously warm expression—one that confirmed what Thisbe had been feeling. That no matter how alone she'd felt, her people had been there. She caught his eye, and he smiled. She couldn't smile back.

Once Thisbe could speak, she recounted her experiences in the catacombs from the moment she'd been snatched up by the Revinir. She told them how scared she'd been about

Fifer. And about dragging the bones and meeting Rohan and discovering Dev in the throne room and being forced to drink the two broths. She showed them her dragon scales. Then she explained how the broths affected her and talked about some of the images that had left her blind and unable to move, and how she wasn't sure what they meant.

As she spoke, Maiven listened intently, especially to the part about the images. When she heard about the one of the girl being snatched away and put on a ship, her face grew wan. But she didn't interrupt. She had many questions to ask, but that time would have to wait. This moment belonged to Thisbe and her people.

Fifer knew a big chunk of Thisbe's story was still missing. "What happened to you and Rohan after you escaped the catacombs? We must have just missed you after you locked the Revinir in the adjoining rooms. And where did you go? Simber saw a seek spell flying by, heading toward the catacombs, so that's why we thought you were still down there. But we decided not to send more because we were so worried about getting you in trouble with the Revinir."

"I got a seek spell from Aaron," Thisbe said. "That must

have been after . . . after the magic came back." She teared up, remembering how receiving it had made her feel. What Fifer said made perfect sense, and if she'd been in the catacombs, the arrival of a seek spell in front of the Revinir or any of the soldiers would have been disastrous, she was sure.

Rohan glanced at Thisbe, who was still emotional, and continued for her. "We made it across the River Taveer and out the cave opening," he said. "Then we climbed down the cliff side thanks to Thisbe's magical hooks."

Thisbe refocused and smiled at him. "Yes. We got water from the lake." Then her eyes widened as she realized she hadn't shared the most important thing. "Oh! And before we starved to death," she said, "we followed our noses to a cave where someone was cooking fish. And you'll never guess who it was." She paused a beat, then said, "Sky."

Another Story

What?" exclaimed several of the Artiméans.

"Sky?" asked Fifer. "How could that be? That's impossible! She's alive? She's okay?"

Before Thisbe could explain, Crow jumped to his feet. "Where is she? I'll go get her!"

Thisbe saw the hope in his eyes and was hesitant to crush it. "That's . . . another story," she said weakly. "You might want to settle back in for this one." She gathered her thoughts, unsure how to start this tale. "I don't think she's dead," she began.

"What?" Crow reached out and put his hands on Thisbe's

LISA McMANN

shoulders, giving her a wild look. "You're killing me right now, Thiz. You know that?"

"Sorry." Thisbe cringed and said hastily, "She's most likely somewhere in another world, or maybe back home."

Seth nudged Fifer. "Another world?" he whispered. "Do you think Thisbe's lost her marbles?"

Thisbe heard him and flashed him a nasty look. "Just . . . let me explain." She coughed, still battling the effects of the smoke, then took a breath and went on, looking exhausted. "So at some point after I was captured, Sky went down the Island of Fire volcano, right?"

Lani nodded. "That's right."

"Well," said Fifer, "she didn't die. That volcano leads to a volcano here in Grimere, in the lake beyond the Dragonsmarche square."

"What do you mean it *leads* to it?" asked Kaylee.

"I mean Sky got sucked down the one in our world and magically pushed up through the one in this world. She made it to shore and has been living down there in a cave by the lake ever since. *Had* been, anyway." Thisbe paused for a breath. "This morning we'd finally given up on you ever finding us, so we decided to try to get back to Artimé through the same volcano network. We were in the water, ready to go, when I looked back and saw the smoke from the castle. Something inside me . . . It's not explainable, really. I just knew I had to get to the castle and save Maiven."

Thisbe looked at the woman, who seemed startled by the revelation. Then she continued. "Sky tried to return to shore with me, but she couldn't swim fast enough, and she got sucked in when the volcano went down. But we know now that doesn't mean she's dead. She's probably okay. We're just not sure where she is."

"This sounds . . . unbelievable." Crow pressed his palms against his eyes, too overwhelmed to say more.

"It's not, though," Lani murmured. "That explains the pirates going other places. Of course. It was right under our noses the whole time."

"So Grimere is where the pirates went to sell the sea creatures from our world?" Samheed asked. "Like the ones we've seen in the market in that big patched-up aquarium?"

"Yes," said Thisbe, growing excited again. "And speaking of the sea creatures, we found Issie's baby! I'm pretty sure I originally saw her in that aquarium when Fifer and I were about to be auctioned off. Remember that, Fife?"

Fifer nodded. "I remember the spotted sea monster. Is that the one you mean? All gray and dark purple?"

"Yes, exactly. Close up, the resemblance to Issie is uncanny. When the aquarium broke and the sea monsters escaped, we think Issie's baby made it down the cliff-side path to the lake. We also think she's the one who helped Sky when she first arrived."

"What do you mean, helped her?" asked Crow, looking up. He was desperate to know where exactly his sister was, now that they knew she was probably alive.

"The ride between volcanos can be a little rough, I guess," said Thisbe. "You get thrown out of the top with the water." She looked guiltily at Crow. "You have to understand that Sky made me swim as fast as I could. She ordered me to go. She knew how important it was that I find Maiven."

The attention in the group swung to the old woman who'd been sitting so quietly with them. Carina seemed puzzled. "Can you explain why exactly it was so important to save Maiven? I'm thrilled you did, of course, but what's going on with these images of yours, and how does that relate to her?" She looked closer at Thisbe. "And do you mind if I inspect those dragon scales on your arms?"

Thisbe held out her arm to Carina and went on. "I'm not sure yet why it was so important for me to rescue Maiven. But I believe she has something to do with the history of this land . . . or something like that. Besides all that, she was very kind to me during my time as a prisoner in the dungeon. And I couldn't bear to know she was trapped there in the fire without at least trying to get to her."

"Perhaps Maiven can give us some answers," Thatcher suggested, giving the woman a warm smile. She'd helped him the last time too, and he'd told her he wouldn't forget her. He gazed at her for a long moment, feeling like she was somehow familiar at a level beyond their brief meeting months ago. Then he glanced at Fifer and suddenly knew why. There was a mild resemblance. "You have black eyes too," he said softly.

Thisbe, Rohan, and Fifer stared. It was true.

Maiven nodded once. She held her body poised and her head just so, as if she were some sort of royalty despite the rags she wore and her decades in the dungeon.

There was something very mysterious about her, and Thisbe was just starting to put it together. "Maiven Taveer," said Thisbe thoughtfully, "are you named after the river? Or is the river named after you?"

Maiven's Story

Once her eyes had adjusted to the painful light and everyone was out of harm's way, Maiven Taveer had noticed the familiar features of the twins immediately. Now she glanced at Thisbe and smoothed her long white hair, which she'd been braiding and coiling around her head for years to keep it off the nasty dungeon floor. It didn't used to be white. And it hadn't been cut in more than forty years.

"This land and the river belong to the dragons and to two families," Maiven said, her voice only a bit disturbed by her time in the smoke. "One of the families was mine. As far as I know, I am the last of them to survive." She gave the girls and Rohan a piercing glance. "I was told there were no more children like you," she said. "But the guards had no reason to tell me the truth. How many of you are there?"

"There were eleven others in the catacombs, including Rohan," said Thisbe. "Plus, Dev came later, so . . ."

Seth, Thatcher, and Simber exchanged glances. They'd seen a few of the black-eyed children go flying over the side of the castle tower. Seth hesitantly offered the information, which made Maiven cringe and lower her head. Thisbe and Rohan looked pained.

"Not Dev, I hope," said Thisbe.

"I don't know," Seth answered quietly.

Then Rohan's face hardened. "It doesn't seem to matter anymore, distant cousins or not. Dev and the other slaves are with *her* now. And . . ." He looked up suddenly. "I am not. I just want to make that clear. I have not had any of that broth."

"Her?" asked Maiven. "Do you mean that dragon-monster?"

"Yes, Your Highness. She calls herself the Revinir. She has no control over me."

Fifer and Seth exchanged a curious glance. Why had Rohan

called this old granny "Your Highness"? Was she a queen or something?

Maiven looked mildly startled at the way she'd been addressed but continued smoothly. "Yes, I've heard of her," she said. "She came in some years ago, and now she's destroyed everything." She looked wistfully in the direction of the castle, which was still smoking, though the worst of the belching black smoke seemed to have ended by now.

"Therrre's not much we can do about the castle orrr the Rrrevinirrr," said Simber. "Orrr Arrrabis, which is a pity. Perrrhaps she'll grrrow tirrred of rrrunning frrrom the ghost drrragons."

"I'm afraid the ghost dragons will soon forget what they're there to do," said Thisbe. "They told Rohan and me that they have really bad memories."

"And those dragons are not able to kill the Revinir," Rohan added. "They said the new generation of dragons and black-eyed rulers must be the ones to overthrow her. The ghost dragons can assist, but they cannot fight."

"So that's what they were doing," said Seth. "They definitely caused a lot of commotion."

Samheed lifted his hand to shield his eyes and surveyed the castle. Several dragons still dotted the skies around it. "They made it possible for you to escape, so there's something to be said for that."

"But I'm afraid she's taking over the castle," said Carina. "And she's got the remaining black-eyed children under her spell so they won't attack her. This land can never be restored to the proper rulers unless the spell is broken." She thought for a moment. "Are the ghost dragons powerful? I didn't get a good look at them."

"They seem to be," said Thatcher. "And the Revinir's bolts of fire go right through them without doing anything."

Thisbe seemed intrigued but not surprised by that tidbit. "They're also huge, and they can breathe fire. But I'm just . . . I'm worried about Dev. I just don't think he would ever do this if he had control of his senses. I . . . I got to know him better."

"Me too," said Fifer. "I'm worried."

Seth wrinkled his nose but said nothing.

"And Arrrabis," said Simber. "What can we do about those two?"

Several of the group instinctively looked to Fifer for answers.

LISA McMANN

Thisbe noticed. Her lips parted in surprise.

"I think we have no choice but to leave them behind," said Fifer decisively. "It's not that I don't care about them. It's just that we have Thisbe now, and we need to bring her home. We need to get back to Artimé to tell them what happened to Alex."

"Home?" said Crow. "But what about Sky?"

"Yes, what about Sky?" echoed Thisbe. "I need to go after her. Quickly, so she doesn't think we've left her for dead again."

"But you said she might be able to go straight to our world," said Lani. "Shouldn't we start by looking there rather than following her down some questionable volcano portal system?"

"But it'll take us days to get there," Thisbe mused. "If Sky is on the Island of Fire, she'll be stranded—it's way too far to swim to Warbler. There's only so much time before she'll get sucked down again, and then who knows where she'll end up. We definitely don't have days to waste."

The Artiméans discussed options for the steps forward. Rohan, feeling awkward, gathered canteens and slipped off to the river to refill them for everyone. Maiven got to her feet and tentatively made her way on shaky legs after him.

Once they were out of earshot, Maiven spoke. "Will you

be going with them?" she asked Rohan as he dipped the first canteen under the crystal water.

Rohan didn't reply at first. He bit his lip as he tried to think of how to answer. Then he turned abruptly to look at her. "You are the rightful queen, aren't you?"

Maiven blinked and lifted her chin. "Right now I'm nothing but a prisoner of my own land," she said. "I haven't been a queen in many years. I doubt I'll ever be one again."

"You are *my* queen," said Rohan. Already kneeling, he dipped his head awkwardly.

"One constituent," said the woman, a smile playing at her lips. "It's a start."

"Thisbe will be your second," he said valiantly, "once she understands who you are. And Fifer, too."

"They have their own land."

"But they are descendants of the black-eyed people," Rohan said, gesturing emphatically. "They should stay here."

Maiven touched the boy's shoulder in a gesture of friendship. "We'd both like that, wouldn't we?"

The boy's face flushed. "I could never say it to her. To them, I mean."

LISA McMANN

"Of course not. It must be their decision if they choose to join us. And only if they feel any pull toward our people at all."

Rohan sighed. "Yes, of course you're right. It's just difficult, Your Highness."

The old woman pursed her lips. "Perhaps just call me Maiven for now, all right? Let's not complicate things for the others." She paused. "Are you from the line of Taveer?"

"No," Rohan said, looking away. "No. I'm from the other family. The line of Suresh."

"Ah, I see. From the land beyond."

"Y-yes."

"I don't suppose you still have a grandmum, do you?"

"No." Rohan looked away. "I'm quite sure everyone's dead over there."

"Then I'll be your grandmum. If you'll have me."

Against his most valiant efforts, Rohan's face crumpled with emotion, and he cried for a few moments.

Maiven let him be and filled a few canteens while she waited for him to collect himself.

Eventually Rohan sniffed and wiped his eyes with his sleeve. "What'll we do? It's beyond hopeless, isn't it?"

"Well, I imagine you'll go off to take on that monstrous dragon-woman, won't you?" said Maiven. "I see the fight in your eyes."

"I won't leave my grandmum behind, though," said Rohan with a small smile. "Will you help me? It's just us two against the world. We'd do better to stick together."

The woman smiled warmly. "Thank you, dear. I don't look like much today, all skin and bones. But with a bit of practice and some decent food to get my strength back, I'll be ready to fight. I haven't forgotten how. I go over my steps, my techniques, in my mind every day to stay sharp."

Rohan looked admiringly at the woman. "Thisbe never mentioned your first name to me until this morning," he confessed. "I've studied all about you in my books. You commanded the army."

"Yes, I did," said Maiven proudly. "And I shall again one day."

"Yes, you shall—even if it is just an army of two," said Rohan. "I believe it."

"And I believe in you."

Rohan's tears began again. He swallowed hard and nodded, then turned back to the river to fill the rest of the canteens.

LISA McMANN

Recovering and Regrouping

I t began to rain as Maiven and Rohan returned to the fire. Talon, Samheed, Lani, Carina, Thatcher, and Kaylee were busy making a shelter at the edge of the forest, while Seth was hastily collecting firewood before it all got soaked. Thisbe napped all curled up, exhausted after the long day. The two from Grimere were tired too. Lani paused in her work and urged them to rest, so they sat quietly near Thisbe. They could overhear Fifer and Simber, arguing in low voices about how they would get everyone home now that Arabis, their main ride, had abandoned them.

"I can only take fourrr plus some supplies," Simber was saying. "What about yourrr hammock? Thrrree?"

"The birds have carried three of us for short distances, but that requires most of the birds to participate the whole time. I think two passengers should be the most for such a long journey since there's nowhere for them to stop and rest." Fifer looked concerned. "And one passenger with Talon for the same reason." She added them up. "That's seven spots. And how many are we?" She looked around, counting. Samheed, Lani, Carina, Kaylee, Thatcher, Crow, Fifer, Seth, and Thisbe. And Kitten, but she didn't take up much space. Plus Rohan and Maiven if they wanted to join them.

"Nine Arrrtiméans," said Simber. "Plus two frrrom Grrrimerrre."

Maiven and Rohan couldn't help overhearing. They exchanged a solemn look, then Rohan nodded. Maiven leaned toward Simber and Fifer. "We thank you for your kind consideration and for selflessly including us in your group without question. But you mustn't worry about us. Rohan and I are in agreement: We will stay here and fight for our land."

LISA McMANN

Simber, who seemed to recognize, or at least suspect, that Maiven was much more than she let on, gazed at the woman with deep respect, and perhaps a bit of guilt, for a long moment. "You'rrre surrre?" he asked.

"Yes," she said with a certainty that Simber didn't dare question.

Rohan concurred. "I can't leave here. The others are in danger—and there aren't many of us left. I have to do something to break the Revinir's spell and bring them back to our side."

"What will you two be able to do against the Revinir?" asked Fifer. "She's so powerful now. I mean, she has wings and breathes fiery lightning spears. It's crazy. She's at least half dragon."

"If there's no other way to break the spell she holds on our people, we will have to find a way to kill her," said Rohan. "That's all there is to it."

"Our magic did nothing to her," said Fifer. "I'm worried that her scales make her invincible against us."

"Then we must find her weakness," said Maiven in a dark voice, "and exploit it."

Thisbe stirred in her sleep.

Simber and Fifer went back to their conversation, softer now so they wouldn't wake her. "We still have too many of us," Fifer whispered.

"And we won't leave anyone behind this time," said Simber. "I can't allow it."

"How are we supposed to do that without Arabis?" asked Fifer, growing annoyed. There was clearly no way to make the math work. There were nine riders and only seven spots.

"I don't know," growled Simber, who was frustrated too. "You'rrre surrre about the birrrds?"

Fifer thought it through again. They'd have to fly nonstop with no place to land for two full days before they even had a chance to reach the Island of Fire, and there was no guarantee that the volcano island would be above water when they needed it to be. So to be safe, they needed to allow three days to get to Warbler.

The birds handled their shifts well with two passengers— half of them flying and the other half resting. Fifer shook her head. "There simply wouldn't be enough rest time for the birds," she stated. "They're magical, but they have their limits, like we all do."

Simber nodded, resigned. "Perrrhaps Arrrabis will come arrround. I'm going to trrry to talk to herrr."

"We all need tonight to recover anyway," said Fifer. "Let's not give up on her. In the meantime, we could send dozens of seek spells all at once to Aaron. Maybe he'll figure out that we need him to come with a new dragon."

"Let's not give all of Arrrtimé a reason to panic again so soon," said Simber, who could imagine all the horrible things Aaron and the other loved ones back home might think if that happened. "Perrrhaps we can somehow summon Spike Furrrious to lend a hand. Errr . . . a fin. Or Pan. We could shuttle a few of us to the otherrr side of the gorrrge and then all go togetherrr frrrom therrre."

"That's a perfect idea," said Fifer. "If you don't have any luck with Arabis, maybe you could cross over and see if Pan or Spike is in close enough range to hear you roar."

"Verrry well," said Simber. He got up and started pacing restlessly, then looked off in the direction of the castle and sampled the air. "The firrre is mostly out, and much of the castle still stands," he said. "The ghost drrragons appearrr to have called it a day and arrre marrrching and flying back the way they came. Perrrhaps they grrrew tirrred of chasing the Rrrevinirrr."

"That's odd."

"*They'rrre* odd."

"Yes. Well, they're not alive anymore, right? They're ghosts. So maybe their perspective has changed."

"They'rrre not alive? Arrre you surrre?"

"I mean—" Fifer stopped and thought about it. "Are they? I don't know."

"They're very forgetful," said Thisbe from her spot on the ground. "Maybe they forgot why they went to the castle and are going home."

"Oh good," said Fifer. "You're awake."

"Yes. I've been listening in for a while now." She hesitated, then rolled over to get more comfortable. "You sound like Alex, talking to Simber that way. Making plans. Figuring things out." Her voice carried a hint of something like an accusation. Or jealousy, perhaps. She hadn't intended it, but there it was. Things had happened to her twin without her. Big things. Fifer had obviously taken Magical Warrior Training and wore the vest now. She'd gotten her dream while Thisbe was stuck

LISA McMANN

in the catacombs dragging bones. And this conversation they were having—planning the future. It was clear that Simber held Fifer in high regard. Much higher than before. Thisbe still had to learn why.

Fifer's heart lurched as she remembered for the millionth time that Alex was never coming back. "You think I sound like Alex?" she said.

Thisbe reached her hand out and took Fifer's. "Yes," she said. "A lot." And they both found a small token of comfort in that.

Simber, hearing them, fought off the lump in his stony throat. Talking with Fifer felt more natural than he'd imagined it could. And while no one would ever replace Alex in his heart and soul, Fifer was making her mark. It was indeed a comfort to have her here.

Sneaking Off

By dawn Thisbe had regained her strength. Rohan and Maiven were feeling better too, and making plans for their future. And Crow was continuing to fret about Sky.

The Artiméans still didn't have a plan in place for getting home, and everyone was restless to do something now that they had Thisbe back. Simber had gone during the night to try to talk sense into Arabis. In the weak morning sunlight he returned to report to Fifer.

"I thought I saw a flickerrr of rrrecognition in herrr eyes,"

LISA McMANN

said Simber, "but then they glazed overrr again and she spit firrre at me. She wouldn't listen."

"Arabis is probably not going to change her mind anytime soon," said Crow impatiently. "So if we're stuck here waiting anyway, I'd like to go after Sky."

"Me too," said Thisbe. She still felt terrible about the way they'd been pulled apart. If only they'd thought to set up a quick plan for meeting up again—like "Take the first exit and stay there" or "Check each one but keep going until you get to the Island of Fire" or something. Anything that would give them a clue to where Sky ended up.

"That's verrry rrrisky," said Simber. "I don't want to split up ourrr parrrty."

"We *won't* split up," agreed Fifer.

Thisbe kept trying. "I know the reason Sky stayed in the cave by the lake was because she hoped someone would eventually figure out the volcano connection. So if she's not at the Island of Fire, I would guess we could find her fairly easily in some other land—if not right back here in our cave in Grimere. She'd stay as close to the portal as possible."

"She'd only be safe on the Island of Fire for so long before she'd be sucked down it and sent somewhere else," Crow said. "And it sounds painful the way Thisbe described it—too painful to do it over and over indefinitely. I'm really scared for her."

"I am too," said Lani, fidgeting a bit. "I hope she's okay. If it were my brother who'd been sucked into the unknown, I'd be worried too."

"We should go as soon as possible," said Thisbe. She glanced at Crow, who looked grateful that Thisbe was advocating for him.

Simber frowned.

Fifer, agonizing over the decision, looked at the statue. "Did you have time to fly over the waterfall in our world to call for Spike and Pan?"

"I did," Simber said. "I wasn't surrrprrrised that Spike was nowherrre to be found, as she prrreferrrs to stay nearrr the inhabited islands. But I hoped Pan would be nearrrby, seeing as Arrrabis is overrr herrre. It would be like herrr to be waiting forrr news. But I cirrrcled forrr a while and called out several times. I thought I saw some movement on the horizon, but eventually concluded it was just the mist rising up off the sea. Therrre was no sign of herrr."

"Strange," said Samheed. "I've never been more torn about a decision in my life."

"What would Alex want us to do?" asked Lani. "Go after Sky. It's pretty clear to me."

"That's not fairrr." Simber got up and started pacing. "He's not herrre."

"Look," said Thisbe impatiently. "I understand and appreciate that we all need to stick together now—I think Alex would want that, too. But I agree with Lani, and I'm sick to my stomach about Sky. Sure, she might have made it through the volcanos back to the Island of Fire, but we don't have a way to all get there. And even if most of us go, she'd be gone by the time we got there because the Island of Fire volcano goes down at least daily." She went to Simber and put a hand on his neck. "Think about it," she implored. "We could *all* take the volcano to find Sky and then go back to our world together— truly all of us who remain. And then fly the rest of the way to Artimé—Talon with two and the birds with three—making a stop on Warbler overnight to let Fifer's birds rest."

"But we'd have Sky, too," said Lani.

"We'd make room," Crow insisted. "I'll carry her myself if I have to!"

Simber's mouth opened as if he were about to argue that it wouldn't make a difference, but then he closed it again. "I could squeeze five on forrr a shorrrt ride frrrom the Island of Firrre to Warrrbler," he conceded. "Then take two trrrips to get to Arrrtimé."

"Yes, that would work," said Crow. "Sky and I could stay back and visit with our mother for a while. We can even take the skiff to Artimé so you wouldn't have to come back for us." He relaxed a bit, and Thisbe bit her lip, watching the giant cat hopefully.

But Simber grew puzzled. "So would Talon and I meet the rrrest of you overrr therrre? That seems too dangerrrous. I won't leave any of you behind. I've made a vow not to."

"No," said Fifer, sitting up and catching Thisbe's eye. "It's a volcano, Simber. It's huge. You and Talon would come with us. It's big enough."

"It was big enough for a pirate ship to go through," Lani reminded them.

"That sounds adventurous," said Talon. "I'm certainly willing."

Simber gave Talon a dark look.

Carina glanced around at the others. "It can't be worse than plunging over the waterfall," she said a bit too casually. "Remember that time?"

"I'll be honest," said Lani. "I'm game to try the volcano. I can hold my breath fine—we all can. I'll just need help if there's any swimming to be done. My wheels aren't equipped for that."

"Of course," said Samheed. "I'm willing too. You and I will stick together through it all. I've got you." He and Lani exchanged a loving glance.

Simber growled. "You want me to go thrrrough the volcano? I don't think so."

Everyone stared. And then Lani's expression cleared. "Oh, I get it," she said. She turned to the others and noticed that Rohan and Maiven were especially puzzled. "Simber doesn't like water," she explained. "He's a cat."

"Oh, that old thing," scoffed Thisbe. "Well, if it helps, Sky told me that when she went through before she felt like she was in some sort of protective bubble. She could breathe the slightest bit, though there was a lot of pressure. But it didn't sound like she was directly touching the water." She covered her mouth and muttered, "Until she landed."

Simber scowled. "That's not it," he said firmly with everyone staring at him. "I simply don't think this idea sounds safe. I'm sorry, Fiferrr, but I'm . . . not forrr it."

"Oh, Simber," said Fifer with dismay. Crow threw his hands up in the air, and Thisbe turned away, frustrated.

Samheed regarded Simber thoughtfully. He turned his gaze to Lani and whispered together with her for a moment, then looked up. "I trust your instinct, Simber," he said quietly. "But there's no way to do what you want. We've exhausted all the options. So Lani and I will stay here while the rest of you go the traditional way. Then Simber can come back for us."

"Yes," said Lani. "We'll be fine here for a week or so."

"But what about Sky?" said Crow and Thisbe in unison, and the others started to argue the options as well.

Fifer waved her hand for silence, a look of alarm in her eyes. "I don't like that idea one bit. We don't need another story about Samheed and Lani getting taken captive in a strange land.

And I hope you realize this war isn't over—it's just beginning. It's not safe here."

Lani was about to protest, but Samheed touched her arm. "She has a point," he said quietly.

Thisbe shook her head, frustrated. "So if Simber won't go through the volcano, we have to split up. And if we're going to take separate routes, then at least let Crow and me go through the volcano so we can find Sky. Then Samheed and Lani can go with you, and none of us get left here."

"Impossible," roared Simber. "You will not leave my sight, Thisbe. If I go home without you on my back, Aarrron will neverrr forrrgive me."

"It's not going to be a problem," Thisbe argued. "Trust me! I know exactly what to do. Sky talked me through it."

Simber narrowed his eyes at Thisbe, clearly not trusting her. He turned to Fifer. "I'm telling you again. I don't think it's ourrr best move. Perrrhaps Samheed and Lani have the best solution."

"Why do you keep looking at her all the time?" snapped Thisbe. "Why aren't you listening to *me*? Your solution still doesn't account for Sky!"

Fifer waved her off impatiently and gave her an *I'm trying to help you so be quiet* kind of look. "Simber," she said, "you're the one who's been so obstinate about sticking together all the time. You're also the one who keeps saying you're not going to lose another one of us. Well, you're just setting yourself up for more problems if you leave any of us here—this country is in a *war!* Come on. Don't you see that leaving anyone behind, even for a week, is way more dangerous than using these volcano tunnels?" She hesitated, then added, "I think you're letting your fear of the water get to you."

Simber emitted a small growl and started pacing again. Then he turned to face Fifer. Everyone's eyes were glued to the fight between them. Who would win?

"It is my job to do what you decide," he said tersely. "But I hope you think about it a little morrre."

Fifer let out a breath. Her heart was pounding. Simber was backing down. And even though she felt triumphant, she began to question her own reasoning. But she pushed those thoughts aside. It was important that she lead. And this was how leaders became great. They made difficult decisions and stuck with them.

"I do have a lot of thinking to do," Fifer said in a cool voice.

"Thinking about my birds and how to get them where we need to go."

The group remained achingly silent, unsure how to react. Most of them agreed with Fifer and wanted to go together to find Sky. But there was no doubt the volcano transportation system was frightening.

Seth thought he detected worry in Fifer's eyes. He scrambled to think of something to say that would help her. "The birds can come through the volcano too," he said after a moment. "We'll wrap the hammock around them, maybe. A few of us could hold on to the ropes."

Thisbe glanced from Fifer to Simber to Seth. This dynamic, with Fifer and now Seth calling shots, was so strange, so foreign. But she didn't want to question it again—not with things going her way at the moment. She stayed silent.

"That'll work, I bet," said Crow. "You said there was some sort of an air pocket. They should be fine."

Fifer nodded. "I think so too. I'll explain to Shimmer what will happen so they won't be afraid." She felt a knot tighten in her stomach. Was this her gut finally telling her something? Was this the wrong move?

"It's settled, then?" Crow said. "We're all going to the lake?"

Everyone looked at Fifer. Fifer looked at Simber. Simber turned his head away and studied some invisible thing on the ground.

"Yes," said Fifer. The word nearly choked her. "We're going. All of us."

Crow blew out a breath of relief. "Thank the gods." Thisbe felt the weight of her guilt about Sky lifting off her shoulders. The others remained still for a moment longer. Then Lani and Samheed moved to pack up their things and put out the fire.

Rohan and Maiven glanced at each other. Things still seemed tense, but the argument was clearly over. And it was time for them to find a home base and continue their planning as well. They picked up their few belongings and a couple of canteens that Fifer had given them.

When Maiven and Rohan were ready, Maiven approached Fifer and Thisbe and the others. "You are incredible problem solvers," she said. "I barely know you, but I shall miss you all. Your attitudes and your tenacity in what seems like a frightening and difficult task all point to the reasons you are successful.

I wish you all the luck. And we hope to see you again someday. Don't we, Rohan?"

Rohan was staring at Thisbe. They'd said their good-byes once. He didn't want to do it again. "Yes, of course," he whispered, his voice choked up. He held out the knife that they'd passed back and forth so many times. On the handle he'd carved a tiny scene of him and Thisbe fishing together by the cave.

Thisbe took it. She stared at it and willed herself not to cry. She had hoped she'd be able to convince Rohan and Maiven to come with them. But it was clear they'd made up their mind, and rightfully so. Thisbe felt like she should stay too, but there was Aaron to think of. She was torn between two lands. "I'll be back," she said, to the surprise of a few of the others. "It might not be right away, but I'll return one day."

"Me too," said Fifer.

"And me," said Seth, shocking himself.

"We'll see about that," muttered Carina. She began to pack up their supplies. "But for now, we need to concern ourselves with surviving a trip through a volcano."

Good-bye, Good-bye

Since everyone was going in the same direction, Maiven and Rohan decided to accompany the Artiméans as far as the city of Grimere. Maiven had hopes her family's village home was still standing after all this time, and if it was, she and Rohan would make it their headquarters.

As they went, the strange-looking troupe took a last look at the castle now that the smoke had cleared. The front of it was charred and the huge drawbridge completely gone. No one knew the whereabouts of the king, but there were new blue flags flying from the turrets today so they assumed he'd been captured or killed. They could just make out the symbol

LISA McMANN

on the largest flag—that of a shimmering dragon with the Revinir's features. It was the land of the dragons again, but in exactly all the wrong ways.

The ghost dragons were long gone. There were still king-supporting protesters near where the drawbridge had been on the outer side of the moat. Blue-uniformed soldiers stood on the inner circle, around the perimeter of the castle. Thisbe imagined Dev among them . . . if he hadn't been killed. Her heart twisted, but she could think of no way to find out—not if they didn't want to be embroiled in another attack. She fell into step with Rohan as they all turned toward Grimere.

"You'll try to save Dev, won't you?" asked Thisbe.

"Sure, if he's among the remaining. Him and all the others."

"I don't know how you'll do it," Thisbe admitted.

"Neither do I," said Rohan. He glanced at her and smiled. Then he pressed something into her hand and gave it a squeeze. "I made you something," he said. "So if you ever need me, maybe you could just send a seek spell."

Thisbe's face grew hot. She slid the item into her pocket without looking at it—she'd save that for a moment all to herself. "I never taught you how to do the spell," she murmured. "I'm sorry."

"I watched you teach Sky how to do it," he said. "You concentrate and hold the item and say 'seek,' right?"

"That's about it. Think about the person you're sending it to."

"That won't be difficult," said Rohan.

Thisbe looked away, a small smile on her lips. "But you don't have anything of mine."

"Well, then," said Rohan, "you must give me something."

"Wait!" said Thisbe. "I gave you that vial of broth, which I made." Then she shook her head. "Or it could have come from Dev's batch. Hmm." Thisbe checked her pockets, finding them empty as usual. She spied some dry bark that had peeled off a tree and ran to get it. Then she asked Samheed for a pencil, since she knew her theater instructor never went anywhere without one. He pulled his notebook from his pocket, tapped it, and a pencil popped out. He handed it to her. A pained look crossed his face as he stared at the blank pages in the notebook. He slipped it back into his pocket so he wouldn't have to look at it anymore, then watched slyly as Thisbe dropped to the back of the group, intent on writing something on the bark.

Samheed glanced at Rohan, who seemed to grow more

downhearted the closer they got to Grimere. He'd witnessed the close bond between him and Thisbe from the moment the two reconnected after the harrowing fire business. And he looked forward to the coming months as Thisbe began to tell more of her stories from her time in captivity. Perhaps they'd all come to know Rohan better through them. He seemed like a good person. Maiven was an unusual woman as well, and Samheed was sure she had many stories to tell. But they wouldn't be hearing them, at least not for now.

They neared the neighborhoods on the outskirts of Dragonsmarche. Thisbe gave Rohan the poem she'd written for him. In a way it was like the poem Alex had written for Sky—not that Thisbe felt *that* way about Rohan, of course. He was just a friend, wasn't he?

Rohan accepted it and did as Thisbe had done: He put it in his pocket for later.

Finally they reached the city. People of Grimere went about their business, though there was quite a bit more glancing left and right now than usual as blue-uniformed soldiers guarded the square—the old ones, not the black-eyed children. There was no market today.

"I wonder what will happen," said Fifer. "Do you think the Revinir will leave people alone now that she's taken control of the castle?"

"Knowing her," said Thisbe, "I hardly think so." Rohan and Maiven nodded in agreement, and Thisbe continued. "She's never satisfied. I don't know what she'll do next, but if I were a resident here, I'd be very afraid." She hesitated. "I'm just glad she's stopped roaring."

"There's no telling exactly what she'll do," said Rohan. "But she is the most power-hungry person I've ever studied. Almost no one else in our history even comes close."

Maiven's face was troubled. "We have a lot of work to do before we can figure out a way to overthrow her." She stopped abruptly to study a fading street sign etched on the wall of a building. "It's this one," she declared, turning down a side street. She looked around cautiously as she walked, then turned again and waded down a smaller alley that was overgrown with weeds higher than the woman's waist.

Maiven counted the doors and stopped at one that was rotted around the edges. A window in the front was broken, and a mangy, dull-eyed cat sat on the sill. Next to the stoop was a flower bed overgrown with more weeds. A thin spiral of smoke rose from somewhere within it.

Fifer pointed at the smoke, and she and Seth exchanged a glance. "Could that be the smoke hole we were looking for?" Seth whispered.

"I don't know," said Fifer. "It doesn't matter now." They had Thisbe and all was well.

Seth peered into it anyway. "I can't see anything."

Maiven Taveer reached into the flower bed and moved a small pile of rocks. She pulled out a dirty, tarnished key, then wiped it off and inserted it into the lock. She turned it hard. It clicked, and the door opened a crack. The cat bolted down the alleyway. Maiven peered in. Satisfied, she looked back at the others. "Thank you for seeing me home," she said. "I wish you success in your venture, and I hope you find your way back here again someday. You know where to find us if you do."

Maiven looked at Thisbe and hesitated, as if she wanted to ask the questions that had plagued her since she'd heard Thisbe talk about the images. But then she glanced at Rohan, who was painfully silent. Perhaps he'd have answers for her.

Seeing his face, she touched his arm and pulled on his sleeve. "Come. You can help me clean up this place."

Thisbe stood at the back of the group. She couldn't bear to see Rohan's face or she might abandon the others immediately, though she knew that would be a bad decision in the long run. Finally she stole a glance at him, and their eyes connected. "Good-bye," she mouthed.

"Good-bye, *pria*," said Rohan. And then he turned and fled into Maiven's house.

Maiven smiled. She lifted her hand to them, her gaze lingering on the twins, and then just on Thisbe. "Thank you for coming back and saving me," she said softly. "I'll never forget what you did." After a moment she nodded her farewell and closed the door.

Thisbe's eyes flooded.

Kaylee clasped her hand to her heart, then silently went up to the girl and offered a hug. Samheed's eyes grew moist. He'd continued watching Thisbe and Rohan, moved by their sadness. Now he pulled out the notebook again. He flipped it open to a blank page and stared at it. Then he produced the pencil and began to scribble a few halting notes. Perhaps he could find words again after all with this most heartbreaking story playing out right in front of him.

A boom in the distance announced the volcano's presence. There was no time for sentiment. The anxious group headed to the edge of the market square, and Thisbe showed them the way over the hill and down to the lakeside. The volcano stood upright and ready, its gaping maw large enough to swallow even the biggest of Artiméans with a single gulp.

Thisbe and the other mages, along with Talon and Simber and Kitten and the flock of red-and-purple birds, all took the short flight through the air to the center of the lake. They hovered above the volcano, watching the smooth glassy surface of the water start to shiver. It was almost time. Fifer glanced at Simber, but he wouldn't look at her. Again her stomach twisted. Was she making a terrible mistake? Perhaps she was letting her guard down too much after being so careful. They weren't home safely yet. What if something awful happened and Fifer ended up losing someone on this journey? Why did this have to be so hard?

The fliers lowered the others onto the base of the volcano.

Fifer spread out the hammock and instructed the birds to stand on it. She wrapped them carefully up inside and gathered the ropes. They rested quietly and waited, trusting their commander.

Thisbe called out a reminder of the plan to her companions: Try to breathe shallowly. Don't panic. Follow her through the first bright hole in the network.

Everyone was ready. The volcano began to descend. The rescue team took huge breaths and held on to one another and the hammock ropes. Then the volcano went under. Water spilled into the hole, and one by one the group got sucked down into the volcano's mouth.

Underwater, zooming inside a thin air pod next to Fifer, Thisbe felt her heart and lungs thudding beneath her skin. The only thing she knew to do was what Sky had told her. She peeled open her eyes against the pressure and speed and managed a glance behind her. She saw several more transparent pods in a line. Relieved, she focused on spotting and guiding everyone toward the first light. Hopefully, their journey would be over in a matter of minutes.

To the Rescue?

Unbeknownst to Thisbe and the rest of her group, Aaron and Pan and their team had been traveling to rescue them. Now the ruler of the sea neared the great gorge between the worlds for the very first time from the air. She soared regally with her new magical wings. On her back she carried six mages from Artimé: Aaron Stowe, Sean Ranger, Scarlet from Warbler, Henry Haluki, and his wards, Clementi Okafor and Ibrahim Quereshi. Clementi wore a serious look as she tried to remember everything Florence had taught her about fighting. She knew that her skills in dance and movement would contribute well to her excel-

LISA McMANN

lent spell-casting abilities. Next to her, Ibrahim was a bit more relaxed. He was an extraordinary painter who'd already managed to create a 3-D door in his first year in Artimé. Both were honored to join this seasoned crew. And they were determined to prove their worth.

Behind Pan, four young dragons followed: Ivis the green, Yarbeck the purple and gold, Hux the ice blue, and Drock the dark purple. Drock, as usual, was a bit of a maverick when it came to the laws of the dragons. He flew a short distance behind the others, occasionally snorting fire in his uncomfortable, unruly fashion.

The Artiméans hadn't noticed the dragons' glazed eyes. They hadn't heard the roars from the Revinir. They didn't have the first clue how powerful she had become. And they had no idea that the real reason Pan and the other dragons had so willingly accompanied them this time was because they were heeding a call from deep within themselves. A call from a single leader that had been controlling them for days. A roar that was due to come again. At any moment.

After crossing the gorge and emerging from the mist, they neared the still-smoldering castle. Aaron pointed to something

507 « Dragon Ghosts

beyond it in the far-off distance to the south. "Look," he said, concerned. "Something else is in flight over there."

"Is it Simber?" asked Henry, scanning the horizon and seeing at first one dot. But then his heart sank—there were several of them. He turned, and kept turning, seeing more and more. Sean Ranger did the same in the other direction. Scarlet, her face alarmed, was first to recognize what they were. "They're dragons," she said in awe. "Coming from everywhere. Hundreds of them."

"More dragons?" asked Clementi. "I didn't know there were more."

"Neither did I," said Aaron. "Pan, did you?"

Pan was quiet.

Drock snorted loudly and writhed in the air.

Aaron's feeling of alarm grew.

Perched at the highest remaining point of the castle, the Revinir surveyed her new realm. She saw the dots too and cackled with delight every time another flight of dragons appeared, coming toward her from one of the lands they'd scattered to years before. Sure, the ghost dragons had turned out to be rogue. But these dragons were all under her spell and had been traveling for days, coming home. The Revinir was ready to rule alongside them. They'd all be under her command, of course. Just like her dragony black-eyed soldiers.

Pan sped up and steered everyone toward the great ruler, ignoring the growing unease of her riders.

"What's happening?" Aaron demanded. "Pan, I think we should turn back. Something's not right."

Pan didn't respond.

"Pan!" Aaron shouted. "Do you hear me?"

Pan continued to ignore him.

But Drock didn't. His eyes were wide in alarm. He darted ahead to the front of the pack, staring at the Revinir.

Then Pan spotted her own dear Arabis the orange at the Revinir's side. Arabis was well! She was in power! Surely the Revinir would restore the land of the dragons to its former grandness and make dragons the rulers of all the worlds. It had to be so, for dragons were coming from everywhere! Would Pan's old friends be among them? Were Gorgrun and Quince and the other ghost dragons here already?

The Revinir rose from her perch on the top of the castle and flapped her wings to make her scales catch the light. Her plan was coming to completion. She'd taken Grimere and the castle away from the king. And soon, with the help of all the worlds' dragons under her spell, she would rule everything in this world and beyond. Now that they were all coming, she just needed to solidify their compliance to her rulership. Ensure complete obedience.

The dragon-woman smiled to herself, feeling the burning in her core. She took a deep breath, then roared out once more to all the approaching dragons. The sound pierced the air and reverberated far and wide, through the castle and rocks and mountains and even under the sea.

At the sound Drock twisted and roiled in the air. He roared too, fire spurting from his mouth. Then he seemed to wrench himself from some invisible grip. He turned in the air and slammed into his mother, jolting the riders.

"What are you doing?" cried Scarlet. Ibrahim clung to Pan's back.

Pan continued flying as if she hadn't noticed.

Drock roared again, then eyed the Artiméans. He drew up alongside Pan, causing her riders to shrink back in fear, and gave Aaron a most serious look. "Something is very wrong here," Drock said gravely. "You must leave my mother and come with me. Immediately. Or you'll all most certainly die."

The Revinir's roar made it all the way into the volcano network, to Thisbe.

Just as the girl spied the first circle of light, the call shook her, stealing her breath. Thisbe's sight left her. She grew paralyzed and panicked in her travel pod as the familiar images bombarded her senses more powerfully than ever before. Her body slackened. Her senses faded away. She couldn't move or breathe or speak. She couldn't tell anybody or do anything but float there, caught in the volcano network.

The first circle of light passed by them without Thisbe aiming for it, confusing the team. Then the second went by as well. By the time Fifer and the others figured out what was happening, it was too late. Thisbe had lost control. They'd missed their stop. Now no one knew what to do. They couldn't communicate. They didn't have a backup plan.

Fifer felt the familiar tightening in her stomach as she reached out for her sister, trying and missing and trying again to grasp the girl's elbow. Finally she got it and hoped the

511 « Dragon Ghosts

LISA McMANN

others behind her were paying attention. Dread filled her. Her instincts had warned her, but she'd turned against them. She'd made a mistake—a terrible, horrible mistake—and put all of these people and creatures in danger. Now they were stuck in a foreign place between worlds with only a little air and a leader who was overcome. More circles of light passed the team by.

Fifer had no choice but to fix this, and no time to plan or strategize. She was in emergency mode, and she had to make a decision fast, before it was too late to save them all. With Thisbe limp and unconscious next to her, Fifer tightened her grip and eyed the next portal, which glowed with an unappealing gray, eerie light. Strange, sinister markings decorated the interior of the volcano's mouth. Despite its uninviting look, Fifer pointed her head toward it and raggedly tried to take a breath, feeling the pressure around her get stronger as the opening grew larger and the gray light became brighter. Fifer hoped all the others would follow. She hoped she hadn't just made the biggest mistake of her life.

She hoped her worst nightmare wasn't about to come true.

Alone and Away

S ky stood on the edge of the Island of Fire, her clothes dripping and her head aching. She hadn't gotten knocked out this time, at least, thanks to Issie's baby.

But she'd made it—she'd made it home. Close to it, anyway. She could see Warbler Island in the far-off distance. If only there were a way to get there. She glanced beside her at her new sea monster companion. Issie's baby had gone down the volcano with her in Lake Grimere, in the land of the dragons. Now the sea monster lounged on the base of the volcano island, soaking up the sun, but keeping a cautious eye on the

LISA McMANN

waters around them—perhaps she knew of the deadly eels that trolled these waters.

Sky shivered. Her clothes were still wet. Knowing the island could plunge underwater with little warning, she considered her options. Should she go down with it and travel through the volcano transportation network again to try to find Thisbe and Rohan? Or stay here and access the enclosure under the island so she could ride out the plunging process and wait for it to come back up?

Swimming to Warbler by herself was out of the question. It was way too far. But what if Issie's baby had the stamina to help her? Sky studied the sea monster. She was about twice the length of a large human—and much thicker, too. The creature was friendly, though in a standoffish way. And she'd been helpful in guiding Sky to the right portal hole, as if she somehow understood where Sky wanted to go. Perhaps the baby _had_ been here before, but the eels had kept her from returning.

Sky had aimed for the first portal, but Issie had blocked her from going toward it. She'd also blocked the next four after that. Sky had fought panic, feeling like she could trust Issie's baby to see her through. After all, the creature had saved Sky before. As they'd gone, with Sky breathing shallowly in her little bubble, she noticed that each circle of light—which was a volcano's open mouth to a different world—had a slightly different appearance. The first two had warmer hues of light shining into the watery network: one deep green, one gold. The third portal was oval shaped instead of round like the others. The fourth was just a thin sliver of light, as if the hole had some sort of loose cover over it. The fifth was the largest hole, with shadowy gray overtones and sinister, glowing, ancient etchings lining the interior of the volcano's mouth.

Issie's baby had steered Sky especially far away from that opening, as if she were afraid of getting too close. But once they'd passed it, she'd veered toward the sixth portal, whose opening shimmered with a ring of fire. Sky had followed her out through that one. The protective air bubble kept her safe from the fiery ring, and as she'd flown through the air and landed hard on the water, she saw that she was home.

Issie's baby was definitely a champion, but that didn't mean she could give Sky a ride all the way to Warbler—the creature had hardly let Sky touch her. Not to mention Warbler was very far away. It could take more than a full day to swim it. Sky

LISA McMANN

wasn't sure she'd be able to hold on to anything for that long.

"But I also don't want to get sucked down into that crazy Volcano Express again," Sky muttered. "Now that I'm here in the proper world, I'm staying." She moved to the part of the shoreline that was directly above the sliding glass door that led to the huge underwater sanctuary. That part had once housed pirates who'd been accustomed to the irregular plunging and rising volcano. The place was deserted now, and parts of it were destroyed. Sky could shelter down there if necessary, but not for long. There was likely no food. No drinkable water. She wouldn't be able to last long. And then what would she do? Grow weak before trying something else? She was in a race against time.

"I'm going below," Sky announced to Issie's baby.

The sea monster sat up. When Sky dove into the water and began swimming down toward the entrance, Issie's baby followed, looking around fearfully.

Sky approached the sliding door and peered inside a small entry chamber and beyond, to the interior of the living space. The place was a shadow of its former self—the gardens were reduced to withered plants and trees. The drop-down seats along the walls, which had been used to keep the occupants of the Island of Fire safe when the island plunged, were in various states of disrepair.

Locating the button, Sky opened the sliding door. She swam inside a small chamber and moved to one side so the sea monster could join her. She closed the outer door behind them, then opened the inner door. The water around them poured out over a large floor grate and drained away.

They walked in, and Sky grabbed an old towel from a hook to dry off a little. Though she'd spent a lot of time on this island studying the causes of the volcano's rising and falling actions, she'd chosen to enter the place only a handful of times. In her work, she'd been intent on stopping that motion, thinking this could be a more stable home environment someday. But now she realized that if she succeeded, this volcano would no longer work in the intricate volcano network. And then Thisbe might never be able to get home.

"I've put so much work into this place," Sky lamented as she and the sea monster went toward the kitchen. "And now I have to stop." She rummaged through cabinets and drawers, looking for anything that could be useful—food, water, or tools. She knew there had once been a few pirate ships tied to this island, but they had all been seized in the final battle between Artimé and Eagala and the pirates. Was there anything here that Sky could use to make a raft? Then, at least, she'd have a chance.

Just then Sky froze, struck by a thought. What would Thisbe do without the help of Issie's baby when she tried to find Sky? Not only would the girl have to know which portal to take, but when and if she did make it back to this world, she'd be just as stuck on this island as Sky was now. Would Thisbe think to come down here? Did she even know how to access this living space?

Sky looked at the sea monster. "When this island shivers, you must go back to Grimere and find Thisbe," she said. "Will you do that? She'll probably be coming . . . though I'm not sure when. It could be a while." Could Sky stay in this forsaken place until Thisbe showed up? There was nothing here to sustain her. How long would it take for Thisbe to save Maiven in the burning castle? It might take days. And would Thisbe return to the lake right away? Sky had no answers.

She reached out tentatively, and the sea monster dipped her

head. "You need a name," she said, pulling back. "How about Isobel? It's like your mother's, but different enough." She tried out the name a few times. "Isobel, will you go down with this volcano when the time comes and try to fetch Thisbe? Look for her everywhere."

Isobel blinked her big brown eyes. Droplets of water still clung to her lashes. The monster seemed agreeable.

Knowing time was of the essence, Sky searched the under-water island as quickly as she could. But if anything useful remained in this place, it was hidden well out of her sight. She wasn't sure how much time she had before the volcano would plunge again, and Isobel needed to be outside in the water when it happened.

When Sky felt a slight tremor through her shoes, she knew they had to hurry. "Through the hatch!" she shouted. "Let's go!" Isobel followed her into the exit chamber. Sky closed the interior door. She held on, staying inside the chamber, and opened the exterior door. Water poured in. When they were fully immersed, Isobel swam out and disappeared. Sky peered out through the murky water, making sure Isobel was staying near the island.

LISA McMANN

Certain that Isobel understood what she needed to do, Sky closed the outer slider, then went back inside. Foregoing the towel in her haste, she ran to the nearest jump seat and buckled in.

It didn't take long. With another slight tremor, the volcano slammed down into the sea. Sky gripped the seat and gasped.

When the motion stopped, Sky opened her eyes. She peered out of the glass walls into the dark sea. She unbuckled and slid off the seat, determined to hunt for sustenance while she waited for Thisbe, and prayed that the girl would quickly return to Lake Grimere so Isobel could find her.

As Sky rounded the main floor, heading for the stairs to the lower chambers, a large, slow movement outside the glass island caught her eye. She turned to look, her heart catching in her throat. Was it one of the horrible eels? But no—an enormous blue creature floated slowly around the glass, as big as a whale.

In fact, it was a whale. Sky gasped. She turned and ran to the glass. "Spike!" she screamed, pounding on it. "Spike Furious! It's me! Come back!"

The whale sped up and circled away from the island.

LISA McMANN

Sky jumped up and down, waving and yelling. "Spike! Spike!"

The creature disappeared into the murk.

"SPIKE FURIOUS!" screamed Sky.

Slowly the outline of the whale sharpened again as she turned back toward the noise. Then one of her big eyes peered through the glass and saw the human who had been lost. The one whom the Alex loved. The Sky.

An expression of pure joy washed over Spike Furious's face for the first time in a long time. And while the intuitive whale knew beyond a shadow of a doubt that the Alex was gone forever, she also knew that the Sky from Warbler was alive. She was here! And Spike Furious had found her!

"Spike!" Sky cried again, and ran for the exit chamber. She smashed the button that had closed the door behind her, took a deep breath, and opened the door to the depths of the sea, hanging on tightly as the water pounded over her.

When it settled, Sky peered out. Seeing Spike waiting, she swam into the murky water and grabbed on to her fin. She rode swiftly toward the top of the sea, gripping the beautiful creature. As they went, Sky pressed her cheek against Spike's silky skin. She began to shake. Soon sobs forced their way out, her tears adding to the salty water.

Spike Furious broke the surface. Sky collapsed on her back, overcome with emotion. Sadness and happiness. Relief. Great joy shrouded in the most devastating ache.

Sky had made it. She'd survived everything that had come her way. And now, finally, after all she'd lost, after all she'd been through, Sky was going home.

Acknowledgments

Thanks from the bottom of my heart to my faithful readers, who keep me motivated and excited to write about Artimé and the seven islands and the land of the dragons. And special appreciation to those who forgive me when I kill off your favorite characters. Your passion is my inspiration!

Thanks also to my husband and fellow kids-book writer, Matt McMann (shameless plug), for putting up with my angsty shenanigans, but mostly for getting me food. Thanks to my kids, Kilian and Kennedy, for your awesome help with these books in so many ways, and to my extended family for your continued support—it means the world to me. Also to Joanne Levy, who is a terrific human.

To my incredible team at Aladdin—you are my heroes! Thank you for your dedication to this book and to all the books you lovingly work on in your various ways. Especially the Batgirl, who is kind and who just gets me. Biggest heart eyes to you. And finally, once again I realize my life wouldn't be complete without Michael Bourret in it. Thank you for being such a great agent and friend and person.

LISA McMANN

Fifer's and Thisbe's stories continue in

THE UNWANTEDS QUESTS

BOOK FOUR
Dragon Curse

Turn the page for a peek. . . .

Aaron Stowe, head mage of Artimé, stared hard at Drock as the small group of mages and dragons flew toward the castle Grimere in the land of the dragons. The dark purple dragon was known to be troubled. He was the least reliable by far of all of Pan's brood. Yet he was the only one making sense right now.

"You must listen to me," said Drock in a low voice. He dropped back in flight so his face was next to his mother's flank, near where Aaron and the other humans rode. "You and your party should leave my mother's back and climb onto mine. I will take you home." He glanced around at Pan and his siblings. All of them had glazed eyes and were intent on heading toward the Revinir and the castle. "It's a dragon curse. She's calling to us with her roar. They're all being controlled by the Revinir, but I . . . So far I have resisted it. I'm the only one."

"But—" said Aaron. A moment ago he'd urged Pan to turn around, and she'd ignored him. And . . . this was *Drock*. If Drock was making sense, did that mean that Aaron might be the confused one? He turned to watch as hundreds of dragons flew toward the castle Grimere, coming from all directions. Drock was right. The Revinir had to be controlling them with her roar. Calling to them, as Drock said. It seemed clear by the way the dragons in their party were all acting, and had been acting lately.

Aaron thought it through again: The Revinir was controlling Pan, the ruler of the sea, and her children. Most of them, at least. Was it possible that Drock could be somehow unaffected? Or . . . could the difficult young dragon be leading them into a trap?

Getting away from hundreds of fire-breathing dragons didn't seem like a trap.

But switching dragons in midair wasn't exactly an easy task. At least they weren't flying over the gorge between the worlds anymore, but a fall to the rocky ground from this height would be just as deadly.

Aaron's face shone with sweat. His lips were pressed tightly into a gray line. "I don't know what to do," he muttered, and turned to Henry. "What do you think?"

"I don't know either." Henry was anxious too. He glanced at Sean and Scarlet and two of his children, Ibrahim and Clementi, who rounded out their party. They all seemed uneasy. Uncertain. And they all desperately wanted to find their fellow Artiméans on the rescue team, who were seemingly lost in the land of the dragons, and bring them to safety. They'd been traveling days to do so! Turning back now seemed like a lost opportunity, a waste of precious time. But there was nothing that felt safe about moving forward into this situation.

Sean leaned in. "This doesn't look promising at all. I know we want to find our loved ones, but we won't last more than a minute against the Revinir and her new dragon army."

"I agree," said Scarlet, then lowered her voice to a whisper. "But how do we know Drock is trustworthy?"

"Hurry!" said Drock, trying to fly steadily close to his mother without knocking into her. Pan seemed not to notice him or what he was attempting to do. She and Ivis and Hux and Yarbeck soared straight and true toward the castle, like all the other dragons. Right into the heart of danger.

Aaron's blood pounded in his ears. He felt light-headed. Dragons were not something to mess around with. And the six mages, no matter how powerful they might be, wouldn't have a chance against this mob. He ripped his fingers through his hair, agonizing over the options, then absently checked his pockets, feeling for heart attack spells. He had plenty of them and was prepared to fight. What if the Revinir was holding the rescue team captive? What if they were in that castle some-where? What if they were so close to them—could they really turn around now? Kaylee was among the ones they sought. What would she think if she knew he'd done that?

Aaron regarded Drock again. The dragon's eyes were clear. He was the only one engaging with the Artiméans, responding to them. And despite the young dragon's salty disposition, he was the only one Aaron felt like he could trust in this moment. Instinctively Aaron knew something was wrong here, and it was obvious Pan wasn't acting like an ally. Their missing loved ones might be nearby, but there was no way this group could take on the army of dragons without being killed. Most of them anyway. Aaron had to be wise in his role. The people of Artimé were counting on him to make good decisions. To bring this rescue team home alive. To be a good, smart leader, even if he didn't want this job. Besides, he couldn't stand the thought of Frieda Stubbs and the other dissenters having even more ammunition against him—they'd made his life miserable enough without that.

The head mage swallowed hard. Holding on to Pan's neck, he crawled along the dragon's back and beckoned to his team to follow. "Let's go with Drock," he said. "Back home. Before it's too late."

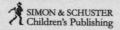 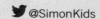

Magic reawakens in this thrilling new series from the
New York Times bestselling author of *Story Thieves*!